PELICAN ROAD

A Novel by Howard Bahr

PELICAN ROAD

A Novel by Howard Bahr

MACADAM CAGE

PELICAN ROAD

MacAdam/Cage
155 Sansome, Suite 550
San Francisco, CA 94104
www.MacAdamCage.com

Library of Congress Cataloging-in-Publication Data

Bahr, Howard, 1946-
Pelican road / by Howard Bahr.
p. cm.
ISBN 978-1-59692-289-1
1. Railroads—Employees—Fiction.
2. Railroads—Maintenance and
repair—Fiction. I. Title.
PS3552.A3613P46 2008
813'.54—dc22
2007050806

Manufactured in the United States of America

10 9 8 7 6 5 4 3 2 1

Book design by Dorothy Carico Smith.

To those who served
the Main Line of Mid-America.
I am proud to have made one among you.

Once, a fear pierced him,
In that he mistook
The shadow of his equipage
For blackbirds.
　　　　　　　—WALLACE STEVENS

English Composition
Miss Glasscock
October 22, 1940

MY UNCLE ARTEMUS
by
Fanny Snowden

My uncle, Artemus Merton Kane, was born in Meridian, Mississippi on September 8, 1895 and is forty-five years old. He is the son of the late Dr. Basil Kane and Elizabeth Merton Kane of this city, and he has one sister, Mary Kane Snowden of this city, who is my mother, and one brother, Gideon, of New Orleans, Louisiana. Uncle Gideon is a well known artist of the French Quarter.

When interviewed for this paper, my uncle was asked about his childhood. He said "it was very cold all the time" and told some interesting stories about the horse and buggy days. He said: "My only ambition as a youth was to be a pirate." I do not believe this.

My uncle served in France in the Marine Corpse during the Great War and was a Corpral who was wounded. My uncle saw actual fighting unlike many of the people who say they did, according to my uncle, who has stated that the Marines won the war for the army. This is contrary to what I have learned in other places. He was awarded the World War Victory Medal with silver citation star. When asked in this interview to explain further about the Great War, he said "it was very cold all the time," that is only my uncle's way of joking.

My uncle has a degree in English studies from the University of Mississippi, which is also my ambition. He also has a tattoo on his arm of the Marine Corpse emblem. He has written many stories and essays but has been rejected each time by the magazines. He could not explain this, though he was asked to. Since 1922, my uncle has worked for the Southern Railway Co. and is a conductor and brakeman and is currently on a fast passenger train of which he is proud to be there. I, myself, have accompanied him on trips between Meridian and New Orleans many times.

My uncle has had the experience of being married to the former Arabella Foster, of this city. My uncle is not married at the present time. When asked about this, he said: "I would prefer to be flogged," but that is only his way of joking. He has a sweetheart whose name is Anna Rose Dangerfield of New Orleans, Louisiana whom is nice and has actually written a book that is published, which aggervates my uncle. Also, he does not own a car but he rides a motorcycle everywhere, which is a very unusual thing for a person to do in the modern automobile age.

In conclusion, I am very proud of my Uncle Artemus. He is very kind and funny, and when I stay with him, I can do whatever I want as long as it is not to dangerous. Once he quoted: "When you are afraid, just grab a hand hold." It is a term or phrase they use on the railroad, and Uncle Artemus thinks it is very wise, and perhaps it is, though I don't know why.

PEARL RIVER MEET

On a cold afternoon two days before Christmas, a freight train waited in a passing track below the Pearl River bridge, just inside the state of Louisiana. The locomotive, number 4512, was shrouded in steam, the dimmed headlight pointing north toward a long curve and the river beyond where soon the fog must rise. The locomotive's tender, heaped with coal and rimed with frost, was coupled to seven cars of LCL freight, two odorous cars of livestock off the Southern Pacific at New Orleans, a government flatcar with a shrouded artillery piece, another with a dismantled Brewster Buffalo pursuit plane, and a wooden caboose once the color of red clay, now almost black with grime. A curl of smoke rose placidly from the stovepipe of the caboose; the marker lamps showed green ahead.

Between the rails, just ahead of the engine's pilot, lay a sheet of newsprint—in fact, the opened front page of yesterday's Baton Rouge *Advocate*, shrill with recent outrages of the Japanese army and the Louisiana legislature. Farther along, almost to the main line switch, a black crow, stark against the white ballast, worked over the last dingy scraps of a dead raccoon. In the manner of crows, he was watchful, and when a vagrant wind plucked at the newspaper, he tilted his eye toward the movement.

Suddenly, the paper spread itself and leapt aloft on the wind, danced, twirled, spiraled upward toward the gray sky as if in panic or joy. In all that still and cold-shrouded landscape, nothing, not even the bird, seemed so much alive. The crow flapped away from his meal and lit teetering in the crest of a short-leaf pine. The paper went on dancing and settled at last over the matted fur and bones of the raccoon. Then the crow, crying his opinion across the afternoon, lifted from the pine and creaked away southward.

The wind died as quickly as it came. In one of the cattle cars, a calf was bawling. The air pump of the locomotive throbbed intermittently, and now and then a white plume of steam jetted noisily from the cylinder heads. Save for these things, the world was silent. The Piney Woods—dense, shadowless, empty of sound and movement—lay close around. Where the passing track joined the main, the lens of the switch target gleamed like a polished emerald.

Pelican Road, whence the train had come and to which it would soon return, was the name given the two hundred and seven miles of ballasted heavyweight main line rail between Meridian, Mississippi, and New Orleans. The name had always been there, older than the railroad, older than any of the men who worked on it now. On a stone in the weed-grown cemetery at Talowah, Mississippi, was an inscription leached by the rains and barely visible under the moss and resurrection plant:

UNKNOWN TRAVELER

MURTHERED BY BANDITS

ON PELICAN ROAD

JULY 25, 1868

There was a road, then, storied and ancient, worn deep by the passage of generations of men, and before them the elk and deer and foxes. Their stories were forgotten, their blood long since raised to heaven in the sap of pines and sycamores, the old road itself swallowed by the vast wilderness it once defied. Only the name remained, and no one could say who first attached it to the railway: an act of collective memory, perhaps, whispered by the voice of time. It was a steel road now, of graceful curves and long straightways, journeyed by fast trains, illuminated for a moment by the bright cone of a headlight, then dark again, or silver under the sun, lying quiet and expectant. The men who traveled it, and those who lived beside, called it by the old name without thought, as if they remembered. Maybe they did, in the same way they remembered sometimes to be afraid of the dark.

A sandy road ran beside the railway, and across it, against the flank of the woods, stood a ramshackle, paintless store, set on brick pilings and fronted with a wide gallery. This was Gant's store, known to all the railroad men. The store's weathered face was plastered with rusty signs for Bull Durham tobacco and Shell motor oil and Goodrich tires. A cotton scale stood on the gallery, and rocking chairs with swayed cane bottoms, and three barrels of empty bottles, and a crosscut saw and a pile of firewood and a wringer washing machine of galvanized tin. Over the door hung a genuine curiosity: a ten-foot alligator skin nailed to the wall, jaws agape, most of its scales fallen away. The door itself, decorated with a barely visible advertisement for Barq's root beer, was shut against the cold.

The interior lay in the perpetual twilight of coal-oil lamps. It smelled of kerosene, of rank hoop cheese, of harness and roach powder and sweeping compound. Salted hams dangled from the ceiling, and seed bins stood open, each with its tin scoop, each giving, even in wintertime, of the sweet, indefinable odor of spring. On the dark shelves were the notions the country people used: Dr. LeGear's Poultry Inhalant; Dr. Kilmer's Swamp-Root; Father John's Medicine; Grove's Tasteless Chill Tonic; Castoria; Sia Smith's Improved Antiseptic; Bauer & Black Corn Pads; Noxema Ointment; Calomel; and Glover's Mange Medicine. Dr. Tichenor's Antiseptic, label printed with the irrelevant image of a charging battle line of Confederate soldiers under the old flag. Lancets. Bleeding cups and eye cups. A jar of leeches (still packed tightly, though all of them had been dead half a century) and a jar of Smith Brothers cough drops. Band-aids and mustard plasters. For rations, the store offered Ball jars of beans and corn, flour in printed sacks that the people could make aprons of, cornmeal sacks with dishes inside. A briny tub of pickles. Fresh Sunbeam bread delivered daily from the bakery in Slidell.

The railroad men could buy their bread at Gant's store. They could buy coffee, ground in an ancient red hand-cranked grinder, and aged cheese, and slices of ham, and warm Coca-Colas. Beyond that, their main interest in winter was the Warm Morning stove whose isinglass window glowed with ferocious combustion. In the shadows beyond the stove, motionless in a chair held together with wire, sat Mister Demeter Gant, his white beard draped over the bib of his overalls, his eyes milky with cataracts. Mister Gant's hands were large and knobby and seemed permanently attached to his knees. He was present in all seasons, immovable and silent like an exhibit of petrified wood. The railroad men regarded Mister Gant with awe. He seemed immortal, old as Pelican Road itself, older than the oaks. It was said that, in the blue-veined, shrunken calf of the old man's leg, a pistol ball from the Confederate War—or the Revolution, perhaps—was lodged like a watermelon seed. No one had ever seen it, but everyone believed in it.

Around the stove, the crew of the freight train, six men, spread their cracked, cold-bitten hands toward the heat. They had come in the store to get warm and to buy some bread and canned beans. As it happened, a diversion had presented itself: a new clerk, a small girl of flawless complexion, her straw-colored hair pulled back in a ponytail, with a face that renewed a man's faith in Possibility. Her name was Allison, they learned, and when Sonny Leeke made her smile, she illumined the dark, cobwebby store with images of spring, of moonlight, of red bridges arcing over quiet water. Four of the crew—Smith, Leeke, Necaise, and Ladner—were qualified to admire her, and they did.

The fifth man, Eddie Cox, the fireman and the oldest of them all, was a black man, so the girl did not exist for him. The space she occupied in the universe was empty as far as he was concerned. He kept his eyes on the window of the stove, and that was all right. The hot fire reminded him of his old lean wife and how her body glistened with sweat in the summertime.

The sixth man, Mister A.P. Dunn, also thought of his wife. He imagined her as she would be in this moment: smelling of detergent, her arms white with flour from the biscuits she would leave on the table for him tonight. She would be playing the radio in the kitchen, and from time to time she would raise her eyes to the foggy window that looked out on the yard. Mister A.P. Dunn had taken such things for granted once, but he didn't now.

Mister Dunn pulled his watch from the pocket of his overalls. Fifteen minutes had passed since they got off the train, and fifteen minutes yet remained to dally in the passing track. As usual, the dispatcher had done them a disservice. They might have easily got to Picayune in all this time, but now they would be stuck for every southbound train. If they got home at all before the hog law caught them, it would be in the deepest shambles of night, in a cold hour long before day. The streets would be quiet under the tin-shaded streetlamps, and the houses would be dark, and Mister Dunn would have to walk home by himself in the silence. He used to like walking through town in the late hours. Everything was still after the noise of the engine, and he would stroll along and look in the store windows and let his mind settle itself. That was before he started getting lost.

Mister Dunn shook the thought away and counseled himself to be patient. Among the many ghosts of the last fifty years were those of men who had fallen under the wheels or taken a curve too fast because they were in a hurry to get home. A man had to be patient, and above all, he had to be philosophical. Time would pass if you left it alone, and even faster if you didn't have much of it left.

The girl Allison awoke in Mister Dunn a yearning that was empty of desire but full of sadness. That came with an aging of the flesh, he supposed. Anyway, even in his youth he had never been good at flirtation, and now he was uncomfortable in the presence of this child who, merely by leaning forward on the counter, could generate more heat than the Warm Morning stove. Worse, he could feel the tension in his comrades, and that embarrassed him. Mister Dunn rubbed his sore leg for a moment, then stood up. "Well, boys," he said, "I am going back to the engine."

The men nodded without comment. Mister Dunn never sat with them long, and sometimes he never left the engine at all. They accepted this behavior in the old man, though they might not have in a younger one.

"I reckon I'll come, too," said Eddie Cox, a broad, stooped, deeply black man in greasy coveralls. His eyes and fingernails were ochre, his hair white and nearly gone, his hands knotted with arthritis. He pushed slowly, stiffly, out of his chair. For most of his thirty-five years of railroading, Eddie Cox had worked on hand-fired engines. Tons of coal, a mountain range of coal, had passed through his hands and worn him out, and now his time was short. He would make his last run on Christmas Day.

Eddie followed his engineer across the groaning wood floor. Neither man looked at the girl. Then they were outside, crossing the gallery, down the steps, and into the lot.

"It's cold, Mist' Dunn," Eddie remarked. "Maybe it'll snow Christmas."

"It has not snowed for Christmas since nineteen and twenty-three," said Mister Dunn.

"Yes, sir," said Eddie. "I remember that, I surely do."

Mister Dunn also remembered the year it snowed. He could remember what he had for breakfast on that vanished morning, and the number of his engine, and conversations held along the trip. Odd that he could not remember what he had for breakfast on the day he was moving in now.

They crossed the lot together. An old bucket of a T-model Ford, painted yellow, sat beside the woodpile. It was the girl's no doubt, for it was lettered with phrases Mister Dunn did not understand, like "Lindy Fool" and "Hold Tight, Mama." More and more young women were driving these days, and wearing pants, and smoking, and things of that nature, even way out here in the country. The radio was the cause of it, he thought, but no matter. Such behavior might have bothered him once, but it seemed of little consequence now.

In a corner of the lot, nearly buried in dead cow-itch and honeysuckle vines, stood an ancient open-cab truck. The tires had rotted from the rims, and on the bed was a load of gray, spongy lumber from which a twenty-foot hickory tree grew. It was told that Mister Demeter Gant had parked the load there a quarter century ago, and there it sat yet, waiting for Judgment Day.

Mister Dunn bit off a chew of tobacco and worked it in his jaw. So many changes, as if the world had shed its old skin like a snake. The Great War, the Hard Times, and now another war coming. Still, Mister Dunn had come to view such things not as change but as the unraveling of a thread old as Cain. Murder and chaos, the loss of faith and decline of morality—all ancient and familiar, though many shouted and wrung their hands as if nothing of the sort had ever visited the race of man.

It was the other kind of change that bothered him, the personal kind that altered the shape of where a man stood and changed the air he moved through. In the last year, Mister Dunn had gone to three funerals, men he had worked with in the link-and-pin days, the coal-oil headlight days, the time before the law kept them from working more than sixteen hours. He could still see them, still hear their voices, but they were gone. After all their striving, thousands of midnights, ice storms, rain, snow, flood, and a million miles, they were gone. Soon Eddie Cox would be, too. Eddie would sit on his front porch in Jumpertown for a year or two, listening to the trains go by, then he would pass like the rest. The Negroes, especially, never survived retirement for long.

Mister Dunn drew deeply of the cold air. It was all of pine and dust and wood smoke, of the odor of coal and steam and the indefinable scent of December, of nights that were long and dark—the dead time, the cold and empty time. Once, in such a time long ago, a star burned steadfastly in the east, lighting the deep blue sky. Mister Dunn once believed that the same star burned for everyone, showing the way out of darkness. He was not so certain now, and that was the change that sorrowed him most. The star was there, no doubt, but if you quit looking even for a moment, you could lose sight of it.

He raised his eyes to the east and considered the gray, motionless clouds over the pine tops. No star there, only a stream of blackbirds moving toward the river. Only the birds, and beyond them the unborn sun of tomorrow. For an instant, he was tempted to go back in the store, take the girl by the hand, and lead her out into this barren, bleached oyster-shell yard where the end of day was falling. Look, he would say, and turn her eyes eastward. He would tell her, There is where the new sun will come, and there ain't many of them before you wake up and find the world has left you behind.

Mister Dunn spat and wiped his chin and called himself an old fool. Next time, he would stay on the engine. That way, he would never—

Never what? he thought. The question floated in sudden darkness. Mister Dunn stopped and turned once in a circle, looking around at the lot, the store, the blur of pine trees. Here was an old colored man watching him, there a freight train standing. He was sure it all had something to do with him, but he couldn't remember. He knew he was supposed to go somewhere, but he didn't know where. He turned another circle, his hands out for balance.

"Mist' Dunn?" said the black man. "Mist' Dunn, what's the matter?"

The engineer stopped turning. "Who are you?" he said. "What you want?"

"It's Eddie, sir," said the black man. "What's the matter."

"Eddie," he said. "Eddie." It came back to him then, all of it, the empty places filling up with the shapes he knew. "Nothing," he said, and went on across the yard. He was halfway to the engine when he heard his name called again, and he turned to see Frank Smith on the gallery.

Smith put his hands in the hollow of his back and stretched. "We didn't mean to run you off, A.P.," he said.

"You didn't."

Smith nodded. He stood a moment more, watching out as men will do, letting his eyes move across the pines and down the main line toward the bridge. Then he was gone back into the store.

Like Mister Dunn, Smith had been raised in logging camps deep in the Piney Woods. But Frank Smith had gone to college, then to the Great War, and so developed along a path no one would have expected, least of all Smith himself, a long-haired, compact, handsome man with a hawkish face that might have been an Indian's. In fact, Smith claimed to *be* an Indian, and not only that, but one who'd been dead for a hundred years. That always troubled Mister Dunn, for he knew that Indians were pagans, and he knew that only Jesus and Lazarus had come back from the dead, and he wished Smith wouldn't talk that way. It was even worse when he went on about how many white men he had massacred in his other life. That always made the boys testy.

Anyway, Frank Smith missed nothing and had an opinion on nearly every subject. He was always reading books nobody else but Artemus Kane ever heard of, and always doing interesting things like flying model airplanes or taking pictures with a Kodak. At home, Mister Dunn had a picture Frank Smith took a year ago: Mister Dunn, Sonny Leeke, Artemus Kane, and Eddie Cox, in their greasy overalls and gloves and watch chains, standing solemnly by the white-trimmed driving wheels of a big Southern freight engine. It was the only time Mister Dunn, at least, had ever had his picture made on the job.

The brakeman Artemus Kane was born to old money and had never lived in the woods; nevertheless, he seemed to be the only one who understood Frank Smith. Some believed it was because they had both gone to college and been exposed to an unusual, even dangerous, body of knowledge not available to ordinary men. Others thought it was because they had served together as Marines in the Great War, from their training all the way to the Armistice, and so were mutually insane. In any event, no one could figure why they chose to wear themselves out on Pelican Road when they could have paper-collar jobs out of the rain.

One time, Mister Dunn and Frank Smith were taking supper in the Bon-Ton Café. Smith was sitting sideways in the booth, reading a thin book written by a Chinaman. Mister Dunn said, What is that book about, Frank?

Smith went on reading. After a moment, he said, It is about how this fellow saw the world a long time ago.

Mister Dunn thought a moment. He said, I am curious how that would be of much use.

Smith closed the book, marking his place with a napkin. Well, A.P., he said, it helps me figure out why it is now.

Why what is? asked Mister Dunn.

Smith shrugged and waved his hand out the café window, at the lighted streets, the people, the black shapes of automobiles. Why all that is, he said.

At the time, Smith's answer seemed overly complicated to Mister Dunn, though the engineer didn't pursue it, since he made it a rule never to argue theology, if that's what it was.

Then, not long after that, they were switching a wood yard south of Hattiesburg when a big thunderstorm came up so quick the men hadn't the chance to fetch their rain gear. The pines were thrashing in the wind, and the thunder pealed in one unbroken crash over the woods, and lightning was everywhere at once, filling the air with the sharp odor of electricity. Mister Dunn had to stop the engine, for the world was white with rain, and he could no longer see the brakemen nor even the cars they were switching. Then, with the storm at its worst, Frank Smith appeared out of the blinding curtain of rain. He was wet all through, his long hair tangled and his shirt and pants covered with mud where he must have fallen down, but he turned his streaming face to the sky and raised his gloved fists and shouted Fuck you! over and over at the top of his voice. The lightning split a pine tree not fifty yards away, and the thunder cracked and rolled, but Smith just laughed, and turned, and disappeared into the rain again, waving his arms and dancing.

In that moment, Mister Dunn feared for Frank Smith and expected never to see him again in this life or the next. Yet, when the storm passed, there was the conductor, looking a little tired, leaning on the coupler of a wood rack. He signaled impatiently for Mister Dunn to come ahead as if nothing at all had happened.

Now Mister Dunn climbed into the cab of his engine, wiping off the grab irons with a rag as he did so—an old habit, for some of the boys were a little careless when they took a leak off the gangway. In a moment, he was in his seat surrounded by the elements of his trade: the throttle and Johnson bar, the whistle and bell cords, the brake lever, sight-glasses and gauges and valves of polished brass, fusees and a box of torpedoes and a red flag. As usual, Eddie Cox had left his tattered King James Bible on his seat, a ritual he observed whenever he got off the engine. In one corner leaned the spike and brush Eddie used to clear the stoker, in another, an umbrella belonging to the head brakeman, Sonny Leeke. On Sonny's seat cushion lay his greasy White Mule gloves and a *Times-Picayune* folded to the crossword puzzle. Affixed to the cabin wall was a rack with Mister Dunn's engraved oil can, a birthday gift from his daughter long ago. In the same rack was Mister Dunn's medical kit, a box of japanned tin he carried from job to job, since the company didn't provide one. It held a tube of hemorrhoid ointment, a jar of Vicks VapoRub, Sloan's liniment, some Mercurochrome, adhesive tape, gauze bandages, a bottle of milk of magnesia, another of Bayer aspirin. These would fix anything short of decapitation or dismemberment. For these last, Artemus Kane had once added to the box a little red paperbacked volume, *Catholic Prayer Book for the Marine Corps.*

> Eternal rest grant them, O Lord, and let perpetual light
> shine upon them. May they rest in peace. Amen.

Mister Dunn did not approve of the Romish book, with its masses and litanies and appeals to the saints, but the dead, he had learned, were ecumenical, and more than once, standing by the roadbed among the smell of overheated brakes, he had read from the little book unashamed while men who claimed no religion at all bowed their heads and were silent.

Eddie Cox came halfway up the ladder. "Pass me down that fine oil can, would you, sir?" he said.

Cox was the only fireman, black or white, who was allowed to use Mister Dunn's personal oil can. Mister Dunn took it from the rack and handed it down. Cox looked at him. "It's just the winter time," he said. "Seem like—"

"Never mind," said Mister Dunn sharply. "I was thinking about something back there. I guess you never done that?"

"Well, no, sir," said Cox, and disappeared down the ladder. He would oil around and check on things. He had a good eye for trouble.

Mister Dunn settled into his seat again and drew his aching leg up under him. It was getting harder to sit now, for his back hurt all the time. Fifty years ago, A.P. Dunn hired out as a fireman for the Newberry Lumber Company, stoking the wood-burning Shays that crawled back and forth through the plundered woods of Lauderdale County, Mississippi. For the last forty years, he had been an engineer on the New Orleans Northeastern, lately renamed for the Southern Railway, and for all that time he had been sitting—ten, twelve, sixteen hours or more at a time—watching ahead, watching for signals, straining into the dark or the rain for any of the numberless disasters that might lie in his path.

Frank Smith made his first trip with Mister Dunn just after the war. Some people would let a new man get run over before they offered a syllable of warning or advice. That was not Mister Dunn's way. He told Smith then, as he told every new man, You can't be afraid, but you got to be careful. You can't ever quit paying attention. It ain't a game, you don't get a second chance. Smith had listened. So had Kane, who made his first trip with Mister Dunn a few years later. Smith and Kane were different from anyone Mister Dunn had ever known, but they were all right. They were smart. They were brave but careful, and they never quit paying attention.

The door slammed across the way. Mister Dunn watched the boys walk across the yard: Frank Smith, with a bag of ham and cheese and French bread and canned beans under his arm; Sonny in his lucky red jacket; Dutch Ladner the swing man. Ladner's nephew Bobby Necaise, the flagman, who was going in the Navy next month, carried the Coca-Colas and a Thermos jug the size of an artillery shell. Young Necaise looked up at a blue jay flying over, and Sonny said something that made the boys laugh. They were all hunched up, for it was sleeting hard now. Mister Dunn heard the pellets sift against the roof of the cab.

It made Mister Dunn feel better to see his crew approaching, these men he had known and journeyed with, on one job or another, for so long. But the feeling brought a sadness with it, too. They seemed fragile and temporary in the gray light, as if who they were and all they had done could be swept away forever by a word, a gesture, an errant thought. Frank Smith would understand that, and Kane would understand it, surely. But they were all good boys, and every one of them approached mortality in his own way. Some, like Artemus Kane, scoffed at it. The Jews, like Ira Nussbaum, believed it was all they had. Others still relied on God's design to explain the mystery, and they seemed satisfied even when there was no explanation at all. That was all right if it brought them comfort. For himself, Mister Dunn could no longer see any design except what people themselves made out of the pure clay of time. Most of them did pretty well in the balance, which was surprising, given what they had to work with, and God still watched from somewhere over the pines, grieving for them all, and loving them. In all his years, Mister Dunn had not seen anything to make him quit believing that, at least. That was the value of remembering, Mister Dunn supposed. It was what the soul was made of.

Mister Dunn pulled his watch. The fifteen minutes were gone, fallen away toward evening with all the other moments of his life. He was not surprised to hear southbound Number 5, the Silver Star, right on time, racketing over the Pearl River bridge. Mister Dunn saw that the girl Allison had come out on the porch to watch the passenger train go by, perhaps to dream that she was on it. He thought, *It is too cold for her out here.* Then he rose and moved across the deck plates. He knelt in Eddie's seat and leaned out the window, his knees against the Bible. Eddie came up and joined him in the window; the others stood down by the pilot, drawing together against the cold. Mister Dunn rolled down the rain curtain, and he and Eddie rested their arms on the window cushion and watched the Silver Star make her appearance up Pelican Road.

Like her namesake, she was first a light glittering against the pines, a moving tremor of light on the rails. Then she was on them, blowing for the crossing. The handsome locomotive, shining like green glass, seemed to lean forward in her haste, rocking on her springs, with a clean hot fire and no smoke from her stack, just a pigtail of steam whirling from the pop-off valve, whipped away by the speed of her going, then another from the whistle as she spoke two short notes in greeting. Mister Dunn lifted his hand.

That close, and at such a speed, a passing train is not seen so much as remembered: a blur of images that the mind retains, though the eye is too slow to follow. Mister Dunn caught the fireman Jean Chauvin's gloved hand thrust out the cab window in greeting. He saw the streak of the long, lighted coach windows and the blurred faces of strangers behind them; the baggage man, Miles Duvall, at his open door; and Artemus Kane. The brakeman Kane, in his blue overcoat, collar turned up, leaned far out the opened top half of a vestibule door. Artemus shouted something at the boys, his arm extended. The train was gone in an instant, pulling its own sound swirling behind it, and the twin marker lamps were gone down the gray afternoon, all gone but for the image of Artemus Kane's face, his hand reaching toward Mister Dunn through the sleet as if sleet meant no more to him than the dust that swirled in their summer passage.

Then silence, a moment when there was no sound at all; then the breathing of the locomotive again and the voice of Frank Smith as he passed under the window: "When you're ready, Mister Dunn."

In a little while, the passing track was empty. No movement, only the cold steel rails and the gray slag, the lamp of the switch target glowing brighter as the daylight failed. The gallery was empty, too, for the girl had gone inside again. The sleet pattered for a while longer, then stopped, leaving a fine powder on the needles of the pines and in the folds of the newspaper. From far away, the shrieking whistle of Mister Dunn's train drifted across the pines, carrying a long way as such a sound would in the wintertime.

CROSSING OF THE WATERS

The Silver Star hurried southward, tunneling through the sleet. Artemus Kane lingered in the vestibule of the coach James River, though he had no official reason for staying where he was. He had come out here to observe Frank Smith's train in the siding at Gant's. Now the train and all the men with it were far behind, and nothing remained for Artemus to see but the roadbed racing by and the Piney Woods—oaks among them this far south, and cypress in the marshy places—marching past on either side, intersticed by deep and mysterious shadow.

Artemus gripped the door ledge with both hands, the steel like a blade of ice under his thin leather dress gloves. Beneath him, the coach swayed elegantly, and the wheels hammered over the rail joints. Artemus was forty-five years old; his hair was beginning to gray and was, at the moment, too long for regulation. The polished visor of his pillbox cap—navy blue, piped in gold—was pulled low over eyes that girls could never tell the color of: sometimes hazel, sometimes brown, depending on the light. He had an angular face that absorbed the shadows and was sculpted by them. It was wrinkled around the eyes from too much squinting, too much laughing, and was marred by a glazed star-like scar on each cheek, the result of an unusual wounding early in the battle for the Bois de Belleau. Artemus, a rifle squad leader, was walking along, shouting at somebody, or giving an order, or maybe just yawning—he could never remember—when a German private, helmetless, coatless, rose up from a shell hole and fired at him with a .22 revolver. The ball passed tidily through his cheeks, leaving his tongue and teeth intact, a lucky shot for Artemus, but not for the German boy, who must have been terrified or crazy. In any event, he made no move to surrender and was taking aim again when Artemus's brother, Gideon, blew him apart with a Winchester Model 12 pump shotgun.

On that long-vanished day, Artemus had worn a khaki blouse—Marines in the line were forbidden their distinctive forest-green tunics—and khaki wool pants, puttees, a steel helmet, clumsy hob-nailed shoes, and all his accouterments, including an M-1903 Springfield rifle and a 1911 Colt .45. Today, Artemus wore a different uniform. The Southern Railway company had issued him a long, tai-lored navy blue overcoat to protect him from the bitter cold of the Louisiana winter; he wore it now with the collar turned up, buttoned to the neck by nine fire-gilt buttons, each bearing the name of the railway company. Under this fine garment, he wore a navy blue uniform jacket with smaller buttons, collar insignia, and gilt service marks on the sleeve; a waistcoat with his watch chain draped across the front; and trousers hung correctly over his polished black high-topped shoes. His accouterments today were a greasy timetable, a company lock key, a box of matches, a pack of Picayune cigarettes, and a pearl-handled Mexican switchblade presented to him by his friend Roy Jack Lucas, a railroad policeman. Lucas had taken the knife from the body of a murderous rider called Jubela after Hido Schreiber, Roy Jack's partner, had removed Jubela from company property, and thence from life, with a shotgun of the exact model Gideon used in France.

In short, Artemus Kane cut a swell figure in the darkening vestibule, though no one was around at the moment to remark upon the fact. This was an empty stretch of country, unrelieved by field or cabin, and the evening was fast closing over it, pulling it away into night so that it might have been any place, or no place at all. Still Artemus, who had ridden Pelican Road for eighteen years, knew where he was by the shape of the land around him. He did not have to look at the mile markers that slipped past like little tombstones, or the tin numbers nailed to the telegraph poles, to know where he was.

The remainder of the universe, however, was less certain in his mind. Though he believed in them, he was sometimes unsure of the spaces that lay beyond what he could see. Once he had thought of them as silent and still, suspended in a blue-gray twilight like the one that was closing around him now. Lately, he saw them as a vast arena of activity where nothing was ever lost, where present and past were happening all at once, a confusion of events that spilled over now and then into whatever place he happened to be standing at the moment. Such was the case now as he thought of the meet below Pearl River. He believed that what he had seen there might only be grasped if he remained in the vestibule amid the cold and sleet that was its context and continuum.

First, there was the girl standing on the gallery, her hand lifted as if in recognition. In his long experience, Artemus had seen no such girl in the dismal store below Pearl River, and he questioned that he had seen one now. Real or not, the girl was important only for what she brought inside his head at the moment of her passage, one of those random memories that Artemus was always meeting in the course of the day, flung out from the vast spaces where the steady ticking of his watch had no meaning.

* * *

A cold afternoon, swirled with snow. A French peasant girl leaves her gate and runs along the column. She goes from man to man, gesturing up the road, crying Le Boche! Le Boche! En avant! The Marines assure her there are no Krauts to their front. They laugh and flirt with her in bad French until she stomps rearward in her clumsy wooden shoes. Then, a little farther on, the scouts discover a prize: behold, a horse-drawn five-nine stuck in the freezing mud, gun and limber and crew all alone on the forest road, left behind by their own fleeing infantry. Le Boche! The Kraut gunners are distracted, lashing the horses, straining at the wheels, when—en avant!—the Marines come howling up the road with fixed bayonets. They shoot and stab until no Kraut is left wanting to surrender, then caper like feral children around the gun. They unhitch the horses and watch them run away, great platter-sized hooves kicking up snow and mud. Someone cranks the gun barrel to full elevation; the Artist rides the muzzle up and drops a hand grenade down the bore. After the breech is blown, the Marines scavenge the dead for souvenirs, especially the much-coveted long-barreled artillery model Luger. No Lugers are found, however: only worthless script, photographs, and letters no one but Squarehead can read. Squarehead, whose real name is Wurtz, is from southern Illinois and fluent in German. He is useful in trench raids, luring the enemy in his own tongue, and useful for bullying prisoners, but he has no interest in letters, so they are left to flutter away along the road. Artemus and Gideon Kane stand together amid the shambles, breathing hard, watching the letters blow away. One of the vagrant pages fetches up at the feet of the French girl who had come back up the road. She is standing with her wooden shoes pressed close together, shawl wrapped tight about her, shivering. When Gideon speaks to her, puts out his hand and takes a step, the child begins to scream. She stands in the road shrieking, and nothing the Marines can do will make her quiet. They leave her there finally, but her shrill voice follows them a long way.

* * *

Artemus knew that memory was the only vessel that could hold both the girl at Gant's store and the French girl who had witnessed, at last, one outrage too many. Beyond that, it was useless to attempt any logical connection between them, or any purpose. In fact, he had long ago given up trying to understand the apparitions that visited him.

The Silver Star pushed deeper into St. Tammany Parish. Artemus leaned out the vestibule window, sleet peppering his cap, and fixed himself in space and time. A house he knew passed by at the end of a long yard, an old hip-roofed French colonial framed in weeping moss. Up ahead, the engine blew for a lonely grade crossing. The "X" of the warning sign flashed by an instant later, and Artemus glimpsed a half-dozen Negro children, wrapped in bright quilts, like a nest of baby birds in the bed of a mule-drawn wagon.

Artemus slammed the vestibule window, then leaned against the bulkhead and, contrary to regulations, shook out a cigarette and lit it, drawing deep. With the window closed, it was quieter. It was still cold, but without the cutting wind. Sleet was sifted in the corners, and the slush on the deck plates was freezing, so pretty soon the porter would come along with his broom and a little bucket of salt. They were all wary of the salt, for it made a mess of the carpets in the coaches, but that was better than having a passenger slip and break his neck and sue the company. The coach lights had come on now, and the single caged bulb in the vestibule ceiling, so Artemus stood in a gloomy yellowish pool of lumination like that of washrooms or billiard halls. The pane of the vestibule window, streaked and grimy as it was, gave little light; beyond it, the world was a blur of indistinct shapes.

When the after coach door opened, Artemus supposed it was a passenger, perhaps the porter and his broom. Instead, it was Vernon Stanfield, a Kane cousin and the second brakeman. Stanfield almost passed without noticing Artemus, but the cigarette smell drew him up. "Ah," said Stanfield. "I been looking for you."

"Well, Vernon, here I am," said Artemus. Both men had to lift their voices above the racket of the vestibule. He and Stanfield looked so nearly alike that they were often mistaken for brothers. "What will you have?"

Stanfield drew an envelope from his coat pocket and waved it. "This is for Eddie Cox," he said. "The company will give him a watch, but he already has a watch." He thought a moment. "I wonder why they do that?"

"Well," said Artemus, "a fellow can't have too many watches, especially when he is retired and doesn't need the one he's got. God damned if I know, Vernon." He bent and dropped the cigarette through a crack between the deck plates. The separation was hardly visible, but the cold swept up through it, and with the cold, the universal smell of the railroad: grease, friction, dust, urine, creosote, dead animals, hot steel, all mixed together in a way that was like no other smell on the earth, and not unpleasant, though some of its constituents might be.

Eddie Cox, the sight of him in the cab of the 4512, was the second thing Artemus had brought away from the meet at Pearl River. Artemus was troubled whenever a man retired, and Eddie Cox would retire in a few days. That would be the end of him, as it was with all the old men. The job crowded their years, then was gone all at once. There was no easing out, and nothing was left behind. They always had big plans: fishing, playing with the grandchildren, making things out of wood— all the things they'd never had time for. What they did, in the end, was nothing. At first, they would show up at the depot or the crews' washroom looking for somebody to talk to, telling themselves they still belonged. In a little while, they realized that time had run off and left them, and they quit coming. Then they died.

Once a man came to this, once he had outlived his dignity and his time, he was a stranger to himself and to all the world. Artemus Kane felt only contempt for such a creature, and a pity that had no kindness in it. He was not proud of the feeling, but there it was. He blamed the old men for reminding him of what he must become himself at last.

"What can I put you down for?" asked Stanfield, waving the envelope.

Artemus looked at the ceiling. A fat winter fly was crawling around inside the light cage. Flies were rarely seen on the Silver Star. "A man would do better dying on the job," said Artemus. "Five dollars. Look in my bag, in the brown wallet."

Stanfield made a note on the back of the envelope. "We all got to die soon enough," he said.

"We should all die out here," said Artemus.

When his cousin was gone, Artemus wondered why he had made such a remark and if he really believed it. Finally, he decided that he did believe it. There was no good way to die on Pelican Road, but usually it was quick, and a man was among his friends, like the Kraut gunners had been on the road. The little French girl had missed that, but Artemus had not.

The coach door hissed open, and a young woman emerged. Artemus looked at her but did not speak. The woman smiled, then her eyes flicked away when she saw his face. She wore a fur-collared red coat, and a little curl of her dark hair slipped across her forehead in a way that reminded him of Anna Rose Dangerfield. "Is the club car this way?" she asked, brushing at the curl with a gloved finger.

It was a ridiculous question, for the club car was always at the end of the train. Where else would it be? But no matter. The woman was slim. She had a smell like clean linen that carried over the railroad smell, and her voice carried over the noise. "Yes, ma'am," said Artemus. "The last coach." He opened the door for her and felt her brush past him, her eyes turned away. Again he thought of Anna Rose, out there now in the empty spaces.

The winter fly circled lazily around the vestibule, lighting, crawling, taking off again. When Artemus was married, his wife could never comprehend why he chose to work on the railroad, an educated man from old money who might yet be written back into his father's will if he would only come to his senses in time. Then Basil Kane died, and two days after the funeral, Arabella hired a Negro man to carry all of Artemus's possessions—there were not many—out to the yard. Artemus found them when he returned from a conductor's run on a broke-dick local. His motorcycle was there, too, kicked over in the grass, a single word scrawled on the tank in dripping white house paint: *Goodbye.* When Artemus lifted the machine, he found another word, one he had not expected, painted on the other side: *Why?*

One afternoon, Artemus told that story to Anna Rose while he lay on his stomach on a quilt, and she rubbed his spine with liniment. They were in the drowsy, mosquito-ridden courtyard of Johnny Lozano's bar on St. Peter Street, with the smell of sewage in the air and a trio of alley cats sporting in the trash cans. Lying next to Artemus was Lozano's dog, for whom the cats were a matter of interest, though of interest only, for his left hind leg had been removed by a streetcar, and he was no longer active. Artemus had called off sick, this time with a legitimate reason: the day before, he had stepped off a moving engine and thrown his back out again, and now he could barely hobble. Moreover, he had hit the cinders, and his face and palms were streaked with cuts. Around one eye was a yellowish bruise.

Well, it's a fair question, said Anna Rose. Why you do what you do, when you could do anything.

How come you never asked it, then?

Anna Rose bore down hard on the clenched muscles between his shoulder blades. I said it was fair. I didn't say it was important.

It was to Arabella, said Artemus, wincing at the pain of her hard little fists, the sting of sweat in his cinder cuts. The dog was attracting a good many flies, and they had a way of daubing in his wounds. At least the liniment kept the mosquitoes off.

Let me put it this way, said Anna Rose. Yesterday, you nearly got killed, when you could have been playing golf instead. So it's a fair question if somebody loves you.

So that's why you never asked it?

She slapped him on the back of his head. So why, already? she asked.

Artemus made no reply, for, in truth, he did not know the answer himself. This was enough: he knew she would not judge his answer, just as he knew she would listen if he tried to offer one. That, Artemus perceived, was a signal difference between marriage and romance. It was the first time he understood, and way too late.

* * *

Artemus left the vestibule and went forward up the train. The consist this evening was impressive: fifteen coaches, a diner, a club car, a baggage car, a post-office car, and four head-end cars of the Railway Express. This close to Christmas, the train was packed, every seat taken. The windows were foggy from the steam heat. All the citizens were well dressed and festive; the dining car was decorated with holly and garlands of pine, and the club car had a lighted Christmas tree cut in the forests of upstate New York. Among the passengers were a good many Army and Navy officers. They were getting more and more of them these days.

The Silver Star was an extra-fare mainline train running daily north and south, superior to all other trains between Washington and New Orleans. It was a splendid craft, beautiful from the white smokebox of the engine through its Pullman-green length to the open observation platform of the club car. The windows in the washrooms were leaded glass. The seats were plush, the aisles carpeted, the end bulkheads painted with scenes of the French Quarter and of the great plantation houses of Louisiana. The dining car, specializing in Creole cuisine, was one of the finest restaurants in the South, its starched and haughty Negro waiters trained in French service. The Silver Star had its own stationery, its own linens and plates and silverware. Passengers could send telegrams to their boardrooms or wives or mistresses while rolling through the countryside at seventy and eighty miles an hour. A steward was on call night and day to take dictation, and the letter stamped and mailed at the next stop.

For all its elegance and style, however, the Silver Star was still tons of steel hurtling along on the dime-sized contact between wheel and rail, drawn by a complex machine that was itself a controlled explosion. Mass, speed, and high-pressure steam were the ingredients, and they existed in a fragile balance that required perfection in a world wildly imperfect, required flawless performance from flawed men and women, required vandals and anarchists to resist their natural impulses. These facts were not available to the passengers. The company wished them to believe that they were in no more danger than if they were in a hotel and went to great lengths to ensure their safety and contentment. The illusion was successful. Artemus knew a number of people, including himself, who could not be induced at gunpoint to board an airplane, but he had rarely known railroad passengers to be nervous. Only the trainmen understood that luck was their sole protection, and that any train—even the Silver Star—could run out of it.

The trainmen guarded that secret, even from themselves. If they thought on it too much, their own luck would suffer. Sometimes that happened. When a man was afraid, he grew self-conscious. He might hesitate or second-guess or fail to act. The irony had played itself out more than once in Artemus's memory: a man, absorbed in thoughts of his own mortality, forgets to look around him, and that is his death warrant.

Artemus found his conductor in the second coach, writing in his trip book. Mister Ira Nussbaum was a lean, handsome old man in his seventies, his close-cut hair gone silver, his eyes quick and black. He had never worn glasses, but his handwriting was cramped and awkward because three fingers were missing from his hand.

Artemus took off his cap and slid into the seat next to Mister Nussbaum, who was riding backward. Artemus did not like to sit that way, for it made him nauseous after a while. The conductor smelled faintly of soap and damp wool and something else indefinable: confidence, perhaps, or the easy mantle of power. Artemus thought of Mister Ralph

Little, a freight conductor of such overwhelming dignity that even the weather deferred to him. His only concession to rain was to allow the water to bead on his polished shoes. He brushed aside the heat and cold and strode through the darkest night as though it were an electric arcade. He never raised his voice, never cursed, never had to give an order twice. His presence calmed good men, or awed them; it turned small, mean men into craven wretches; it silenced the loudmouthed, humbled the braggart, drained the powerful of their vanity. By his own testimony, Mister Little considered only Ira Nussbaum to be his equal in the operation of trains.

Mister Little died of a heart attack in the overstuffed chair he always carried on his caboose. His friends were gathered about him. The flagman, Sonny Leeke, held his hand while he passed and took the old man's last farewell to his wife and married daughters. Artemus believed that Mister Nussbaum would go in a similar way. He would be borne off the Silver Star like an elder knight, hands crossed over his watch chain, hair ruffling in the wind.

Mister Nussbaum, then, was among the last of a dying species, along with men like A.P. Dunn and Rufus Payne and Eddie Cox. When they passed, whatever they had been, good and bad, would pass with them—time, another world, a different vision of what it meant to be a man—and there would be nothing to replace. For Mister Nussbaum, the end would be complete, for he had left no kin to follow and disappoint him. His wife, Rebekah, had been ill of cancer a long time, and on Christmas Eve last, she died in the hospital. Ira Nussbaum had her body placed in the baggage car of the Silver Star for burial in New Orleans. He did not lay off that day. He took out the Silver Star himself and worked the whole trip without a word.

Artemus had forgotten the anniversary until he took his seat by the old man. Around Mister Nussbaum's uniform sleeve was a thin band of black cloth, awkwardly pinned, his only concession and announcement. Artemus wondered what he should say, or if he should say anything. In the end, he said, "Slidell coming up, Captain."

"Is it?" said Mister Nussbaum. He leaned close to Artemus and sniffed the air with his long, chiseled nose, and quivered his white moustache. "My boy," he said, "if you're going to smoke on duty, have the courtesy to take a little breath mint afterward so I don't have to know about it."

"Sorry, sir," said Artemus.

"You need a haircut also."

Artemus passed his fingers through his hair. "My God, Captain," he said. "You sound like my daddy."

Mister Nussbaum closed his trip book and folded his hands across it. "I *am* your daddy," he said.

"Huh," said Artemus. "And you let mama raise me Catholic? She never mentioned—"

"It is a figure of speech, Kane," said the old man.

"Are you rich?" said Artemus.

"Not any more," said the conductor. "I have spent it all on psychiatrists, trying to figure out how such a smart woman as your mother, God rest her soul, could raise such an idiot."

"Ah," said Artemus. Once, in the last days, Arabella had made him see a psychiatrist in New Orleans. She wanted the doctor to figure out why Artemus got so angry at times, and why he broke things. After three visits, Artemus told his wife that it would be just as useful, and far cheaper, to subscribe to the *Reader's Digest*.

"I'll get a haircut tonight," he said to Mister Nussbaum. "I promise."

The conductor went back to his paperwork, and Artemus looked past him out the window where the woods, the moss, the houses—some of them on stilts now—passed in winter array, made soft and ephemeral in a light the color of old pearls. Artemus spotted a big red-tailed hawk on the company wire, his feathers huffed against the cold, and now and then clouds of white herons, startled by the train, erupted from the marshes. Then Ogee Womack, one of the porters, appeared in the door of the coach. He rocked down the aisle, hands brushing the seat backs. "*Sli*-dell!" he announced grandly. "Slidell, Lou'sana, comin' up!"

They rolled into town with brakes squealing and sparks rimming the wheels, the locomotive bell tolling, tolling. The trainmen—Artemus and Mister Nussbaum, Oliver Bomar, Vernon Stanfield—watched from half-open vestibule doors, and some of the postal clerks, tired of the dim, ink-smelling grotto of the post-office car, stepped out to take the air. Miles Duvall the baggage man slid open his door and leaned against it. When the train ground to a halt, Artemus stepped down and savored the damp air and the steam swirling from beneath the coach. It felt good to stand on solid ground, away from the swaying confines of the train. It was full dark now, and the sleet had turned to rain. The platform lights reflected in the wet bricks below, and the streetlamps and Christmas lights of the town glittered on the wet streets, the roofs of automobiles.

A red-capped porter in a voluminous overcoat pulled a baggage cart down the platform, the iron wheels grating on the bricks. The station agent, Mister Jefferson Davis Danly, walked beside. The cart bore a mahogany casket.

Mister Nussbaum came down the steps carrying a lighted lantern. He indicated the casket as it disappeared into the baggage car. "We used to think that was bad luck," he said.

Danly was a short, round, baldheaded, bespectacled man whose handwriting on waybills and train orders was so elegant you could hardly read it. "I'm surprised at you, Ira," he said. "I would have thought you above superstition at any age."

The conductor adjusted his cap. "I used to think of it as imagination."

Artemus said, "Well, call it what you will, it is bad luck for that fellow anyhow."

"In fact, that's a woman," said Mister Danly.

"Ah, me," said Artemus. "A young woman?"

"Not so young," said Mister Danly. "I knew her for a long time. She used to have a café in the old days, then—" He stopped, shrugged his shoulders and looked away.

"What?" asked Artemus.

Danly had the waybill for the coffin on his clipboard. He slipped it loose and folded it, then tapped it thoughtfully against his cheek. After a moment, he said, "She ran a sporting house down on Bogalusa Street for a number of years. Couple of days ago, she made all the girls leave, then soaked her bed in gasoline and burnt the house down around her. She had…a sickness, so I'm told." He gave Mister Nussbaum the way-bill. "You might have seen it in the papers."

The three men stood in silence, staring at the waybill in the conductor's hand. Artemus wanted to smoke again. He felt like he was inside the coffin himself, shut away from the air and light. Finally Miles Duvall waved from his open door, signifying he was ready to go.

"Very well, Jefferson," said Mister Nussbaum. He lifted his lantern and was answered by two short notes from the locomotive. All at once the train was moving. Mister Nussbaum disappeared into the coach. Artemus swung aboard after his conductor and was about to raise the steps when the agent called his name.

"I could have billed her out on the local," said Danly, walking alongside. "I just—"

"I know," said Artemus. He raised the steps and closed the lower half of the vestibule door. "This is the Silver Star," he said. "Everybody rides first class."

Artemus watched Mister Danly grow smaller and smaller as the depot fell behind. The agent waved a last time, and in a moment, he was gone. The town slid past, growing leaner and poorer, and then they were in the dark again, gathering speed among the pines and cypress and weeping moss toward the cold waters of Lake Ponchartrain.

Artemus went forward to the baggage car. Miles Duvall was hunched over his desk, a lamp illuminating his face. He wore a green eye-shade, like a bank teller. Miles had a face no one would remember long, were it not for his prodigious black mustache. His sleeves were rolled to the elbow, and on his left forearm was a faded tattoo of an anchor and the name, nearly illegible now, of a long-forgotten ship of the line. Miles looked up at the closing of the door. "Hey," he said, swiveling in his chair.

Baggage jobs were bid on by trainmen, and Miles Duvall had been a trainman once. Five years previous, he was working a train that struck a car at a crossing—a big Chrysler driven by a young woman schoolteacher, carrying half a first-grade class back from their field trip to a cotton gin. Duvall and the engineer and fireman ran back down the train, arriving just in time to hear them all burn. After that, Duvall worked as a crossing guard in Hattiesburg and only lately came back to the road as a baggage man.

"Hey, Miles," said Artemus. He took off his overcoat, for the baggage car was warm after the brisk night. The car was lit by electric bulbs, each in a little wire cage, that ran along the ceiling. By these lights the casket, still wet with rain, was illumined. It seemed to glow among the boxes, trunks, and luggage. Artemus thought of a Mark Twain story, the one with a coffin in a baggage car, a hot stove, a box of Limburger cheese. The story did not seem so funny now. Artemus knelt and touched the smooth, rounded top of the casket.

Duvall said, "I was just fixing to wipe it off."

"I'll do it," said Artemus. He took out his handkerchief and wiped the beads of rain away.

The swivel chair creaked. "Did you know this person?" asked Duvall.

"Oh, no," Artemus said. "She was a friend of Danly's." He took off his coat and gloves, and sat down on a steamer trunk. He was not about to tell Miles Duvall that the woman in there was burned up. He said, "I ain't talked to you in a while. How you like being back on the road?"

"It's all right," said Duvall, "so long as I can't see what's going on up ahead."

"Well, good," said Artemus. He dropped the subject then, but he thought about what the man had said. There was no real safety in the baggage car, and Miles Duvall knew it. He could still die any number of ways—by derailment, telescoping, boiler explosion, crossing accident, what have you—and the matter was out of his hands. A man could be careful, pay attention, do everything right, but some things were still out of his hands. In all his years on the road, Artemus had never, not once, known an engineer not to blow for a crossing, no matter how lost and insignificant the road might be, no matter if anyone was watching or not. When a whistle post went by, the engineer reached for his whistle cord, and he or the fireman rang the bell, and there was an end on it. Yet time after time, gravel trucks and tanker trucks and cars full of schoolchildren—cars driven by the old and the young, stake bodies loaded with corn or bananas or sugarcane, cement mixers and buses and taxis and cotton wagons—insisted on ignoring the shriek of doom. Artemus wondered why they did that, and if it was better for the train crew to see it coming, or better not to. In the end, he thought Duvall was right. It was better not to.

Duvall rose and stood beside the coffin. The train swayed into a curve, and he took hold of one of the leather loops suspended from the ceiling of the car. He nodded at the coffin and said, "The porter told me about her. He didn't much like putting his hand on the box."

Artemus made no reply.

"Your church won't bury her," said Duvall.

"Somebody will," said Artemus.

After a moment, Miles asked, "Do you remember the barber?"

"Indeed," said Artemus.

It was a long train that day, and Artemus, the swing man, was riding up front to help Miles Duvall with the switching: a cotton compress, a wood yard, a pickle plant in Enterprise, Mississippi. They were drifting into town, bell ringing steadily, whistle blowing for the crossings, and Miles and Artemus were pulling on their gloves when all at once the engineer stood up and said, Look out—what's this? and dynamited the brakes. The fireman hit the boiler backhead and was knocked cold. The wheels squealed in protest, and the train bucked hard. The men in the caboose were knocked flat, and the flagman broke his arm. Artemus caught himself and leaned out the cab window, peering down the long boiler of the engine in time to see a man standing in the middle of the rails, head bowed, hands clasped before him, but only just in time. The train would take a long time to stop, and all Artemus could do was watch as the man disappeared under the lead truck. There was no jolt, no bump, only the inexorable and indifferent progress of the heavy freight engine over the place where the man had been.

The main line was tied up for three hours while the ambulance came and took the injured away, and the coroner collected all the pieces of the man from under the engine—a barber, they learned, whose shop was just down the street, whose wife had left him two days before.

Now, in the baggage car, Miles said, "I wonder how in God's name he thought that would fix anything. And this woman—"

"Yeah," said Artemus.

* * *

Frank Smith finds Kane drawing ammo in the CP. Come with me, he says. Kane gathers up his bandoliers and follows the platoon sergeant. They pass down the line in a fog so dense it swirls like smoke around them. The company has been here for twelve hours, dug into the mud, waiting for orders to move. A light rain is falling, and through it, the Marines can hear the weakening cries of German soldiers wounded last night and left behind by their comrades. The Marines have already killed a German medic caught by the dawn in open ground. They will shoot all Kraut aid-men now, in retaliation for a Marine corpsman shot by a sniper yesterday.

This morning, the weather is unsuitable for snipers, but they are out there just the same, watching for movement in the fog. Kane and Smith keep their distance from each other. They move quickly, silently, bent over to make poor targets.

A half mile to their front is the tangled patch of woods from which the Krauts must be driven soon. Orders have arrived at last, and Smith has come to pass the word: over the top in thirty minutes, fog or no fog. Most of the men are watching the line, their rifles propped on the parapets of their holes, bayonets fixed. In one hole, a boy is praying, his rosary wrapped in his hands. Get ready, says Smith, and the boy nods and goes on moving the beads through his fingers.

At Kane's squad position, they are beckoned by Squarehead, the Marine from Illinois. Listen to this, says Squarehead, and waves them down. Smith and Kane lower themselves to the mud and listen. Somewhere out front, invisible in the fog, a man is talking. The voice rises and falls in the liquid syllables of the German tongue, as if the speaker were delivering a lecture.

What? says Smith, straining to hear.

This guy, the Marine says, shaking his head. This asshole—apparently, he came back to get his buddy last night and got shot himself. Ever since, he's been cussing the other one, blaming him for making orphans of his children, making his wife a widow, shit like that. He won't shut up.

What does the other one have to say? Kane asks.

Nothing, says the Marine. He ain't said a word. Hell—what would you say?

Well, says Smith, we go over in thirty minutes. Somebody will shut him up then, I guess.

I'll shut him up, says the Marine from Illinois.

Kane leaves the bandoliers of ammunition with his squad and follows the sergeant. Presently, they come to a hole where the young Marine they call the Scholar is cutting up his face with a straight razor. The boy is a graduate of the state university of California, well-spoken, of good family, a philosopher. He has always been brave. Now he sits in a filthy pool of water, his helmet and rifle and all his 782 gear thrown every which way, drawing the blade of the razor down one smooth cheek, then the other, cutting deep enough to spring out little curls of fat. He has fouled his pants, and the blood and rain run down his face and stain the collar of his tunic. While Kane gathers up the cartridge belt and haversack and helmet and rifle, Smith kneels in the foul cold water and takes the boy's razor away, carefully, and tries to wipe the blood off, though it keeps running, for the cuts are deep. What you doing, Winstead? demands Frank Smith, who never uses nicknames and does not have one himself. What the fuck you doing? he says.

The Scholar looks at Smith as if had made a stupid joke. Why, it is the rules of hell, Staff Sergeant, he says. You ought to know that.

The corpsmen are summoned to take the Scholar away. He makes a good deal of noise and attracts a burst of machine gun fire from the wood. Smith and Kane squat in the Scholar's hole, rifles across their knees, while the rounds snap over their heads. They have one cigarette remaining between them, and they light it under a poncho and pass it back and forth, savoring the smoke.

How you feelin? asks Smith.

Kane touches the scabs crusted on his cheeks. He says, The corpsman took the stitches out. I'll be all right long as I keep my mouth shut.

Fat chance, says Smith. Away off in the wood, they can hear the Maxim gun running through its slow cycle of fire, a leisurely Tat-tat-tat, tat-tat-tat, and far behind them, the rumble of French 75s firing by battery. The sky is low enough that the guns flash yellow on the bellies of the clouds. Smith says, Winstead was right. It makes sense when you put it the way he did.

Kane nods in agreement. When you are in hell, you play by the rules of hell.

Smith appears ready to say more, but time has run out. The artillery rounds are sighing overhead, making bright splashes off in the fog when they land. The Marines can hear the growling and clanking of the hinky-dinky French tanks that will support them in the attack.

Time to go, Smith says, while, in the wood line, the Maxim gun opens up again: Tat-tat-tat, tat-tat-tat.

* * *

Now Artemus looked at the baggage man in the dim, rocking car. He said, "When you are in hell, Miles, you play by the rules of hell. You cannot expect them to be the same as ours."

Miles Duvall took off his visor and laid it on his desk. "Tell that to the church," he said. "You want some coffee?"

"Sure," said Artemus. "Coffee would be good."

When the Silver Star began to slow for the span over Lake Ponchar-train, Artemus put on his overcoat and moved back through the train. The people's faces were reflected in the windows as they watched for the glow of the city. Artemus passed through the club car. The girl was there at a table by the Christmas tree, but she did not look up.

Artemus emerged onto the rear platform. A cold mist rose off the lake. On the platform rail was a lighted drum sign with the train's name. Out on the water, Artemus could see the lonely winking lights of buoys, the running lights of a tug, the dark shoreline where the houses were like distant candles.

On the crossings over and homeward from the Land of France, Artemus had discovered that the one darkness which could not frighten him was the profound, ancient darkness of the sea. He would stand alone at the rail as the transport plowed into solid blackness, her bow wave churning constellations of phosphorous to mimic the stars. When the shrouds and stays creaked in the wind, when the stars danced and whirled with color and the sea lights took the faces of men he had known, or of girls, or of strangers, Artemus felt only a deep reverence, as though he were on the brink of the Great Mystery itself. It was a darkness like no other, and Artemus came to believe that if he could only reach the heart of it, he would find there the answers to love and Possibility, to why you lived and what happened when you died. Artemus Kane relished the crossing of Lake Ponchartrain as he had the crossing of the sea.

On the south shore, it was different. The Silver Star crept through the ragged edges of the city: junkyards, boatyards, warehouses, dark streets lined with ramshackle bungalows and shotgun houses. Dogs howled like the sentinels of barbarian tribes. In an empty lot, men had built a fire in an oil drum, and their shadows leapt over the rubble, over the brittle grass, while the smoke, stinking of old rags, curled over the train. Ancient cemeteries drifted by, crumbling tombs and angels brown with moss and feathered with resurrection plant. A flare danced at the lip of a tall factory chimney, and boxcars and tanks and gondolas lay in sidings, their flanks scrawled with the mysterious chalkings of switchmen, yard clerks, hoboes, all the faceless minions of a thousand train yards spread across the night—all strangers to Artemus, like the souls in the warm, lighted coaches whom he would never see again.

Rain streaked the red glow of the marker lanterns. The drum sign cast a pale light over the rails behind. Artemus saw a possum they had run over. The wheels had sliced it neatly in half. The train slowed, then groaned to a halt so Vernon Stanfield could line the switch onto the terminal tracks. When the train was still, Artemus felt the dangerous night close around him like a damp garment. A house stood by the track side, windows darkened, with a barren yard and a dog that Artemus hated. This creature was chained, and every time they stopped here, the dog lunged at the train in silence, fell back at the end of his tether, rose from the mud to lunge again. A devil dog. Artemus always snarled and cursed at him, which only maddened the dog. One of these nights, Artemus thought, he was going to take the pistol from his Gladstone bag and send him to the Valhalla of mean dogs. And if the people came out, maybe he would shoot them, too, for being the kind who would make an animal like that.

Tonight, Artemus ignored the dog, though he could hear him slathering out there in the dark. He pressed against the bulkhead and lit a cigarette, feeling a prickle at the base of his skull. He took a fusee from the rack and twisted off the cap. Next to the entrenching tool and the bayonet, Artemus knew no better close-quarter weapon than a fusee dripping phosphorous. He held the flare ready to defend himself, not against the futile sorties of the dog, but against a vision he often had at such moments: hands reaching for him through the stanchions; dark, helmeted figures clambering aboard, their uniforms caked in mud, faces slashed by the wire.

It seemed a long time before the cars glided into motion once more. In a moment, Artemus would drop to the ground and line the switch for the back-up movement. He would be vulnerable and alone, but it would be over in an instant. Shortly after, they would see the lights of Basin Street and the train shed where Anna Rose would be waiting.

Artemus pulled on his gray cotton gloves and popped the fusee. The flare sputtered, then spread its hellish red smoking light over the rails, over the vacant lots, gleaming in the windows of an abandoned house. "Fuck alla you," said Artemus. He leaned out and signaled for a stop while the switch target slid beneath him like a lizard's eye.

COPPERS BY MIDNIGHT

He felt no pain—that was good. Lucky it was dark, too; that way, he didn't have to see what was going on, though he could hear it—smack, smack, smack—and that was bad enough. Really, though, all he had to do now was rest his elbows on the drawbars and wait to die. If he hung on long enough, of course, it would start to hurt—the nerves would wake up, look around, realize what was happening, say Whoa, man, we in some deep shit here!—but he wasn't going to stick around for that. Before that happened, he would be dead. He was already drifting in and out, his soul pulling against the cord that bound it to life. Pretty soon the cord would break, and he would float off toward the stars, toward Orion and the Seven Sisters walking overhead.

If he looked straight up, he could see plenty of stars in the open space between the tall black ends of the boxcars. That was funny, because a while ago it hadn't been any stars, just the low gray clouds and the mist. But he could see the stars now. They had moved in the time he had been here, shifting in the heavens, going on about their business. He didn't know many, but he knew the ones in Orion that his grandpappy had taught him, and he thought he would travel toward those when the time came. Now and then, when his soul assayed out into the dark, he could see the stars get bigger, brighter—could see that they were blue, not white, and could feel the heat from them. They were not cold, as he had always imagined. That was an important discovery, he thought, and he wished somebody was around to tell it to, but he was alone except for the dog.

Beyond the railroad yard was a screen of willows and cypress, a marsh, and beyond that the lights of houses; his own house, too, where his mother lived. The dog had come from somewhere over there. He hadn't got a good look at the animal but knew its kind well enough: a nigger dog, bony, short-haired, with a broad head and big muzzle, eat up with fleas, bare patches on his ass where he'd gnawed at himself. He had seen a thousand such dogs in his day and hated them all, worse than white people's dogs. Now this one had found some of his guts that were looping down under the couplers and chewed them loose and was eating them—he could hear it, even if he couldn't see or feel it.

"Go on, you son bitch," he said. "Be enjoyin' yourself, fuckhead dog." Then he forgot about the dog and found himself listening to the spring peepers in the marsh. That was a good sound. He heard whip-poorwills, and now and then an owl up in a cypress tree, and some-where a mockerbird singing. A long time since he paid any attention to sounds like that. He could smell a sweetness—dewberry vines blooming in the yard, and privet on the edge of the marsh. That was funny, too—it was late December, almost Christmas, and who had ever smelled such things and heard such things in the deep wintertime?

Way off among the houses, voices and laughter, maybe a joint over there, people having fun. He wondered how much time had passed since the switch engine left the yard. The locomotive had steamed right past on the next track, lighting up the rails long before the engine passed. Switchmen were riding the footboards—he called out, but nobody heard over the noise, and pretty soon they were blowing for the crossings in town, and he was alone for a time until the dog came.

He closed his eyes and felt his soul drift out into the blackness; it was gone a long season, tugging at the cord. Or maybe it was just the dog pulling out some more of his guts. He supposed it didn't make much difference either way. In a little while, he opened his eyes again and saw the headlights of a motorcar on the road.

* * *

The motorcar, a Chevrolet, belonged to the police department of the Southern Railway. One night last August, all the side windows had been broken out by some mischievous person with a crowbar, right under the noses of a half-dozen detectives on stakeout. The chief special agent, annoyed beyond measure, refused to order any new windows until the perpetrator was caught. Nobody looked very hard—in fact, no one looked at all—with the result that now, in December, the two detectives in the car were freezing their asses off, even with the heater going full blast.

The wipers, clicking and clacking, smeared the mist on the cracked windshield. The interior of the car was clammy and littered with brittle leaves of the autumn past, together with fusees, red and blue and white lanterns, a jug of coal oil, empty root beer bottles, yellowed sports pages from the *Times-Picayune* and *Meridian Star*—cheap novels, train manifests, and switch lists of freight and passenger cars long since dispatched into the dark of other nights. For weeks, a mildewed, round-faced doll had been propped in the back seat, smiling faintly, her glassy eyes gazing at her strange chauffeurs, or beyond them, or at nothing at all, just as the doll's little girl had been when they found her dead in an abandoned house by the right-of-way. Around the doll, like opened birthday presents, lay dozens of green .22 long-rifle boxes, some faded to the color of spring foliage, all discarded by Special Agent Hermann Schreiber, called Hido, who burned up two boxes a night shooting any living thing in the lower orders of creation that showed itself on railroad property. Schreiber was engaged in an experiment to determine whether God could produce vermin faster than the Remington Arms Company could produce ammunition. So far, God was winning.

Tonight, as usual, Schreiber was behind the steering wheel. He loved to drive a motorcar, for it was always a novelty, always a challenge, and he always made the thing go fast. Until he became an American, Schreiber had never driven a car or even sat in one. In another life, he had been a gamekeeper on the forest preserve of a Bavarian nobleman. His business was the hunt, and he was a first-class marksman over iron sights. When the army conscripted him for the Western front, he was thirty-eight years old, but his eye was still sharp. The army gave him a K-98 with a weighted barrel and a telescopic sight, and he put his old skill to good use: French, British, Americans, who knew how many? God perhaps. He felt no weight from those years, though sometimes in a dream he perceived an intermittent shadow moving across a narrow window—the arms, dripping rain, of a windmill—and heard machinery creak and groan far beneath him. Eventually, he was captured by murderous, wild-eyed United States Marines in the last days of the war. Schreiber, who was scared shitless of the Marines, dropped his scoped rifle down a well and stepped forward with his hands empty. His captors, who were in a hurry, never knew he was a sniper, or they would have put him against a tree and shot him. In fact, Schreiber had never told anyone about his adventures, not even his partner, Roy Jack Lucas, who had not been in the war, and who, right now, was slumped against the passenger door, rubbing his forehead as the car banged and jolted over the muddy track that ran along the south yard in Meridian, Mississippi.

Hido Schreiber carried an old .45 revolver, a cheap owl-head .22 throw-down, and a set of brass knuckles. He wore a gray wool overcoat, gray suit and vest, gray spats over black shoes, and a gray fedora. He carried three cigars, a Hamilton 992 pocket watch on the end of a gold chain, a folding wallet with twelve dollars, and a wrinkled photograph of his wife and two infant daughters who died of influenza while he was cooling his heels in a PW camp in Belgium.

Roy Jack Lucas wore a brown fedora, wire eyeglasses, a cheap rain-coat, a brown tweed suit and vest, a Hamilton 992 pocket watch on the end of a gold chain, and, in a shoulder holster, his .38 caliber Smith & Wesson revolver. He carried a pack of Half-and-Half cigarettes. Some matches from the Bon-Ton Café. A Case clasp knife. A pint bottle of bootleg whiskey and an invitation to his son's wedding at St. Patrick's Church, which he did not attend. The back of the invitation's creamy cardstock was scribbled with notes regarding the theft of three hundred pounds of U.S. Government cheese from reefer IC 5909 on a moonless night in November. The two detectives knew very well who had done the deed—a common thief, George "Sweet Willie Wine" Watson—but they were not about to tell anybody, for it would mean a Federal rap and endless paperwork. Instead, they chose to be patient, thinking that one night Sweet Willie Wine would wander into the sights of Hido Schreiber's .45 while committing a felony.

Lucas liked old Willie. He hoped the man would keep out of sight so Schreiber wouldn't have to drill him.

Roy Jack Lucas was sixty years old. At nineteen, he was hired as a patrolman on the Mobile & Ohio. Before that, he could not remember much. He might if he thought about it, but he didn't think about it. Now he was a detective on the Southern. Had he been asked, he would be hard-pressed to tell how such a thing had come to be. He was married once, but he wasn't married now. He didn't remember much about that, either, except that his wife had not spoken to him in the thirty years since their divorce; she would, in fact, cross the street when she saw him coming, even after all this time.

Lucas did not hate her in return. Years had passed since he had the energy to hate anything except the way his partner drove. Schreiber knew only two speeds: all ahead and dead stop. "Jesus Christ, Hido," said Jack, cradling his head in both hands. "You missed a hole back yonder."

"Jackie, Jackie," said the other. "You ought to get your brains looked at. Hurting all the time, I think you got a tumor."

"Good," said Roy Jack, then had to put one hand out to catch himself when his partner stomped suddenly on the brake.

"What the fuck?" said Schreiber. He ground the gears, searching for reverse. The car lurched backward, then slewed back down the road, the transmission whining. When it stopped, Schreiber reached over and shone his flashlight across the main line. "My God," he said.

A man was shielding his eyes from the mist-swirled stab of the light. For an instant, Lucas thought the man was floating between the cars. Then he understood. He pushed open the door and stepped out into the mud. He had his own flashlight now, and saw the dog crouching, saw the black blood on his muzzle, saw what he was guarding between his paws. The dog looked up and snarled at him, his eyes flashing red in the torch beam.

"Be careful of the shit-eater," said Schreiber. He called all dogs shit-eaters.

"I will," said Lucas.

"Hold on, Jackie, I'll get him," said the other, struggling to reach his delicate, almost toylike doubled-barreled sporting rifle in the back seat. "Don't look him in the eye."

"I won't." Lucas pulled himself onto the raised ballast. The dog snarled again and stood up, bristling. He drew the Smith and looked the dog in the eye and shot him six times.

"Well, shit," said Schreiber from the car. "You never give me a chance even."

Lucas stepped over the trembling body of the dog and put his flashlight on the man dangling in the couplers: a light-skinned Negro, perhaps forty, in an old barn coat and wool trousers and brogan shoes. The pants and shoes were soaked in blood and glistened wetly in the torchlight. The man's face was lean and bristly, and he still wore his hat. The couplers had caught him just under his diaphragm, and his shoes were dangling a inch from the slag.

"Gahd *damn*, Cap'n," said the man, laughing. "You ain't fool around with no dog, does you."

The detective had a ringing in his ears from all the shooting. He shook his head. "What?"

Schreiber was there, breathing hard. He looked at the dog, then at Lucas, then at the man. "What the fuck happen here?" he said.

The man shrugged. "I be crossin' through the cut, be stoppin' to light a weed. Now here I is."

"Shit," said Schreiber. He looked to the west where the yard was swallowed in darkness, no lights but the eerie red and green of switch targets, blurry in the mist. "They must've kicked in on the cut," he said.

"What?" said Lucas. His breath made a cloud, like the others, like the dog had made when it was still breathing.

Schreiber didn't reply. He went away, and in a moment returned with a blue lantern from the car. He knelt and lit the wick with a match, then handed it to Lucas. He did not look at the man in the couplers. "You go flag the head end. I'll get to a telephone. Jesus."

Lucas took the lantern and walked up the cut, past the black maws of boxcar doors, past a string of greasy black oil tanks and a half-dozen loaded gravel hoppers, their flanks silver with moisture. Now he realized what Schreiber meant. The cars in the track weren't coupled up when the switch engine shoved the hoppers down. The impact drove the two boxcars together just as the man was standing between them lighting his cigarette. Bad luck and stupidity. Colored people traveled up and down the yards all the time. The railroad was their path to town and back to home; it was where they picked dewberries in the spring; it was where they set out from when they left for Detroit or Chicago, huddled in an empty box or gondola, or underneath on the hog rods. They knew about switching cars. They knew the rules as well as the railroad men themselves, and they knew what could happen if the rules were forgotten.

There were lots of rules: Don't stand in the middle of the rail. When you get off, face in the direction of movement. Always grab a long ladder. Don't wear rings—you could pull your finger off. Listen for the rollout. Watch out. Pay attention. Check the oil in your lantern. Never shine your lantern in someone's face. Always pass signals just like they are given to you. Don't put a placarded car or a car of poles next to the caboose. Don't leave a knuckle closed on the head end of a cut. Pay attention. You can't see a flatcar rolling at night. Don't put your foot in a switch frog. Turn the angle-cock easy. Make sure the engineer can see you. Stay in sight. Stay out from between cars. Don't couple air hoses in a cut that's not blue-flagged. Don't be afraid. Don't hesitate. Pay attention. Watch out. Watch out. Death is always there—in the slick grass, in the moment when you think of your girlfriend, in the great wheels turning—waiting for you to forget. So don't forget.

A brake cylinder was moaning air, and the cars were groaning; Lucas paused long enough to set a hand brake so the cut wouldn't roll out on them. His ears were still ringing, but he could hear Schreiber grind the company car into reverse, then heard it whining backward down the road. Lucas hung the blue lantern on the first knuckle and started back again. He could see the car's headlights bobbing and blinking. He could hear the windshield wipers, click-clack. By the time he returned to the man, Schreiber had reached the lower crossing and was gone.

"I be breakin' the rules," said the man. "Ought not to been crossin' through, and them workin' up there. I know better'n that. Say, you ain't got a weed, has you? I can't get to mine right now."

Lucas shook out two cigarettes, lit them both, put one between the lips of the dangling man. "Smoking ain't good for you, what they say," said the detective.

The man nodded. "I know *that's* right," he said. "Done killed me once already. Ain't it a bitch."

Lucas was sliding fresh cartridges into the cylinder of his revolver.

"What's your name?" he asked around the cigarette.

"Is you rai'road police?" said the man.

"Naw, we the god damned Red Cross," said Lucas. "What you think?"

"Well, I think you might's well shoot me, too," said the man.

"Naw," said Lucas. "We'll get a ambulance up here, fix you up."

"Huh—I know *that's* right," said the man, laughing. "What we gone do in the meantime? We could play catch."

"I ain't got a ball," said Lucas. He slipped the pistol back in its holster, tight under his shoulder, under the tweed coat. "What's your name. I ain't seen you around here."

"Naw, Cap'n. I been off in Parchman ten years. They 'cuse me of killin' a nigger with a screwdriver, but it wasn't me."

"I'm sure it wasn't," said Lucas, though he was sure it was.

Parchman prison farm was up north of Jackson in the strange, flat, lonesome Delta country. The man must have ridden down to Jackson on the IC, then over to Meridian on the A&V. Only God knew why he ended up in the Southern yard. It was no easy trick, that traveling, and it left a man filthy and exhausted and maybe a little insane. Lucas had rousted many a 'bo, and they were all crazy.

The man in the couplers waved his arm at the sky. "Hey, you know them stars ain't cold, like you think they is."

Lucas did not have to look up to know there were no stars out, just the gray scudding clouds and the mist. "I didn't know that," he said.

The man looked up at the stars and began to sing:

> Gimme copper penny, boss, lay it on the rail,
> Little copper penny, boss, lay it on the rail,
> Jes' a little copper penny,
> Tha's enough to go my bail.

While the man sang, Lucas took hold of the dog's hind legs and dragged the body across the cinders, laid it out between the rails of the main line. He would have thrown it into the water, but he lacked the energy, and anyway, the thing was coming to pieces. He stood a moment, smoking, and looked out into the marsh, at the black water and the cypress, all smelling of decay. The town lights made a dirty yellow stain on the clouds. Lucas could smell the dog's blood and the man's, and the bile soaking the man's trousers. He flicked the cigarette away. He looked at his watch, then took out his notebook and wrote down *1201 AM* and *Cut in #1—negro male caught in couplers.* He turned and shone his light on the boxcar numbers, then wrote, *L&N 4139—B end—L&N 4250—A end.* "What's your name?" he asked.

The man stopped singing. Lucas tapped his pencil on the pad. "You'll get a stone from the county," he said. "They'll put a name on it or not, it's up to you."

"It's Watson, sah. Be June Watson," said the man. He spat blood, wiped his mouth on his shirt sleeve. "A stone would be nice," he said.

"Watson," said the detective, and wrote it down. He moved closer to the man, trying to ignore the smell. "You any kin to Willie Wine?"

The man's eyes lit up. "Sweet Willie *Wine!*" he said. "He my baby brother! You know him, Cap'n?"

"Yeah," said Lucas. "Yeah, I know him." He played the flashlight along the drawbars and couplers, then climbed the ladder and set the hand brake on the B-end car, just to be sure. Beyond that, he could do nothing. His hands were greasy now, but he pressed them to his temples anyway, pressed hard until he saw lights behind his eyes.

"It sho' a small world, ain't it?" said the man. "Here I come all this way, see could I find him, first white police I come across be a friend of his."

"Look, you in some deep shit here."

"Willie, he all right," said the man. "He done some bad things, but he ain't no bad boy. He just need somebody—" The man stopped and drew in a deep, ragged breath. Lucas closed his eyes and waited. In a moment, the man said, "Whew! That was a long way."

"Aw, man," said Lucas, and put his hand against the sill of the car and vomited in the gravel.

"How come a mockerbird sing at night?" asked June Watson after a moment.

"'Cause he can, I guess," said Lucas, though he heard no mockingbird. He heard them often in the spring and summer when he couldn't sleep, their caroling loud down the quiet streets, a lonesome sound, but not in the deep wintertime. Lucas looked down the road, hoping for headlights. He said, "How come your little brother is so no-account?"

"He ain't had a chance to be nothin' else," said June Watson.

"You believe that?"

"I believe I want another smoke," June Watson said. "I wants to get in all I can while I can."

Lucas lit another cigarette and put it between Watson's lips. The man sucked at the smoke, and the red tip glowed and hissed. "Mmm," he said. "Half-and-Half. That's a premium weed."

"You'll have plenty of time yet to smoke."

The other laughed around the cigarette. "You know better," he said. "Soon's they uncouple, I'm a dead son bitch."

Lucas knew that was so. He had seen two other men caught up like this. One was a switchman who hadn't paid attention; he had summoned his wife, spoke to her coolly, made her promise to get all she could from the railroad company. The other was a kid maybe fifteen years old. He cried the whole time and fainted when they opened the couplers. They never did get his name, and in seven years nobody had ever called to ask about him. Man and boy, they had lived only a few minutes after they hit the ballast. The sound of the lift lever was their death knell.

"You gone stay with me?" asked the man in the couplers.

"I'll be right here," the detective said.

"I want you to do it," said the man. "I want you to pull the pin."

"Aw, man," said Lucas. "I—"

"Nah, nah," said the man. "You the only one I knows. Needs to be somebody I knows."

"All right," said the detective.

"'Less you want to shoot me first," said the man. "I wouldn't mind that."

"I ain't going to shoot you," said the detective.

They were silent for a moment. The yard was like a cold slab of iron. Nothing was moving, and no sound but their breathing and the creaking of the cars. Finally, June Watson said, "You hear that mockerbird? I love to hear—"

"Shut up about that, god dammit," said Lucas. After a moment, he said, "Look here, you got any folks? Somebody you want us to send for?"

The man thought a moment. "I got a mama," he said, "but I wouldn't want her to see me all like this. Can you find Willie Wine?"

"Not unless he wants to be."

"Well, I know that's right," said the man. "He'll get the news tomorrow, I 'spect."

"I'll make sure he does," said Lucas, "one way or another." He would leave word at Wimpy's Café in Jumpertown, but the truth was, they probably knew already, the word going around in the juke joints and ramshackle houses of the Negro district. Things came to them on the air, Lucas believed, like radio waves.

"I wisht I had a drink," said the man around his cigarette, squinting his eyes at the smoke. "A drink'd be a good thing 'long 'bout now. Steady my nerves."

Before he thought, Lucas had his bottle out. Now he would have to let the nigger drink. Well, fuck it. He could wash the bottle. When the man had finished his cigarette and spat it out, Lucas reached up and put the bottle to his lips. The man drank, his Adam's apple bobbing up and down. "Take it all," said Lucas. He could smell the whiskey where it was dribbling out of the man's insides and mixing with the blood on his pants legs.

The man couldn't drink it all. He started coughing and spitting up blood, and Lucas took the bottle away. He wiped the neck on his shirt sleeve, then tipped it up and drank it dry in one long draught that burned all the way down. Then he flung the bottle into the marsh, heard it splash in the dark water. Lucas waited until the coughing was finished. He put his flashlight on June Watson's face. The man was grinning, his eyes crossed, the edges of his big white teeth rimmed with blood. "You a good man," he said. "You awright." Then his face took on a puzzled look, and he lifted a pointing finger. Lucas felt a tingle in his spine and made himself turn around.

He thought at first it was an illusion of the uncertain light, a shifting of some vagrant shadow where the dark was rearranging itself. Then he lifted his light and saw that it was the dog. It was dragging its hind legs over the rail, slavering pink foam, the teeth bared and rimmed with blood like the man's. In the flashlight beam, its eyes gleamed red, and its breath was harsh and wet, coming in long gasps and plumes of mist. Roy Jack Lucas took out his pistol again and emptied it into the broad head. The shots were loud in the silence, echoing off the cars, but even at that, Lucas heard the rounds strike wetly and the skull crack. The dog jerked and trembled and died at last with its muzzle an inch from Lucas's shoe, and the black blood pooled outward over the gravel.

"Gahd *damn*," said June Watson.

Lucas's ears were ringing again. He stood with his pistol against his leg. Steam rose from the bloody rents in the dog as if it were smoldering deep inside like a slag pile. Down the main line, Lucas could see the headlight of the switch engine returning. Lights were turning into the road, too: a car, and another with a swirling red bubble. That would be Hido in the company car, and the ambulance from the Negro funeral home. A third car bumped over the crossing—the coroner, probably. It was unlikely they'd bring a doctor, not for this.

"It'll be okay," Lucas said. "It'll be jake in a minute."

"I know that's right," said June Watson. "It be gettin' cold. You gone stay with me?"

"Huh?" said Lucas. Then, "Yeah, yeah. I'll be right here."

Watson laughed, then choked again. He put out his hand, the pale palm turned up. "Christmas gif', white folks," he said. "I got you. Gimme a penny."

"God almighty," said Lucas.

"I got you," said Watson. "C'mon. Little somethin' to carry across, pay the ferry man with."

Lucas dug in his waistcoat pocket, produced a penny, laid it in the open palm. Watson closed his hand around it. "You a good man," he said.

"You owe me that, now," said Lucas.

* * *

That was all right, then. Everything was jake, though the cold was settling in him. Pretty soon, a whirling red light was in his eyes, and he couldn't see a god damn thing. Heard men crunching through the slag, heard their voices, but no words. After a while, words didn't mean anything anyhow. He tried to listen to what the white police was saying, but again it was no more words than the mockerbird singing.

The switch engine coupled so gently to the east end of the cut that he didn't feel so much as a nudge. The engine's headlight was dimmed, but still bright enough to hide the stars above him. That was all right, too—he'd be up there soon enough. He heard the mechanical clank and breathing of the engine, then he heard some words—"I'm gone give you some morphine, boy"—but he couldn't see the face of the man talking. He felt a little prick in his arm, and a warm feeling ran through his veins.

The white police had his hand on the lift lever and was looking at him. "Can you hear me, June?" he said.

"I can hear you," said June Watson. "Go ahead—pull it."

The police jiggled the lever, then turned his head, spoke to a switchman with a lantern. "I need some slack," he said quietly. The switchman moved his lantern up and down, and the engine gave a little push. The couplers tightened, but it was still all right—no pain, just a squeezing— it felt pretty good, in fact, like an embrace, and June Watson drifted out a long way. When he returned, a mockerbird was perched on the drawbar, little gray and white fellow, flicking his tail, cocking his eye at June Watson. He smiled at the bird, then at the police man. "Go ahead," he said.

"Goodbye, June," said the white police.

"I'll see you over yonder," he said.

The police man nodded. He turned to the switchman. "Back 'em up," he said, and lifted the lever.

CHRISTMAS EVE, 1940

When Mister A.P. Dunn awoke, he had no idea where he was. He knew he had been sleeping, for a vast empty space lay behind him, but he could not say where he slept, nor what dreams he'd had.

The windows were gray with daylight, the room crowded with the indeterminate shapes of furniture. A telephone rang insistently. Mister Dunn closed his eyes, and a collection of images came to mind like photographs in an album: a radiator with a rope tied to it ("Fire Excape" read the hand-lettered sign) under a window pale with the first light of morning; a threadbare rug, an iron bed, a naked lightbulb dangling from its wire; a gallery overlooking a street. He believed he heard a radiator clanging, and outside, the clash of couplers and the chatter of a switch engine backing under a load. He had seen and heard these things somewhere, evidently, for they seemed a part of him. Then the pictures went away, and the sounds with them. He opened his eyes again and found himself in a different room, a different time, and somewhere a telephone ringing. He sat up and looked around. Here was a sewing machine heaped with cloth, there a chiffarobe, a rocking chair, a wash stand, a green plant on a table by the window. In the fireplace, a gas heater burned with blue flame. The bed where he lay was of wood and fancifully carved, and someone besides Mister Dunn was in it: a woman whose back was turned to him, her gray hair spread across the pillow.

Mister Dunn rose carefully lest he wake her, and while he sat on the edge of the bed, he thought how he must have been dreaming after all, for it was just last night he met the girl in the café. He tried to think of her name, but could not grasp it. He and the girl took a walk in the late summer night—it was Slidell; he remembered that—and the room must be a hotel room. He searched his mind in vain for a reason why he might be in a hotel. Ah—he had brought the girl here. With that, the shame chilled him. He had dreamt of a long time passing since then, but it was a dream only, for the shame was fresh, and the knowledge of what he had done pressed on him like a stone.

Then he thought, *But her hair was black last night.* It was bobbed, too, and that had shocked him even more than her sudden naked- ness—he had never felt a girl's hair like that. He glanced at the woman beside him, thinking it was only a trick of the light, but her hair was gray and grown long. He looked at his hands, translucent and spotted, the knuckles swollen, an old man's. The summer night was gone, too, and winter was at the window pane. How many seasons had he slept in company with a sin so great it would rob him of life? It's not fair, he thought, shivering. I didn't mean to do it.

Then he understood. Deep in the house behind him, the telephone went on ringing. Mister Dunn knew it was ringing for him. Neither sleep nor sin had robbed him—not of time, at least. He had been living, and now he was old and changed forever. He was not in a hotel, and the woman beside him seemed to belong here. Still the shame pressed on him, heavy as on that distant morning when he woke to find that a girl—whose name he had long since forgotten—had left him in the night and taken all his money with her. It wasn't fair, he thought. Time should have healed him by now.

God won't let you forget, he thought. When A.P. Dunn stood at the final Gate, he would have to answer for it.

He found a robe and drew it on, and moved across the cold floor, touching the furniture to ensure he was in the right time, whatever it might be. He went to the window and looked out on a blue-gray sky and a silver curtain of sleet. Beyond a privet hedge rose the shape of a white house, windows ablaze with electric light. The smoke from its chimneys was thin and gray and lay flat against the roofline.

He needed to answer the telephone, but he found it hard to leave the window. He saw an overturned wheelbarrow in the yard and a concrete birdbath glazed with ice. The dull leaves of the hedge were growing heavy with ice, their limbs bowing, and a white powder was collecting among the drifted leaves. It was peaceful, and he thought how he could go out and lie down in the yard and sleep under the ice. Then the woman's voice rose drowsily behind him.

"Mister Dunn, the telephone is a-ringing."

The words opened a door in his mind. He had heard those same words, in that same voice, almost every day he was home, in all weathers and seasons, since the call boys in Meridian began to use the telephone. They still came to the hotels out on the road, lads in knickers and caps and coats too thin, barging into sleep with their brisk young voices, A.P. Dunn! Call for Engineer A.P. Dunn! Call for 4:30 list on Number fifty-two! Rise up, rise up! But in Meridian they used the telephone now.

So he was home, he thought, and with that knowledge, all the empty places began to fill up. He was not in Slidell, but in the house he bought before he married, and the wife Nettie he'd lived with for forty years—who never knew he had betrayed her once, and once only—was speaking to him from the dim margins of sleep, and he was a locomotive engineer on the Southern Railway, and the insistent telephone was for him.

He left the window then, and went out through the door and down the long hall. The telephone was squat and black and sat upon a table under a painting of flowers his daughter Eileen had made. He picked up the horn. "Hello," he said. "This is A.P. Dunn."

In the gray parlor, a Christmas tree sat by the window, looking for-lorn with all its lights turned off. Eileen used to love the Christmas tree. She was in Gulfport now, married to a lawyer, and she never wrote nor called on the telephone.

The call boy's voice was clear and plain, as if he were standing in the door. Mister Dunn was called for Extra 4512 South at 7:30.

"Thank you," said Mister Dunn, and hung up.

The job was designated an extra so that it might work along the road at will. It appeared on no timetable, and every train had rights over it. Mister Dunn could not have said why he preferred such a job when he could have had almost any on the road. Maybe it was the waiting that appealed to him, though he chafed at times, as he had yes-terday at the Pearl River bridge. Waiting made time stretch out longer, and sometimes, when you were old, that seemed to be a good thing, as if you could put off the final call, the one you had to answer no matter what. But you couldn't put it off. *We live way too long anyhow*, thought Mister Dunn.

Shuffling in his robe and worn slippers, he returned to the bed-room. He was all right now. He was in the right time, and he remembered where he was. Anybody could be confused at waking, he thought.

A set of clean, starched overalls and a clean shirt and cap and neck-erchief were laid out on a chair where Nettie had put them the night before, like she always did. Sometimes he wished she wouldn't, just once. Sometimes he got weary of the familiar and the predictable.

On the chiffarobe was his Hamilton watch, the gold worn thin, the porcelain face cobwebbed with tiny cracks. The hands were blue and delicate. It was a model 992, the only watch he ever owned, and for half a century it had never failed him, never lost a minute. The inside back cover was crowded with inspection marks from crotchety old shade-wearing jewelers, some of whom had been dead for three decades.

The girl in Slidell had taken his money but left him his watch, though it was in plain sight on the bedside table. He had always been grateful to her for that, at least, for he would have been hard-pressed to explain its loss to Nettie. In fact, he would have told her the truth—he had never been able to lie to her. As it was, he didn't have to say anything at all, which was worse than a lie, or the same thing, he supposed. He had almost told her a hundred times, but he never did, and now he knew he never would.

Like most people, Mister Dunn had been ruled by time all his grown life. The difference was, citizens structured their days around the mill whistle, the posting of mail, the clock on the office wall, the movement of the sun over the cotton or corn—they painted time in broad strokes, by the hour, by the passage of morning, afternoon, night. For them, a minute more or less had no meaning, the deviation of a man's watch with his neighbor's of no consequence. For the railroad men, however, tiny increments of time were the stuff of life and death.

Men died for a moment lost, or because they were tired and misread a train order in the dark. Time was everything, and trust was everything. You had to pay attention, not only for yourself, but for the other fellow. Graveyards were full of men who were there because they hadn't paid attention, or because somebody else hadn't. That's why you had to do right, for every man had the lives of others in his hands. Still, they were only men, flawed, sometimes hungover, usually tired, often distracted, and the wonder was that someone was not killed every day.

Mister Dunn picked up his watch and hefted it, letting the chain dangle. Carefully he wound it, not too tight, and held it to his ear and listened for the little ping-ping that meant a faulty mainspring. He was glad to hear that all was well among the gears and levers that moved inside the brass case on the twenty-one jewel bushings. The hands said six-oh-four and twenty-five. Twenty-six. Twenty-seven. Time was moving right along.

His wife said, "Mister Dunn, I put the coffee in the pot. All you got to do is light off the eye."

"I know how to do it, Nettie," he said. "Now go back to sleep and don't be troubling yourself." Once upon a time, she would rise at four o'clock, or three, or midnight, and cook eggs and biscuits, and fry ham, but for a long while she had been sick, and she needed her rest. It had taken Mister Dunn a good deal of arguing to get her to stay in bed, to convince her that he could get his own breakfast—and even now he sometimes found her up before him, rattling around in the kitchen. Nothing, however, could persuade her to use his first name. It was an old way she had learned from her mother.

Mister Dunn believed in the words he spoke forty years ago, when he stood with Nettie before the pastor of the Anchor Baptist Church. He still believed in them, even if he had betrayed them once. He hoped that belief would count for something when the death angels came.

After he was dressed, Mister Dunn made his coffee. It was always Luzianne, strong and black, but not the chicory kind. He drank it at the kitchen table and had some cold biscuits and ham and a wedge of cheese. He gave some of the biscuit to his dog Missy, a little rat terrier who spent most of the winter lying under the coal-oil range. Sleet rattled against the window, and Mister Dunn wished he could stay all morning in the warm kitchen. He had wished that many times, and wished he could go to his daughter's piano recitals and her graduation and her wedding, but the job had kept him from these things. Well, he would retire in a few years, when he had saved just a little more money, and then he could sit in the kitchen any time he wanted. Trouble was, his daughter was grown and gone now, and there was too much he couldn't get back.

He took his coffee and went to the window. It was sleeting hard now, and the day was so dark that the houses still had their lights on. Probably it wouldn't get much lighter until afternoon, and by then they would be down south, and it would warm up and start raining. The grab-irons and stirrups would be slippery today, and the rails slick, and it would be hard to see, and everybody would be soaking wet and chilled way down in the blood. He wouldn't miss that, he thought. He would be glad to be shut of it.

He would get a hobby, he thought. He would take up fishing and gardening in the summertime and rabbit hunting in winter. Maybe he could make things up to Eileen, and maybe she would let him and Nettie see their grandsons. Anyway, the weight of memory alone should sustain him, he thought—and after all, Pelican Road would still be there, something he was a part of, and he could go and see it any time, for the old men were always welcome around the depot.

But not yet, thought Mister Dunn quickly, and reminded himself that he was still a locomotive engineer. Pretty soon, he would be setting his watch, reading his orders, talking about the day to come. Then he and Eddie and Sonny would mount the big steam engine that waited for them at the roundhouse, and the world would be in perfect order for a while longer. Mister Dunn didn't have to worry about missing it yet.

A.P. Dunn had enough age on the road to keep an engine when he found one he liked. The 4512 was a Mikado with eight stubby driving wheels and a firebox that burned cleanly, with the power and air to handle a hundred cars if it had to. It was stoker-fired, which meant that Eddie Cox did not have to shovel coal. It had a melodious whistle. The cab roof was painted red, the boiler black, the gangways and drivers trimmed in white. The 4512 was a handsome machine and a testimony to Mister Dunn's age and reputation.

The old men always talked about how locomotives were living things—that somehow, through some mysterious infusion, each took on a peculiar character that matched those of men. An engine could be weak, strong, stubborn, or eager—it could be snakebit or lucky, clumsy or full of grace, forgiving or demanding. To a civilian, all engines looked the same, and the notion of life in a machine was dismissed as romantic conceit. The fact was, you could feel the life when you laid your hand on the throttle. You could feel it in the vibration of the deck plates in the cab. You knew then that you were in the company of something immense and profound.

The effect was never so great as when an engine was coming along by itself. From a distance, it might seem elephantine, clumping and swaying down a yard track, its mass reduced by perspective. Then it was on you, and it was no longer a machine but a living creature whose single eye never closed, joints leaking steam, drive rods moving in solemn articulation, tall as a two-story building, dark and implacable, with a purpose and destiny all its own. When it passed, trembling the earth, it hissed at you, and you could hear the workings of its heart, the deep drawing of its lungs, and the man up there in the cab window seemed no more than an inconsequential organ, something easily removed and forgotten like a polyp or a bad tooth. Then, when it gave voice—

No sound on earth was like that of a steam engine crying, though the sound was so common that the ordinary civilian rarely paid it any mind save at a grade crossing—and not even then, perhaps, if his mind was on other things, and the windows of the motorcar were rolled up, and the radio playing, children squabbling, wife nagging. But it came to every person—in a pause of stillness, on a shadowed porch maybe, or in some anonymous hotel room high above the city—that moment when he did listen, for he could do no else. Then the sound plumbed deep inside him to the place where every unborn dream still lived, where the oldest memory of all understood that life was passing, and no hand could stay it. The sound echoed off the dark fronts of buildings, or drifted over the fields and wood, and in that moment it became the soul's own voice, crying all that was ever lost or dreamed of.

In the early days of the Depression, when he was laid off in spite of all his seniority, Mister Dunn took a chance and went out west to work a lumber boom on the D&RGW. He found himself a member of a vast fraternity of jobless men riding the rails in those days. Near the end of the journey, he fell in with some other travelers, and they made a camp one evening on a high ridge north of Durango, Colorado, in the San

Juan range. The Río de los Animas Perdidos lay serpentine in the valley below, and as far as they could see, clear to the silver, snow-topped mountains, the air was a crystal globe of silence. Nothing—not wind, not the creak of a branch nor the rustle of needles in the tall junipers— broke that momentary stillness, and after a while, Mister Dunn felt it down inside him, deep in the secret country of his heart, as if it were silence, not air, that he breathed. Then, as they listened, there arose from far down the valley the mournful cry of a steam engine on the narrow-gauge railroad. They could see no smoke, no movement; there was only the disembodied voice, as if the lost souls of the river were calling out in the twilight. The sound hung in the air like a drifting hawk, then died out in echoes among the far ranges, leaving the stillness again. In a while, the falling sun lit the distant, eternal snow and creased it with blue shadows, and the long fingers of coming night crept across the valley until only the coils of the river held the memory of day, and the boys marveled at how all that could happen in silence. The weight of time beyond measure settled on them, and they could feel the mountain breathe and stir itself, pushing a little closer to the darkening sky, lifting their tiny palmful of days closer to the mystery that dwelt above them, closer to the stars that spread in their myriads across the sky like fireflies rising in the dooryard of heaven. Only when the moon rose and the wolves began howling from the valley below— only then did they make a fire, and when Mister Dunn slept at last beside the dying coals, he heard the whistle again, and dreamed of silence, of moonlight, of the river when it had no name, shining in a distant age with a light no man had ever seen.

Mister Dunn turned away from the window, shut off the stove, and washed the coffeepot and his few dishes. He thought about going in to sit with Nettie a while and watch her sleep. Only she wouldn't sleep; she would know he was there, and wake, and trouble herself. Anyway, time had caught up with him, and it would be a brisk walk to the roundhouse. He left by the back door, closing it softly behind him.

* * *

The consist for Extra 4512 South was four empty boxes and a car of hogs. The switch engine had coupled the cars to caboose X-630 just before five o'clock that morning, then shoved the cut in the clear, rattling the caboose where Frank Smith lay awake on the hard bench cushions. In the half-dark, he listened to the voices of the switchmen, the air groaning in the brake line, the click of the wheels beneath him, the huffing and chattering of the switch engine, and at last the pop of the air hoses separating when the engine was cut off. Then it was quiet but for the sleet bouncing off the stovepipe and pattering on the windows. He felt around on the floor until he found the watch in the breast pocket of his overalls: five thirty-two, it read, and no use lying down again, for he knew his train was listed soon.

The X-630 was a relic of the last century, a grimy wooden box with side and end doors and a tiny cupola. Its platforms fore and aft were just wide enough for a man to stand on. It was a shack most conductors scorned—a reject, rough to ride in, unlovely and unloved—and for that reason, and with little difficulty, Frank Smith had made it his own.

Soon gray light would spill down from the cupola and fill the square windows and illumine the stove, its blackened coffeepot and coal pile; the rack of fusees and red flags and torpedoes, hot box powder and journal box hook; the conductor's desk with its spoked chair and a coal-oil lamp suspended on gimbals. The crew's rain gear hung like shabby, penitent ghosts from pegs on the washroom bulkhead. Smith had built bookshelves with a chicken-wire door: on the shelves were Faulkner and Twain and Hemingway, a dictionary, the current *Old Farmer's Almanac*, *Leaves of Grass*, Drake's *Indians of North America*, Sonny Leeke's collection of detective comics, and a half-dozen pulp westerns. On the bulkheads, secured by thumbtacks, were photographs Smith had made: group photos of the boys, a swamp at daybreak, family pictures, a photo taken from the back door of the caboose of rails receding between walls of pine trees. There was a portrait of Red Cloud, a copy of the famous Busch lithograph of Custer's massacre, pictures cut from magazines, a chart of world history, and a pinup calendar from Bergeron's Auto Repair on Camp Street. The girl for December 1940 was lounging before a fireplace in a white peignoir and Santa hat, smiling.

The caboose was freezing cold, which might explain the prominence of the calendar girl's nipples on this Christmas Eve. It smelled of kerosene and coal smoke and rubber slickers and the wax on the fusees. Under that layer of smells were those of coffee and red beans and generations of fried meat, sweat and old piss, the acrid perfume of Octagon soap, and the ephemeral odor of dark nights, weariness, movement, and of men who had come and gone—ghosts that no amount of Pine-Sol or paint could banish.

The coal fire was banked in the stove. Smith threw off his Navy blanket, and barefoot, shivering in his long drawers, went over and stoked the fire under the granite coffeepot he had filled with grounds and water the night before. When the coffee was made, he pulled the blanket over his shoulders and sat cross-legged on the cushions again, the tin cup of coffee steaming in his hand, and waited for the shack to warm up. It was good to drink morning coffee in solitude with the world coming awake outside—a little suspension of time when your mind was clear and you could think about the day ahead, though it rarely turned out the way you supposed. In that moment, familiar things seemed new and fresh again, and Smith took pleasure in looking around him. The gods gave you a new chance every day, he thought. Trouble was, you pulled the old days behind you like a long freight train.

He had lived in the caboose for nine weeks now, ever since Maggie suggested strongly that he leave. Sixty-three days, each one crossed off in ink on the Bergeron calendar. It was not uncommon for men to live in their cabooses for a day or two—on a work train, for example, or in a place where there was no hotel. But two months was way beyond anything the rules allowed, and Smith felt like a fugitive. He bathed in depot washrooms and did his laundry in the sink and ate in cafés or cooked for himself on the caboose stove. So far, he had escaped the attention of the railroad police, except for Roy Jack Lucas and Hido Schreiber, the night men, who did not give a shit anyhow; who, in fact, stopped by to visit and warm up on occasion, or listen to a ball game on Smith's battery-powered radio.

On his off days, Smith went by the house and picked up his girls, Iris and Dahlia. They were ten and eight, and had red hair like their mother's, and such a temper and a sweetness about them, and a Celtic imagination that thrived on fairies and ghosts and shadows. They had their names from two old-maid aunts of Maggie's who had gone to New York in the '80s and lived out vivid, often scandalous, careers as actresses. Frank Smith suspected that the "old maid" was merely honorary, a family title conferred on two beloved souls so that they might be spoken of and not forgotten. But no matter. Smith was glad to have such peregrine blood in his children, and he hoped they would blossom like the flowers in their names, like the two aunts who had not been afraid of anything.

Smith gave his children what he could. He bought them books of fairies and butterflies, he read to them, he told them stories. In return, they brought to him the tales they wrote in their childish hand, and the pictures they drew, and the things they made of clay. They liked to go to the picture show and, after, on a scavenger hunt in the trash behind the Temple Theater where they could always find old movie posters. If the weather was good, and if he could borrow a car, they would go to Highland Park. The children loved to ride the carousel out there, and Smith liked watching them go around and around on the bright-painted, cheerful horses plunging to nowhere. Sometimes he brought them down to the yard to watch the trains. Whatever they did, the time always came when he had to take them home. At first, they asked why he couldn't stay, but lately they had quit asking. They had their own ways of understanding.

But Frank Smith couldn't live on company property forever. Pretty soon he would have to get a boarding house room, which would put him right back where he started. That was funny, he thought. A capital joke.

On the other hand, he could move in with Artemus Kane, who had offered a room in the house he owned on 7th Street. Smith had most of his things over there already, though he had little outside his married life save the Harley-Davidson motorcycle which he kept in the shed next to Kane's Indian Chief. Artemus Kane had been born and raised up in the 7th Street house; it was almost paintless now, ramshackle and drafty and comfortable, full of books and worn furniture, with a broad front porch shaded by oak trees. Moreover, it was close to downtown— you could hit the Kress's store with a mortar round, if you had a mortar—and it was a short walk down through the Catholic church playground to the Southern yards, and maybe it wouldn't be a bad place to hide out for a while, Smith thought.

Kane stayed married for eighteen months to Arabella Foster, a match no one ever understood. Arabella was a childless divorcée when she met Artemus in New Orleans—a beautiful, elegant, well-educated woman who should never have been expected to adjust to the railroad life or to a place like Meridian, Mississippi, and especially not to Artemus Kane. Arabella refused to live in the old house, so her daddy bought them a place out in the new Lakemont subdivision. She hired a designer to "do" the house and refused Artemus permission to smoke inside or take a leak off the porch, not even the back one. Arabella had ambition. She got in with all the right people, making her way by sheer force of will into the closed ranks of Meridian society, who did not approve of her but who could not, apparently, resist or dissuade her. Finally, she began to worry at Artemus to get off Pelican Road and start a respectable business. Everybody else thought the idea of Artemus Kane running any kind of business, much less while living in a lake subdivision, too grotesque for words, but Arabella insisted on seeing in Artemus something that was not there. When she surrendered that notion at last, Artemus crawled away from his marriage as gratefully as he would from an opera.

So Artemus was back on 7th Street again, and for two years he had been with Anna Rose Dangerfield, another New Orleans divorcée who was not so beautiful as Arabella, but prettier and smarter. Anna Rose was a novelist. She was calm, mostly, and had a sense of humor. Best of all, she was not the kind of person who would aspire to live in a lake house. Kane's romance with her proved a record of endurance more remarkable than the Key Brothers' flight; nevertheless, the boys had a betting pool on how long the affair would last. To Kane's credit, he had so far cost his detractors, as well as his friends, a lot of money. In fact, Smith himself had lost ten dollars at a year and a half.

In the car ahead, the crowded hogs grunted and squealed. Coupling a livestock car to the caboose was ill-mannered in Frank's view; the shack was already beginning to smell like a hog lot, and the sensation would only increase when the train began to move. Wrapped in his coarse blanket, Smith wondered how the animals must feel, what they talked about, if they reassured one another. Perhaps the wisest among them knew they were going down to death and so would calm the rest, speaking of unfenced cornfields and troughs of turnips at the journey's end, all the while their hearts breaking with the truth.

* * *

In the summer, when the trouble with Maggie is just starting, Frank Smith and Artemus Kane take a trip to the Gulf Coast on their motorcycles. They make camp on the beach, go out on a long hotel pier and drop some crab nets and fish for croakers and speckled trout, then build a driftwood fire below the seawall and fry their fish and boil their crabs. While they eat, the night grows around them in a way Smith would never forget, as if it could stand for all nights' coming. The orange disc of the sun falls slowly at first, then drops all at once when it touches the horizon, leaving the sky empty but for the black shapes of pelicans beating homeward. Little by little, the water drains the color from the sky, calms and smoothes itself until it seems a vast, polished floor, the distant barrier islands hovering like airships. Soon the evening star burns bright and for a little while solitary until the night is accomplished. Then the last reluctant purple slips from the sky, and the stars straw themselves like silver dust across the darkness.

The two comrades sit with their backs to the fire, warming the muscles and the fragile spines that always ache. The dark water laps softly at high tide, and now and then an L&N train, bound for New Orleans or Mobile, blows monotonously for the myriad crossings to the north. Their motorcycles gleam in starlight; automobiles hum along the glittering arc of the coast road; the old beach houses, haunted by time, draw deep into the shadows of palms and moss-drenched oaks. To the east, the Biloxi lighthouse probes with its revolving beam. Smith squints toward the blackness that lies over the sea beyond the red channel markers, clear to the rim of the world. The breeze off the Gulf ruffles his hair and whips shoreward the rank blue smoke of his cigar. After a moment, he waves his hand at the bright shaft of the lighthouse beam. He says, We come from the dark, but we always think the truth is in the light.

Lux aeterna, says Artemus Kane.

Why couldn't it be the other way around? says Smith. The truth is in the dark maybe.

But not just any dark.

No, says Smith. Now he points his cigar at the starlit Gulf. Look how smooth the water is, like you could walk across it same as Jesus. If we could do that, maybe we'd get to where the truth is.

I tried it on a ship, says Kane. Twice.

I know, says Smith. I was there. You can't get to it on a ship. You'd have to walk.

You saying it ain't possible?

I'm saying you'd have to walk, says Frank Smith.

The truth was never easy, and it was never simple, and it had a way of breaking your heart. Thus men chose its imitation whenever possible and made the world fit the shape that suited them best. Smith believed man created God and Truth both in his own image, and he attached no blame to that. He had long ago decided that most people got along as best they could, trying to be brave, trying to be good, trying to subdue the terrors of life with whatever expectations lay easiest to hand.

In a little while, Artemus Kane, always restless, stands up and shakes himself and begins to pace in the sand. He lights a cigarette, his face lit momentarily by the glow of the match in his cupped hand. Finally, he walks off toward the water, the tip of his cigarette arcing up and down like a lantern signal. Smith follows and catches up with him at the water's edge. Once, camping out on Horn Island, they had seen the phosphorous race along the wave tops, and a bright arrow pointing to the moon. Here they have the grimy water of the Sound lapping half-heartedly at the sand, and a darkness relieved only by the shrimp boats' distant twinkle and the red blink-blink of the channel buoys.

They walk a while, a chancy business barefoot, for the wrack line is littered with broken glass, with dead catfish and stingrays who always wash up with their spines lifted, it seems. All at once Kane says, I am sorry for your troubles, Frank.

They have been avoiding the topic, and Smith would like to go on avoiding it, though he knows it is useless. He says, Don't blame Maggie. I brought it on myself.

I don't blame her, says Kane. And, no, you didn't. It's the fucking job.

In fact, Smith does not blame the job. If it was the job alone, A.P. Dunn and Ira Nussbaum and Eddie Cox would have been living in rooming houses and cooking on hot plates for years. The real fault lay somewhere else, maybe in a man's refusal to examine himself. There was too much pain for it to be otherwise.

The pain, when it comes, is empty and still like a room someone died in. Right now, Smith feels nothing, and he is glad, for the pain draws him inside to prowl through landscapes he doesn't want to visit. He nudges an oyster drill out of the sand, picks it up and examines it. As usual, the shell is occupied by a hermit crab who withdraws behind the armor of his legs. Smith throws the shell far out in the black water, hears it splash. He says, Let's talk about something else.

Sure, says Kane, but he presses it anyway. He says, All I know is, freedom's worth whatever price you have to pay to get it.

I guess you would know, Smith says. You remember that when you get tired of Anna Rose.

Smith is sorry at once, but he doesn't take it back. He watches Kane move out into the water, hands in his pockets, a dark shape against the stars. An airplane passes high overhead, engine droning, invisible save for its running lights.

When Kane speaks again, his voice seems far away. Maybe I won't get tired, he says.

I hope not, says Smith. I got money on you.

Kane doesn't answer. He is way out in the salt, and Smith judges the water would be up to his waist by now. Smith can hear Artemus Kane sloshing ahead as if he meant to reach the channel.

Heave about, fool, says Smith. You gonna fall in a hole out there, or step on something.

The sloshing stops. Smith can just make out his comrade's shape in the starlight. Kane says, I'm just following your advice. Trouble is, I don't know what to look for in the dark.

They are silent for a while, each man standing in his own narrow portion of night. Finally, Kane begins to move shoreward again. In a moment, he is on the hard sand, bending over, his hands on his knees. Christ, he says. You can get lost out there.

* * *

Now it was Christmas Eve, and the hot summertime journey was like a half-remembered dream. Smith got dressed—yesterday's greasy overalls and shirt, a flannel-lined jacket, his old striped cap—and went out to the back rail of the caboose with a fresh cup of coffee.

The yard was bleak and solemn, little pellets of sleet bouncing off the rails. Full daylight would be late coming, and then only a mockery of day. Lights were on in the stores and cafés and second-story offices along Front Street, and the switch targets burned brightly in the gloom. Christmas carols crooned from a loudspeaker at the Webb Funeral Home. Many of the buildings downtown were draped in fat colored bulbs, and the windows of the stores shone with tinsel. In the caboose, Smith had some presents for his children, wrapped in green and red paper by lithe and impossibly beautiful high school girls hired by the department store for that purpose. He would deliver them tomorrow after his train got in, whenever that might be. Right now, it was pleasant to look out on the quiet yard and listen to the sleet pattering down.

Mister Earl January came limping up the train. A long time ago, when Earl was a brakeman, he somehow let the wheel of a hopper car roll over his foot. Earl jerked away too late and pulled off the flesh of his toes like taking off a glove. The rest of the crew came looking for him, following his voice. They found him sitting in the gravel, the five white bones of his toes plucked clean and gleaming in the lantern light. Now Earl was a carman in the shops where his job, among other things, was to inspect all outbound trains and give each one its air brake test. He kept his toes in a jar of formaldehyde on the table beside his bed, or so he told anyhow, whenever he felt compelled to explain why his wife went to the grocery one day years ago and was still gone. Mister Earl had raised their daughter, Pearl River, by himself. Now Pearl was thirty years old, a trim woman with fading auburn hair and a tired face, who still lived at home and waitressed at the Bon-Ton Café. She had never married, and she never stayed with a suitor for long before she ran him off. She was a cold one, they said. Then one man admitted what the others in their shame would not. She ain't cold, he said, but she bleeds twenty-five days a month. Then he, too, ducked his head in the shame of telling, and not he nor any man spoke of it again.

The carman pulled himself up on the bottom step of the platform. "You got any more that 'ere coffee?" he asked.

Inside the caboose, Earl sat on one of the cushions, drinking his coffee. "This here's a bad time," he said. "Too many things goin' on."

Smith leaned back in his chair. "It ain't so bad," he said.

"Huh," said the other, and waved his arm at the caboose. "Look at you, livin' like this."

"I been in worse," said Smith. "What else is happening?"

"Well, maybe you didn't hear about that nigger in the south yard last night," replied the carman, with the satisfaction of one about to deliver catastrophic news.

"No," said Smith. "Something bad, I reckon?"

"Bad? I guess it *was* bad!" The old man sipped his coffee, watching Smith over the rim of his cup.

"Aw, it was bad," Earl said at last.

"God dammit," said Smith.

"All right," said the carman, "I'll tell you since you want to know. Carlton Wigley's job is makin' up a cut, way late. What you think happens? Nigger's crossin' over, gets squeezed in the joint." Earl laced his hands together to signify the couplers coupling. "Didn't nobody know he was there 'til Roy Jack and Hido come along."

"Well, shit," said Smith. "That's bad, all right."

"Goddamn right," said Earl. "Tell you who it was. It's Willie Wine's brother, June." He took another sip. "I'll tell you somethin' else, too."

"What?"

Earl peered into the cup, blew on the coffee, took another sip. Grimaced. Shook his head. Frank Smith tapped his fingers on the desk.

Finally he leaned forward. "Damn you, Earl," he said.

"Roy Jack was the one pulled the pin on him," said the carman.

Smith leaned back again and considered that for a moment. He said, "I thought June was still in Parchman."

"If he was, son bitch wouldn't be dead," said the carman. He rubbed his foot. "Man, it hurts in the cold," he said.

Smith said, "You ought to quit, Earl." He had said it a thousand times before, and he was tired of saying it.

"I can't yet," said the carman. "I got somebody else to look out for."

Smith had nothing to say to that. He moved toward the door. "I got to go uptown," he said.

"No!" said the other, in a way that made Smith turn and look at the man. Earl January wasn't looking at him, though. He was staring at the stove, scratching the bristles on his chin with his thick yellow nails.

"What is it now, Earl?" asked Smith.

"Nothin'" said Mister Earl, waving his hand. "Just…nothin'. You go on."

"Earl, I swear to God—"

"It's nothin', I tell you," said the carman. "Go on."

Smith was too tired to press it. He passed out the door and into the cold morning. He shoved his hands deep in his pockets and made his way up the train, past the grunting hogs and the mute boxcars, noting the numbers as he passed. One empty Southern car and three round-topped boxes from the Western Maryland, the kind they called covered wagons. No military freight this time—although the hogs might be going to Camp Shelby down below Hattiesburg, now that he thought about it. Shelby was an old training post from the Great War, and it was a busy place again since the Germans had rolled into Poland, and the Japanese were swarming over the Pacific Rim, and National Guard out-fits all over the country were being called to active duty.

Smith hunched his shoulders against the sleet and pushed through the gravel, through the smell of coal smoke and rotting fishmeal. A war come again, the whole world choosing sides. Not long ago, Smith and Kane took a notion to join up again just to get away from things. They agreed that it would be useful to do something different, kill some people, tear up some shit, call in some artillery on a medieval farm-stead—reduce it to piles of god damn bricks and then pound the bricks to powder because a twenty-year-old Kraut machine gunner was holding up the company's advance. They could do that again, they thought. They were still in good shape, and they were smarter now—smart enough to pay attention this time, maybe even write a book about it. Smith would pay attention and see the truth, and Kane would write it down, and people would listen.

When they called on the Marine recruiting sergeant at the post office, the man had listened, leaning back in his chair, his fingers steepled together. He was older than either Smith or Kane, and fatter than both of them together. When they had finished their appeal, the sergeant said, So you boys was in the Great War together, huh?

Seventy-three Company, First of the Fifth, said Kane.

Well, that's real good, said the sergeant. I got your names and numbers. Fuckin' Japs land in Palm Springs, we'll call you.

Neither Artemus Kane nor E. Franklin Smith would be running away to war this time. Too bad, really, for it made everything so simple and solved all immediate problems. For them, there would be no killing of Japs or Krauts, and if Kane wrote about it, he would have to make it up. When you got old, you couldn't run away from anything anymore, and killing was for the young.

Walking along the train, Smith thought about the man who had died last night, June Watson, who hadn't paid attention. The railroad would take you like the war would take you. You fucked up, it would snatch your ass away to the spirit world, and goodbye. You didn't fuck up, it would take you anyway, sooner or later, one way or another—break your back, cut your leg off, wear you out.

He thought about Roy Jack Lucas and wondered if he had really pulled the pin. Whatever the truth, somebody had done it, had held a man's life through the cold iron of the lift lever until the slack ran in. I'm glad it wasn't me, Smith thought.

He thought about Earl January's troubled daughter, wishing he didn't know the truth about her. She wasn't a girl anymore, but Smith always thought of her that way. Mister Earl had always loved the beautiful shady reach of the river Pearl down in Louisiana, and he had named his child for it. He had named her rightly, for when you didn't know the truth, she made you think of shade and green light and slow water. Now she was in a jam, probably, and the old man wanted to tell about it and couldn't, and Smith had given him no chance.

Somebody was hunkered down in one of the empty boxcars. Smith couldn't see him, but he could feel him in there, hiding in the shadows—a soul, a body, a sorry bundle of aspiration looking to get out of town. Frank Smith had never been mean to the riders, and every day he asked the gods to give him the same consideration.

He pushed on toward the depot where he would have time for a quick breakfast in the lunchroom, where he would buy a New Orleans paper and a half-dozen White Owl cigars at the newsstand. Then, when Ladner and Necaise came, he would sign the register and set his watch and get his orders, and they would all wait for Mister Dunn and Eddie Cox and Sonny Leeke to bring the engine down. Ladner and Necaise would be grateful for the hot fire in the caboose stove. They might comment on the hogs, or they might not. Either way, life was good, mostly, if you didn't fuck up.

* * *

George Watson had been in the boxcar most of the night, sleeping warm and comfortable under a big sheet of cardboard until the carman passed and woke him up. He didn't want to leave Meridian, but things were getting too hot for Sweet Willie. He knew Roy Jack Lucas was looking for him. That hurt some, for he and Lucas had been friends for years. He heard, too, that the city police were hunting him for the Club Moondog robbery, where all he did was drive the car.

These were the least of his problems, however. Last night, Sweet Willie Wine looked up from shooting pool and there was Lucy Falls watching him through the curtain of smoke. She was a small light-skinned woman with tight bobbed hair, and because she was light-skinned, she could paint her mouth and not look like a bluegum on a syrup can. A few months before, in a grocery in Jumpertown, George gave her the eye. She smiled at him, then passed him by and went up to a man named John Price.

Hey, baby, she said. What's this I been hearin'?

Aw, baby, said John Price, I didn't mean nothin'. I was just messin' 'round.

It's all right, baby, she said, and gave him a big hug and rubbed up against him. The man was getting into it, almost smiling, his face slack with relief, when Willie saw his face change. The couple turned as if dancing, and Willie saw the back of Price's white shirt blooming in little red flowers where she was stabbing him with an ice pick. He dropped to his knees, and she let him go. When she left, she passed Sweet Willie with a smile. Hey, baby, she said.

This was the woman who told Sweet Willie last night, in the smoky back room of Wimpy's Café, that he had knocked her up. She leaned hip-shot against a pool table and pointed a long red fingernail at him. What you mean to do about it, Willie? she said. Sweet Willie Wine knew that marrying was not what she meant. She wanted him to carry her to Orleans or Memphis where some doctor in a back alley could fix her problem with a coat hanger. God damn Lucy Falls. Sweet Willie said, Let me just get you a nice drink, baby, and we'll talk about it. His coat was hanging right there, but he dared not take it. He slipped out front, and when he got out there, George Watson just kept on slipping down the road, house to house, until he came to the Southern freight yards, then over the fence and the rails and through the slag and into the first empty boxcar he came to.

New Orleans was looking good, or Miami, or Cuba, maybe, if he could get there. South America would be even better. Sweet Willie Wine knew he was bound for an early death; he just didn't want it to come from an ice pick.

He was dressed in a wool snap-brim cap and checkered wool suit and brown and white two-tone shoes. He had a linoleum knife in his pants pocket, a .38 pistol in his jacket, and five dollars. His warm raccoon coat was, so far as he knew, still hanging on a hook in the pool room. Everything else was left behind in his crib across the alley from Wimpy's Café. It was easy to leave, for Sweet Willie Wine had never left anything he could not steal over again.

Sooner or later, time would move past the place where they knew he'd be back, and somebody would push open the door, gather up the bedsheets and his few clothes and burn them out back—they would keep the raccoon coat, of course, when they found that—and sweep the dead roaches into the alley. They would find his cut from the Moondog job, two hundred dollars stuck behind the drawer in his chiffarobe, and whoever found it would spend it quick. Then nothing would remain to show that anybody had passed there. They would find the letter from his brother, and if they chanced to read it, maybe they would hunt up June and tell him not to bother calling on Sweet Willie Wine, for he was gone and took George Watson with him.

Down the train, some hogs were grunting and squealing in a livestock car. George Watson could hear music playing downtown, and that reminded him it was Christmas Eve. He risked putting his head out the boxcar door—nobody in sight, nothing moving but a curl of smoke from the stovepipe of the caboose. Lucy Falls would be looking for him pretty soon, but by then, he'd be gone. So long, Lucy, he thought. So long, June. Then he went back into the shadows and crawled under the cardboard again, and after a little while he slept, shivering in his dreams.

* * *

The office of the railway police was on the second floor of the freight house, up a flight of creaking, spider-ambushed stairs illuminated at night by a single Edison bulb, and in the daytime by a pair of tall windows that looked out on the yard. A porter cleaned the stairs every Saturday, but to little purpose, for the grime on the windows was too deep, the spiders too crafty, and too many men passed that way. The detectives' office was behind a door with a frosted glass pane. It was a landscape of littered desks, telephones, gooseneck lamps, bulletins, wanted posters, old newspapers, and overflowing ashtrays. The walls were painted the universal sickly yellow of the Southern Railway, and across one of them was a rack of pump shotguns and Thompson sub-machine guns left over from Prohibition days. Mister Charlie Granger, the chief special agent, kept the key to the gun rack in a locked drawer all its own, just so the Kraut couldn't get to the Tommy guns.

At this early hour, all the lamps in the office were still burning, and now and then a gust rattled sleet against the windows. The radiators hissed and clanged. Chief Granger—a portly man in suspenders and bow tie and scuffed shoes, with horn-rimmed glasses and a balding head over which he combed the last strands of his hair—sat at his desk and watched Hido Schreiber caress the oiled walnut stock of a Thompson chained in the rack. Shreiber's partner, Roy Jack Lucas, slumped at his own desk, smoking, with a cup of coffee before him. Both men stunk of wet wool. Granger had just finished telling them that the day squad was off on a suspicious derailment at Livingston, Alabama, and the two night detectives would have to double over. Neither man had said a word, but Lucas began to turn his cigarette lighter in his fingers, tapping it against the desk, always a sign that he was unhappy. His face was slack, his eyes fixed on some point over the chief's shoulder.

The chief had a division to run, no matter that Lucas was unhappy.

Still, he was not without sympathy. He knew how Lucas had pulled the pin on the colored man. People would tell that story a long time hence, even when nobody was left to remember Roy Jack's name. But that was last night, and there was nothing anybody could do about it. Today ought to be slow, and at the end of it, the chief would go home to find his grandchildren by the Christmas tree, and his wife and daughter making supper in the warm kitchen, and his son-in-law listening to the Ole Miss–LSU game on the radio. Neither Lucas nor the Kraut would be so lucky. The chief didn't want to forget how lucky he was.

"Well, anyhow, it ought to be a slow day," he said, and rose from his chair and walked across the gritty floor to the windows. "You prob'ly won't even have to go outside," he said. Across the yard was the Meridian Hotel; on its red brick flank were painted the words *European Plan. Fireproof.* For years, Granger had wondered what the European Plan was. He had always meant to walk over there and ask, but he never got around to it.

An Alabama & Vicksburg passenger train lay at the depot, steam swirling around the cars. The windows of the hotel and the windows of the coaches were still alight, as if the day had never come. A man was coming down the yard. The chief recognized him: Frank Smith, one of the Southern freight conductors. *There you are, Frank*, said Granger to himself.

"Hell, Charlie, don't worry about it," said Lucas. He clicked his lighter once, twice, then slipped it in his vest pocket. "Everybody's got to be somewhere."

Granger watched Frank Smith pass out of sight in the yard. "Ain't it the truth?" he said.

Hido Schreiber rattled the lock on the gun rack. "Hey, Charlie," he said. "C'mon. It's Christmas Eve. Lemme have one, just for the day."

"Forget it," said the chief special agent.

Schreiber laughed. Outside the window, a switch engine chattered by, hauling a cut to the yard.

CRESCENT CITY

These things Artemus Kane knew first in his waking: a street-lamp—no more than a fat, cloudy bulb under a tin shade, its halo in the fog the delicate transparency of watercolor—hanging from an iron bracket outside the window of Anna Rose's flat. The streetlamp shone through the jalousies in yellowish slats, breaking up the shapes of the water stains on the ceiling, rippling over the slow-turning blades of the overhead fan. The flame of the gas heater made shadows dance over the mantel: books, a Chinese jar, a figurine of Pierrot. Occasionally, the headlights of an automobile, reflected in the wet stones of the street below, swept like ghostly comets over the ceiling, the wall, to burn themselves out in the mirror of the dressing table. Finally, the glass rectangle of the transom glowed dimly by the Edison bulb that had burned in the hall night and day for thirty years.

Artemus listened to the nocturne of the city: a police siren on Canal Street, a switch engine on the batture, boats hooting on the river, the horn of a ferry and the answering moan of a ship passing down to the sea. The clatter of garbage cans. A delivery truck shoving through the fog. Voices, arguing or intimate or laughing, of strangers passing on the banquette below, their footsteps fading away into what-ever world they had made for themselves out there in the night. Johnny

Lozano's dog was barking down in the courtyard, maybe fussing at the roaches, or a rat, or maybe he saw Hecate in the fog. Artemus Kane said once, when he was in a bad humor, that dogs only barked because they are stupid. Anna Rose told him they are not stupid. She told him that Hecate walked in the night, and only dogs could see her. Hecate was the Goddess of Night, she said. Artemus was silent for a while, working the muscles in his jaw. He was angry as he often was, though not at her. Never at her. Then he said he knew Hecate well enough. He saw her in the deep watches all the time, he said.

Anna Rose's laundry hung down there among the palms and Spanish Bayonet and the urns that, when summer came, would drip with flowers. The urns were empty now, and the walls slick with mold. Black roaches, even in December, scuttled over the bricks.

Christmas Eve had arrived hours before on the solemn chime of the cathedral where candles burned for the dead and their light cast dancing shadows over the sorrowful faces of saints. The bell rang to no real purpose, however, for the ghosts here had outlived time, and the turning of day and night was only an illusion for the living. St. Peter Street was yet closed and shuttered against the night, the galleries draped with yesterday's laundry and twined with the wisteria of a hundred years. The bricks and plaster were glazed with damp like the tile roofs and the chimneys that curled little plumes of smoke. The drooping telephone wires were beaded with moisture. The banquette and the stone-paved street reflected the streetlamps and the dim lights burning over the doors.

It was still dark, but not long before the gray winter dawn. This was the hour when Artemus always woke, coming to awareness all at once as though waking were a door he stumbled through. Whenever he came out of sleep, his dreams, remembered or not, lingered like smoke around him. His head ached—he believed that pillows, no matter how arranged, cut off the flow of blood to his brain—and he was always angry, always afraid, as if something were about to happen, or already had.

Now, in his waking, he looked at Anna Rose and felt the anger and fear pass away. She had thrown the covers off the small swelling of her breasts and flung out an arm and dangled a slim ivory leg off the bed. The sight of her stilled the anger and fear that he could never put a reason to. He wanted to touch her breasts, touch the delicate bones of her face, the ridge of her nose. He wished she would open her eyes and turn to him. But Artemus would not waken a person from sleep, no matter how restless, and especially not Anna Rose once she found it.

* * *

In the line, at first, they can never sleep, or only enough to leave them bleary-eyed, stumbling phantoms of men who move as if walking in sand or water. Then, after a while, they discover they can sleep anywhere: in the mud, the rain, on the march, even in company with the dead. Finally, at the end, when they dare to believe again they might live, sleep becomes too much like death for some, and they grieve for fear of it and for the want of it.

Gideon Kane is one of these. Just after the Armistice, when the regiment is in cantonment, Gideon goes four nights without sleep. It is the silence, Gideon says. It is too god damned quiet to sleep, he says.

On the fifth night, Artemus is making his rounds as Corporal of the Guard when he hears a hacking cough in the darkness, nothing unusual, half the men in camp have a cough, but this one he recognizes. He searches among the pyramidal tents and at last finds his brother sitting on the duckboards with a .45 service revolver in his lap. Artemus brings his rifle down to port arms. Gideon, he says. What the fuck you doing?

Gideon hawks and spits and looks up at the shadowy figure in the dark. Fuck off, buddy, he says, and cocks the pistol and puts it to his temple.

No, you don't, says Artemus, and slaps his brother with the butt of the Springfield, a quick upward expert stroke, the kind they use on prisoners sometimes, that sends the boy sprawling but doesn't kill him. Gideon lies quietly in the mud, moaning a little. Artemus says, Well, I guess you'll sleep now, you little shit. Then he drags Gideon off to sick bay where they give him a dose of morphine. The next day, and the next, Artemus comes around to find him sleeping, still loaded up with morphine. His head is swaddled in a bandage, his mouth agape, his nose running, the pillow-ticking soaked with drool. On the morning of the third day, Gideon is sitting up but refuses to speak. Artemus sits by the cot, waiting, until, at last, Gideon points to his bandaged head and says, It's not this, Brother.

Well, what, then? asks Artemus.

Brother and fool, says Gideon. It's that I don't want to wake up again.

* * *

Over the simple curve of the footboard, Artemus watched Pierrot's shadow dance on the plaster wall with its partner, the fat shadow of the jar. Overhead, the fan wobbled on its stem, kinetic in the barred light like an old moving picture of a fan. The blades were pitched to drive the heated air down from the ceiling, and Artemus could feel the warm breath of it. He heard mice in the walls, and his Hamilton watch ticked on the bureau. Beside him, Anna Rose talked in her dreams, like she did the first night of the first day he ever saw her.

* * *

She comes in the midst of an early summer squall that has swept unexpectedly off the Gulf and, in a matter of minutes, left the gutters awash, overloaded the drains, and pushed up manhole covers on the streets. Artemus, in a saggy linen suit, tie loosed, a watch chain looped from his coat pocket, has been drinking whiskey and paregoric, and he cannot be sure if he is sleeping or awake. As the storm diminishes, he watches from an archway that drips rain like a beaded curtain, flanked by the heavy, lashing fronds of banana trees. The courtyard is filled with the sound of water. Gray-green light suffuses from the stippled pool in the center where bright fish live. The light creeps into the shadows of oleander and ivy, touches the face of a melancholy statue of Our Lady whose hands, black with mold, are spread in a gesture of benefaction and forgiveness, as though she were expecting a caller with bad thoughts.

Gideon Kane's Creole house is often the destination of such persons, including Artemus himself. The people who know Gideon, who have been drawn into his circle, come when they want to, but more when they need to. They come with their faces shining like Moses' to spend an afternoon, a night, a week. They pass through the rooms, share the cooking, make love in curtained alcoves, smoke dope, sleep on the couches, drink and talk through the dark hours and play jazz on the Victrola. They take up collections for the gas bill and leave their toiletries in bureau drawers. They are plasterers, defrocked priests, pastry chefs, bartenders, novelists who have never sold a novel, musicians who play in back-alley clubs, painters and sculptors, Tarot tellers, horse trainers from the Fairgrounds track—people who are driven to make things, or shape or tell them, who share those compulsions and one other, the most dangerous, the one that guarantees bad thoughts: they all want to know Why.

They believe there is an answer, though they understand that it is not to be found at Gideon Kane's or anywhere else. God is unlikely to whisper it anytime soon. The Christ will not proclaim it from the housetops, and nature is mute. Toward these silences they are grateful, for they understand this, too: the answer, were it ever attained, would admit them, not into the ineffable light, but into a loneliness too great to bear, into a garden of stony despair worse than Gethsemane. The question, in the end, is all that matters, and the fact that they can ask it at all.

Thus comes Anna Rose Dangerfield through the gate with its iron scrolls and pineapples. The rain has caught her on the street, evidently; she is not dressed for foul weather, but in a cotton jacket and knickers and cotton stockings and a broad snap-brim hat that makes her look like a newsboy, all soaked through and through. In fact, Artemus supposes at first that she *is* a boy. Then she steps to her ankles in a cold puddle and curses and slams the gate shut with an awkwardness that betrays her. Artemus wakes from his drowse then. He jabs a finger at her and says, Stay right there, and turns away. The girl follows him under the arch and waits. In a moment, Artemus returns with an umbrella. He frowns out into the courtyard, puzzled, then sees her standing beside him. A cigarette dangles from his mouth, and around it he says, I thought you were going to wait.

I was standing in the rain, she points out.

Ah, says Artemus. It's just as well, for I am a man who does not approve of umbrellas as a general thing. If you have come to see Gideon, you should know that he is inside wearing a gas mask.

Why is he doing that? says the strange girl, and steps forward, watching his face. Now that she is close, Artemus can tell that she, too, has been drinking. It is Sunday, after all, the day appointed for bad thoughts.

Well, he was gassed one time, Artemus says. He claims he can still smell it, more on rainy days.

Who are you? she says. The rain is coming harder now, hammering on the courtyard bricks, overflowing the gutters. Artemus is swaying a little, and he takes the girl's arm to steady himself. The girl frowns. What happened to your face? she asks, and raises her hand and touches Artemus on the cheek.

He says, First, let me tell you about this one time. It was late October of '18. You think this is rain? Think again! We were in the yard of a big old church, but no dry place in it, you see, nor in the church either, of course, because the god damn roof was gone and the walls knocked down by our own artillery. Imagine that!

Who are you? she says, but he goes on talking, and the rain beating down. He says, Oh, you wouldn't of known Gideon then. He was a fair-haired, delicate boy, but a good Marine just the same, one of the best, next to myself. The day I'm telling—I remember like it was yesterday, he was in his garrison cap and overcoat with a Winchester twelve-gauge slung muzzle-down over his shoulder—he always carried a shotgun, wouldn't have a thing to do with a rifle. Mud everywhere, in big clumps on his shoes and puttees. His weapons squad was in the church making coffee. They had a brace of these half-ass French machine guns, I forget what you call 'em, chambered .30 caliber U.S. and prone to jamming. They were called—

We need to go inside, she says.

—Chauchat guns, says Artemus. They were no good. They... He falters then. He has forgotten the point of his story. He says, I'm sorry. I didn't mean to bore you. Did I mention the windmill?

You are Gideon's brother, she says. I know about you.

The windmill is important, he says.

I don't want to hear about it, she says.

All right, he says. But first—see here, are you a girl or a boy?

She laughs. I am a girl, trust me.

Well, thank God for that, he says, and pulls her close and kisses her full on the mouth. She lets him get all the way done before she slaps him.

* * *

At midnight, they are alone in the studio amid the smells of oil paints and turpentine. Artemus has not taken a drink in hours and is almost sober, and now he paces the pine floor among his brother's canvases, smoking a pipe filled with the cheap drugstore tobacco he prefers.

Meanwhile, Anna Rose watches from a pile of silk pillows where she sits with her legs drawn up. She has removed her wet shoes and stockings and her feet, bare now, are crossed at the ankles. She is smoking a cigarette, a china cup in her hand to catch the ashes lest they fall on the pillows. Behind her is an ancient Japanese screen brushed delicately of egrets and a mist-shrouded river, all fading yellow with time. The jalousies are open; the rain streaks the windows and patters through the leaves of a live oak outside. Voices rise from the house below, and someone is playing a guitar.

* * *

When they first came into the studio, Artemus showed her his brother's recent art: streetscapes mostly, leaning about on canvas stretchers, unframed. They are not of the Quarter but of downriver neighborhoods and the Irish Channel, Magazine Street, Algiers. The paintings have little negative space, not even the sky; they are solid with houses, with buildings and complicated galleries and windows, rooflines and ironwork, jutting dormers, laundry on the line, finials and urns and swags, automobiles and streetcars. Everything is touched by low sunlight, the tilting of day to evening, and a dark play of shadow. Kinesthesia, Anna Rose called it. Look here, she said. Look how the light and shadow make the buildings live and how they make the people move.

Artemus has perceived this in Gideon's work, how restless it is, and full of movement, but he has never understood how the effect was achieved. He looked closer, a little humbled, a little jealous, trying to see it through the girl's eyes.

Gideon has crowded his streets and sidewalks with people. Their faces, black and white, are animated, their garments bright splashes of color, their gestures arrested in time, but just barely, as if everything were about to shift, as if the composition itself was about to change.

Can you hear it? asked Anna Rose. She took Artemus by the arm and guided him close to a busy street slanted on an easel. Listen, she said. Do you hear that? It's the hardest thing to do, making sound where there should be no provenance of sound, just paint or clay or words on the page. She frowned then. That's hard for me, writing, she said. It's hard to make it live so you can hear it.

One painting is different from the rest, quickly done, and loosely. In it, the sky is white, the shadows stark. A railroad boxcar in three-quarter wedge, slightly canted, sits by itself on a yard track in a pool of dark cinders. The air hoses hang correctly, the knuckle is rusty, brake chain slack, and the lettering on the car, and the chalk markings, are indistinct but exact, like the eye might catch them if the car was in motion. The light glances off the rail and the roof walk and the circle of the brake wheel, but it is a neutral light, and everything in the painting is still, and there is no sound.

Look at this one, Artemus said. I was there when he did it. He set up his easel right in the yard and would of got run over if it wasn't for me. What do you see?

You tell me this time, she said.

Artemus lit his pipe, and the cloud of rank smoke swirled across the painting like ground fog from the marshes. He said, There was a hundred cars in the yard that day, but he chose this one and cast it apart from all the others. He got it just right, but he altered the universe for it.

Why you think he did that?

Artemus pondered a moment, feeling a little stupid. Finally, he said, It's what he saw, what he wanted to see.

Yes, she said. It's about something different. This one is about some*body*. Maybe about him. Maybe you.

What? said Artemus. *I am a stranger to you*, he thought. What makes you say that? he asked.

We are the only reason to do any art at all, she said. To do anything at all.

They left the paintings then, and Anna Rose sat on the pillows and took off her shoes and stockings, lifting each leg just a little, a simple, thoughtless, graceful act, ordinary and beautiful. You got an ashtray? she asked, and Artemus found a china cup with a smudge of dried coffee in the bottom. He gave it down to her. Thanks, she said, and lit her cigarette.

* * *

It is a little while before she speaks again. The only light comes from a fanciful lamp, a Nubian hermaphrodite bent gracefully backward and holding in her palms the globe of the moon. By its lumination, Anna Rose's face, when she lifts it, is small and sharply planed, fragile even with the broken nose, the dark crescents under the eyes. The black curls of hair along the nape of her neck are damp with sweat. When she speaks, her voice is barely audible over the rain.

I was going to stay home this afternoon, she says. I went walking instead. I didn't know I was going anywhere until I got here.

That often happens to people, he says.

She smiles at that, but the smile drops quickly away. She says, Before it rained, the sun was just under the clouds, like in the paintings. Maybe that's why I went, because it was a soft day, because it smelled like rain but I thought it wouldn't rain. People were everywhere in the street, and all their voices were crowded together, and music—the pie lady was singing, a guy was playing a horn. You know what I mean?

Yes, says Artemus.

Anna Rose waves her hand. She says, The sun touched everything, all the green leaves and the buildings and the people's faces. The light made me want to cry, it was so perfect. I thought…I looked out and I knew I had to be in it. If I could just get into the light, then it would touch me, too, I thought. I would be there in the middle of time, like all those people, and I would see everything the way they do, and I would feel something.

Her voice is drowsy now, and she has turned her head toward the window. All those people, she says.

She yawns then, and lies back on the pillows. Artemus is no longer pacing, the pipe has gone cold in his hand. He waits for her to speak again, but she is sleeping now, curled on her side, her legs drawn up.

In a corner of the studio is a still life that Gideon has set up for his students: oranges, a pomegranate, a clay pitcher laid out on an ample square of muslin. Artemus sets the arrangement aside, shakes out the cloth, and spreads it over the girl. She stirs and takes the edge of it in her hand and pulls it to her chin.

Artemus watches for a long time. He paces to the window, to the door, around the canted easels, all quiet lest he waken her and she leave. He turns off the lamp after a while, and when his eyes adjusts, he finds Anna Rose nearly vanished in deep shadow. He sits down on an over-stuffed sofa, among fringed pillows and damask throws, in company with a pair of tabby cats who reluctantly make way for him. Anna Rose snores lightly and talks now and then in her sleep: a name he does not know, a phrase he cannot decipher. He listens to the rain, listens to the oak leaves brushing the window pane, and as he drifts into sleep at last, he understands what Gideon meant in the hospital long ago.

* * *

Now he had known her across seven seasons. By now, he should not have been able to abide the touch of her naked foot under the covers. He should be lying in the bed rigid as a plank. Usually, he could count on three months to the moment when he discovered that the person he desired so ardently yesterday was the last one he wanted to see today, and the voice so lately musical was discord now, like the screeching of a parrot.

He sat carefully upright and looked at the girl beside him. She was sleeping with her eyes half-open, which always made him uneasy. At such times, he listened closely to assure himself she was breathing. It was a foolish thing, but he was afraid he could lose her that way, afraid

Hecate would steal her away in the dark.

He stood up then, and suddenly there was his own shadowy self in the mirror of the dressing table. He was going a little paunchy around the middle, but he was still trim enough, he thought. For a while, Artemus had the notion that surely the Corps would take him back for the new war—he was, after all, an experienced rifleman—and he could return to the Land of France and smite the Hun all over again. Only they didn't call them Huns now, did they? The god damned Krauts, thought Artemus. All that trouble, and they hadn't whipped them after all.

He moved closer to the mirror, and in the dim lumination of the streetlamp considered his face. He touched the pale scars, first one, then the other. Too old, Artemus, he told himself. The Marine recruiter had made that plain to him and Frank Smith when, not long ago, they had gone to see about reenlisting. Try the Army, the man had said. They take old guys like you. That was funny, considering the recruiter was older and fatter than either of them.

When Anna Rose found out he had tried to reenlist, she did not bother to ask Why. She called him a god damned fool and would not speak to him for three days.

Now Anna Rose moved restlessly and frowned. "I'm cold," she said in her sleep, and Artemus lifted her leg back on the bed, and crossed her arms over her breasts, and pulled her grandmother's knitted afghan to her chin. "Thanks," she said, and murmured a name Artemus did not know. Artemus didn't hold that against her; he had plenty of names she didn't know either. Everyone did, he supposed, and it was nothing to worry over. He put on his robe then and turned up the gas heater. The apartment had no stove, but no matter. Anna Rose couldn't cook anyway, or wouldn't, which was all right with Artemus, who cared little for eating. There was a hot plate, however, and Artemus turned it on and watched the coil glow red. He started a brew of coffee in the glass percolator. When the water began to boil, Artemus moved quietly over the worn Turkish carpet. He eased open the jalousies, eased open a window—wincing at the sash weights clanking in their grooves—and stepped out on the gallery. The cold slapped him, and he drew the robe close. He lit a Picayune and drew on it, exhaled and watched the smoke drift away with the vapor of his breathing, watched it mingle with the heavy fog.

He tried to fix things for Anna Rose—a leaky sink, a door that wouldn't close, a shorted-out lamp. He had broken things, too, like the original percolator that he threw against the chimney breast, like the slats in the jalousies that he put his fist through one night. During these episodes, Anna Rose watched him without a word. Sometimes afterward, when he was calmed down and feeling foolish, she would tell him to leave, though she never made him leave. Sometimes she would ask him what he was mad at. To this, he never gave an answer. The one thing she never did was cry. In any event, Artemus had bought a new percolator and replaced the slats and oiled the hinges of the jalousies so they wouldn't wake Anna Rose if he opened them, though she always woke anyhow.

* * *

In the late summer, on a night too hot for sleep, Artemus stands naked in the open window, smoking. He can feel the sweat run down his back and down the inside of his legs. The ceiling fan is useless, and no breeze comes from the river. Across the street, a door opens in a rectangle of yellow light, and a man steps out on the gallery, his black bow tie undone around his neck, his white tuxedo shirt stained dark under the arms. The man leans on the iron balustrade for a moment, then straightens and lights a cigarette. His hair is slicked and parted in the middle, and it gleams like wax in the match's flare. His face, shiny with sweat, is pale and bloodless as a painted doll's. He looks across the narrow space of the street, but if he sees Artemus, he gives no sign. The red tip of his cigarette raises and lowers, and the blue smoke drifts away.

Artemus hears the whisper of the mosquito barre, hears the bedsprings squeak when Anna Rose gets up. He says, I'm sorry. You ought to be asleep.

She comes to stand behind him. Her damp breasts brush against his back, and her arms slip around him. There is no fog this night; otherwise she would not have come near the window. Anna Rose hates the fog. It's too hot, she says. I can't sleep.

He steps back a little, taking her with him. Who's the sheik yonder? he says.

Anna Rose peers over his shoulder. Oh, he's a horn player out by one of the clubs on the lake, she says. He's married, and right now he's thinking about what a shitty life he's got.

Artemus laughs, a little. Across the way, the man jumps at the bark of a woman's voice behind him. He shakes his head and arcs his cigarette out into the street, then goes back through the door and slams it shut. Anna Rose says, Be glad you ain't him.

I used to be him, says Artemus.

Not any more, says Anna Rose.

Artemus turns and pulls her close against him with his hand tight against the back of her neck. He hears himself speak, and all at once he is talking about the fog, though there is no fog. It is the bloodless man across the street, maybe, the way he moved like a marionette. Artemus tells about how the fog crawled over the wheatfields in France and shrouded the wounded, and how their cries rose out of it, and men moved through it like phantoms. He tells her how, sometimes when he is flagging in the Piney Woods, the fog creeps up over the roadbed, and the distant markers of his train gleam like the eyes of a watchful beast. Anna Rose listens, her arms tight around his neck, her cheek pressed to his breast, until he is quiet.

* * *

Tonight, there was a fog. When the Silver Star backed into Basin Street Station, Artemus was on the rear platform, watching for Anna Rose. He was nervous, jittery, still hearing the dog lunging against its chain in the dark. He found Anna Rose in the crowd, and when she saw his face, she said no word but only pressed herself against him, her hand closing on his lapel. They took supper in the lunchroom, then went over to Immaculate Conception and lit candles for the dead. All the while, Anna Rose kept hold of him, and all the way back to her flat on St. Peter Street. Anna Rose was built for speed, not comfort, but tonight she made love quietly, the whole time watching him, clinging fiercely to him, making small sounds. Her eyes never closed, never left his face, even as she came, and afterward she would not let him go. Don't you leave me alone, she said, over and over. Don't you leave me alone yet. Not yet.

I don't mean to leave you at all, he said.

You will one day, she said.

Everybody leaves one day, said Artemus. You will leave one day.

No, I won't, she said, and turned away from him.

Now, hours later, Artemus stood at the window. The foggy street, the river, Anna Rose's little flat, all were gone strangely quiet in the turning of night to day. In that moment, Artemus could hear the blood in his ears, and he thought maybe this is what death was like—silence and fog, scattered halos of light, an eternal suspended moment in which the universe, paused and breathless, waits for something to happen.

Frank Smith believed that all of time ran together and that nothing was ever lost. The spirit was not lost, he claimed, but lived on in the shadows of tomorrow, just as it lived in the shadows of the past.

For a long time, Artemus disagreed, arguing that everything died. Values and manners and ways of life would die. Love died, and youth. Churches and religions must pass away—Christianity must die, and Islam, and every other creed—and one day the earth itself would turn dark and icy and roll away toward the disc of the perished sun. Meanwhile the spirit, if there was a spirit, was lost.

Not so, argued Frank Smith. Something essential would remain always, he said, even in the final emptiness. He looked at Artemus. Why else would you light candles in a church? he said.

Because Anna Rose believes in it, replied Artemus.

They were sitting on a flat car waiting for the engine to return, sitting in the glow of their bug-swirled lanterns in the heat of a Louisiana midnight. Smith said, All right, try to imagine the universe without you in it.

I can do that, said Artemus.

No, you can't, said Smith.

So Artemus thought about it. He pictured in his mind a street, people in a picture show, cows grazing in a pasture, all in the future. I can do it, he said.

No, you can't, said Smith. You are seeing everything through your own eyes, in a way that nobody but you sees them. You are there right along. You are a spirit, you see.

Now, looking out at the quiet street, Artemus could easily imagine the darkness active with striving shadows. No one ever finished his business, he thought. No one ever got it right. Certainly Artemus Kane had never got it right, nor ever would. No wonder the spirit remained. No wonder he saw apparitions.

"Who you talking to?" said Anna Rose in a sleepy voice harsh from the night's cigarettes. Artemus winced again. He hadn't meant to be speaking aloud.

"Frank Smith," he said, and backed inside and closed the jalousies quickly.

She pulled the afghan up to her chin. "Do you always talk to Frank when he's not around?"

"That's the only time I can get a word in edgewise," he said. He sat on the bed. The room smelled of coffee now.

She backed up against the headboard, drawing the afghan with her. Artemus shook out a Picayune, tapped it on his thumbnail, and put it between her lips. In the flare of the match, her face was lined with shadow. Artemus brushed a curl of hair from her forehead. "What were you dreaming about just now?" he asked.

"I dreamt I was cold," she said. She drew on the cigarette and exhaled. "Don't talk about leaving any more."

"I won't," he said.

"People do too much of that," she said.

They sat quietly for a while, smoking, watching the daylight creep into the corners of the flat, listening to the sounds grow again. Things were always better by daylight, as if it were another country, one you could travel in without looking over your shoulder.

Artemus poured a cup of coffee for each of them. While they drank, he brushed his shoes and got into his uniform and wound his watch carefully. In a little while, the call boy knocked on the door. All the call boys knew to find him at Anna Rose's now.

"Call for brakeman Artemus Kane," said the boy through the closed door. He rapped again, and Artemus opened it to find a stout lad swathed in an overcoat and muffler, wearing a checkered cap the size of home plate. "Nine o'clock list for Number Six, Mister Kane," squeaked the boy, craning his head to peer into the room.

"Thank you, Elmer," said Artemus. He put a quarter in the boy's hand. "Now beat it," he said.

"Mornin', Miss Anna," said the boy around the closing door.

"Mornin', Elmer," said Anna Rose, who was hiding beneath the afghan.

When the boy was gone, Artemus picked up his grip. "These god damn swains," he said. "They never give up."

"I should give the poor lad a glimpse one day," said Anna Rose, sliding from the bed.

"Elmer?" said Artemus, and laughed. "It would blow all his fuses."

Anna Rose pulled on her thin dressing gown and robe. She crossed the room and stood before him with one bare foot atop the other. "This is not the same as leaving," she said. "I know that."

"I'll be back tomorrow," he said. "I get double time for Christmas Day. I'll buy you something pretty."

She looked slantwise at him, in that way she had. She kissed him once, deeply.

"You are not false to me," she said.

"Until the sun don't rise, baby," he said, and then he was gone.

PINEY WOODS

Frank Smith was having breakfast at the counter in the depot restaurant. That is, he was looking at the fried eggs, the sausage, the grits. So far, he had not been able to eat any of it.

Outside, the cold sleet came down. There did not seem to be anyplace under the gray sky where it did not fall, slanting with the wind, cold as crystal. The rails and slag and the tops of cars were dusted with white. Steam billowed from the maroon flanks of the A&V passenger train. Travelers and car inspectors and trainmen moved through the scene, obscured one moment, revealed the next, like figures in a great battle.

Charlie Granger came in, brushing the cold damp from the sleeves of his overcoat. He nodded to Smith and climbed on the stool next to him. The counterman set a cup of coffee before the chief. Granger laid out a pipe and a tobacco pouch on the white marble countertop and cradled the coffee in his hands. The presence of the chief special agent made Smith uneasy. He liked Charlie Granger well enough, but Granger was police, and in Frank Smith's view, police never made polite conversation.

Granger took a sip of his coffee. Without looking up, he said, "I hear you been camping out in the shack. What's that like?"

Ah, shit, thought Smith. He picked up his fork, examined it, then laid it down again. "It ain't so bad," he said. "It's just temporary."

Granger nodded and took another sip. "You going south with A.P. this morning?"

Smith made no reply, aware that Granger already knew the answer.

The chief sipped his coffee. "Old A.P.," he said after a moment. "I hear he might be a little nervous now days."

"You seem to hear a lot, Charlie," said the conductor. He swiveled on his stool to face the other man. "I don't know how much of it is anybody's business," he said.

Granger slid his coffee away. "Let me tell you something, Frank," he said. "For two months you been living on company property in violation of about a hundred rules. But you know what? I don't care. I'll let that be your business. But a engineer piles 'em up in the trees, that's *my* business. You understand what I'm saying?"

"A.P.'s all right," said Smith, staring at the counter. "He wasn't, I wouldn't ride with him. When he can't do the job, you'll be the first to know."

"Well, I appreciate that, Frank," said the chief. A plate of steaming eggs and bacon and grits was laid before the chief special agent. He took up the salt shaker and examined it. "Don't confuse your loyalties," he said. "It's dangerous for everybody."

"You don't have to tell me that," said Smith.

Granger nodded. "Yeah, you been around a long time," he said. "That's why I trust you." He picked up his fork and prodded his eggs. "You ever notice how ain't nothing like it used to be?" he said.

"All the time," said Smith. He looked at the chief's plate, then at his own, cold and congealed now. He pushed the plate away and counted out thirty-eight cents in nickels and pennies on the counter and rose to leave.

"Long day ahead," said Granger. "You not gonna eat?"

"I ain't hungry," said Smith. "I'll see you, Charlie."

Granger caught his arm. "Hold on," he said. He picked up the coins one by one, weighed them in his palm, then dropped them back in Smith's overall pocket. "It's on me," said the chief. "Come by the house when you all get back tomorrow. It'll be Christmas. Maybe we can find you a good supper."

* * *

Mister A.P. Dunn had no idea where he was. He seemed to have traveled a long way from somewhere, through a kaleidoscope of lights and music in an alien city crowded with buildings. Along the way, men he recognized had appeared, and that was good. Old, familiar voices were welcome in a strange place, and old remembered faces. Bruce D. Herrington. T.L. Jacobs. Tom Utroska and Ralph Little and John Marquette. They stepped out of doorways or passed right through the glass of store windows and traveled a little with him, one giving place to the next, talking about the old times in such a way that it was easy to believe no time had passed at all. In fact, they each made it a point to insist that time had fooled Mister Dunn and that nothing lay between what he was now and what they had been once.

Mister Dunn wondered why they brought up such a thing. The old men who had lived out their years might have something useful to say on the subject, but Bruce Herrington was not yet twenty when his foot slipped through the stirrup of a tank car and he was dragged a quarter mile while the ties beat him to death. What did a boy know about time who never had any himself?

Now Mister Dunn was alone in the shadow of a great dingy building he did not recognize, on a brick sidewalk that bounced with sleet. He paused, thinking about Bruce Herrington. In heaven, ye shall know all things, he thought. Up there, even the least would possess the wisdom of the ages. Still, it was hard to think of young Herrington being so wise. Mister Dunn remembered how the boy used to have fun, how he never gave a thought to any moment but the one he was living in. It didn't seem right he should be weighed down with so much wisdom now, heaven or not.

It's all a mystery, thought Mister Dunn, and took a step on the icy walk. A moment later, he was flat on his back, staring up at the tall flank of the building. His head hurt, and he knew he had struck it in his fall, but it didn't seem to matter much. Mister Dunn lay content on the brick sidewalk, growing warm and comfortable, until a man leaving for home found him. As the man helped him to his feet, Mister Dunn protested. "I'm all right," he said. "It ain't nothin'." He stood on the sidewalk, his head bent, and watched the dark nickel-sized drops of blood splat on the bricks. He was astonished at how quickly they froze. He looked up at the brick building looming before him. What is this place? he thought. He didn't remember until the man took him inside.

* * *

Roy Jack Lucas stood at the freight office window, smoking, with a cup of red-hot coffee in his hand. The coffee was steaming up the pane, and Lucas had to keep rubbing it clear, not that he was looking at anything in particular. He had been standing at this window for thirty years, and the scene below had little about it to engage his interest.

Lucas was alone in the office. When the chief went off to breakfast, Hido Schreiber had snuck away to the bootlegger's to get some more whiskey, in violation of Rule G which forbid employees to partake of alcohol on duty. Lucas thought this was a good rule for everybody but himself and Hido Schreiber.

A gust of wind rattled the glass, and the detective tried hard not to think of June Watson's face last night. When the couplers opened, at the moment he died, the man's face grew peaceful, no fear in it anywhere, and his eyes lit up as though in recognition. Roy Jack Lucas refused to be inspired by that transition. He did not care to be deceived by hope.

He did not want anything or anybody to be waiting for him on the other side.

God damned mockingbirds, thought the detective. What was that all about?

Lucas's head was hurting, but the coffee helped. The window steamed up again, and he wiped it away with the sleeve of his overcoat. Down below, a car inspector, oil can in one hand, pulling hook in the other, moved along a cut of Railway Express cars, checking the journal boxes. Through the window, Lucas heard the box lids creak as the man pulled them open, and clank as he kicked them shut. Creak-clank. Creak-clank. A baggage wagon rumbled down the platform below. A switch engine backed through the yard on an outside track, bell ringing, with a cluster of switchmen on the footboards. In another ten years, maybe Lucas would be able to retire. He wondered where he could go so that he never had to see or hear a railroad again.

God damned mockingbirds, he thought again, and all at once stepped back from the window as if he had seen some awful thing. He turned, his eyes searching the air around, then stumbled away among the desks, hurrying, trying to remember where they had left the car. He slammed the glass-paned door behind him and nearly fell going down the long steps.

* * *

In Jumpertown, Eddie Cox pulled his cap down against the sleet. The streets were empty, the mud glazed with ice. The houses he passed were paintless, gray as the sky. No flowers bloomed on the galleries, and no children played in the yards, and the trees were bare. That was the worst trial of winter, Cox thought. In winter, you saw how everything really was.

"Two more days," he said aloud. "Two more trips, all you got left." He repeated the words to himself, waiting for them to make him feel good, but they floated away without meaning. Two days, and he could walk out here and not have to go anywhere he didn't want to. He tried to think of where such a place might be, but he couldn't, because Jumpertown was all he knew. Three days, and the houses would still be poor, the yards muddy, the window cracks stopped with rags. Eddie Cox would still be himself—only somehow different. He could not fathom how he would still be himself, but not himself. Well, that was for later. For now, he had to go fire an engine for Mister A.P. Dunn, something nobody else in the world could say. For now, the cold was real enough, and the icy water that trickled down his collar.

Cox passed the funeral parlor. The lights were burning inside, and he wondered who was dead this early in the morning. A man he knew was smoking on the porch, and Eddie asked him. The man, dressed in a black suit, his hair shiny with pomade, came down the steps and told him. After that, Eddie Cox felt colder still.

* * *

Downtown, the sleet rattled on the mildewed canvas top of Sonny Leeke's motorcar as he stopped at Ladner's tiny bungalow, then at Necaise's mama's house. Miz Necaise waved at them from the porch. "You all look after my boy," she called, as she did every time, and Necaise said, "Aw, Mama," as he always did, and they all laughed.

The morning was so dark that it seemed no morning at all, and the three men, crammed in the ancient single-seat T-model with their grips and lunch pails and bulky clothing, speculated about the weather. Maybe it would lighten up soon, they said. Maybe it would be warmer down south.

Necaise said, "Hey, you all think I could ride the head end today?" He told them for the hundredth time how he was going to be a boilerman in the Navy. "I bet A.P. and Eddie could tell me about boilers," he said. "I never thought to ask 'em before."

Leeke said, "We'll see what Frank says."

"Well, I didn't know if you'd want to swap," said Necaise.

"Shee-it," said Leeke, and ran the car up on the curb, as he did from time to time for no apparent reason.

* * *

The three comrades' hope for warmer climes was in vain, of course. In New Orleans, the sleet and rain had dissolved the night fog. It was not sleeting now, but a sullen, dreary mist hung in the air, waiting to turn to rain again, and sleet after that.

Artemus Kane walked up Royal Street in a bad humor, hands deep in his pockets, overcoat collar turned up, shoulders hunched. For the space of a block, his mind was noisy with irritating thoughts. He envisioned the half-dozen umbrellas Anna Rose kept by her door, and how he could have taken one but for his own hard and fast principle that umbrellas were unmanly. Artemus worried about his uniform. He hoped his cap would not lose its shape. He had a rain cover for it, but never wore the thing, for it looked absurd, like a woman's bathing cap—another matter of principle. He tried to keep his shined shoes out of the puddles. He thought about his motorcycle waiting outside the trainmen's washroom in Meridian and worried if it would start when he got back. He wondered if the pipes in his house had frozen, if the Silver Star would be on time, if Anna Rose was mad at him, if his hair was turning gray, if he had cancer…

"Jesus H. Christ," he said aloud to himself, and stopped under a gallery heavy-laden with bougainvillea. The red flowers still bloomed despite the frost, and in an apartment above, someone was playing a piano. The air was rich with the smell of new-baked bread. A trio of nuns hurried by, their long rosary beads swaying at their waists.

"Good day, sisters," said Artemus, and lifted his cap, hoping they had not overheard his blasphemy. The women smiled in return as if it really were a good day. They were all three young and pretty, and

Artemus thought What a waste of pretty girls, as they passed on. Then he crossed himself in contrition and remembered how people ought to be respected for their choices. What is it like, being married to God? No doubt they had a better chance than if they were married to Artemus Kane.

The iron storefronts shone with rain; the cobbled street was streaked with lights like the aurora borealis. Shopkeepers and waiters lounged in doorways or under their unrolled awnings and watched the morning come. A pair of aproned dishwashers, taking the air, argued in the patois of the West Indies. Citizens hurried on their way, drawn into themselves like sullen birds, the smoke of their cigarettes trailing behind.

Despite the winter dreariness, Artemus felt the energy of the city around him, quickening his heart. I am part of all this, he thought. I belong here. It was a feeling that seldom came when he was alone, away from Anna Rose and his comrades. Then he seemed a part of nothing, isolate, shut off from the world like an insect in a glass jar. When a man was alone too much, he had only himself to look into, and what he found there was all manner of darkness. Thus Gideon kept his salon, where people sought the company of others to redeem them. Thus, perhaps, Anna Rose embraced Artemus Kane so desperately in the long nights, who had been too much alone herself.

Being solitary was not the same as being lonesome. Solitude was a condition of circumstance that railroad men rarely entered for long, and when they did, it was often a blessing. Sometimes it was good to lie in your bed at night in some cheap hotel and let the silence and dark close around you, let the voices grow still, let movement cease. Artemus believed that was why so many of the men loved fishing, when they could go off by themselves in a pirogue on the brown waters.

Lonesomeness, on the other hand, did not depend on circumstance. It was bolted in the heart and seized on a man's weakness, a vise that squeezed all possibility out of time, that crushed hope and rendered meaningless anything tomorrow could offer. A man had to be careful around it. On the job, he had to shuck it off and make himself pay attention. Men had died because their eyes were turned inward toward some yearning memory.

He caught a streetcar on Canal. The car was crowded with people going to work. The wheels ground and rang on the thin rails, and the catenary wire crackled and filled the varnished interior with the smell of electricity. Artemus had a window seat beside a large woman bundled and scarved like one of the refugees they had met along the road to Soissons. The woman grunted from time to time, and jabbed Artemus with her elbow, but he ignored her and watched the lights.

Artemus wished that Anna Rose might be sitting by him now instead of the refugee woman. He would let Anna Rose have the window seat; she would put her gloved hand against the glass and talk about the streaming lights and the people she saw across the dark morning.

Hell and damnation, thought Artemus, cursing the lost chance.

The large woman glared at him. "Tut-tut, m'sieur," she said. "It is Christmas Eve, the nativity of Our Lord."

Again, Artemus was surprised that he had spoken aloud. "Je vous demande pardon," said Artemus. "Pardonnez moi…I don't know the word for sin."

"Peche," said the woman, and smiled a little. "You should perhaps light a candle," she said, and turned back in her seat.

* * *

Cold sleet fell on the woods of South Mississippi that lay between Artemus and his home in Meridian. These were the old Piney Woods that gave the district its name, that were being harvested by thousand-acre plats for flooring and framing and paper. The cut-over land was a tangle of fallen saplings and stumps and dead vines; among these, the sleet pattered and froze, driving the rabbits and squirrels and deer that still clung to the land, and the men who had ravaged it, into deep cover.

The sleet sometimes gathered in the top of a pine and bowed it over until it broke in two with a crack like an artillery round in the winter silence. Such a sound, the death of a tall yellow pine, woke Donny Luttrell from his sleep in the telegraph station at Talowah, Mississippi. He had been the operator here for six months now, so passing trains no longer stirred him, nor the voice of birds, nor the scuttling of a rat in the pantry. But he would start awake if his call sign came over the wire, or if some unusual noise intruded itself. Now he groaned and sat on the edge of his cot, shivering in his long woolen underwear. He pulled his blanket over his head like a penitent monk and dreaded the cold passage he must make to build up the fire in the stove.

The station, which operated from six in the morning to midnight, was one hundred and ten miles from Basin Street. It was not a building, but an antique link-and-pin boxcar covered with tar paper and set up on cedar bolts. Between the boxcar and the rails of the main line lay an apron of cinders that in summer was strewn with weeds. A single drooping wire linked the station to the broad world through the company telegraph poles marching past. Inside was a scattering of chairs, a file cabinet, and a desk for the telegraph key. In one corner was the Army cot where Donny was shivering, in another, the woodstove he had to get to before he could warm up or make his breakfast. The station had no waiting room nor baggage room, for no passenger trains ever stopped here. It had no running water, but it did have a privy on the lee side—another destination that Donny dreaded every cold morning, and worse in the pitch-black nights.

For a while after the Civil War, a sawmill village thrived here. Exploring in the scrub pines along the railroad, Donny had discovered brick pilings, a mound of rotted sawdust, some rusted machinery, a bank safe discarded in a gully. Early in the winter, he found a burying ground with a few slanted markers beside an old sunken road. Now, the sole purpose of this lonely outpost was to provide an interchange with the narrow-gauge Richfield Lumber Company line that wandered for miles through the woods. At Talowah, the logs brought out behind wheezing Shay locomotives were transferred to standard-gauge cars of the Southern Railway. The station also controlled a passing track a mile to the south. For this reason, the station was fitted with a creosoted pole and a semaphore signal arm that would drop and show red if a main-line train had orders for the passing track. The semaphore had red and green glass lenses illuminated at night by an oil-burning lamp that was forever blowing out, which the operator had to rectify by climbing the ladder in all weathers with a box of kitchen matches.

On this Christmas Eve morning, the timber crews had all gone back to the mill in Hattiesburg for the holiday. The interchange yard was empty, and the Shay locomotives brooded in the engine shed with their fires out. The sleet sifted down, the pines sighed in the wind, a gang of crows muttered to one another from their perches. Donny wondered what they spoke of, high in the cold solitude of the trees.

Donny Luttrell had not come to the railroad by choice. He origi-nally set out to be a University Man and a Captain of Finance like his father Jacob. Unlike his father, however, Donny spent his first year of college carousing with his fraternity brothers in Memphis and Jackson. In the spring semester, when he realized he was failing all his courses, Donny took comfort in the arms of a girl he met at the spring mixer. Her name was Rosamond Lake, a Chi Omega from a good Greenville family. One night in early May, she sat crying under a streetlamp and told Donny that she had "missed her time." She had to explain to him what that meant. The same night, Donny went home on the midnight train, leaving all his possessions in the boarding house room he had taken a month before.

His father fixed it, of course, for he was a man who knew how to get things done. Mr. Luttrell arranged for the procedure and made sure the young woman had recompense for her pain and discretion. Then, to get Donny out of the picture a while, he had a conversation with an old

Shrine brother who happened to be the superintendent of the Crescent Division of the Southern Railway. The superintendent was interested that the boy knew telegraphy, even if it was only from a Boy Scout merit badge. Before Donny knew it, he was an operator on the extra board of the Crescent Division. Furthermore, with the serendipity that follows the rich, the job at Talowah, so lonesome and remote that nobody ever bid on it, was open. The superintendent worked it with the telegraphers' union so that Donny could be posted there as long as he needed to be. The job was mostly checking the yard, inspecting loads, taking wait orders for the siding, and keeping the depot swept out, and it was unlikely Donny would get into any trouble down there.

Donny had a few days' breaking-in at Meridian, then went down to Talowah like a doomed man. When the local passenger train dropped him off, he stood in the hot sunlight with his suitcases and a bag of rations beside him and a horsefly buzzing around his head, and his only thought was, *I can't do this*. It would be easy enough to run away, for, along with a switch key and cipher and rule book, the railroad had issued him a pass good on any second-class passenger train on the Southern system. That meant New York, Washington, New Orleans. The trouble was, old Jacob controlled his bank account; worse, most of his railroad salary, when he started drawing, was already garnished to the old man, who expected Donny to pay back the medical and discretionary fees resulting from the one damp spring afternoon when God had allowed him to know Rosamond Lake.

A half-dozen men in the log yard had stopped work and were staring at him, so he went inside. No one had been at Talowah for three months—in that time, the siding and interchange had been controlled out of Purvis—and the place was in shambles. Every corner of the ceiling had a big nest thick with wasps who began to dip and dive around the moment the door was opened. The floor was covered with leaves and rat pellets. The desiccated body of a squirrel lay on the desk. Mice had pulled the stuffing from the cot mattress to line their home in the stove and had chewed the semaphore ropes in two. Donny looked around and said aloud, "I can't do this." He took his telegraph key from his suitcase and plugged it into the wire with shaking hands. *This is Talowah*, he tapped out. *Send janitor immediately*. A long silence followed on the line, then the sounder buzzed to life: *19. 19. 110, copy two*.

Donny jumped back as if the sounder were a rattlesnake. He had caught the message all right, but he could not think of what it meant. Ah—"nineteen" meant to clear the line for orders. "One hundred ten" was the call sign for Talowah. In a panic, he rummaged through the desk until he found the order tablets and carbons and stylus. Everything he had learned at Meridian fled away like birds, and his hand trembled as he reached for the key. *Ready to copy*, he sent, slowly and painfully, for he could not remember the code nor the cipher.

After several false starts, during which the sounder seemed magically to communicate the dispatcher's annoyance, Donny was able to copy a wait order for a train that even now was approaching. He found a pad of clearance cards and filled one out as he had been taught. Now what? he thought, and remembered. He would have to hand up the orders to the engineer and conductor of the passing train.

A telegrapher up at Meridian had shown him how to fix an order hoop and warned him that he had to get close to the train. Get in close and don't miss, said the man. Everything depends on it, he said. Then he said it again: You have to get in close. Unfortunately, in the rush to bury Donny Luttrell and his sins at Talowah, the boy never got a chance to practice or observe. No matter, he thought. He had seen trains all his life, had even stood next to them waiting to board—and where was the difficulty? Besides, the matter of handing up orders was just one among a thousand things he did not know and did not plan to know.

Now he fixed the hoops all right, and stepped out on the cinders and stood close by the track as he had been instructed. The approaching train was no more than a headlight gleam to the north, and Donny waited, thinking *I can't do this*, and *Why do I have to do this?* and the train coming closer all the while, rails creaking, the engine whistling for signals over and over, which made no impression on Donny since he had forgotten all about whistle signals. He shut his eyes and willed the sound away, willed himself away, back to school, back to the last possible moment when he could have kept his pecker in his pants—

And all at once, the engine loomed over him, its bell tolling, tolling doom. The earth shook, and the very air seemed pushed out of shape as if by a towering storm. The engine erased the sky, extinguished the sun, filled all the universe with darkness and spitting steam, moving fast, the drive rods like great mechanical arms reaching for him, the white-trimmed wheels higher than his head, the long boiler higher than God almighty himself.

Donny was stunned by this apparition. He cried out and flung himself backward, the order hoop forgotten. He heard voices, saw the blur of faces, then the brakes began to squeal and after an eternity, the train ground to a halt in a cloud of dust.

He waited. The train stood before him like a great wall, brake cylinders groaning, wheels tick-ticking with heat. He waited a long time for something else to happen, long enough to think about how much he had fucked up, long enough to unravel the order from the hoop and contemplate the ways in which a little square of waxy paper could alter the nature of existence. Then the engineer, whom Donny would come to know as Mister Cuthbert Streiff, appeared.

Mister Streiff—who must stop his train, put out the flags front and rear, and walk back twenty car lengths to get his order—had the face and build and posture of a dangerous bulldog. Donny watched him approach, saw him stumble in the ballast, watched him pause to stamp out a grass fire kindled by the sparking brakes. Donny noticed that the smoke from other fires was beginning to weave its way among the cars.

Only when Mister Streiff stepped onto the cinder apron did his eyes fix on Donny Luttrell. They narrowed to little slits under the black brim of his cap and never left the boy's face. Mister Streiff came closer. The crickets sawed in the grass, and a mockingbird sang from the signal pole, and Donny felt as he did when he stood before his father: an emptiness where his heart should be, a readiness to embrace whatever guilt the old man assigned him so long as this moment could be over. When the engineer stopped, he was so close that Donny could read the label on his overalls. The man seemed incapable of speech. The veins in his neck were swollen thick as pencils, and a sinister purple blotch crawled out of his collar and up his throat. Then he shut his eyes and gathered himself, and when he spoke at last, his words were calm and deliberate.

Who are you? he asked, and the boy told him.

The engineer plucked the order from Donny's hand and read it. Then his eyes raised again, and Donny could not look away. Are you a coward? asked Mister Streiff.

In Donny's mind, a sudden image took shape: Rosamond Lake on an iron bench, under a streetlamp, crying. Yes, he said.

Yes, *sir*, said the engineer.

Yes, sir.

Let us be clear, said the engineer. Are you a coward, or were you only afraid?

When the boy gave no answer, Mister Streiff took off his cap and drew a starched sleeve across his brow. He said, Find somebody to teach you the difference. You can be afraid out here, but you cannot be a coward.

The engineer turned then and was almost to the grass when he stopped and spoke, his back to the boy. If I have to do this again, he said, you best light out for the woods. Then he was gone.

Donny Luttrell was left still waiting to be made small, but the man who should do it was walking off. Donny waited, half-expecting the man to return, but in a moment he was alone. After that, Donny didn't know what to wait for.

Eventually the train jerked into motion, the slack running out bam-

bam-bam. All manner of cars marched endlessly by, rolling faster and faster, until at last Donny saw the outstretched arm of the conductor on the caboose. Donny crept timidly to the track and held up the order hoop, and the conductor, in crisp overalls and spectacles and fedora, reached far out to snag it. He did not look at Donny, but only shook his head in disgust.

When the train had passed, Donny began to stamp out fires in the tall grass. It didn't take long for the flames to get away from him, and some of the loggers came running with shovels and axes and swing blades. They shoved the boy aside and set about putting out the fires, then went back to their work without saying a word to Donny Luttrell, who stood amid the stink of ashes with tears of anger running down his face.

* * *

The mice were easy to evict from the stove, but the wasps were a different matter. He finally had to close the damper and fill the stove with journal box waste to smoke them out, which meant that his first night was spent sleeping in the engine shed on a pile of tow sacks among a cloud of mosquitoes. The next day, he found a broom and figured out how to sweep and, after many trials, how to make coffee, eggs, bacon, beans. He learned about chiggers and ticks, though not how to keep them off. He memorized the railroad cipher and built up his speed on the key—anything to make the time pass. Donny was nineteen years old. It would be two years before he could get out of Talowah, and until then he would be stuck with the ignorant peckerwood loggers and railroad men he had to deal with, who could hardly write, and who, he believed, had never entertained a thought either coming in or going out that wasn't about "backtime, overtime, or pussy."

His resentment of them was matched by ample resentment of their own, a reverse snobbery that had conditioned them all their lives to look down on the educated and privileged, on those who were unlikely to be crushed beneath a fallen tree or die under the wheels, who would not end up broken and stooped and drawing a pension barely enough to keep them in whiskey. The College Boy, as they called him, no doubt had connections in high places. He would do a little time in the Piney Woods, then move up in the company. As a superintendent or vice president, he would return to that unimaginable world of comfort and accommodation, perhaps to roll past one day in the parlor of the Silver Star and say to himself, Now this seems familiar—but no, how could it? then turn back to his Cuban cigar and his newspaper.

The summer, languid and hot and rainless, passed slowly. The pines were loud with the serenade of cicadas, the logs on the cars whirred and ticked with secret life, and every evening the sun grew round and orange and seemed to hang forever just above the trees. The solitude was almost palpable, made of dust and resin. It was interrupted only by the narrow-gauge log trains crawling out of the woods, or the passing of the big trains on the Southern main line. Now and then, one of these would stop to pick up cars or drop off empties, and Donny might speak perfunctorily with a trainman. Other times, he went to the yard and pretended to inspect loads that had been transferred from the narrow gauge. In fact, he had no idea what he was doing. The loggers spoke to him not at all, but sat under a shade tree and watched him.

Donny got better at copying orders, but he could not make himself stand close to moving trains. He had to shut his eyes and hold up the order hoop and hope that the engineer caught it, then wait for the cars to pass and shut his eyes again and hold up the hoop for the conductor.

Sometimes, sitting in the open boxcar door on a hot night, Donny would think of Rosamond Lake and wonder if she knew of his fate, if she knew how much of a failure he was, cuckolded by his own cowardice and his father's purse. Whenever he took the local to Lumberton or Purvis for supplies, Donny used the depot telephone to call her, but Rosamond was always out. He had written a dozen letters, but tore them all up. What could he say to her, after all? Why didn't you ask me first? Why did you take the money? Did you think I was without honor, Rosamond?

He was, of course. It was he who left on the midnight train and proved himself a coward. Honor, indeed. The word mocked him even as it crept into his consciousness. As an idea, it formed slowly, for he was used to thinking himself above it. His father always said that honor was for fools not interested in making their way in the world. Honorable men were those who did not know that you had to take what you got, no matter the means. Honor! his father shouted when Donny had offered the possibility. It was his father's final lecture before Donny left for Talowah, held in the office of the Merchants and Farmers Bank, of which Mister Luttrell was chief officer. Honor! the old man cried. Are you so stupid that you hide behind an illusion? The girl is gone. She has forgotten you, and what you call honor will not cause her to remember, only to despise you more. She is no longer an object of your desire. She is beyond your concern. Look to yourself, boy, for I assure you no one else will.

But Donny could not forget Rosamond Lake, no matter if she gave up their child, no matter if she took money for her silence. He was, after all, the one who ran away. Every morning through the summer, he sat on the edge of his bunk and thought of blonde Rosamond and her heart-shaped face, her full, hard breasts and strong legs. Rosamond would be soft asleep that early, nestled in her room in the old home place in Greenville near where the great River flowed. Their secret would be vanished now, put away like a bundle of clothes you would give the housemaid, just as his father had said—and later (he could see this clearly) Rosamond and her mother would dress in hats and gloves, and walk into the streets to shop for her return to school in the fall, to call on neighbors for tea, and give no thought to Donny Luttrell.

As the summer drew on, he began to understand how honor could be the property of those who had striven and lost, yet did not regret the loss. Donny was sorry he had not striven harder, but he was striving now, in spite of himself. The knowledge of what is right and true will come in its own time, he thought, even if it's a hot, stinking morning in the wasteland of the Piney Woods.

This understanding came in solitude, and with it another gift. Slowly, imperceptibly, his father's voice began to die away, and his mother's returned. It had been years since he'd heard her, but there she was in the static of the wires, the creaking of the steel rails, in the little sighs and whispers of the woods at night.

He was seven years old when he stood watching the sexton shovel dirt into her grave, when he heard the clods striking the box far below. He remembered coming home to the quiet house that still smelled of her, full of the things she had touched, the plates she had eaten from, the mirrors, empty now, that had borne her image in fleeting glances. Nevertheless, she stayed long with him in the night, in the air around him, like the pale query of the moon through his bedroom windows. Then she had faded quietly as he grew older and his father's voice argued louder and louder against the dreaming, the reading of books that were not true, the boy's effeminate love of gardens and poetry. In the end, it took the military academy at Port Gibson to break Donny of all that. After four years, he came home prepared to demonstrate what he had been taught, by fistfights and scorn, about what it meant to be a man. The next fall he entered the university, and now here he was.

His mother's voice returned when he most needed it. She asked him to forgive her for leaving him, and he did, though he thought it unnecessary. She asked him to forgive his father, too, and he could do that. Then he understood that he could forgive even himself, for he knew somehow that forgiveness was only an act of admission, of looking in the mirror and seeing your own true face. Maybe he had learned that in college. Maybe he had learned it because he was afraid not to. In any case, his mother's voice comforted him, and in time, his father's voice ceased altogether. After that, he dared to look around him once more at the things he had allowed himself to forget. The woods around the station were full of light and shadow. He listened once more to the call of birds, saw their colors, hearkened to the secret stirrings of the hot nights. He marveled at the season's dying as though seeing it for the first time.

Nevertheless, the engineer's question remained: Are you a coward, or are you merely afraid? To find the answer, Donny began to push himself into the trains. He ran straight at them, tempting vertigo, forcing himself through his fear into a zone so dangerous, so insane, that all his nerves and muscles screamed in protest. In a little while, his fear began to wear away. Eventually, he could stand an arm's length from the engine, the rocking cars. He began to enjoy the danger, the rush of air, the brush of drive rods in his face and the sudden heat of steam. He found himself looking forward to the smell of friction and steel and grease, the clatter over the rail joints, the heralds and slogans of the craft: Southern Serves the South; L&N, The Old Reliable; Illinois Central, Main Line of Mid-America; Cotton Belt Blue Streak; Lackawanna, Route of Phoebe Snow; Southern Pacific; Missouri Pacific; the Great Northern goat; Katy, the Bluebonnet Route. He began to see how all these powerful roads were connected in a single net of commerce, and that he, Donny Luttrell, the lowly operator at Talowah, was part of it. Getting in close. Moving freight. Moving trains, never mind the time and weather. It was the first time in his life Donny understood himself to be part of something larger than he was. Not even the Methodist Sunday School had taught him that.

As he was learning in solitude, Donny began to look at the men around him in a new way. Having decided that honor was a virtue after all, he began to learn its cousin, humility. It was impossible, he found, to take his pants down in a privy in deep August and go on feeling he was better than anyone else. He discovered that the loggers' stink on a hot day was his own stink. He began to listen to the men's talk, and he saw the way they accommodated themselves to a hard and unforgiving world that he, Donny Luttrell, had always imagined had nothing to do with him. He watched the Southern trainmen, how they stepped down from their engines, their cabooses, and went about their job with careful ease. He studied their hand and lantern signals, and, once he found the courage to ask, they let him help with the switching. They taught him how to get on and off an engine or a moving car. They showed him how to throw a switch and how to "drop by" and how to set a hand brake. They taught him all the myriad rules that a man must follow if he were to stay alive and quick.

Once Donny had chosen this direction, the ultimate trial followed naturally: a boy his own age, in overalls and a felt slouch hat, strode out one afternoon where Donny was pretending to measure a load. He threw his hat down and said, College Boy, you are a god damned pussy, and I am a-fixin' to whup yore ass. Donny replied by breaking the boy's nose with the measuring stick. They fought a good fifteen minutes while the men shouted encouragement. They rolled and slugged and bit in the dust of the lumberyard until Donny's ass was comprehensively whupped, until he was unable to stand, until he was bleeding from his mouth and nose and ears. He had to be put on the local and taken up to Purvis for repairs, while one of the lumbermen, an old Western Union telegrapher, watched the station for him.

They still called him College Boy after that, but at noontime, they invited him to sit with them under a shade tree and take of cheese and crackers and Red Devil potted meat, and of good spring water that came from back in the woods somewhere. One man showed him how to make pancakes on the stove. Another showed him how to keep the chiggers off with rags soaked in kerosene. When they told stories, he was allowed to laugh along with them. Though he had no stories of his own to tell, he began to adopt the others', as if they were part of him, too. They showed him the right way to inspect a load, and they let him ride in the cab of a Shay locomotive so that he could see what went on back at the cutting.

Autumn came all at once with a sudden frost that shriveled the blackberry vines and turned the sky a deep and cloudless blue. By then, Donny had developed a signature, what telegraphers called a "fist." No longer did he have to ask for a repeat or for slower transmission. He went up to Meridian one day and charged a gold Waltham watch and chain to his father's account. He went to the stores department and talked them into giving him a cap with a brass plate:

SOUTHERN RAILWAY

AGENT

Finally, he finished a letter to Rosamond Lake and posted it on a passenger train. He received no reply.

One afternoon in October, a local stopped at Talowah to pick up some cars. While the brakemen were switching out the empties and picking up the loads, the conductor came up to the depot to sign the register and pick up the waybills. He was a man Donny had seen before: not a tall man, but compact, with long hair and a sharp handsome face. Under the bill of his cap, the man's eyes seemed to miss nothing, though they ignored the telegrapher standing in the boxcar door. The conductor took the bills out of the box and signed his register ticket, then stood for a while, thinking. Finally, he looked up at Donny Luttrell. He said, Have you ever tried to imagine the universe without you in it?

I beg your pardon? said Donny.

Think about it, said the conductor, then walked away down the main line toward his caboose.

Donny thought about it, and the next time the conductor came to sign the register, the boy said, There can't be a universe if I am not in it.

Why is that? asked the conductor.

Because, said Donny. He waved his hand at the woods around them. Because nothing ever dies.

The conductor nodded. All right, he said.

Now you tell me an answer, said Donny. What is the difference between being a coward and being afraid?

Are you talking about yourself? the conductor asked.

Yes, said Donny.

Well, said the conductor, if you were a coward, I'd be talking to somebody else right now.

On Christmas Eve, Donny put a shovel of coal on the fire and made his coffee and listened to the chatter on the telegraph. The boys were talking out there, moving trains. During a pause in the traffic, Donny closed his key and tapped out *110, 110, 19*, signifying that Talowah was open and asking for orders. From the dispatcher, he got the word *Intelligent*, an inquiry about cars ready to be interchanged. Donny was happy to reply that there were none. *Merry Xmas*, the dispatcher returned. Then the sounder, in its elevated wooden box, amplified by the customary Prince Albert tobacco can tucked behind it—the sounder was still, and Donny closed his key. Outside, the wind moaned around the corners of the boxcar, and a southbound train whistled for orders. Donny made sure the green board of the signal was displayed, then stepped out in his long flannel underdrawers and agent's cap to watch the freight train by.

DEVIL DOGS

George Watson slept troubled under the cardboard in the empty boxcar, and there a dream came to him, full of ice picks and mean dogs and laundry flapping like ghosts in the yards of Jumpertown. He saw Lucy Falls naked, her skin slick and brassy in the lamplight, and he smelled her, felt his hardness grow, felt the heat of it. She said, Hey, baby, what's this I been hearin', and put out her hand. George said, Aw, I ain't really leavin', baby, and was about to come into her when the dream shifted. Lucy was gone, and there was George's lost brother rising from the tangled weeds of a ditch by the cotton mill road. There was a low fog over the road and fields, but June was bathed in light like an angel might be. Music was all around him, like when the people used to sing at church when they were boys, all the people with sweat running down their faces even when it was cold, the fat women fanning themselves, singing and clapping.

'Fore God, said George. How long you been out?

While ago, said June. I come all this way to find you.

George didn't know what to think, and he could hardly think anyway for all the singing. He put out his hand to touch his brother, but his hand went right on through, and all he felt was an icy coldness. He knew then. He said, You dead, ain't you, June?

It's all right, said the other. I'm here, ain't I?

George thought it seemed all right, even if it shouldn't. The singing made it seem all right. In the old times, George had never understood what the people were singing about. He said, I never did know what all that meant, June, and his brother said, That's all right. It's always there, bigger'n anybody. Bigger'n you, even.

You talkin' 'bout the devil, he can kiss my ass, said George.

I ain't talkin' 'bout the devil, said June. He took a step closer, and George could smell cedar and linseed oil. What about mama? said June. How she doin'?

George stepped back in the road, the mud pulling at him as if it didn't want him to move at all. You dead, you ought to know, he said. Dead peoples know everything.

The singing stopped then, and the light went away, and June stood before him cold and pale, solid as a statue in the fog. All at once, George was afraid. He tried to move again, but the mud held him fast. June Watson said, I *do* know. That ain't what I asked you.

I ain't seen her, said George. Leave off with that.

She never give up on you, said June. I ain't either. I told a man last night, a police—

You don't be talkin' to no *police*, said George, all at once angry. Ain't you learned nothin'?

You don't know what I learned, said June. Now, look at you—where you think you goin', anyway?

George Watson made to answer, but found he could not. He could not see himself beyond the margins of the winter day. At last he said, I swear I don't know.

Course you don't, said June. You never did.

Don't say that, said George. Don't you ever say that.

The music came again, but softer now. June began to fade, to take on the color of the fog around him.

Are you really dead, June? asked George Watson.

I'm dead, George, said the other. I'll see you on the other side.

When will that be? asked George, but no answer came. The road was empty, and the singing now was the shrill of the cotton mill whistle, calling the people to work.

When will that be! cried George again. Then he sat up and cried out the question one last time in his waking. The words echoed in the empty car. Sweat poured down his face in spite of the cold, just like the faces of the people in church long ago.

* * *

The cars ahead of George Watson were empty, and the cars behind, though riders had been in each once upon a time, and would be there again. Strangers to the world and each other, they had carved their names and their runic signs into the wooden bulkheads and built fires on the floor. In the last car stood the doomed hogs, grunting and shoving. They were miserable in the cold, but not so miserable as they would be when the train began to move. Now and then, one would poke his snout through the slats of the cattle car and sniff at the cold air.

Finally, at the end of what was not yet a train—it would not be a train until the engine was coupled up and the marker lamps hung out—the caboose curled the usual black smoke from its stovepipe, and the window over the conductor's desk glowed from the lamp.

Whenever a caboose was shown in the cartoons or funny papers, it was always cute, red, and bouncy. Magazine illustrators usually portrayed it quaintly, a New England cottage on wheels. Among ordinary citizens, the word "caboose" evoked whimsy as if it were a childish diminutive like "horsey" or "moo-cow." Perhaps for that reason, and unconsciously, railroad men hardly ever used the word. It was a cab, a shack, a crummy, a hack. On the Northern roads it was a cabin, a way-car, a van. You would see "caboose" written down any number of places—manifests, switch lists, timetables, train orders, and so on—but you would go a long time without hearing the word spoken.

Frank Smith's X-630 was neither cute nor red, but it was bouncy; in fact, the crew could hardly stand up in it when the train was at speed, and using the toilet underway required courage and skill. A.P. Dunn was a smooth engine driver. He was good to keep the slack stretched out, and when slack was inevitable, as on a descending grade, he used the air skillfully to keep it at a minimum. He was always mindful of the boys back there, especially when they were walking the car tops. But even the best engineer could not make the X-630 a Pullman ride. The crew accepted this and joked about it, as men will often do about a thing they cannot change.

Mister Earl January sat by the caboose stove, drinking the last of his coffee, warming his feet, waiting around to give the 4512 its air brake test. When he heard George Watson cry out, Earl thought it was a hog at first, but decided at last that it was a man. He accepted without question that a man would be crying out somewhere in the cold morning. Earl January had seen and heard many odd things in his thirty years' service, and he had long ago given up wondering.

He had seen strange lights moving in the yards at night, heard voices, witnessed shadows following him on the other side of a cut. He supposed these were the spirits of those who had been on this ground before. They did not frighten him anymore, though once they had made the hair rise on his neck. He saw one strange thing this morning, just before daybreak, when he came out to the kitchen: sweet Pearl River lying naked in the corner, all curled up, her mouth bleeding and frothing, and a big orange-and-blue can of Gulf bug spray empty beside her. He had no doubt she was dead right then, but the sight of her did not fit with anything in the world he could imagine. That's what he wanted to tell Frank Smith, to get his view on it, but in the end, he couldn't tell. He didn't want anybody else's view. He wanted to hold on to his belief that when he got home, she would be all right again. In fact, he could see her clearly, making supper in the steamed-up kitchen, listening to Christmas music on the radio.

Mister Earl had worked alone for a long time, but for a while he'd had a helper named Joe Chiney to work with him. Chiney was old, but nobody knew how old, not even Joe Chiney himself, and he was so black, and his clothes so greasy, you could hardly see him at night—his lantern looked like it was floating around all by itself. He had about twenty children, and a half dozen of these waifs would often trail along after their daddy, picking dewberries, asking questions, throwing chunks of slag at one another. Mister Earl liked when they did that, for it kept things lively. That was when Pearl was young, and sometimes she would come out, too, and play with the nigger children, and Mister Earl would buy them all cheese and crackers and Big Orange drinks for their supper. He and Chiney always watched them closely, making sure they stayed safe in the yard and the shop and the rip-track.

Joe Chiney didn't show up one day, and the children quit coming. Pretty soon word came that he had died, but everything was kept down in Jumpertown, and Earl never knew where his partner was buried. Not that he would go there anyhow, for he did not think it appropriate to visit nigger cemeteries. In any event, it was of no consequence, for Earl knew Joe Chiney had come back from the dead. Earl had seen him a couple of times up around the scale house, and more than once had caught a glimpse of him in the yard. If an old nigger could do that, surely Pearl could. She would come back, and Earl would find a good man to help her and love on her.

Mister Earl January bowed his head and prayed silently, his lips moving with his thoughts. Lord Jesus, he said, I have asked you a thousand times. I have begged and pleaded. Now you want me to think she is dead, that's fine. Whatever lesson you want me to learn, I have learned it. You make her well again, and I promise I will look out for her.

Mister Earl found himself weeping. Usually, praying made him feel better, but this time, he had the sense that no one was listening. He wiped his eyes and forced himself to remember that the Lord could fix anything. Surely, if he could bring a nigger back, he could resurrect little Pearl. Then he thought about how he had been on the jury that sent June Watson to Parchman. What if this was a Judgment for his act? What if it was a punishment brought down on Earl in his old age, and his own daughter to bear the pain? Oh, these god damned niggers, he thought.

* * *

Frank Smith left the depot restaurant and entered the crowded waiting room. The place smelled of damp wool and newspapers and an odor that belonged only to railroad stations. A blue cloud of cigarette smoke clung to the ceiling, and through it the globes of the overhead lights hung on their stalks like yellow moons. A porter leaned on his broom. A clerk was chalking in arrival times on the train board. So many people: mothers and fathers and sleepy children, soldiers, sailors, old women huddled in their heavy coats, a man in a wheelchair, another passing out tracts. The lines were long at the ticket windows, and Smith thought, *Jesus, don't anybody stay home for Christmas anymore?*

He had to stand in line at the newsstand to get his paper and cigars. While he waited, he thought of his conversation with the chief special agent. Mister Dunn's circumstance was no secret among the men, but now the bosses knew it too, as they inevitably must. If something bad happened, E. Franklin Smith would be the first one they hauled on the carpet. *Mister Smith, how long were you aware of engineer Dunn's condition? Did you not think it detrimental to the operation of your train? Did it not compromise the safety of your crew and that of others? Yet you never reported Mister Dunn. Can you tell us why?*

The prospect was not funny, but he laughed anyway, thinking about it. Frank Smith owned one suit and tie, twenty years out of fashion, that he kept around for funerals and the like. He would wear that, borrow some eyeglasses, borrow one of Kane's briar pipes maybe, and present himself to the board of inquiry at the trainmaster's office among the spittoons and typewriters. *Gentlemen,* he would say, *I would like to point out that loyalty is not so much a matter of confusion, as Mister Granger says, but rather one of balance wherein the Railroad Company, the assholes who work for it, and the individual asshole each demands his portion.* He could share these thoughts with the officials while he turned in his switch key and rule book and lantern. He could develop them further as he rode out of town in an empty boxcar.

Of course, the bad thing hadn't happened yet, and maybe it wouldn't. Maybe Mister Dunn would straighten up, maybe he would be all right—*probably* he would, and the questions would never be asked. Meanwhile, Smith's loyalties would go on being what they were.

One thing was certain: Frank Smith would have to break camp in the X-630. It would be a simple matter of locking the caboose door and walking across town to Artemus's house. He would do it tomorrow when he got home, and then he would go see the girls.

Smith got his paper and his cigars and made his way through the crowd. He had never worked in passenger service a day in his life, and he expected to be able to say the same thing when he was old and retired, if he lived that long. He loved to be among people and talk to them, find out what they had done and what they believed in. He felt that everybody was a traveler on the same journey, and a person should be interested in what others had learned along the way. But the Public was a different matter. The Public was too delicate, too selfish and self-absorbed, a loud collective Voice clamoring with complaints, demanding attention. Freight service was better. The hogs in this morning's consist might complain, but they would never report him to the company for offending their sensibilities.

Outside, the air was damp and cold, a good feeling after the over-heated restaurant, the crowded depot. Smith walked along the platform toward the crews' washroom where his orders would be waiting. The other men ought to be there by now, and they would compare their

orders and their watches and sign the train register. Smith supposed
that, while he was there, he ought to get word to Artemus Kane that he
would be moving in.

Halfway down the platform, Smith met a pair of soldiers. They
leaned against a stanchion, smoking, in their heavy wool overcoats and
garrison caps. One boy had a smooth face; the other's was blistered
with acne and his nails were bitten. They had no rank, but on their
overcoat sleeves they wore the stylized propeller flash of the air corps.

"You boys coming or going?" asked Smith.

The two soldiers dropped their cigarettes and came to attention.
"Just passing through, sir," one said.

Smith laughed. "Stand at ease," he said. "Where you from?"

Omaha and Detroit, they told him.

They talked a while. The lads were going to New Orleans before
reporting for duty, and they asked about places to see down there.
Smith gave them his *Times-Picayune* to study. He learned about their
families. He learned they had both been to junior college, to basic
training in Oklahoma, and to aerial gunnery school. They were part of
a B-17 squadron that was to train at the new Army field in Biloxi. They
would be waist gunners, they said, and explained to Smith what that
meant. Then they had to go back and explain what a B-17 was. The
conductor listened with interest, though the concept of standing in an
open fuselage, six miles above the earth, was difficult for him to grasp.
"How can you do that?" asked Frank. They told him about oxygen
masks and flight suits, then admitted that neither had seen an actual
B-17 or flown in an airplane in his life.

Jesus, thought Smith. "Well, that's all right," he said. "I haven't
either." He dug in his pocket and found the coins that Charlie Granger
had returned to him. "Go get you some coffee and donuts," he said.
When they protested, he said, "That's an order." They took the offered
coins then, and thanked him, and went on toward the waiting room.
They were a few steps away when one of them turned.

"You were in the last one," he said.

"Yes," said Smith. "Fifth Marines." He thought a moment. "Maybe there won't be another one," he said.

The other boy stopped and turned now. "Devil dogs," he said. "That's what the Germans called you, isn't it?"

Smith was impressed. "Yes," he said. "That's what they called us."

The boy shook his head. "How did *you* guys do it?"

"It was easy," said Smith. "We had dirt to dig in. You fellows should carry some dirt along."

The first boy laughed and saluted. "If it comes to that, sir." Then they turned smartly and were gone.

* * *

Frank Smith, who has commanded the platoon for three weeks, is standing under the mildewed canvas fly of the CP, watching his new platoon leader, Mister Carmody, pore over maps. The lieutenant wears leather leggings instead of puttees. He displays his bars on his overcoat epaulets and keeps his helmet strap buckled at all times, and he smokes cigarettes like a Frenchman. He has been absorbed in the maps since his return from officers' call. The maps, drawn during the Franco-Prussian War, are only marginally useful, like the lieutenant himself, who has been here less than a day. This is his first command out of the Academy, their fourth platoon leader since the regiment entered combat. By the statistics of the Fifth Marines, the lieutenant has, on the outside, three weeks before he is killed or wounded. Smith wonders if the officer knows this, and if so, what it must be like to know it.

Corporal Artemus Kane is in the CP, too. An hour ago, while the lieutenant was away, Kane showed up demanding to know where his squad was. He had his Springfield rifle, all his 782 gear, and a haversack stuffed with Mills bombs. He was still addled by hospital morphine, and Smith wondered how he had gathered all that equipment, how he had found the platoon at all. In any event, the sergeant ordered Kane to remain at the CP as a runner. Sit down here where I can keep an eye on you, he told the corporal. And for Christ's sake, keep your fucking mouth shut. Compray-voo?

Since then, Kane has been sitting quietly, smoking, drinking coffee. In fact, he has drunk nearly two pots of coffee and has visited the sinks a half-dozen times. Smith is encouraged, for a man coming down out of the morphine clouds often craved coffee, and pissing purged the system. The lieutenant does not know Kane from Adam's house cat, but thinks he is an actual runner. He does not know that the corporal is AWOL from the regimental hospital. Men often leave the hospital and return to their companies, a breach of regulations that everyone accepts, though no one fully understands until he has done it himself. It is a reality the lieutenant will need to learn, if he lives. In any event, Smith sees no need to trouble him with it now. Kane's cheeks are still plastered with dirty white bandages, however, and the lieutenant keeps glancing in his direction. Luckily, the maps have proved a distraction.

Squarehead arrives suddenly, ducking his head under the fly. He has been interrogating prisoners at battalion. He takes off his helmet and scratches the greasy mat of his hair. Fuckin' Krauts, he says. Guess what they're callin' us now.

Suddenly, Kane brays with laughter. If they're dead, they can't call us anything, he says.

The lieutenant looks up sharply. Smith thinks, *Goddammit!*

Squarehead beholds Artemus with surprise. Where the fuck did you come from? I thought you were—

Smith glares and draws a hand across his throat. Squarehead looks at the sergeant, then at Artemus, then at the lieutenant. He grins. Right-o, Staff Sergeant, he says.

So what do they call us? asks the lieutenant.

The Marine looks at Smith, who nods his head. Squarehead laughs. Teufelhunden, sir, he says. Fuckin' devil dogs. Can you beat that, eh?

I rather like it, says the lieutenant. He adjusts his glasses and considers the men before him as if he were seeing them for the first time. His gaze rests for a moment on Artemus Kane, then moves away. Do we have any more of that coffee? he asks.

Smith pours the officer a canteen cup of coffee from the new pot simmering on the fire, then slings his rifle. Permission to check the line, Mister Carmody, he says. The lieutenant lifts his hand. Carry on, he says, and, with a last curious glance at Artemus, goes back to his maps. Smith points to the corporal. You come with me, he says.

Smith walks out of the CP, pulling through the slick, glistening mud. He does not look back, but he can hear Kane following behind, his shoes squelching in the mud. The day is dark and gray. They have not seen the sun in a long time, and they all talk of it as if it were some mysterious star that the ancients once knew. It must rain again soon, and when it does, the Germans will most likely make a raid.

Presently, Smith comes to the line. The men are sitting on the parapets of their rifle pits. They take turns cleaning weapons, writing letters, combing the lice from their tunics, while the others watch to their front. Out there, the artillery has blasted away every tree and landmark save for the chimney of a ruined house. The ground is laid with staked concertina that wiring parties set out during the night, always a touchy business under the illumination flares.

The Marines are lean and hardened by their long marches, hollow-eyed from lack of sleep. They are running out of cigarettes and ammunition, and rations are short. They have been fighting for weeks without relief, and that, too, shows in their eyes. They have seen too much. They are nervous and watchful, quick to react to any sound, any sudden movement, so that it is unwise to approach them unannounced, even from the rear. Frank Smith whistles tunelessly; they look up, expectant and motionless.

Smith hears a tap-tap-tapping behind him. It is Artemus Kane, moving slowly, tapping a Mills bomb against the steel breech of his rifle. The men relax at the corporal's approach, and they shout greetings. One of them makes a joke about old Lazarus risen from the dead. My Lord, he stinketh, says the joker.

Fuck you, says Kane. Fuck alla you.

They are all caught in a fog of time, and sometimes men emerge from it, and sometimes they don't. Three weeks ago, the company was in a patch of tangled woods heavy with smoke, leaves and branches falling from the bullets thick among them. Everybody was mixed together in time, Krauts and Marines, all yelling, firing every which way, clubbing and stabbing. Most of the company officers were dead or wounded, and Smith had command of his platoon. He was trying to move the men forward when he came upon Gideon Kane. The boy was sitting on top of Artemus shouting Corpsman! Corpsman! and struggling to keep his brother's hands away from his bloody face. Smith glanced at Artemus's wound, the blood, the exposed teeth, and felt a sickness well inside him. Nevertheless, he pulled Gideon up by the collar, had to fight him until he stood erect. You got to leave him! he shouted into Gideon's ear. We got to keep moving! He kicked the boy in the seat of his pants, kicked him again until he was lurching forward, Smith close behind, prodding with his bayonet. To stop was to die in a patch of fucking woods nobody ever heard of.

Later, Gideon returned to the place where his brother was shot. Artemus was gone, of course, and Gideon spent two days tracking him down to a field hospital in a grove of linden trees. When Gideon returned at last, their third platoon leader, a nervous OCS graduate who had been with them eighteen hours—Smith could not remember what his name was—declared he would have Gideon court-martialed for desertion in the face of the enemy.

But, sir, said Smith, Mister Baylor gave Private Kane permission to seek out his brother.

Lieutenant Baylor was their second platoon leader, a promising officer come up from the enlisted ranks and thus well liked and trusted by the men. He had granted no such permission, of course, for he was killed by machine gun fire in the opening moments of the Belleau Wood fight, and long before Gideon went over the hill. But Smith felt it was the sort of thing Mister Baylor would have done.

Why was I not told of this? demanded the fresh lieutenant, who did not know Smith's name at all.

Sir, I did tell you, said Smith, though of course he had not.

Well, by god, Sergeant, you keep me informed, said the lieutenant.

Aye, aye, sir, said Smith.

The next morning, the new lieutenant was struck in the forehead by a single sniper's round while inspecting the line. When Smith removed the officer's identity disc, he learned that his name was Cantwell, Joseph C., that his service number was NG7954862, that he was a Protestant. Smith promised the dead officer that he would learn the names of all those who followed him, no matter how long they stayed.

Now Smith takes Kane's grenade away and returns it to the haversack. I told you to stay quiet in the CP, he says. You never listen, goddammit.

In the gray light, Kane's face is pale and sunken. The bandages have kept him from shaving. Sorry, Staff Sergeant, he says. When I came up, I was hoping Mister Baylor was still the boss.

Mister Baylor is dead, says Smith, and tells the story.

My god, says Kane. I stayed away too long. You got any fags?

Smith lights a cigarette for himself and one for the corporal. How you feelin'? he asks.

I got a headache, is all, says Kane. He unslings his rifle and rests the butt on his shoe. What about Gideon?

Smith nods to the right. Still with the weapons squad, he says.

I meant to ask *how* he was, says Artemus.

He's all right, says Smith. He drops his cigarette in the mud and lights another. After a moment he says, Gideon has a bad cough. The corpsmen say it's bronchitis. I told him to go to the hospital, but he don't listen any more than you do.

The rain begins, slowly at first, then harder. The men curse and begin to reassemble their weapons and tuck their letters away. The clouds seem all at once to settle on the ground to their front, and the wired and shell-pitted landscape, already ghostly and foreboding, takes on an even more sinister air. Then a green flare goes up over the German lines. The men watch it rise and sputter out. They all know what it means.

Here we go, says Kane.

Welcome back, says Smith. They are the only ones standing erect now. The others are lying in their holes, rifles cocked and locked and pointed toward the ground that lies before them. Kane and Smith fix their bayonets. The staff sergeant knows full well that it is useless to order Artemus Kane back to the CP. Most likely, Mister Carmody will not notice Kane's absence. If he does, and if he makes inquiry, Smith will lie, and all will be well. Smith says, Can you handle the squad?

The cigarette is drooping from Kane's mouth, and he squints against the smoke. He rests his Springfield against his chest and, with both hands, pulls the bandages from his cheeks. Underneath, the wounds are blue and ghastly, smeared with ointment, dangling with stitches. Kane drops the bandages in the mud. How does it look? he says.

Like shit, says Smith.

Is it corrupted? Any pus?

Smith peers closer. He lays two fingers against Artemus's cheeks, one then the other, to test for fever. Not so I can tell, he says, but you prob'ly should of stayed.

Fuck that, says Kane. Too much time on my hands. I'll be careful.

All right, then, says Smith. You know what's fixing to happen. Your boys are on the left, up against first platoon. I'll keep Wurtz as a runner.

Aye, aye, says Kane, but he doesn't go. He stands fast, twisting his hands on the muzzle of his rifle, the rain bouncing comically off his helmet. Thanks for looking out for me, he says.

Go on, says Smith. We're out of time.

All right, says Kane. He slings his rifle, hesitates, turns to the right.

Artemus, says the staff sergeant. Not that way.

I know, I know, says Kane. He turns again and walks slowly, painfully away, like old Lazarus, toward the left where his squad lies waiting. The staff sergeant watches him go, then turns back to the CP, where he must inform Mister Carmody that he is about to meet armed Germans for the first time.

* * *

Alone on the depot platform, Smith looked at his watch. Time was growing short. He set off down the worn bricks; beside him lay the rail yard which, for all his reading, all his pondering, remained the one place on earth that made any sense to him.

The two young airmen would be drinking coffee in the depot restaurant by now. If Charlie Granger was still there, he might well buy them breakfast. Granger's eldest son was buried somewhere in the fields of France, but his name was engraved on the monument that loomed in the middle of 23rd Avenue—a cairn of stone crowned by a bronze infantryman arrested in the moment of attack, Springfield rifle in his left hand, right hand poised to throw a Mills bomb, coiled barbed wire and the old familiar junk of battlefields strewn about him. How unlike the Confederate monument by the courthouse, where the soldier stood at rest, youthful and contemplative and sad.

SWEET PEARL RIVER

Not long after he met Anna Rose, Artemus got bumped off the Silver Star and bid on a daylight freight job as conductor. One afternoon, southbound, they were stopped on the main line waiting for a northbound local to get out of the way. The local had pulled a drawbar and had to set the car out and had lost time, and Artemus's train was stuck. His drag was so long that the engine was at the south switch of the passing track, and the caboose was stopped in the middle of the Pearl River bridge. Max Triggs the flagman was flagging behind, Hubert Craft the swing brakeman was reading *Field & Stream* in the cupola, so Artemus filled his pipe and went out back to smoke. He was glad to have the chance, for he loved rivers, and he usually passed quickly over the Pearl, the iron bridge trusses flickering by and gone. Now he could study it for a while, take the evening air, sit on the porch as he might at home.

It had rained in the early afternoon, so the river lay under a fine mist. The water stretched away on either side, but Artemus sat down on the west-side steps, among a whine of mosquitoes, so he could watch the sun fall. In fact, it had already passed below the trees, painting the feathery tops of the cypress and pines with a delicate bronze light. Cypress and pine and oak were all draped in gray moss and hung with vines. In the shadows below, in the rank grass where white and yellow flowers bloomed, the fireflies were rising. Among the shadows, too, a single great sycamore leaned from the bank, whose silver leaves and white trunk seemed to hold still to the light of day. The leafy top of the sycamore dragged in the water, and Artemus thought he saw movement there. In a moment, a graceful pirogue poked its nose out, parting the mist, rounding the tree slowly. A boy sat in the stern, paddling lazily. He looked up at the bridge, and when he saw Artemus, he lifted the paddle from the water. "Hidy," said the boy.

"Hidy, yourself," said Artemus.

"Say, can I come up there?" asked the boy.

Artemus beckoned, and the boy landed his boat and scrambled up the bank. The steps of the caboose were so high above the bridge timbers that Artemus had to pull the boy up by his hand. When he was aboard, the boy sat down next to Artemus, comfortable as if he were an old friend. He was about ten, a black-haired lad with a solemn face tanned the color of dark walnut. He smelled of fish and child-sweat, and Artemus remembered how his niece Fanny sometimes smelled that way at day's end in the summer. The boy wore a cotton shirt and jeans britches rolled to the knees. His legs and bare feet were spotted with chigger and mosquito bites, some bloody where he had scratched them. "Dern these muskeeters," he said. "It ain't been a breath of air all evenin'."

Artemus laughed. "What's your name, sport?" he said.

"Sturgis Montieth the Third," said the boy. He pulled a corncob pipe from his pocket. "You got a Lucifer?" he asked.

"I do," said Artemus, and gave the boy a match, which he lit expertly with a flick of his thumbnail. He puffed great clouds of acrid smoke, then rested his elbows on his knees and squinted into the twilight. "That'll do for the 'skeeters," he said. "They can't abide Injun terbaccer." Then, after a moment, he looked at Artemus and asked, "What's *your* name?"

Artemus told his name, and the boy put out his hand, and they shook. "Pleased to meet you," said the boy, then pointed with his pipe stem as an old man might. "The river's pretty, ain't it?"

"Yes, it is," said Artemus. On the sandbar, a green heron—Artemus had not noticed him before—posed motionless, one foot raised. In the yellow sky, swallows darted and chirped to one another. Artemus and the boy could smell the warm creosote from the bridge, and the old rank smell of the slow-moving water. They heard the secret voices in the long grass, the voices of night, and a bull frog tuning up, and his lesser cousins making a loud chorus: the leopard frogs, the spring peepers, the trilling of toads courting on the muddy banks. Here a kingfisher came darting down the tunnel of trees, there a flight of egrets crossed the sky. Silver minnows flicked and dodged in the shallows, and a snake traveling upstream scattered them. A big snake doctor came and perched on the pigtail whistle of the cab and watched them with his quick, bulbous eyes.

"Say, can I see your watch?" asked the boy.

Artemus was wearing overalls, and his watch chain was looped across the bib. He took out the gold Hamilton and showed it to the boy who said, "I wish I could have one like that."

Artemus was suddenly aware of the piece, the weight of it, the delicacy of the numbers and the fine deep blue of the hands. The watch was ticking away, and time was passing, and right now Anna Rose was maybe going to Mass, passing through the doors of Immaculate Conception with her hat on and a little veil of netting over her face. Artemus could see her dip her hand in the holy water font, make the sign of the cross, walk down the nave alone with her head bowed.

"You will, one day," said Artemus, and slipped the watch back in his pocket.

"Huh," said the boy. "It's always One day this, and One day that—I'd like to know what day you all are talkin' about."

Artemus laughed, for he knew the feeling well. He said, "Well,

Sturgis Montieth the Third, what you doing out here on the Pearl River with night coming on?"

"Well, I was scoutin', sir, mostly," the boy said. "Too much fresh water to fish. We live on the county road about a mile upstream. My daddy is the game warden. I pretend a lot, to exercise my imagination. This evenin', I am a Royal Canadian Mounted Po-lice."

"I expect that is a good trick in Louisiana in the summer," said Artemus.

"Well, it's summer in Canada, too," said the boy. "I guess they got muskeeters, too, and they speak French like Daddy. I learned that in school."

"All right," said Artemus. "I see your point."

"So why are you-all settin' here on the bridge?" asked the boy.

Artemus explained that his train was delayed by another train, and sitting on the bridge was all they could do at the moment. He said, "I cannot begin to tell you how much I am disappointed by this state of affairs."

The comment was lost on the boy. He said, "How you know to do it? How you know to stop?"

"We got a train order at Picayune," said Artemus. "It said to stop at the south switch of the siding, so that's what we did, and here we are."

"Huh," said the boy. He smoked for a moment, then said, "I hear you-all in the night, and I hear the engines whistle for the crossin' down at Gant's store. Such a lonesome sound in the dark."

"Yes, it is," said Artemus. "You don't ever get used to it."

* * *

Artemus Kane, at least, never got used to it. He loved to be out on the car tops on a warm day while his train rambled through a town: cap cocked over one eye, hands in his pockets, posing in the same careless, infuriating way that sailors have. He never missed a chance to lean from an engine cab or the cupola of a caboose and wave at the poor mortals down below—citizens in motorcars huddled like sheep at a crossing; children racing the train on their bicycles; pretty girls hanging laundry in their backyards—as if to say, *Why, this is nothing. I do this every day.* He believed he saw the envy in all their eyes—the longing for motion and speed, for freedom, for the privilege of walking always on the edge of doom that could make even ordinary moments of life a sweet possession. And late on a moonless night, when the lamplit windows of houses winked across the fields, and the whistle of the striding locomotive drifted back from some nameless crossing, Artemus thought of himself and his comrades as the last tragic heroes, traveling forever into the darkness, forever apart, with nothing for their passage but a hint of coal smoke borne away by the wind, the glow of their marker lamps fading and gone, and this: a deep silence that embraced all the sorrow and mutability of a race that had owned Eden once.

He never got used to sixteen-hour days, pitch-black nights, clouds of mosquitoes, surly hoboes with knives and guns lurking in empty cars. He remembered slipping on ice-caked ladders and stirrups—once trying to grab a hand hold but feeling the grab iron slip away, falling between the cars, catching himself at the last possible instant before the wheels had him—and how it was to look for car numbers in the dark, and switch in the blinding rain, and walk the tops at fifty miles an hour against a wind that slashed like a razor and blew your lantern out, or what it was like to work the head end, to be in the engine cab on a hundred-degree day with the firebox doors opened and a gasoline truck racing you to a crossing.

The world the railroad men inhabited was an alien masculine world with a language all its own—the runic timetables, the peculiar idioms, the complicated rules. Hecate was real, and death was real, and the landscape was wrought of solid things, of iron, steel, gravel, piney woods, weathered freight offices and scale houses—a lonely, complex, unforgiving place.

One night. One day. One afternoon. That's how the men told their stories, every incident a particular moment in time, captured forever, immortal, always dressed in weather, in light or dark, full of voices and the quick, moving shapes of men. It was sleeting, raining, hot, cold, pitch-black dark; trains were always moving, wheels groaning, the clock in the freight house ticked for no one, and something was about to happen—something *was* happening. Ghosts spoke, laughed, did mischief, got hurt, were stupid or clumsy or annoying—but in the telling they were not ghosts, for you could see their faces, see their arms move, see the pencils in their pockets, the grease on their pants, see the rain running off the bills of their caps, smell the whiskey on their breath. You could see a black yard engine coming down in the blinding rain, all the crew in sou'-westers so it looked like a shrimp boat, but never mind the rain, for the trains had to move just the same. Here a man grinned at you from the line of a story, and you knew he was real, no matter he died two decades ago from too much drink. You saw a man sitting amazed in the welter of his own blood—a man lying dead, cut to pieces, among the tall spring grass—men shambling up the yard in circles of lantern light—or running, taking a leak, choking on a chaw of Red Man, hanging off the side of a car—a man framed in the window of a locomotive cab or riding the footboard—bending to throw a switch, stepping off a moving engine or caboose, setting a hand brake, climbing a long ladder, walking the tops—each one real, all real in their grace, their sweat, their stinking in the heat, their noses running in the cold, their hemorrhoids and hangovers. Here a man flings his cap down and stomps on it in frustration. There a man throws a cup of water in another's face, and everybody tenses for a confrontation that never comes. A man curses, one fires a pistol in the air for no reason, another vomits bootleg liquor out the cab window, another cuts you with his meanness, then an hour later says something kind that saves you.

This is what he might have told the boy, but he didn't for there was no time, and no words to tell so a boy might understand. He wanted to

tell Anna Rose, too, and maybe he would, for he hoped to have the time
for that. Someday pretty soon, anyhow, if he didn't lose her.

* * *

"Sometimes I like to come up here to watch the trains go by," said the
boy, and pointed with his pipe stem. "I stand right over yonder."

"Well, you must be careful," said Artemus. "These things will hurt
you."

"Oh, I stand 'way back in the grass. I always give the fellers on the
engine a highball." He waved his hand in the way that signified a highball, the universal signal to proceed. "They always like that," he said.

"All right, I will teach you something," said Artemus. "When you
watch a freight train by, you always look for sticking brakes and hot
journal boxes." He pointed out the journal boxes on the caboose, and
the brake shoes against the wheels. He said, "One makes fire around the
wheels, the other makes smoke, maybe fire, too. You see something like
that, here's what you do when the shack comes by." Artemus showed the
boy the hand signals for sticking brakes and for a hot box. "Then the
boys will know they have trouble," he said.

Sturgis Montieth practiced the movements. "Now, that's somethin'
like," he said, pleased with himself.

"Only," said Artemus, "if you give those signals just for fun, the lord
God will strike you dead with a lightning bolt. You understand?"

"Yes, sir."

"You can't be fooling around out here," said Artemus.

"No, sir." The boy thought a moment. "What if it's night?" he said.

"You can signal with your lantern, but never mind that, because
you better not be up here at night. Now, pay attention." Artemus
showed the boy the hand signals for coupling air hoses, cutting off,
backing across, and the signs for numbers one through ten. The boy
picked them up easily.

"That's good," said Artemus. "You learn quick."

"One day, I would like to be a railroad man my own self," said the boy.

"I thought you wanted to be a Royal Canadian Mounted Po-lice," said Artemus.

"Shoot," said the boy, "that was only pretend. Don't you think I'd a whole lot rather ride up here like you, with a fine watch, on a fast freight train?"

"You think so?" said Artemus. He wanted to tell the boy about Anna Rose, about the pain of craving her and how he wouldn't see her tonight or tomorrow night, maybe not for a long time, because that's how it was on the railroad, and you had to accept it or get out. However, this was only a boy, and he would not be moved by a sentiment of that kind. Artemus Kane would not have been moved when he was a boy, standing by the high iron, watching the trains go by and dreaming of travel and speed. In that distant time, Artemus believed in a future that owned no room for yearning, and speed was all that mattered.

Far ahead, the engine's whistle blew a series of long and short notes.

"What's that?" asked the boy.

"The engineer is calling in the flags," said Artemus. "It means the local is tucked away in the hole at last, praise God, and we are about to leave." He dug in the pocket of his overalls and produced a rubber ring, its diameter a little larger than a dollar coin. "This is an air hose gasket," he said, laying it in the boy's palm. "You keep it. When you hire out, show it as a sign. You'll be that much ahead."

The boy looked at the gasket as if it were the Holy Grail. "Mankind!" he said. "Thanks, mister!" Artemus laughed.

From the rear, Max Triggs the flagman was trotting toward the caboose. The engine gave two quick notes on the whistle.

"That's the highball," said the boy.

"Time to go," said Artemus. He helped the boy make the long step down. "Stay off the bridge, now. Maybe I'll see you again sometime."

"I'll watch for you," said the boy.

In a little while, the Pearl River and Gant's store and the local in the siding were far behind them. Hubert Craft was still up in the cupola, reading, lifting his eyes now and then to watch for trouble along the train. Artemus and Triggs stood on the back of the caboose, holding fast to the handrail. They were making good time now, and the rails slid rapidly beneath them, the caboose wheels clicking on the joints. The air smelled of coal smoke and friction and rain. It was dangerous to linger this way on the narrow platform and the train racing along. It was against all the rules. Sometimes, though, and especially on a summer evening, you just had to do it, just for a little while.

Triggs asked, "Who was that little feller you were talking to?" He was a droll man whom Artemus had never seen disturbed or agitated. Hubert Craft was the same way, and sometimes their calmness drove Artemus crazy. Neither Hubert nor Max Triggs ever raised his voice, and Triggs didn't raise his voice now, so he was all but inaudible over the noise of their passage.

Artemus shouted in return. "Just a boy, though a smart one. He has ambitions to be a railroad man."

"Huh," said Triggs. "He ain't *that* smart, then."

IN HOC SIGNO

The roundhouse was not round, but octagonal. On six sides were the stalls where locomotives were serviced in preparation for their next runs. The seventh side held the office, the shop, and the trainmen's washrooms. In the center of the octagon was a turntable, which was not a table but a section of track on inverted trusses set down in a pit. Southbound engines had to back out, those nothbound had to head out. If necessary, a locomotive could be set out on the table and turned slowly to the grind of electric motors and grease squelching in the gears and cogs. Thence it would head or back through the yawning doors that led to the maze of tracks in the yard.

The roundhouse was a monument to the age of heavy machinery. It reverberated with the clang of tools, the whine of motors, the thump of air compressors, the mechanical breathing of the locomotives. Its vast floor, and the floor of the pit, were of cinders and beds of ancient, petrified grease. Everything was under a common roof and lit constantly by electricity, since not even the white sun of August could penetrate the smeared and blackened skylights. Every surface was coated with a fine dusting of soot so that, in time, the clothing of the men who worked there was the color of soot and so deeply penetrated that no Oxydol or Clorox could redeem it. In rainy weather, water dripped through the smoke vents in the roof, the soot turned to paste, black tears coursed down the walls, and the old grease beds glistened with beads of moisture, each one an oily rainbow.

Meanwhile the locomotives, large and small, yard and freight and passenger, brooded in their stalls, fussed over like thoroughbreds, gleaming and polished like nothing else in that ashen place. Engine wipers used their rags and brushes and steam hoses against the grime of the road. They shined headlights and gauges and sight-glasses. They raked clean the mud drums and fireboxes, and restored the white-painted rims of the great wheels. Oilers oiled and greased; machinists tinkered and measured; hostlers moved the engines to and fro. In the office, the roundhouse clerks bent like monks over maintenance forms and pay rosters and orders for parts and tools. The office in winter was always blue with cigar and cigarette smoke and blistering hot from the iron stove. In summer, the ceiling fans wobbled on their stems and stirred the smoke around and blew papers everywhere, in fact stirred everything but the heat thick as tar in the air. In living memory, only one woman had ever entered there: an aggrieved wife waving a little automatic pistol around. No one was injured.

The men lived on the ground, but nothing else did: not a blade of grass, neither roach nor rat. Even jimson weed, which throve on concrete, could find no purchase on the toxic floor of the roundhouse. Yet life is persistent, and here it took hold among the timbers of the roof where lived generations of bickering sparrows and cooing pigeons. The rafters were white with droppings and dripped with the remnants of ancient nests. The birds seemed to enjoy the smoke and soot that rose at all hours around them. They seemed frantic to perpetuate themselves and mated and brooded even in the winter, so that, in any season, a man was likely to be shat upon or have a spindly, featherless nestling drop in his coffee. Hido Schreiber, on his days off, sometimes visited the roundhouse with his double-barreled rifle and boxes of rat-shot cartridges. He worked great slaughter among the birds, but when he left, they only seemed more numerous than before.

* * *

Bobby Necaise was a round, freckled, good-natured boy whose accent was that of the Gulf Coast, kin to the urban dialect of New Orleans, which in turn was kin to certain dialects found in New York City. Bobby did not know this. He had not seen New York City, but he hoped to during his adventures in the U.S. Navy. He wanted to see everything. He wanted to go to Europe, to Italy and France especially, and walk among the stuccoed, sunwashed villages of the Mediterranean. He wanted to steam across the blue waters of the Pacific and visit islands where coconut palms thrashed in the offshore breeze, where girls with naked bosoms cavorted in grass skirts and flowers. He had read about all these places in *National Geographic*, and they were set like jewels in the vast, endless future he was about to embrace. He could see himself clearly in an image informed by the recruiting signs at the post office: standing on the deck of a warship in his dress blues, a white hat cocked on his head, the wind whipping his neckerchief, the sea beyond marbled and foaming. For now, however, Bobby Necaise was a brakeman on the Southern Railway in a greasy barn coat and overalls and a polka-dotted cap with the brim turned up. He carried a cracked leather Gladstone bag and a lantern. His gloves were stuffed in a coat pocket along with a timetable and a ham sandwich his mother had made. The conductor had given him permission to swap with Sonny Leeke, so Bobby would be working the head end today, and he could talk to the enginemen about the mysteries of steam propulsion.

They were in the crews' washroom when he asked about swapping. At first, Frank Smith was reluctant. Necaise hired out at fourteen as a messenger boy, but, as Smith pointed out, he had only been on the trainmen's board for a year, and this local was the first regular job he had been able to hold.

Just this one trip, begged Necaise. It's Christmas Eve, ain't nothing going to happen.

C'mon, Frank, argued Sonny Leeke. It's an easy day, and you got to let the boy break his cherry sooner or later.

You always have an elegant way of putting things, said Smith. He looked at Necaise. You better get your ass moving, he said. It's a long walk to the roundhouse.

So here was Bobby Necaise, crunching over the cinders of the roundhouse floor, nodding to the sooty drones whose lives were spent among the grease. When Necaise worked the back end of the local, Frank Smith always looked out for him, teaching by example, hovering and watchful. Now Bobby was on his own. He would be the man who rode the footboard of the engine, who made the cuts on the head end, who would read and interpret train orders and switch lists and watch for danger lurking past the long black boiler of the engine. It was a school of responsibility shaping him for his own future, and he was fully conscious of the trust placed in him. The thought made young Necaise glow with pride and left him unprepared for the sight that greeted him beyond the washroom's rusty screen door.

* * *

Once Frank Smith had made up his mind about Necaise, he had no second thoughts. A train conductor was not allowed second thoughts; he was supposed to be right the first time. When he made a mistake, he had to stand by his own judgment and take the rap. That was the hard part of the job. So far, Smith had not found the easy part, except that he got to be in charge.

The rear-end crew had returned to the X-630. On the desk of the caboose, under the white glare of the Aladdin desk lamp, lay the train's brief consist and three waybills. Sure enough, the hogs were on a U.S.

Army waybill and were to be set out at the packing plant in south Hattiesburg. The second bill was for the empty boxes, all going to New Orleans, and the third was for a single car of logs they must pick up at Pachuta. With so little work, Smith wondered why they were running the extra at all, why they had not annulled it. He considered ignoring the log car, but knew that, if he did, he would be nagged by the unresolved task all night. Anyway, it would only take a few minutes to pick up the car at the saw mill.

On a clipboard over the desk were the orders Smith had been given at the crews' washroom. They were stapled together with a pink clearance slip listing the number of each order and that of the train to which they were addressed. This morning, they had three slow orders, copies of which were given to every train to indicate sections of the road where speed was currently restricted:

TRAINS WILL NOT EXCEED 15 MPH BETWEEN
X TOWER AND LITTLE WOODS.

And so on. The particular order that governed the movement of Smith's train read

ENG 4512 RUN EXTRA SOUTH YARD MERIDIAN TO
L&N JCT 730 AM TO 1130 PM.

By this means, Smith's southbound local would be subject to the demands of the dispatcher between their departure point and the yard limit in New Orleans, and this for sixteen hours, the maximum time a crew could work. After that, they were due eight hours rest and an hour-and-a-half call before reporting again. This was the Hours of Service Law, which the men called the Hog Law, though no one knew why. It was a rule strictly observed. If a crew's sixteen hours were up, they stopped, no matter if they were a hundred feet from the yard limit or ten miles out in the swamp. If the Hog Law caught them, they shut down, put out the flags, and waited for a relief crew to come and get them. For obvious reasons, the dispatcher always tried to get the men in under the law, but it was not uncommon for a train to go dead after accidents or delays.

This rule, which often seemed absurd to the common citizen, grew out of the days when men were unprotected by unions and had to work as long as the company demanded. Smith had heard old men like Mister Dunn tell of working two or three or four days straight, catching a little sleep when they could on the steel deck plates of a locomotive cab or the cushions of a caboose. Men so used would reach a point when they could hardly walk or see. They could not judge distances nor decipher orders nor remember the rules. They missed signals, or misread them. Their minds wandered, and they ceased to care what happened to them. Trainmen were run over, losing fingers and legs, more often losing their lives. Firemen no longer heeded the water level in their boilers and kept on shoveling coal until everybody on the engine was blown to kingdom come. Enginemen ran too fast or too slow. They sideswiped cars and jerked out drawbars and collided with other trains.

Once, when he was new to the job, Smith asked Mister Dunn if such an attitude on the company's part was not only cruel but counterproductive. Mister Dunn merely smiled and left his brakeman to discover for himself that greed always trumped kindness and reason, a lesson Smith should have learned in the Great War but missed somehow amid the confusion.

Frank Smith was glad he did not belong to that fraternity who worked in the days when the companies fought every safety device and treated their employees like chattel. He was glad to have missed a time when a man's experience could be judged by the number of fingers he had lost to the link-and-pin. The job was hard enough without all that, and sixteen hours on the cholly was long enough for anybody.

Some of the old men, in the way of old men, spoke fondly of a time and circumstance they no longer had to deal with. They held their experience up as a test of character which the younger, softer, more pampered generation could only fail. Not Mister Dunn, however. He might get confused, but he was never fooled by the softened edges of memory. He taught his young charges to fall on their knees every day and thank God for Westinghouse brakes and safety couplers and electric headlights. He taught them to be loyal to the unions that had forced these changes, sometimes with violence, always with difficulty. He told them, Boys, it ain't no romance in widows and orphans.

Their train had another running order this morning—an unusual one:

EXTRA 4512 WILL NOT REGISTER OR
REQUIRE CLEARANCE AT TALOWAH IF THE
TRAIN ORDER SIGNAL INDICATES PROCEED.

Ordinarily, conductors were required to sign the register at Talowah, or throw off a register ticket if their trains did not stop. Thus Smith felt uncomfortable with the order; he preferred that everyone know where his train was all the time. Still, it was Christmas Eve, and things were slow, and there should be no problem. At least they had cleaned out the log yard at Talowah last night and would not have to bother with it today.

Talowah was a strange place. Not only was it hard to switch, but Smith always felt uncomfortable there, as if someone were looking over his shoulder or walking just behind. Last night, standing in the circle of light from his lantern, he felt it especially strong in the whispers and stirrings of the barren woods. He never told anyone about the feeling, not even Artemus Kane. It seemed an oddly private thing. On the other hand, Smith had come to like the young operator there. He hoped Donny Luttrell was relieved for Christmas; in fact, Smith would be glad to take him down to New Orleans on the caboose. Such a thing was unlikely, however, for the boy was at the stony bottom of the extra board. Christmas in godforsaken Talowah would be solitary and lonesome, but maybe it was something the lad needed, something he might profit by in time to come. Smith felt himself qualified to make such a judgment, having been sufficiently lonesome himself on a good many occasions.

Pretty soon, Mister Dunn and Cox and Necaise would bring the engine down. In the meantime, Ladner lit the marker lanterns and hung them out, red to the rear. He and Sonny argued about baseball for a while, offering to include Mister Earl January in their debate, but the carman ignored them. Sleet pecked at the stovepipe, and now and then a cold gust pushed against the windows. The caboose was warm and smelled of coffee and coal and damp clothes. And hogs. The boys had found a great deal to say about the hogs.

Smith looked up from his work and considered the scene being played out in the narrow, lamplit aisle of the X-630. Mister January went on staring at the hot stove as if it were about to speak, or dance maybe. Sonny was lounging on a bench, and Ladner was doing pull-ups on the handrail that ran along the ceiling. Smith could see the shiny red and green paper of his children's Christmas presents under the rack of fusees. It was one of those moments when lonesomeness stepped back a little and a person could feel comfortable in the world, when common experience and hardship clad each man in the robe of kinsman, when every detail seemed in its proper place. Such moments came but rarely, and they never lasted long, but they were sufficient to remind Frank Smith of how fortunate he was. The others, if pressed, would agree, though they might not be able to articulate the feeling, or even want to. In any event, they would not mistake it for cheap sentimentality. Every man knew that harmony on the job was a matter of chance and luck, for one rarely got to choose those he worked with. A great many assholes found their places on the railroad, and sooner or later, every crew ended up with one or two.

Most of the men Smith worked with were not assholes. True, they were deeply flawed. They drank too much, they argued and bickered, they got into fights, they were run off by their wives, they sought the company of lewd women. But they were not mean or hateful. They were not interested in power, and while some of them, like Smith himself, preferred to be in charge, they used authority only so far as the job demanded. Their confrontations burned with the bright incandescence of fireworks, and faded just as quick, as when Sonny and Artemus Kane got into a fistfight and tore up the Purvis depot and terrorized the waiting passengers. Next day, Artemus and Sonny stood together before the trainmaster, hats in hands, and received their week's suspension. Then they went home and packed their bags and caught the next train for New Orleans where they spent the whole week laid up at Artemus's brother's house. Neither one ever mentioned the fight again, though they enjoyed hearing others tell about it.

Sonny Leeke was out on the rear platform, peering into the sleet and gray morning. In a moment, he returned and demanded to know where the engine was. "We ought to be coupled up by now," he said. "Ought to be leaving town."

Smith leaned back in his chair. "I told you, goddammit, to stay on the head end, but you wouldn't have it, so don't be complaining to me."

"That's right, Sonny," said Ladner. "Because of your lazy ass, Necaise and A.P. are prob'ly halfway to Tuscaloosa by now."

"Well, fuck alla you," said Sonny.

In truth, Frank Smith, now that he thought about it, was a little peeved himself. He pulled his watch and studied it as though the white face might reveal some answer. All it told him was that they were five minutes late. That was not a good sign.

* * *

Smith would have been irritated indeed if he knew how, at that moment, Mister A.P. Dunn was sitting on the floor of the roundhouse washroom with a dozen men, including Eddie Cox, gathered around him. Someone had bandaged Mister Dunn's head, but he had torn the bandage off, and now he was bleeding again. Moreover, Mister Dunn, who never swore, was swearing. All the bad words he had heard in fifty years of railroading were suddenly boiling out of him like a volcano, and Bobby Necaise was stopped cold.

Since he came out on the railroad, Necaise had grown accustomed to foul language. Lately, he had been practicing it on his own, for he knew that sailors used colorful speech, and he wanted to be up on it. In addition, Artemus Kane had instructed him that cursing was a useful language all its own and, in its pure form, had nothing to do with good or evil. Artemus was the best at it that Necaise ever heard, and Sonny Leeke was second, but they rarely ever swore around Mister Dunn. Now to hear that gentleman rain obscenities and curses himself was beyond imagination. The roundhouse men stood about in shock. With anyone else, it might have been funny, but no one was laughing now. This was too much. This was like hearing Jesus tell the Pharisees to fuck off.

"What's the matter?" said Necaise. No one paid him any mind except Eddie Cox, who looked surprised to see him. Necaise said, "I'm the head brakeman on the job. What's the matter with Mister Dunn?"

The engineer said, "God damn it to hell, I will whip all your goat-fucking asses!"

"Lord!" said Necaise.

"It ain't nothin' to it, Mister Bobby," said Eddie Cox. "He just feeling bad this morning."

"Shut up, Eddie," growled a big man in a brown suit and bowler hat. Necaise knew this man to be Tom Brody, the roundhouse foreman. Brody shoved forward and punched a finger in the boy's chest. "Where is Sonny Leeke?" he demanded.

"Working swing today," said Necaise. "What's the matter?"

"Well, this is a hell of a thing," said Brody, looking Necaise up and down. "Sending a goddamned cub up here."

Necaise pushed through the men and knelt down and took hold of

Mister Dunn's shoulder. The old man knocked his hand away, but Necaise took hold again and shook hard.

"A.P.," he said. "Look at me. We got to go. We're late. Look at me!"

"He ain't goin' nowhere," said Brody.

"Yes, sir, he is," said Necaise, standing to face the man. "He's got more sense right now than you ever had."

"Sonny boy," said the foreman and was about to step forward when Mister Dunn got to his feet.

"Now, hold on there, Tom," said Mister Dunn, stepping between the two. He turned to Necaise. "Hello, Bobby," he said. "Are you on the head end today?"

After that, Mister Dunn appeared to pull himself together as if nothing at all had happened. He allowed Necaise to bandage him up again while he read his orders and had a cup of the roundhouse's foul coffee. Necaise was chafing, but Mister Dunn seemed to think they had all the time in the world. He explained to Necaise that he had slipped on the ice and hit his head, but he had been hurt lots worse than this any number of times.

"Can you run the engine all right?" asked Necaise. "Because you don't have to if you don't want."

"Nonsense," said Mister Dunn.

Eddie Cox eased up to Necaise and whispered, "Maybe we best get on. I'll carry his grip."

As Necaise was leaving the shack, the foreman stepped out of his office and caught him hard by the arm. He said, "You ever speak to me like that again, I will haul your freight."

Necaise shook off the man's hand and followed Cox and Mister Dunn across the cinders to the pit where the 4512 was being turned.

For all his bravado, Bobby Necaise was not feeling well at all. In fact, he was scared shitless and wanted to be gone. He wished he were waiting on the caboose with Frank Smith. He would never have suspected that an engineer could lose control of himself like Mister Dunn had. Certainly, Necaise never thought he would lay a hand on an engi-neer, much less call one by his first name, much less give him advice on what he might do. Furthermore, he had sassed the foreman in a way contrary to all his raising, and on top of all that, they were running late. Bobby Necaise had collected a good deal of experience and made the first enemy of his life, and he was not even out of the roundhouse yet.

The hostler was moving the 4512 off the table. The rails groaned and creaked under the weight, and the drivers turned with a stately slowness. The engine, white flags hanging limp on the pilot, was clean and elegant and beautiful. It seemed small under the shed, and Necaise realized for the first time how cavernous and forbidding the round-house was.

In a moment, the engine was off the table with the tender pointed toward the big doors that led to the yard. Eddie Cox was already in his seat, having satisfied himself that the fire was laid correctly. Meanwhile, Mister Dunn had paused at the foot of the gangway. When Necaise approached, the engineer turned on him, his face so clouded with sudden anger that Necaise pulled up short.

"Did Smith say you and Sonny could swap out?"

"Yes, sir," said Necaise. "I asked him because—"

"Never mind why you asked him," snapped the engineer. "I don't want to hear any god damned excuses. Did he ask *me* if I wanted a new man up here? Did he?"

"Well, no, sir," said Necaise. "I guess he thought—"

"I don't give a damn what he thought!" shouted Mister Dunn. "Fucking trainmen think they run the show. Did you come up here to spy on me? Smith thinks I can't do the job—is that it?"

For an instant, Necaise thought the old man was going to strike him, and the boy cocked his arm reflexively. Then he caught himself. *No, I won't do it*, Necaise told himself. *If he hits me, I will take it.* He came to attention then, as the recruiter had taught him to do. He was ready to accept the curses, the blow even, without complaint. This is like training, he thought. This is a test.

Then Eddie Cox appeared in the gangway. "Mist' A.P. Dunn," he said. His voice managed to be firm and deferent at the same time. "Miss Nettie be waiting to hear your whistle in the yard," said Cox. "You ain't going to be late, is you?"

All at once, Mister Dunn's face changed as though he had taken off a mask. He smiled at Necaise. "Well, Bobby, you're on the head end today?"

Necaise nodded in a tentative way.

"Have you met my wife Nettie?" asked the engineer.

"Well, no, sir," said Necaise, finding his voice.

Mister Dunn narrowed his eyes and looked about, puzzled. "Well, she was here just a minute ago," he said. Then he smiled. "Maybe another time," he said.

* * *

Frank Smith was waiting at the head end of the cut when the engine backed down. He stood with arms folded and watched Necaise make the joint, watched him couple the air hoses and turn the angle cock slowly so the air would flow smoothly into the brake line. He remained silent while Mister Earl made his brake test and Necaise stood waiting with cap in hand. Finally, when all was done and engine and cars were officially a train, Smith said, "What happened to you all, Bobby?"

Necaise lowered his eyes. "Well—" he began.

"Don't talk to the cinders," said the conductor. "Talk to me."

Necaise looked up and put his cap back on. He told all that had transpired in the roundhouse, leaving nothing out. When the story was finished, Necaise said, "I guess you have to tell somebody now."

Smith began to walk up the length of the tender, pulling Necaise along by the sleeve. He said, "Listen. I have noticed that most people would rather run and tell on a man than to confront him. That is not our style out here."

"No, sir," said Necaise. "I know that. I just thought—"

"You handled the situation as good as anybody," said Smith. "Just do your job, and we will get through all right."

Now Mister Dunn was high above them, leaning out the window with his elbows on the sill and his watch in his hand. The white bandage stuck out from under his cap. "Hello, Frank," he said, his voice light and cheerful like that of a young man. "I have seven forty-five and ten."

Smith drew his own watch. "All right," he said. "And fifteen, sixteen—"

"On the money," said Mister Dunn, and put his watch away.

Necaise clambered up the gangway and disappeared into the cab. Smith said, "A.P., is there anything you need to tell me?"

"Yes, Frank, there is," said the engineer, and smiled. "We're late, so grab a hand hold. I mean to run and stink like a gourd vine."

Smith walked back to the caboose without saying more. Again he sensed the presence of the traveler in the boxcar, but the man was no longer of any interest to him. The conductor was unnerved by Mister Dunn's behavior. It angered him, as if some blithe stranger had come among them claiming a kinship he did not deserve. Smith was considering second thoughts, weighing the safety of his crew against the protection of his engineer, knowing all the while there was only one choice. It was Christmas, and the trip should be easy. They were late. Eddie Cox could run the engine if he had to. In the end, Smith could not bring himself to humiliate A.P. Dunn by calling for a replacement.

Tonight, however, he would gather the crew in his hotel room—even Eddie Cox, though Smith would have to sneak the Negro up the fire escape. Mister Dunn would require a special invitation, a note perhaps, for trainmen did not summon engineers without some decorum. At least, Frank Smith did not. Then, under the dim overhead bulb, among the cigarette-scarred furniture, Frank would address his engineer in the presence of them all. Mister Dunn would have to face the truth, and Frank Smith would be its instrument. If

A.P. didn't step down, if he wouldn't admit that his running days were done, then Smith would have to call the superintendent.

Farewell, Mister Dunn. Merry fucking Christmas. All your courage come to this, and in whatever your years remaining, you will remember that Frank Smith betrayed you.

At the caboose, Mister Earl January stood a little distance from the steps, favoring his bad leg. "You all be careful," he said.

In his irritation, Smith waved the man away. Then he paused, one hand on the grab iron, his foot on the bottom step. Foolish, he thought, to let a kindness pass unnoticed. "Thanks for your good help," he said.

Mister Earl made no reply, but turned and set off toward the roundhouse, his shoulders slumped, his figure suddenly small against the bleak expanse of the yard.

Smith swung aboard and waved his hand in the highball signal. The engineer, watching from the cab window, replied with two short notes on the whistle, and immediately the slack ran out and the short train eased into motion, a smooth start, the signature of Mister A.P. Dunn. Smith watched as Earl January passed away behind. *I hope I am not fucking up*, said Smith to himself, to the gods, to whoever might be listening.

Sonny Leeke was standing on the narrow platform. "About goddamned time," he said.

Smith leaned on the rail and made no reply. Sometimes Sonny crawled on his nerves.

"What's the matter with Mister Earl?" asked Sonny Leeke. "He acts like somebody put a hose pipe up his ass."

"Somebody did," said Smith.

"How's A.P. this morning?"

"He's all right," said Smith.

Out of the gray, solemn light they came, moving slow, the headlight shimmering on the rails, past the M&O freight house where a porter was sweeping the platform with a big push broom. The porter waved, and the two trainmen waved back, a timeless salute that recognized no distinction of race or class. Lines of waiting freight cars and empty passenger coaches echoed their passage, and the green and red switch targets glided beneath them, and all the while the caboose wheels of the trailing truck kept up their steady rhythm on the rail joints, click, click…click, click. The engine whistled for the crossings, tossing its melodious cry across the morning, the sound racketing off the vine-covered backs of tin-roofed warehouses and mill buildings where lights burned in the windows.

Pat Murphy's track gang had moved aside for the local to pass. Murphy carried a slapjack and pistol and worked his men, summer and winter, like a chain gang. Mister Dunn greeted them with two notes on the whistle, then in a moment they appeared to Smith and Sonny. Swaddled in wet, ragged coats, black faces turned up grinning, they leaned on their steel lining bars and lifted their wet, gloved hands. Old Pat himself sat under the sleet-bouncing canvas top of a yellow handcar a track away. The black men waved, but Pat Murphy made no sign, his red face dull and disinterested under the broad felt brim of his hat.

The train jerked a little as Mister Dunn grabbed another notch and the speed picked up, the click of the rail joints faster, click-click, click-click. They were past the yard limit now, rolling ever a little faster past the gray houses and backyards of Jumpertown where laundry stiffened in the cold, and dogs barked at them, and last summer's gardens stood in weedy ruin.

Dutch Ladner came out on the back porch then and breathed deep of the sweet coal-scented air. Frank Smith, leaning on the rail with the old X-630 swaying gently beneath him, saw once again, as he often did in dreams or at odd moments of the day, the muddy streets and raw, unpainted houses of the lumber company town where he grew up. Strange it was, how such images arrived unbidden out of the air.

Time was passing, and old men like Mister Dunn and Earl January were passing with it, and the old camp days, and the days of youth. Soon enough his turn would come, Smith thought, and Artemus's, and

Sonny's, and all of them who were now quick and boastful, who believed they owned the world. Smith supposed they did own it for a while, but not for a long while, not even as long as the old men had, for the world was changing, twisting, beyond anything they could grasp or imagine. In France, in Poland, in Russia, the Krauts had dropped a big rock in the water, and the ripples were crossing the pond, and soon all this fine, familiar world would be washed away, and no one of them could say what might take its place.

The train jerked again, leapt forward, and the three men grabbed the rail as the cab began to rock and bounce. Sonny Leeke laughed and pulled on the pigtail whistle and made it shriek. Mister Dunn, true to his word, was rolling fast on Pelican Road, making the ties and ballast flick beneath in a blur, making the fencerow trees and telegraph poles jump past and fall away behind in stately procession, bringing the wheels on the rail joints down to a steady hammer. Smith peered careful around the flank of the cab as the train went into a gentle curve. He saw the drive rods work, back-and-forth, back-and-forth, the black engine making smoke and raining cinders as Mister Dunn opened the throttle and teased out a little more speed, as much as he could without beating his train to death. Mister Dunn himself leaned far out the window with his cap turned backward and his goggles on, the white bandage fluttering behind like an aviator's scarf. Smith thought, By God, but he is a first-class engineer, and he will make the time. Smith took out his watch and gauged their passage by the white mile markers flicking past: they were doing almost a mile every minute now, the boxcars swaying and rocking. Smith thought of the hogs huddling in the frigid wind, shifting their weight, each one accepting whatever the moment brought. The traveling man in the boxcar would shiver too, but at least he was there by choice.

Ladner and Leeke had done the sensible thing and gone inside, but Smith stayed a moment longer, clinging hard to the rail. They were out amid the flat, fallow cotton fields, passing bare patches of woods and scattered tenant houses with smoke rising from the chimneys, passing unpainted barns, fencerows covered in dead honeysuckle vine. The urgent whistle blew for the little lost and unnamed crossings, and the sound of it echoed across the empty land as whistles like it had for years, and all one sound, one voice crying out of time.

Smith was about to turn away when he noticed a sudden change in the light. To the southeast, the pale disc of the sun appeared ghostlike and fleeting, its broad rays slanting down through the riven sky to touch the earth, as if to remind them all that it was still there. Then, just as quick, it was gone again, hidden by the driving clouds.

Maybe that is a good sign for us, thought Frank Smith, who believed in signs. He prayed again, *Don't let me fuck up. Don't let me fuck up.* Then he turned and went inside to the warmth and light.

HOW THINGS ARE MADE OF TIME

June Watson was laid out in a casket of soft pine, the new wood neither stained nor painted, but rubbed down with linseed oil by the carpenter's smooth palm. June Watson's head, empty of thoughts, rested on a baby-blue sateen pillow, his body covered to the chest with a baby-blue cotton blanket. He was dressed in a suit coat that a few hours before had been hanging on a rack in the Jew store. His long-fingered hands were crossed on his breast, his face peaceful, if a little puzzled, as though, even with a brain pumped full of formaldehyde, he were trying to remember where he was.

His mother Nandina did not know that only half her son lay in the casket; nothing under the blanket but old pillows where his legs used to be, the legs themselves burned to ash in the funeral home furnace. She did not know how it had been unnecessary to purchase the trousers to the suit. Her daughters knew, but they kept the knowledge to themselves. Three o'clock that morning, Nandina's minister, roused from bed, had rapped softly on her door. Miz Watson had not seen her boy in ten years, and now she was looking at him dead, and that was enough for her to bear right now, her daughters thought. Maybe enough to bear forever, though she had one son yet, somewhere down in the cribs and whorehouses around Wimpy's Café. The minister had gone hunting

George Watson in the dead of night, but George was vanished and no one to tell where. Now the mother's wails could be heard on the street outside the funeral home in Jumpertown, whence many a woman's lamentations, raised for her lost children, had drifted out over the mud of winter, the dust of summer.

Miz Watson, a birdlike woman with a tight knot of white hair under a black pillbox hat, stood before the casket invisible in the midst of her daughters, her cousins, sisters, aunts, and nieces. The women were a blur of hats and fur collars in a cloud of Blue Waltz perfume, an island of mourning from which the men, all but the minister, kept their distance. The people, scattered in the pews, blinked away sleep and talked softly in their weariness, their disbelief. Only, they did believe, really. They were not surprised. This was the end that men from Jumpertown always came to, and the women left to mourn.

The funeral home parlor where June Watson lay, and where he would lay for a week to come until distant kinsmen could arrive from Chicago and Detroit and Cleveland, was illumined by dim electric bulbs dangling from the ceiling. A cold draft made the cords sway so that the shadows of the people danced back and forth on the puncheon floor. The windows gave a little light, but not much on this gray Christmas Eve. The bier was surrounded by pine and cedar boughs cut hastily before dawn, and the scent of these, and the heavy scent of the women's perfume, masked the odor of formaldehyde and linseed oil.

A slim woman, the mahogany skin of her face stretched tight over her cheekbones, sat at a pump organ in the corner. The pedals wheezed and thumped. She was playing "How Sweet the Name of Jesus," though with difficulty, for some of the keys no longer worked. The neighbor women in the dark pews hummed in company to the song, finding harmonies written in no book, and other women made the words, softly, deferent as the light itself.

The undertaker, who had worked all night snipping and draining and sewing, stood stiffly by the door in his worn black suit with the silk mourning band sewn permanently to the sleeve. He was lulled by the women's voices. Many was the time, in days-long mourning, he had gone to sleep on his feet. He was drifting away now into a realm of angels and tombstones and dark cedar trees—nowhere, he believed, could there be more peace—when a presence stirred him, a newcomer who brought with him the smell of damp and the unaccustomed reek of whiskey. Thus the undertaker was the first to see the white man who stood just inside the door in a cheap raincoat, sleet melting on the shoulders. He held his fedora in one hand; under his arm was a round-faced smiling doll.

"Sir," said the undertaker in surprise. White people often came here to bid farewell to maids, butlers, yardmen, nannies, but the undertaker did not expect any white people would come to see June Watson. "Sir," he said again, shaking off sleep.

The man made no reply, nor any sign that he had heard. Now the people had sensed him, and their faces turned, and their glances fell. The organ wheezed into silence, and the voices, all but the wailing of the women. In a moment, that too died away, and the women turned together toward the door. Nandina Watson, her hands twisting a lace handkerchief, stepped forward expectantly as if some messenger had come. Her daughters, handsome yellow women with angry faces, held her back. The oldest, Dicey, said, "What you mean, comin' here."

The people drew a breath and waited, uncertain and afraid. A moment ago, they had been in their own world, but the white man changed everything. He brought the other world into the parlor, and it was that world, not the man himself, that Dicey was bold to challenge. Still, the man said nothing, only drew back his raincoat and jacket so they could see the badge pinned to his waistcoat and the butt of the pistol in his shoulder holster. The gesture did not threaten. The people understood that it was made only to establish once and for all the relationship that existed between them.

"We don't need no po-lice," said Dicey. "Not no more."

"Let it be, Dicey," said her mother. She stepped away until she was alone in the aisle, between the rows of people watching. She said, "You come about George, ain't you, Mister."

"No," said the white man.

Nandina Watson closed her eyes. The sisters made to close around her, but the old woman waved them back. She looked at the policeman again. "Maybe you can find him for me," she said. "Tell him what happened. Tell him to come home."

"I will do that," said the man. He was looking past Nandina to the casket. "I promise."

They watched as the white man walked down the aisle. He passed Miz Watson without a glance, nor seemed to pay any mind to the people nor to the women whose eyes followed him like the eyes of wolves beyond a fire, menacing but helpless in the presence of a power they could fear and despise but never comprehend.

The white man came to the casket where June Watson lay. There he stood a long moment with the silence heavy around him. They saw him take up the doll as he might a living child and lay it in the casket where June Watson slept. They watched him turn. They looked away when his eyes swept across them. At last, they watched him go, down the aisle past Miz Watson again, and out the door. They felt the cold wind as he went out to the street and heard, in the same instant, a freight train's whistle as it left the yard southerly bound. They had heard train whistles countless times before, but this one made them shiver all together as if spirits had come among them.

* * *

On the passing train, George Watson sat with his legs dangling over the sill of the open boxcar door and watched the gray houses of Jumpertown pass by. He no longer had any mind for Lucy Falls; instead, he was remembering the dream that had visited him. The dream had told

George Watson that his brother was dead.

Perhaps one day he would find out how it happened. Probably he wouldn't. News didn't carry far about somebody like June, and George Watson did not plan to return to Meridian nor anywhere else in reach of a woman who carried an ice pick. He wanted to leave all that to the gray morning falling behind, and he wanted to bury Sweet Willie Wine. From now on, he would be only George Watson, for better or worse. Probably worse, for the time was long past when he could have changed even George Watson from what he was.

He saw the backyard of his mother's house. It was all mud and dead weeds, and the fence leaned over nearly to the ground. He thought of a little brown dog he kept in the yard for a while. June hated that dog, but George used to play with it all the time until it bit him once. He killed it with a brick and had no more dogs after that.

Nobody was stirring at the house. The windows were dark, and no smoke curled from the chimney. That was a strange thing, for his mother always got up before daylight. George wondered if his brother had got home before death came for him. Goodbye, June.

George thought that when he got to wherever he was going, he would find somebody to write his mother. He would tell her farewell and not to mourn. He would ask her to think of him as already dead, far away in a place where she could not reach. It would not be a lie. George Watson had learned long ago that the world was full of people still walking around, still talking, who were dead just the same. Goodbye, Mama.

The sleet was gone now, and a flurry of snow was falling, tentative flakes that melted when they struck the ground. It was getting colder, though, and pretty soon the ground would be white. George had not seen snow for a long time, and where he was going, he would never see it again.

The train rambled on, picking up speed, and the snow slanted past the boxcar door. George scooted back from the sill and clasped his arms around his knees and watched the country of his youth pass by, and he knew it was the last time for that, too. He tried to fix it in his mind in case he ever wanted to recall it, but the snow was like a curtain between him and the world. He saw lights burning in corner groceries where he used to steal apples, and in Hung Fat the Chinaman's garage where he learned about motorcars. The lights were clear beacons in the morning, but the buildings themselves, the houses, even the telephone poles, were so gray and indistinct that they might already be nothing more than memory. The streets were empty, not a soul in sight, no one to wave goodbye to as he passed.

The lights were on in the funeral parlor, too, and George wondered who could be laid out so early in the morning. For most of his grown life, George believed he would end up in that funeral parlor himself, but he wouldn't now. Some other place awaited him: a piece of ground he hadn't seen yet, or a cold river, a field, a ditch by the road. It didn't much matter one way or the other. Sweet Willie Wine was already dead. George Watson would be cut or shot one day, or dangled from a lamppost.

He was alive right now, though, and hunger gnawed at him. He hadn't taken breakfast, of course, and he would have no chance at dinner. That was all right, too: he had been hungry before, and he could take supper in New Orleans where it wouldn't be snowing. He knew a colored café where his three dollars would get him a good meal and a room, and he knew a dark alley uptown where the .38 would get him three dollars more. Maybe ten or twenty if he could find a fat white man. A cold steel barrel in a fat man's belly always got the prize.

George Watson got to his feet and went back into the dark where the cardboard was. He was cold, and he was done with watching, and he no longer cared whether he remembered anything or not. If he could only get to sleep, he wouldn't know he was cold and hungry. He might dream, of course, but no matter. A dream was a dream, no more real than anything else.

* * *

By the time Roy Jack Lucas returned to the freight office, the snowfall was heavy, and the glass had dropped five degrees. Last night, the track gang had brought up a load of sand from the sand house to cover the bloody patches where June Watson had died. Lucas thought how the snow would finish the job. Sand, water, blood—in the spring, the dewberries would be lush there, but the Negroes would not pick them, Lucas knew. They would give that place a wide berth for years to come. He had known the people a long time, and he knew how, for them, the earth held the memory of death forever.

The detective switched off the engine of the Chevrolet; it coughed, coughed again, rattled, and finally died. A black cloud of soot rose from the tailpipe as though the motorcar's soul were escaping. Lucas glanced over his shoulder; the back seat looked empty now, and lonesome, where the doll had been. Lucas let his hands fall to the bottom of the wheel and sat back in the seat. He still had the smell of the funeral parlor in his nose, an odor of perfume and mothballs and cedar boughs. He could still feel June Watson's cold hand when he lifted it and lay the doll beneath.

Roy Jack Lucas watched the snowflakes fall. He watched them take possession of the ground, folding themselves over bricks and cinders, dusting the roofs of freight cars and buildings, everything growing whiter and whiter with each moment. He imagined how excited the children must be out yonder in the town. Sometimes, Lucas wished he could believe in Providence just so he'd have somebody to complain to. He'd petition the Almighty to let the snow keep falling, let it pile higher and higher until everything and everybody was covered up, and then leave it for a thousand years. He imagined the round globe of the earth floating through space, silver with snow and mist, glinting in the light of the sun as the ages turned. Then, one day, God might let the snow melt again and find once more the pure rivers and seas underneath, and maybe He would start all over then, maybe do it better this time.

Lucas settled down in the car seat, watching the snow sift through the glassless windows. In a little while, he closed his eyes. His head was hurting bad now, and he hoped that Hido was returned with the whiskey. Even with the pain, he had to laugh at the thought of praying for eternal snow.

Roy Jack Lucas sat in the car a long time. He grew sleepy and strangely warm, and the thought came to him that he might freeze to death right there in the company car. He was comfortable with the idea and was just about asleep when Hido rapped on the windshield and brought him back to the world.

* * *

Mister A.P. Dunn had been rolling fast, trying to make up time. Snow was falling briskly now—he hadn't expected that—but not so bad that he couldn't see. It was pretty, in fact, even if it was cold on his face when he leaned out the window. The long black boiler of the engine swayed and bounced, and the day was dark enough that he could see snowflakes swirl like delicate white moths through the headlight beam. The white-trimmed drivers were a blur, and the complicated back-and-forth motion of the drive rods was, to Mister Dunn, a beautiful, precise, mesmerizing display of which he never grew tired.

Houses slipped past, shuttered against the cold, some close enough that he could see the brief reflection of the passing engine in the windows. In some yards, children played in the snow. These little ones had emerged into a world transformed, a landscape of purity and silence that drew them forth in awe. Many of them had never seen snow, but they seemed to know instinctively what to do with it. An audience of elaborate snowmen stood by the right-of-way, and now and then a company of sweating, overdressed midgets, white and black, boy and girl, would swarm from a backyard to pelt the engine with hard-packed snowballs. As the train announced its coming, these urchins would wait in ambush, snowballs piled like artillery shot, enough for the engine and the caboose, too, while their folks would wave from the porch.

Trouble was, the cold was making Mister Dunn's head hurt. A few months ago, he had been struck between the eyes by a chunk of ballast thrown up by the wheels. The pain now was the same, but he could not remember being struck lately. It is only the neuralgia, he thought, and when he had a chance, he would take some of the Bayer aspirin from the first-aid tin.

Mister Dunn enjoyed running fast when it was appropriate and safe, on a good rail with the engine rocking beneath him. Nothing wrong with running fast if a man knew what he was doing, if he was making up time.

Once, in the early fall, the crew was sitting amid the din and clatter of a noon café, crowded into a narrow booth—save Eddie Cox, of course, who had to take his meal on the engine—when Frank Smith, out of the blue, proclaimed that he would no longer allow the phrase "making up time" to be used on his train. He said it was misleading, even heretical, since time was a sacred commodity that could not be reclaimed.

Well, Frank, said Ladner, what would you have us say?

Well, just don't say anything, replied the conductor. Just don't talk about it.

Sonny Leeke, cooling his coffee in his saucer, said, That is ridiculous. If you are five minutes late at one station, and two minutes late at the next, then you have made up three minutes, as any god damn fool can plainly see.

No, said Smith, it is not time, it's the train moving *inside* time. It's only an illusion, he said. It's a trick. There's only one time, and that's now. Now, now, now.

Aw, fuck that, said Sonny Leeke.

Of course, no one paid any attention; in fact, the conductor himself seemed to forget about it after a couple of trips, though it did take that long to get the idea out of his system. Now Mister Dunn had made up two minutes, and southbound 4512 was approaching Pachuta, Mississippi, where they were to pick up a solitary car of logs which seemed attached to an inexplicable urgency.

Mister Dunn thought about Frank Smith and the conversation they had earlier in Meridian. The conductor had seemed truly angry about something. Smith would often bluster—everyone expected that—but he rarely got mad. Moreover, thought Mister Dunn, the men on the engine were behaving in a peculiar way.

Eddie Cox had not said a word since they left the roundhouse. He worked the stoker and the water valves, the fire was clean and hot, but when he was in his seat, he stared straight ahead out the narrow front window of the cab. Necaise, too, was silent. Now and then, he looked at Mister Dunn and smiled, but that was all. The rest of the time he sat with his chin in his hand and looked out the window. True, it was hard to talk amid the racket of the engine, but usually the men would shout at one another over the noise, making a joke, calling attention to something by the roadside, cursing the motorcars and trucks that raced the train to a crossing. The men stayed connected by what was happening to them, but now they were not connected, and Mister Dunn did not like the feeling.

When they passed the yard-limit sign at Pachuta, Mister Dunn backed off the throttle and let the train drift and whistled for signals. They came around a long curve, and there was the same squat, hip-roofed, bilious-yellow depot where John Marquette had been shot dead by his own fireman in the year 1921. Mister Dunn had not thought about that in years. That it was so long ago, a lifetime ago, seemed impossible.

The red arm of the semaphore was down as expected, and the agent was on the platform. Mister Dunn brought the train to a slow, squealing stop. Necaise had his gloves on and was out of the gangway without a word before the engine cleared the depot.

The cab was silent now but for the hiss of steam and the throb of the air compressor. Mister Dunn looked over at his own fireman. Eddie Cox was staring straight ahead, his hands folded in his lap, and Mister Dunn thought how maybe this was the same thing old man Marquette had seen in the last minutes of his life.

Mister Dunn said, "Well, Eddie, it is snowing for Christmas."

The fireman nodded but did not reply. Back in the train, a hog squealed angrily.

Mister Dunn took off his cap and goggles and was about to run his fingers through his hair when he touched the bandage. Puzzled, he unwound it and saw that it was bloody. "Eddie, what is this?" he asked, but again the man said nothing. Mister Dunn was not accustomed to being ignored by colored people, but he and Eddie Cox had been together a long time. He dropped the mysterious gauze out the window and watched it flutter to the ballast.

Around them lay the shuttered town, given over to the cold. West of the main line was a long siding crammed with empty wood racks and log flats, all dusted with snow. A single paintless frame house, broad-galleried, smoke curling from all its chimneys, sat in a grove of barren oaks. The house shared the grove with an ancient Reo truck, its empty bed and log yokes like the skeleton of some supine beast, and a muddy lot with a dozen or so overturned barrels—the homes of fighting roosters. Another truck was parked in the middle of the gravel road with both doors hanging open and the hood raised. Arranged beside it was a canvas fly littered with greasy tools that were rapidly disappearing under the snow.

The village itself huddled to the east at the junction of the state highway and an unnamed gravel road: a dozen buildings, some brick, some frame, some with a gallery and some without, all fronted with a plank sidewalk that rose and fell according to the level of the door sills.

Robinson's Dry Goods, with a string of fat colored lights draped around the gallery. Pachuta Feed & Seed. The Please-U Café. Dingle's Drugs. A white Methodist church with double spires and a wreath of new pine boughs on the door. In a vacant lot, someone had left a trash fire burning, and the smoke drifted eastward in a rank cloud.

The paved highway stretched north and south toward the wide world. Like the railroad, the highway offered escape should anyone think of it. The gravel road that crossed the highway led deep into the piney woods from which the town drew its meager bounty. Beside the depot was a historical marker erected by the D.A.R. Once, years ago, Mister Dunn had climbed down off the engine to see what it said:

> *Pachuta*
> Named for a prominent Chief
> of the Choctaws. Once a relay
> station on the old Pelican Road.
> Incorporated 1889.

The Choctaws were gone to the reservation or off to Oklahoma. The teams of strong horses and the swaying, yellow-wheeled stage-coaches had long been replaced by railroad and motorcar. A single bulb burned deep inside the café, and a pair of motorcars coated with mud were shoved against the curbing, but no living persons were in sight save the railroad men. Necaise and the agent were stamping their feet in the cold, while Frank Smith walked up the train with his hands shoved deep in his pockets. A quarter mile behind, Ladner stood between the rails with his red flag.

Mister Dunn knew he had a moment of grace. He spun in his seat and said, "Eddie, now you must tell me what is eating you and young Necaise. If I have done you a disfavor, I will try to correct it. In any event, you need to speak up."

Eddie would not look at his engineer, but his face grew long and mournful. He had white bristles on his chin. The collar of his coat was

ragged. "Beg pardon, Mist' A.P. I just got lots on my mind this mornin'."
He took off his cap and peered into it. Mister Dunn could see the
cracked leather of the sweat band and the BLF button on the crown.
Then, in a sad voice, still without looking up, Eddie said, "Mist' A.P.
Dunn, they's blood just running down your face, sir."

"What?" said Mister Dunn. Sure enough, he could feel the warmth
of it on the cold, dry skin of his nose. He wiped at it with his hand. A
snowflake came through the window and settled amid the blood
smeared on his fingers and for an instant was colored by it, like a red
doily, then vanished. Mister Dunn looked out again at the snow falling,
and he was all at once taken with a deep chill, one of those where your
teeth start chattering, and you lose control of your muscles, and it
seems your blood must freeze in the veins. He stood up and crossed
unsteadily the iron deck plates and pressed against the boiler backhead,
feeling the warmth calm him. He wiped at the blood again. The pain
was growing in his head, and now he seemed to remember how the
wheels had thrown up a rock and struck him between the eyes. Was that
today, or another time? Something else troubled him, though, another
pain he did not understand the need for. It lay over his heart as though
a great weight were pressing there. He thought, Oh, it's just time, Eddie.
That's all it is—just time that's hurting.

The fireman started as if Mister Dunn had spoken aloud. Eddie
Cox stood up with his cap in his hand. He tapped the sight-glass and
ran his long fingers over the water valves and stared at the firebox
doors. "Mist' A.P.," he said, "you ain't ever done a thing in your life to
hurt anybody."

"You can look at me, Eddie," said Mister Dunn. "You can say whatever you need to."

"All right, sir," said the other. He raised his eyes then and let his
hand drift until it barely touched Mister Dunn's shoulder. "Sometimes
lately you ain't yourself, is all," he said, and let his hand drop. "Like
today. Maybe you ought to rest a while. Let me run the engine 'til you

get yourself back."

Mister Dunn tried to remember when he wasn't himself. He knew Cox was right because he *couldn't* remember, and the blank spaces in the morning scared him. Frank Smith had been right, too: nobody could really make up time. But, thought Mister Dunn, a person ought not to *lose* it either. Still, A.P. Dunn was an engineer on the Southern Railway. He had been tired before, more tired than this. He wondered if he should take a Bayer aspirin. He said, "No, Eddie, I am only warming my back. I can run just fine."

Eddie Cox nodded. "I know you can, sir," he said. He smiled a little. "You done already made up time."

Mister Dunn took his seat again and leaned backward out the cab window. Frank Smith and the agent were passing into the depot. Necaise was behind the first boxcar, his hand on the lift lever. "Gimme some slack," shouted Necaise, and Mister Dunn backed the engine a trifle. Necaise lifted the lever. "Let's go to the sawmill," he said.

They did not put poles next to the engine or caboose, which is why they came out with the boxcar. They rambled a quarter mile down the main and cleared the switch to the sawmill. Necaise, riding the stirrup on Mister Dunn's side, signaled Stop. He lined the switch and crossed over—the curve was on the fireman's side—and signaled Back Up.

"Back up," said Eddie Cox, for he alone could see the brakeman now. Mister Dunn put the 4512 in reverse, backing gingerly down the spur. This track was the property of the sawmill and was not well maintained, and even at their slow speed, the boxcar swayed on the light rail, pushing it down into the rotten ties. Mister Dunn drew the air off until they were barely creeping along.

Necaise rode the stirrup, though he might as well have walked, they were going so slow. Eddie called the brakeman's signals to Mister Dunn.

"Two cars," said Cox, signifying two car lengths to the coupling. The flanges of the wheels squealed on the tight curve, and the branches of trees, closing overhead like a tunnel, scraped the roof of the boxcar.

The locomotive seemed to grow in the tight space.

Mister Dunn said, "I am not coming in here again until they cut the brush and fix this track."

"One car," said the fireman. "No, sir, we got no business up in here with a heavy engine." He leaned far out the window. "Easy," he said. "That'll do."

The log flat lay solitary in the muddy sawmill yard, and they made a good coupling. The brake line wheezed as Necaise cut in the air. When the coupling was complete, Necaise walked along the car and pulled at the chains that held the logs. Then he climbed onto the back end of the flatcar on Eddie's side—it was uncomfortable and dangerous to ride the stirrup on a flatcar—and waved them on. "Go ahead," said Cox.

They were almost to the main again when the light rail twisted and turned over beneath the heavy load of logs. Cox saw the car lurch sideways, shouted "Big hole it!" and Mister Dunn without question or thought slammed the brake lever and blew out the air. Cox saw the chains snap and flail like snakes and the logs spill out over the mud and he cried "Look out, Necaise!" though he and Mister Dunn were already out of their seats and down the gangway.

They were moving inside time all right, but the substance of it had changed. It was no longer like air or water, as it seemed sometimes, but like oil, thick and viscous, or like time in a dream. They did not take the gangway steps but slid down the handrails, these old men, and it was a long way, and they struck the ground hard so that Eddie Cox bit his tongue and spat blood, and the both of them trying to find purchase in the mud, swimming in time and light that seemed to congeal around them, and the snow drifting through the trees, and the flatcar canted over, the ground plowed up. What filled their minds now, what occupied the universe around them, was the expectation of what they must find, what they did not want to see, yet could not get to fast enough, just to get it over, to see it and be done with it. They climbed over the spilled logs like old spiders, their legs and arms made heavy by the ponderous weight of time they did not have.

Then the weight and the closeness and the expectation all lifted off them in a second as if they might leap skyward, high as the hidden sun, the invisible stars. Time folded into its accustomed shape again, and the old men stood panting and bleeding among the jumbled logs, staring at Bobby Necaise climbed halfway up a cedar tree, clinging to the limbs like a possum.

"Holy Jesus' name," said Necaise. "Holy fucking shit."

BELLE ROMAN MEET

In the Pachuta depot, the coal stove hissed, and now and then a clinker fell down through the grates. The agent's chair in the shallow bay window creaked monotonously as the man pecked at a typewriter wide and heavy as an upright piano. Tat. Tat-tat. Tat. The agent's desk was piled with papers and great cloth-bound books. Above it hung a Union Pacific calendar adorned with a color print of a long bright-yellow passenger train winding through the western mountains behind a matching quartet of diesel locomotives. Frank Smith thought the picture beautiful and romantic. He had always wanted to go out West and see the mountains and the deserts. For years, he and Artemus had planned a motorcycle trip out there, knowing all the while they would never have time for it unless they lived to retire. By then, of course, they would be too old and stiff, their spines too far gone, their joints too frozen, to ride motorcycles anywhere, but they agreed to try it anyhow. Surely it would not be a bad way to go out—a pair of broken-down ex-trainmen lurching off on their antique machines into the kind of sunset they often saw in cowboy movies. That would be a proper end, far better than a pair of iron beds in a ward of the Soldiers' and Sailors' Home.

The picturesque setting of the calendar was a long way from this dismal village in Mississippi. Smith wondered if the UP men ever took note of their surroundings, and if any of them ever dreamed of riding motorcycles to view the moss-draped oaks and brown bayous and New Orleans street scenes depicted on Southern and Illinois Central calendars. What would they think of Pachuta? No doubt they had Pachutas of their own out there.

Smith studied the picture and wondered what it was like to work on a diesel engine. He imagined they were smooth and quiet and comfortable, like riding in a Hudson Hornet. He was calculating the trade-off between diesel and steam power when it occurred to him that his crew had been gone a long time, too long to fetch a single car from the sawmill. Apparently, the agent had the same thought, for he looked up from his typewriter and said, "Where's your boys, Frank?"

No sooner were the words spoken than Bobby Necaise stumbled through the door like a messenger from Roncevaux. The boy was excited, breathing fast, blood smeared on his face. At the sight of him, Smith felt the warmth evaporate from the room, and all notions of romance fled with it. Something bad had happened, and all at once Smith was cold with fear. He thought, Somebody's killed, I should have been there, I should have gone with them…

The news, once Necaise settled down and delivered it, was not so bad. The log car had turned over, but the engine and boxcar were still on the rail. Nobody hurt.

The agent was already telegraphing the dispatcher that the main line was blocked by the 4512. Smith and Necaise stepped outside where they found Sonny Leeke come up from the caboose with his umbrella. When Leeke heard what happened, he looked at Frank Smith. Then he said, "Bobby, go tell Dutch. Tell him to move the flag back a ways and be careful."

Necaise took his hat off. "I'm sorry," he said. "Maybe if you—"

"Never mind," said Leeke. "That's a bad place in there."

The boy nodded and walked away. He was half a car length away when Sonny Leeke spoke again. "Bobby?"

"What?" said the boy, turning.

"You didn't fuck up, did you?"

Necaise looked from one man to the other. "I did everything I knowed to do," he said. "I swear to God."

"Then let it go," said Leeke. "Get your head back on. And stay with Dutch on the flag."

Necaise nodded again and turned, stumbling a little in the slag as he walked. Smith knew that Sonny Leeke was right: the boy's nerves were touchy, and the walk back would do him some good, and Ladner would make him laugh. He also knew that the boy would not let it go, not right now, and that was good, too. That would make him careful.

"Do I have time to take a piss?" said Leeke, tilting his head at the depot.

"Piss away," said Smith, "then hurry on down."

On his way up the train, Smith forced himself to accept his own circumstance. Most likely he would not get back to Meridian before tomorrow evening when his children would be tired and worn out with Christmas. The overtime pay would be a consolation, however, and it would have to do. As he was adjusting to this new reality, Smith came upon a pile of feathers where a hawk had slain a pigeon. From the scattering, he picked out a long gray wing pinion and twirled it in his fingers as he walked.

*   *   *

George Watson had a sense that something had happened. The drag was sitting too long on the main, and he could hear no sounds of switching. He eased up to the boxcar door and peeped around just in time to catch a glimpse of Frank Smith passing forward. A bad sign. They were stuck in some cracker town south of Meridian where a strange nigger would be slapped in the jailhouse the second he appeared. He stepped out into the frame of the open door, thinking he might tell where they were, when he came face-to-face with another man passing up the train.

Ah, shit, he thought. He had violated the rider's cardinal rule: stay out of sight.

The man was carrying an umbrella. A burned-down cigarette dangled from his lip. He said, "Well, if it ain't Sweet Willie Wine. What the fuck you doin' out here, Willie?"

George recognized the man in return, but couldn't remember his name. "Oh, just riding south, mister," he said, dragging off his cap. "I ain't hurtin' a thing, I promise."

The brakeman had dropped his smoke and was lighting another with a silver Zippo lighter. George said, "I hope nothin' bad's happened."

"Naw," said the brakeman. "We turned over a car in the woods, is all." He laughed.

"Meanwhile," he said, "they's a load of hogs back in the train. Maybe you smelled 'em. One of 'em already froze to death."

"Well, sir, that's some bad luck," said George, trying to keep the cold shiver out of his voice. "That's just some bad luck for a hog."

"Hogs ain't got any luck," said the man. "How about you?"

"I'm fresh out myself," said George.

"Stay warm, Willie," said the brakeman. Then he laughed and passed on, and George thought maybe he had some luck after all. He remembered the man's name, Sonny Leeke. He wished he had asked for a cigarette; Sonny Leeke would have given him one. Frank Smith would have, too.

Pretty soon, the trainmen came walking back. As they passed, one of them—George didn't see which one—tossed a Prince Albert tin in the door. It banged against the bulkhead and came to rest in the far corner. He picked up the tin and popped open the lid and looked inside. The tin was half full of tobacco. There was a book of matches, a sheaf of OCB wrapping papers, and a folded dollar bill. George Watson laughed. That Prince Albert tin was as good as a first-class ticket to the promised land.

* * *

The log spill was a mess, but it was well clear of the main line. The lumber company would try to blame the incident on the train crew, of course, but Smith was certain they could beat that. Mister Dunn explained in detail what happened, then mixed up some salt water for Eddie's bitten tongue, and gave Smith a vial of Mercurochrome from the first-aid kit to daub on Necaise if he needed it. When the train was together again, Smith called in the flag and had them back into a clear track in the Pachuta yard. Smith expected to be held at Pachuta for Number 65, a reefer train hauling bananas out of New Orleans. The green fruit was high revenue but perishable, and the profit was balanced against the per diem charge on the refrigerator cars that carried them. Every second the reefers stayed on the property, the bananas grew riper, and the per diem tipped toward the red, which meant that the Southern Railway Company wanted to get rid of the whole affair as quickly as possible. No wonder, then, that Number 65 was a train so hot that it had superiority over everything but the extra-fare Silver Star.

The crew gathered around the front of the engine, warming themselves in the steam from the cylinder head, waiting for the official order that would hold them at Pachuta. They had been lucky, and they all knew it, and the knowledge subdued them. Nobody, not even Sonny Leeke, complained about the wait. Smith sat on the pilot and took out his trip book, a little bound notebook where, in the course of a trip, he wrote down everything that happened. Every conductor did this, the information later recorded on the conductor's wheel report, and finally on the dispatcher's train sheet. Smith wrote,

Pachuta 845 AM. IC 61708 derailed @ sawmill
acct bad rail turned over. Waiting for orders re. 65.

Presently, the agent came down from the depot with their order:

EXTRA 4512 SOUTH WAIT AT BELLE ROMAN FOR
NO. 65 UNTIL 9:51 AM.

This was hardly the order they expected. Smith read it and shook
his head. "This can't be right," he protested. Belle Roman was a passing
track fifteen miles to the south. They might have waited there for 65
had they been on time, but they were not on time, and the dispatcher
knew it because the agent at Pachuta had told him. They were delayed,
and delay meant changes. What was the dispatcher thinking? "This
can't be right," Smith said again. "He ought to hold us here."

"I asked for a repeat," said the agent. "I guess he wants to get you
over the road."

"But why?" said Smith. "All we got is some empty boxes and those
god damned hogs."

"Must be some valuable hogs," said the agent.

"I can make it," said Mister Dunn.

They all looked at him in surprise. At the derailment, Mister Dunn
had behaved well. He had been professional and done everything right,
and Smith had begun to hope that maybe he would not have to bring
down the gods on A.P. Dunn after all. Now the engineer was proposing
a risky fifteen-mile dash for no useful reason.

"I can make it, boys," said Mister Dunn again.

Smith knew he could refuse the orders. He could still call for a relief
engineer. He looked hard at Mister Dunn, searching for any trace of the
brash intruder he had detected in Meridian. He saw only the old, good
man in his starched overalls, watch in one hand, cap and goggles in the
other.

"Let's go, if we're going, for Christ's sake," said Dutch Ladner.

"Okay," said Smith, and turned toward the caboose. "When you are ready, Mister Dunn," he said.

* * *

Now they were rolling, the white flags fluttering into rags on the pilot. Mister Dunn had abandoned the niceties of train handling and was flying along without regard for anybody's sensibilities. He and Eddie Cox were trying to fit the fifteen miles into a ten-minute passage. They had the 4512 blowing black smoke, and the caboose was bouncing like a kite. The locomotive whistle blew for crossings with the high-pitched urgency of a passenger train. Smith held on and watched the snow slant horizontal past the closed window of the cupola. Whatever happened was out of his hands now; everything depended on the old man at the throttle of the locomotive. Smith had to trust his own judgment and that of his crew. Most of all, he had to believe that Mister A.P. Dunn, crazy or not, was a first-class engineer.

Across the aisle, on the other side of the cupola, Sonny Leeke was smoking one cigarette after another and drinking coffee from the Thermos jug he brought from home. Leeke could not abide Frank Smith's coffee.

Leeke had not spoken since they left Pachuta. Now, all at once, he said, "They's a nigger riding in one of them Maryland boxes."

"I figured somebody was," said Smith. He had to shout over the racket of the train.

"It's Sweet Willie Wine," said the other. "I saw him."

"Well, I'll be damned," said Smith, surprised. "That was his brother was killed last night." Sonny hadn't heard about the incident, so Smith filled him in. "You reckon he knows?"

"He's a bad nigger," said Leeke. "You reckon it would make any difference?"

Smith thought that was a valid question. If you were a bad man, the whole universe must look different. He was studying the gray pigeon feather when Sonny Leeke spoke again. "Necaise might've got himself killed," the brakeman said.

"The boy is doing fine," said Smith. "I don't know what you'd of done different."

"I didn't mean that," said the brakeman. "Anyhow, I might call off when we get home."

Again, Smith was caught by surprise. Men rarely laid off for no reason—money was tight, even for bachelors like Sonny Leeke and Artemus Kane. Experienced men, however, knew when they needed time. When a man got shook up, maybe he would quit paying attention. On the other hand, the derailment at Pachuta, though a close thing, was not unusual. Sonny Leeke had seen a hundred such incidents in his time. If Leeke was troubled, it was not what did happen, but what might have happened, that shook him. That was bad thinking.

"You were not on the head end," said Smith. "If you had been, the rail would have turned over just the same."

"I told you," said Leeke, "that's not what I meant. Bobby might've—"

"I know what you meant," said Smith. "Don't start thinking too much. You can't stand the strain."

The slack ran in with unaccustomed violence as Mister Dunn began to slow for Belle Roman, now a bare quarter mile away. The brakeman drained his coffee cup and screwed it back on the Thermos jug. He opened his window and put his head out into the cold wind, and Smith knew that, up ahead, Leeke could see the green lens of the passing-track switch.

"Are we going to make it?" asked Smith.

The brakeman laughed. "Look yonder," he said.

Smith slid open his own window and leaned out. Sixty-five's light was already in view, jiggling with speed. *Jesus Christ*, thought Smith, *he expects us to be in the clear already*. There was no stopping now. They had to get in the hole, off the main, out of the way, or there would be dramatic results when the two locomotives collided.

Sonny Leeke was enjoying himself. "That A.P. Dunn is a high-rolling son bitch," he laughed. "I take back everything I ever said about him."

"You're a pussy if you lay off," said Smith.

The brakeman pulled on his gloves, a fresh cigarette dangling from the corner of his mouth. "Fuck you, boss," he said as he swung down from the cupola. "We fixing to die anyhow."

Smith's instinct was to get up, find his gloves and coat, start being in charge. In fact, all he could do now was watch. The boys knew what they were doing, and no order Frank Smith could give, no instruction or advice, could change whatever was about to happen.

* * *

Like Sonny Leeke, Mister A.P. Dunn was having a good time. His head had quit hurting—indeed, his whole face was numb from the cold wind—and the locomotive cab was filled with excitement. Necaise and Cox were speculating on whether they would beat 65 to Belle Roman, and what would happen if they didn't.

"Man tell you to jump," said Cox, "you best be jumpin'."

Necaise looked out the window. "Hell, I ain't jumpin' from way up here."

"We'll see when the time comes," said Cox.

They made the fifteen miles in eleven minutes by Mister Dunn's watch, but when the green switch target came into view, there was the headlight of the opposing train just topping the hill.

"God Almighty," said Eddie Cox. "He thinkin' we in the clear already."

"He won't stop that big train now," said Necaise.

"You got that right," said Eddie.

"Then we better do this smartly," said Mister Dunn. "Bobby, I am not stopping. You'll have to beat me to the switch."

The boy looked up in surprise. "I can't do that," he said. "What if—"

"There is no 'what if'," said Mister Dunn. "You'll just have to do it."

"That's what I'm talkin' about," said Eddie Cox.

Necaise pulled on his gloves. In a moment, Mister Dunn pushed the throttle forward and drew off a little air and said, "Now, Bobby."

"Aw, shit," said Necaise, but he launched himself out the narrow front door of the cab and began the long, slippery walk down the boiler gangway to the pilot. In a moment, Mister Dunn saw Necaise on the engineer's side, watched him drop off the pilot and run for the north switch to line them in.

Eddie had crossed the cab to look. Necaise was lifting his knees high, arms pumping. Eddie laughed. "That boy is round, but he sho' is fast," he said.

They watched the boy grab the tall switch stand and key the lock and shake loose the chain and line the switch red in the last possible instant before the 4512's lead truck entered the points. Necaise didn't need to signal "come ahead," but caught the pilot step as the engine went by.

Eddie went back to his seat and leaned far backward out his window. "Now we get the back end in," he said.

Number 65 was passing the south switch, and the engineer was blowing his whistle in frantic bursts, by way of saying that he couldn't stop now. The 4512 curved into the siding and Mister Dunn pulled back a notch on the throttle, praying to clear the north switch in time. 65's headlight was a dozen car lengths away when Sonny Leeke dropped off the caboose and unlocked the north switch and lined it green, jumping back as 65's engine, whistle shrieking, thundered through the points an instant later.

"He got it!" cried Eddie.

Mister Dunn never brought his train to a stop, but ran down the long passing track while the yellow reefers roared and rattled past them on the main. The fruit train's caboose was a blur; no shouted greetings nor waves this time, although somebody lifted his hand from the cupola window. By the time the 4512 neared the south end, the switch was clear. They could stop now, if they wanted to, but Mister Dunn thought, *Let's see what happens.* Sure enough, Necaise dropped off the pilot and ran ahead once more to line them out. He turned the switch, again at the last possible moment, then caught the gangway steps and climbed aboard, grinning, his face flushed. "Man, oh man," he said.

"Wasn't even close," said Eddie Cox.

The train curved out onto the main, and as it straightened out, Sonny Leeke closed the north switch and locked it behind them and ran for the caboose yelling, "Don't leave me, you sons of bitches!" so loud they could hear him on the head end. Mister Dunn, looking back, saw Frank Smith's highball from the cupola and knew that Leeke was safely aboard. Mister Dunn answered with the whistle and drew back on the throttle, and in a moment they were rolling fast again down the main line.

Necaise was pulling off his gloves, trying hard to act like nothing had happened. Cox was working the stoker. Mister Dunn got the train settled down, then sat back in his seat and took off his goggles. If they had been thirty seconds later, if Leeke or Necaise had stumbled on the icy ground, if the locks or switch points had been frozen… But these things were not what you thought of, Mister Dunn told himself. He turned to his companions. "Well, boys," he said, "that was some first-class railroading."

* * *

In the caboose, Frank Smith sat at his desk, making note of the meet at Belle Roman in his trip book, in the same dry, cryptic language he had used to record the derailment at Pachuta:

BRmn 945AM met No. 65 no signals.

That was all. That was sufficient. This time, however, since this was his own personal record in his own personal notebook, he added,

A close thing, damned well done.

Smith understood that when Mister Dunn argued for the meet, he was not asking for a chance to prove himself; he was asking for a chance to prove them all. Neither time nor loss could erase what they had done at Belle Roman, though nobody would ever know it but themselves. It was like so many things the men did out of courage and decency, in the process of lives that must vanish one day and leave no trace behind.

The train rolled smoothly now, for a freight train. They were between places, suspended in distance and time, and the rails and the snow-dusted roadbed spooled out mile after mile behind them. Sonny and Dutch were in the cupola, each man wrapped in silence, watching ahead. The smoke of their cigarettes drifted down and mingled with the gray odor of the coal stove. Again, Smith felt strangely without purpose. He lit a cigar off the top of the lamp chimney and tapped his pencil on the scarred slope of the desk. The pigeon feather lay there, shivering a little in the moving air as if it remembered flight.

* * *

Frank Smith is nine years old on the cold, yellow January day when his mother whips him soundly with a willow branch for breaking the only ruby-glass vase she had ever owned, or was likely to. Banished aloft, Frank broods a while among the brothers' close-packed beds, then slips out the window and down the drainpipe. He has a blanket, a wedge of cheese, a tin of sardines—rations the older boys keep on hand for their nocturnal excursions—a box of Lucifer matches, and a Barlow knife. He believes this to be all a man needs to get over to Pelican Road, then out to the Territories where vases have no relevance. His assumptions are right enough, for many a person has made the trip with less.

He walks a hundred yards or so through the pine barrens to a bend

in Black Creek, to a familiar sandbar littered of driftwood, where, wea-
ried of travel, he decides to make his first camp. Of the driftwood, and
of rich lighter knots, he makes a fire. He gathers a pallet of pine straw
and sits down cross-legged, the blanket wrapped around him. They
would all be sorry, he thinks, when they read about his exploits in the
Hattiesburg paper, how he is made a chief of the Cheyenne and leads
them to his death against the cavalry.

Before long, he has eaten all his cheese and all the sardines. The fire
is warm, and he is comfortable, except that the wind keeps soughing
through the pine tops, a mournful sound, and a flock of crows has followed him. These have set up a camp of their own in a dead oak tree,
from which they offer doleful warnings. Frank understands the language of crows, and he wishes they would go away and find someone
else to torment. Finally, he falls asleep, wrapped in his blanket, with the
muttering of the dark birds interfering in his dreams.

When he wakes, the fire is only a pile of coals, and the early night
has settled among the trees. A remnant of day remains trapped in the
waters of the creek; beyond that, the Piney Woods are thick with darkness. His mother is there, still a girl, slight and black-haired, draped in
a shawl, sitting on her own pallet of pine straw with her dress arranged
around her.

Some wild injun, she says. I could of run a drove of cows through
here, you wouldn't even notice.

The boy sits up and draws the blanket over his head. It smells of
wood smoke, and through the opening, he can see the new moon over
the trees.

I think you dropped this on the way, says his mother, and puts out
her hand. The boy cannot see what she holds, but he puts out his own
hand and closes his fingers on hers. There he finds a bird feather, not a
crow's, but a blue jay's. Up close, it seems to be lit from inside, like the
blue lanterns the car-knockers use sometimes on the lumber company
railroad.

They sit a long time and watch the moon rise. His mother tells him that when a full moon walks across the woods, the trees turn up the underside of their leaves in greeting. Later, on the way home, she tells him that feathers are signs, dropped in a person's path for a reason. It was not necessary to know the reason; all that was required was to pay attention.

* * *

Over Smith's desk, in a gilded frame, hung a picture of his mother when she was a girl, yet unmarried, no record yet on her smooth, smiling face of all she would come to know and do, of the children she would bear, of the wisdom she would earn in the hardship and grace of her long life. In her summer frock and straw hat, she poses in the yard of her father's house in Hattiesburg, her hand draped languidly over the chair arm. The trees are heavy with leaves; the frame house, windows open, drowses through the hot, long-forgotten afternoon. In the background, across the dusty road, lie the rails of the Southern Railway.

So many summers and winters gone, and his mother was dust, as they would all be dust one day. Smith settled back in his chair in the X-630. He held his feather to the light and listened, and in a moment it came to him what the feather had to tell.

The pigeon had been waddling along, minding its own business in a world of gray and white. It pecked at the snow, remembering some spilled corn that was around here yesterday. Up above, a little rustle, the wind passing over outstretched wings, a dim shadow. The pigeon did not know what death was until it came for him, and even then it was nothing, no trouble really, not even pain.

HOW THINGS VANISH INTO SILENCE

Donny Luttrell finished breakfast by eight o'clock, and at eight fifteen he took an order for train 171, southbound:

NO. 171 WAIT AT TALOWAH FOR NO. 22 UNTIL 9:15 AM.

Number 171 would ordinarily wait for Number 22, a passenger train, at Lumberton, but the southbound freight was running late and would be stuck in the hole at Talowah instead. Donny filled out the clearance card and, with the lever at his desk, lowered the order board just as 171 whistled for signals. He jumped at the sound, for he had not expected the train so soon; in fact, he dropped the semaphore arm in the engineer's face, and brakes began to squeal as Donny shot back his chair and reached for the order hoops. This was too close, and Donny cursed the dispatcher as he moved, and cursed the engineer who should have known he would have an order at Talowah. Donny stumbled out the door and down the steps to the cinders. The engine was on him, but he kept running. The head brakeman stood in the gangway with his arm out, and Donny pressed close to the big turning wheels and held up the hoop just in time for the man to catch it. The brakeman shouted at him. The clamor of the engine's passage swept his words away, but

Donny could tell from the man's face that he was greatly annoyed at such a near thing. They would blame him, of course, until they looked at the time on the clearance card.

As the long train rambled by, Donny had leisure to fix the second hoop for the conductor. Finally, the caboose came swaying past with the conductor standing on the bottom step, smoking a cigarette. Donny held up the hoop and shouted "It ain't me, Cap'n!" and the conductor caught the order and laughed and waved, and Donny knew it was all right then.

The train left behind a haze of coal smoke and a vast silence broken only by the keening of a pair of hawks. Donny looked up and saw them wheeling at a great height. In the summertime, a pair of kites had nested in a tall pine tree behind the depot. Donny liked to watch them hunt for bugs in the air, two graceful black arrows against the blue sky. The kites were gone now, though, following the weather southward, and the hawks had taken over.

Donny wondered about the town that once lay here, and the people who had dwelt in it, and if any of them ever suspected, in their own deep winters, that all they had built would vanish into silence. Of course they did, he thought. They had no illusions, for the evidence lay not only in their own lives, but in the old wisdom of man that told them all their striving would come to this: a few bricks, an old safe, a burying ground hidden in the vines, and no one to look upon it but the high circling birds. The virtue, however, lay not in their knowing, but in their refusal to yield to what they knew. Men strove and strove, and it all came to naught, but no matter, for only in the striving could they prove themselves worthy of anything. This was a truth that had come to Donny Luttrell in his solitude. It was the single truth that allowed him to push himself into the passing trains, and the one that made the solitude bearable way out here among the pines. Not the loneliness, but the solitude. One could do worse, he thought, than the company of ghosts.

It was Christmas Eve, and somewhere the world he knew was lighted and merry. All that seemed far away now, but again, no matter. Next

Christmas, or the next, he would be in the world again. For now, he would learn from the silence. He would suffer it so that he would never forget it, and carry into all his life the memory of solitude, something to lay at the feet of the little Christ Child as proof that he had striven, too.

Later, he thought, he might visit the lost cemetery and put some green boughs on the graves for Christmas. For now, he turned back into the boxcar depot. A family of wood rats lived under the floor, and by this time they would have stirred and come up through the crack by the stove. They would be sniffing around in there, wondering where their breakfast was.

* * *

During the night, while Artemus slept and Anna Rose dreamed, the fifteen heavyweight olive-green coaches of the Silver Star were moved to a service track and washed of road dust and grime. The aisles were vacuumed, linens changed, windows and brass polished, lightbulbs replaced, roller bearings oiled, generators and batteries tested, wheels inspected. The diner took on ice, clean linen, tea bags, coffee, French bread hot from the bakery, fresh trout and shrimp and crabs. Toilet paper came aboard, and hand towels and washrags, stationery, and a bundle of this morning's *Times-Picayune*. Clean sheets and pillowcases. Clean neck cloths and towels for the barbershop. Typewriter ribbons, fresh-cut hothouse flowers, shoe polish, ashtrays. The bar in the club car was restocked and made ready—tomato juice and vodka and crisp stalks of celery for early-morning drinkers; whiskey, beer, gin, liquors from the Caribbean. Though the Silver Star traveled through dry states, the club car was never dry. The law aboard the Silver Star was the law of the State of Louisiana, and a white person could get a drink any hour of the day or night according to his choosing.

When the cars were ready, a switch engine drew them out of the service yard and, with a switchman riding the rear end, backed them down against the bumper post of their appointed departure track. There the cars were connected to steam pipes and electric cables. There they rested through the long hours of darkness until the time when ceiling lights were lit and vestibules opened. The cooks arrived before dawn to light the stoves and start breakfast, the stewards to set the dining car tables, the porters to ensure that all the seats were turned the right way, that every headrest was clean, every ashtray in every armrest empty, and every roll of toilet paper brand-new, the ends folded in a little triangle and affixed with the stamp of the Southern Railway. Clerks armed with revolvers set to work in the RPO car and supervised the loading of mail sacks, a goodly number this Christmas Eve. The road engine, swirled with steam in the cold air, shiny and clean and polished, backed down from the roundhouse and coupled to the head end, while iron-wheeled carts piled high with trunks and suitcases began to grate across the bricks to the baggage car where Miles Duvall waited.

* * *

At Basin Street station, the trainmen's shack was down among the REA and baggage rooms along one flank of the smoky train shed. Artemus Kane stood at his locker door, studying a photograph taped there: a book-jacket portrait of Anna Rose Dangerfield from her novel *The Virtue of Indifference*. Artemus had gone down to the *Times-Picayune* offices and bought the file copy, since Anna Rose would not give him one. In the picture, she wore a dark turtleneck and silver earrings shaped like dolphins. The photographer had turned her body slightly to the left, then tilted her fine, narrow face back to the camera so that she looked out from the corners of her eyes. Her hair was short, cut above the ears, combed so that strands of it fell across her forehead in a reckless way. Her cheekbone was defined by the same shadow that softened her broken nose; her eyebrows were arched, her lips parted in a smile that women must have envied.

This morning, Artemus took little comfort in Anna Rose's smile, but only a yearning for something far away and lost. He leaned against the bank of lockers, stricken with sadness. It had to be the cold of deep December, he decided. The cold and the sleet and the gray sky and the early darkness. It was about the lost woman in her casket and Miles Duvall. It was about Arabella, a woman whom Artemus no longer knew or even cared to know. All at once, Artemus wanted it to be spring. He wanted to take Anna Rose down to the Pearl River, to a sand bar he knew where they could make a picnic and she could wade in the water. He had wanted to do that for a long time, but never had, and now Artemus tried to imagine what it would look like. He closed his eyes. There was Anna Rose in a straw hat, there was the picnic basket, a sycamore tree, white butterflies—except he could not find himself any-where in the scene, nor could he make the elements fit together in any kind of tomorrow, as if time had suddenly lowered a curtain beyond which he could not see.

Yesterday, however, was a different matter. The past was always right there to hand, mostly when you didn't want it, Artemus thought. In fact, he could see little use for it, for he rarely ever learned from it, and all it did was torment him, and there was not a god damned thing he could do to change it. Nevertheless, it was all his own.

Artemus knew his sadness had no real focus, no reason, unless it was simple guilt. The past was full of reasons for that, as far back as memory could reach. Artemus looked one last time at the photograph. *Grab a hand hold*, he told himself. *It is only the cold and the dark, and they can't last forever.* In testimony, he drove his fist into his locker door, adding another dent to the half-dozen already present. Then he gath-ered his overcoat and bag, slammed his locker door, and went off to find the others.

* * *

At eight thirty, the train crew entered the telegrapher's office in the Basin Street station. From the radio, they learned that a storm was moving in from the northwest and that snow was likely. The operator laid their orders out on the scarred counter. Nothing unusual. The Silver Star would run by the time card, she had rights over everything movable or immovable, there were no flag stops.

"Kane," said the operator, "I have a message here for you and you alone." He looked at the others and said, "Boys, it warms my innards when two young people just can't bear to be apart."

"Damn," said Oliver Bomar the flagman. "It ain't been thirty minutes since he seen her last."

"Thank you, Mike, goddammit," said Artemus, snatching the folded paper from the operator's hand.

"Let's see what little Anna says," said Stanfield, pressing close. "I know it's poetical."

"Step away, rodents," said Artemus, his heart beating fast. The image of Anna Rose on the sandbar returned to him. Suddenly the morning was not without hope, nor the clouds their silver linings. He opened the paper.

> Kane—Am being evicted from X-630.
> Will move in with you tomorrow. Don't wait up.
>
> E.F. Smith

"Aw, fuck me," said Artemus, and crumpled the message into his coat pocket.

"Well," said Bomar, "that was not the response *I* expected."

Artemus ignored his comrades. He allowed himself a moment to let the disappointment fade and to get used to the idea of Frank Smith moving in. Then it was all right. It was a good thing, and he gave it no more thought.

Mister Nussbaum took no part in this exchange. In fact, he had hardly spoken to his crew since they gathered outside the washroom, and he did not speak now. He read over his orders, looked at the men's faces, and walked outside.

Oliver Bomar said, "The captain is a mite peevish today."

"I will see about it," said Artemus.

He found Mister Nussbaum leaning against a stanchion, head bent, arms crossed. As Artemus approached, it occurred to him that he had never seen his conductor lean against anything.

"We should have a good trip today," said Artemus.

Mister Nussbaum looked up at the sound of his brakeman's voice. "You still need a haircut," he said.

"I forgot my promise," said Artemus. "I went to church last night with Anna Rose, and then…I got distracted."

"I can understand that," said the conductor. He turned and pressed his back against the stanchion. The mourning band on his sleeve drooped awkwardly, and the safety pin showed. In the dim gray half-light of the terminal, Mister Nussbaum looked old and tired, and Artemus thought of his own image in Anna Rose's mirror a little while before. Don't leave me now, thought Artemus. Not yet.

"My ancestors used to blow rams' horns in the mountains," said Mister Nussbaum. "They would summon God and speak to him as I am speaking to you, and he answered in a voice terrible, like thunder, but a voice nevertheless. Then, all at once, he quit speaking. Do you believe that?"

"No, Captain," said Artemus. "I don't believe he quit, because I don't believe he ever spoke at all."

The conductor nodded. He said, "You were in the war, Kane—did you ever pray?"

"Yes, sir. All the time."

"Any good come of it?"

"None that I could tell," said Artemus.

Again, the conductor nodded. He said, "Millions of your kind pray every Sunday for peace. They are praying for it right now. They will pray for it tonight and tomorrow in great Christmas hosannas. Do you suppose any good will come of it?"

"No, Captain," said Artemus. "It only gets worse over there."

"You're an educated man, Kane. What do you make of that?"

"Are you being…ironic, sir?"

"I am long past that," said the conductor.

Artemus walked out to the edge of the platform. The Silver Star lay beyond three empty tracks and as many empty brick platforms. All the vestibule doors were open, waiting, and steam curled from her heating pipes. The windows and the steel cars gleamed in the terminal lights. On the head end, Mister Rufus Payne was walking around his engine with an oil can in his hand. The train was together, and time was already pulling at it. Time was hounding them all. Artemus said, "I noticed last summer no flowers in your yard. That was the first time in all these years—"

"She was the one who made the garden," said Mister Nussbaum quickly. "I had no opportunity, gone all the time—"

"Yes sir," said Artemus quickly. "I shouldn't have mentioned it."

Mister Nussbaum looked across the terminal at the waiting train. "After she died," he said, "I thought how, if I ever got my gold watch, I would take the time to make a garden again, put out all the things she loved, just like she had them all those years, and in that way I might keep some portion of her. Now I know that is folly." He smiled. "I don't even know the names of any flowers."

"Maybe that's what happened to God," said Artemus. "He only planted one garden, and that was a long time ago. Maybe he forgot."

"I wish he had not," said Mister Nussbaum.

"Don't we all," said Artemus. He stepped down into the grease-stained gravel, where the smell of Pelican Road rose around him. In the high rafters, pigeons cooed and rattled their wings. He thought about Anna Rose, how she had asked him not to leave her alone. He thought about when he left this morning, how she stood in her bare feet on the cold floor and looked into his face and spoke his name. Now he said, "I would ask a delicate question, sir. I would not ask it if it were not important."

"All right," said the conductor.

Artemus paused a moment, collecting his words. At last he said, "All those years together, you and Miss Rebekah. Were they worth what you are feeling now?"

"Yes," said the conductor.

"Thank you, sir," said Artemus.

* * *

A half hour before boarding time, the trainmen strolled across the terminal rails in their blue overcoats, carrying their Gladstone bags, to the track where the Silver Star waited. While Mister Nussbaum went forward to compare his watch with the engineer's, the trainmen climbed aboard the fresh coaches to stow their bags and speak to the porters. When everything was ready, they took their stations along the tall, riveted flank of the Silver Star. Artemus and Vernon Stanfield stood by the bumper post. Mister Nussbaum, with Oliver Bomar the flagman, waited on the platform midway down the train. The porters stood lordly by their cars.

So it was that, one hundred and ten miles from Talowah down storied Pelican Road, Artemus Kane made ready to depart the crowded rooftops, the neon, the rainy streets of the city he loved and the place where Anna Rose lived. This was always a surreal moment for Artemus. The overhead lights of the train shed and the lamps along the platform winked in the flanks of the coaches and gleamed off the rails in a strange, mechanical lumination that made Artemus think of dynamos and power plants, though, in fact, he had seen neither except in pictures. Visible beyond the arched opening of the train shed was the morning, the afternoon, the darkness, each in its season, but beneath the pigeon-haunted steel girders, the light partook of neither day nor night. The train itself seemed created anew, fresh as Eden, no trace of yesterday's long travel anywhere in evidence. Not like a freight train, whose every inch was a record of months and years, of deserts and forests, green valleys and smoke-grimed cities. The train occupied space, profound in its stillness, solid and eternal and unmoving, yet, soon enough, there would be only emptiness here, and the train itself vanished down the stream of time.

At nine o'clock, the train caller's voice echoed among the marble vaults of the station: "Southern Railway Train Number Six, the Silver Star, now boarding on track three for Hattiesburg…Meridian…Birmingham…Atlanta…and *Wash*-ing-ton. All aboard!"

Then the waiting room doors opened, and a flood of people emerged. Not one of them gave thought to how the handsome cars had come to be there, nor that his crossing depended on luck, nor that his safety, his well-being, his life itself, was now lifted out of the hands of God and placed squarely in those of the likes of Artemus Kane and Vernon Stanfield. The thought always made Artemus laugh, as he supposed God did Himself.

As Artemus had anticipated, a good many college students were riding today: boys in ties and letter sweaters, girls with bobbed hair in stylish coats that did nothing to conceal their slim legs and trim, coltish bodies. Artemus watched them and marveled. He understood well the cruel and fundamental mathematics of time, but never, he thought, had he been so young as these little ones, nor so comfortable with himself. Artemus loved all the girls. On the other hand, he viewed the young men as predators without redemption, and their confident manner, their awareness of themselves, nudged Artemus with jealousy and a vague sense of loss. God damned college boys, he thought. Of course, he had been a college boy himself after the war, but that was different.

Vernon Stanfield seemed to read his cousin's thoughts. "I guess most of these boys'll be fighting the Japs in a year or so," he said.

"Ha," said Artemus. "Not these swains. In *my* time, we had plenty of university men in the ranks, but you wait and see, cuz. These boys got too much money nowadays. They are too soft, and they don't care about anything. Their daddies will get 'em off."

A boy approached diffidently. He wore a Tulane football letter, the knot of a fraternity tie just visible over the V of his white pullover sweater. He was tall and handsome, his unblemished face quick with intelligence. "Beg your pardon, sir," he said. "Which is the car for Atlanta?"

"Three cars ahead, sir," Artemus said. "Merry Christmas."

When the boy was gone, Stanfield laughed. "Hypocrite," he said.

"Well, hell," said Artemus.

The student's name was Jeffrey Brown. The trainmen did not know this, of course, nor suspect that they would ever know it, nor that the prim, well-dressed man in the straw boater, hurrying down the platform, had just embezzled a comfortable fortune from the Hibernia Bank. The girl in the black dress was going to her father's funeral in Tuscaloosa. The couple clinging to one another were engaged against her father's wishes. The little boy in knickers and miniature Norfolk jacket was taking his first trip alone, and the Redcap who carried his bags had twelve children at home. Businessmen on company errands. A nun traveling to a new parish, frightened by the change. A woman who had booked passage on a ship from New York. An opera singer. A gambler. A man who felt like weeping, and another glad to be free. The crowd swept by, each person more or less anxious, each trailing a complicated life, long or short, that had brought him to this moment. For them, the Silver Star had nothing to do with the process of their lives; a train was only a bridge over time to a place where life would be continued, the journey itself only a hiatus, a passage to some other morning, afternoon, darkness where love or decision or catastrophe awaited. The trainmen understood this, and they were aware of the secret lives that passed before them. Yet, with few exceptions, the passengers would remain faces only—pretty, handsome, frightful, studious or bored or fearful. There was little time to know them, and little inclination, a fact which Artemus, at least, regretted sometimes.

Stanfield was right, of course: the boy in the Tulane sweater was traveling toward a destiny he could not begin to imagine. He was an instrument of the world's changing, and he might well pay for it with his life in some distant place that no one, on this winter morn, had ever heard of.

When Artemus went to the university, he had already been in a war and believed that he had taken all the chances he would ever have to. In fact, for all his adventures, he had found himself innocent of a world where life and death were not the only choices. In the end, being in a war hadn't prepared Artemus Kane for a god damn thing. Maybe the Tulane boy, having done things in reverse—as Frank Smith had done—would be luckier. Maybe, in his extremity, he would understand something more about what was happening around him. Maybe he would see the terrible waste in it, and maybe he could redeem it all in a way that others could not. For an instant, Artemus thought of following the lad, of giving him some warning of what his responsibility might be. But it was too late. The boy was gone, the moment passed.

Artemus pulled his watch. Eight fifty. Oliver Bomar appeared on the observation platform where Artemus had stood last night by the light of his flare. Oliver hung out the two lighted marker lanterns and turned the switch to illuminate the drum sign. By this means, the abstractions of the timetable were made reality, and the Silver Star a train.

Mister Nussbaum paced nervously on the platform, something he rarely did. Finally, he walked over to a stanchion and snatched open a telephone box. The line connected him with the terminal yardmaster in his glass gallery over the waiting room doors. Mister Nussbaum listened a moment, then slammed the telephone into its cradle. He waved to his crew. They were cleared to depart on time.

In his years of train service, Artemus had known many vicissitudes.

His past girlfriends had been a torment. The night his mother died, he was switching way down in Hattiesburg. He had missed every one of his wife's birthdays, most Christmases and Easters and Sunday mornings at Mass. He had known times when his heart was leaden with sorrow for no reason, and times when the old war crowded out every other thought, when the dead were more real than the living. He had been hungover, exhausted, angry, frustrated. He had struggled in the shadow of mistakes and irrational behavior. Through every difficulty, however, he forced himself to pay attention. He made himself set aside whatever troubled him and planted himself firmly in the moment, knowing that was the only way he could survive. His reward for this diligence was an excitement that never failed him when a passenger train, no matter how humble, no matter if he belonged to it or not, was about to sail.

This morning, the departure of the Silver Star from Basin Street was heralded by Mister Nussbaum's drawn-out cry—"All aboard!"— that set tardy passengers to running and made mothers pull their children close. Porters swung their yellow footstools aboard and pulled up the vestibule steps with a clang. Miles Duvall stood in his open door, the trainmen and porters and dining car waiters peered from the vestibules, Mister Nussbaum stood erect on the platform glaring at his watch as if it had insulted him somehow. At the appointed moment, the exact instant when the fine blue arrows of his watch indicated nine o'clock and one second, the conductor lifted his hand, and the engineer, Mister Rufus Payne, answered with the whistle, the shrill notes echoing in the vaulted shed. Then the train began to move, an almost imperceptible gliding without noise. Mister Nussbaum swung aboard, and a porter pulled the steps up behind him. Steam shrouded the watchers on the platform. Passengers waved from the windows. The trainmen waved to children and smirked at pretty girls. Only the aged, white-haired conductor remained aloof, peering intently up the length of his train like a ship's captain in the shrouds. The Silver Star emptied the space it had occupied, and in a moment it was curving away through the switches, its headlight bright in the gray morning, shimmering on the rails. Smaller and smaller grew the drum sign, the awning and gilded rail of the club car, the red markers, until all that remained was a haze of coal smoke and an empty track where once the Silver Star had made ready, and those left behind began to drift toward the waiting room and the world beyond where their lives awaited them. If any were listening, they might have heard the shriek of the whistle one last time. After that, the train vanished into silence and was no more.

* * *

Artemus stood on the back platform, watching the arch of the train shed pass away. The heavy cars thumped on the rail joints and rattled through crossovers and switches. Dwarf signals and lighted switch targets glided past, and trackmen in their greasy overalls, and carmen with their oil cans, and switchmen waiting by their fat, stubby-wheeled yard engines—all lifting their gloved hands in farewell, acknowledged in return by Artemus Kane, a brakeman on the Silver Star, anointed and privileged, but their brother just the same.

The train moved slowly through the east end, following a freight train that was itself following another freight. Artemus and Oliver Bomar and Stanfield joined their conductor in the vestibule of the forward coach, each man in turn peering impatiently up the train. They could see the caboose of the drag ahead. The lighted fusees dropped by its flagman passed beside.

"This is unusual," said Mister Nussbaum. "Highly irregular."

Artemus thought this a splendid understatement. The dispatcher in Meridian was fucking up: nobody but God delayed the Silver Star. Still, there was nothing they could do.

At X Tower, a station that controlled access to the Ponchartrain bridge, they got some bad news: emergency repairs were underway on the long trestle, and the yellow slow-order flags were out. Artemus returned to the platform while they crossed the lake. At the far end, he found a bridge gang huddled around their handcar on the safety platform. This was cold work for them, out here in the wind amid the lashing spray from the gray, troubled waters below. As the men waved, and Artemus raised his hand in return, he felt once more a brush of guilt for his dashing uniform and the warmth of the coaches.

Thus the Silver Star passed from that place, too. The bridge gang admired her going, and watched her lights grow smaller and smaller. They watched the lanky brakeman's figure diminish until it was like a little blue doll. A flock of pelicans drifted overhead in elegant formation, and before they were gone, all that beautiful train had vanished into the mist of the far and distant shore.

THE CORBIES

Almost two hours out of Basin Street, and forty-five minutes late, the Silver Star, still following closely on the heels of the northbound freight, paused at Slidell. Artemus and Mister Nussbaum stepped off the last coach in time to watch the porter and the baggage cart labor up the platform. No coffin this time; only the piled trunks and luggage of citizens who wanted to be someplace else. The colored waiting room was crowded with black people waiting for a train everyone called "Ol' Zip Coon" that ran in at least three sections every Christmas. This was good revenue: a Jim Crow day-coach special carrying Southern blacks to visit kinfolk in Detroit or Chicago or Milwaukee.

Jefferson Danly strolled behind the baggage cart as usual. He was dressed in a brown tweed suit with a red waistcoat and a green bow tie. "Hello, boys," he said. "Merry Christmas."

"Somebody needs to clear the road," said Mister Nussbaum tightly.

"Just be patient," said Danly, "we are putting that drag in the hole for you up at Gant's store."

"That's real good, J.D.," said Artemus.

The agent patted Artemus's lapels. "I'm your Santy Clause," he said. He turned to Mister Nussbaum. "Starting next year they are installing block signals on the main line to keep you fellows from running into each other. Not a minute too soon, if you ask me."

"We have never made a practice of running into each other," said Mister Nussbaum.

"Well, you can't be too careful," said Danly. "Never fear—someone's watching over you." He went on then, moving forward to the baggage car. On an outside track, invisible beyond a switching cut, a south-bound freight slipped by like a child trying to leave the room before he is noticed.

The trainmen could not see the sky, only the underside of the passenger shed. Empty sparrow nests were tucked into all the braces, and the paint was peeling. Mister Nussbaum moved away a little and stood in silence, rubbing the stubs of his fingers. He had remarked to Artemus once that he could still feel them when it was cold, the ghosts of his fingers come to ache and accuse him as if they blamed him for their loss.

"Why don't you go inside, Ira?" said Artemus. "I can—"

"Leave it alone," snapped the conductor, and thrust his hands deep in his coat pockets, out of sight.

* * *

Ira Nussbaum, seventeen years old, has been on the extra board for a week, and this is his first trip without supervision. The train, a local, has been on the road fourteen hours, longer than the boy had ever done anything at one stretch. The engineer, John Marquette, is a sturdy, blockish man with a face that seems carved out of some workable but impervious stone. In all that time, Marquette has not spoken a word to his brakeman nor glanced in his direction. The Negro fireman might as well have had no tongue at all; the whole trip, he has moved about his tasks like a shadow, his fear of John Marquette filling the cab with a smell like sour sweat. Ira has never learned his name.

At midnight, Ira lines them into the hole at Nicholson for a south-bound train. The engine winds slowly into the passing track, and Ira, waiting on the ground, makes a mistake. When the engine reaches him, Ira steps onto the narrow footboard beside the pilot, an awkward perch with no good hand hold, not meant for riding, especially on a forward movement. But Ira is tired and confused and angry. The sweat is burning in his eyes, and he is half-blind from the headlight. Now he is bent half-double, balancing himself, holding on with one hand, trying to keep his coal-oil switch lantern steady in the other. He can see the engineer leaning from the cab window, watching him. Ira tries to signal for a stop, but Marquette won't stop. Instead, he reaches for the throttle and gives it a jerk. The engine coughs and leaps forward.

When the boy falls, his overall strap catches in the footboard. He cries out. His dropped lantern passes under the engineer's window, but still the engine does not stop. The boy is dragged along the roadbed that cuts him, along the ends of the ties that dig into his back. He can feel the rail under his shoulder, and the white-rimmed wheels of the leading truck are squealing on the rail beside him. Then he is free, lying on the slag, looking at his hand. He feels no pain yet where the fingers were, only astonishment that they are gone. When he holds his hand up, the blood seems black in the starlight. It soaks down his sleeve as the train passes, looming over him, shaking the ground.

He does not hear the air hissing in the brake line as the train stops, nor the men coming back, nor any of their voices but one. Mister John Marquette bends over the boy, his mouth against his ear. How you like that, Jew? he asks, and then he is gone, and the pain and the darkness take his place.

* * *

Artemus turned away from the thought of the conductor's hurt; there was nothing for it anyhow but to make fatuous remarks and accept the rebuke such remarks deserved. Instead, he thought of Anna Rose, thin and small, who burned the gas heater even on warm nights in winter, who shivered in the fog of all seasons. Most likely, she went asleep again after he left, and likely she would not have wakened yet. When she did, she would do her matins. Artemus imagined her crossing the room, barefoot, in her pale gown, with a lighted taper in her hand. She knelt before the crucifix on her dressing table and lifted the candle. Artemus imagined himself standing behind, watching her face in the mirror, her thin shoulders, her slim, hipless boy's buttocks under the dressing gown, her long legs. Nymph, he thought, in thy orisons be all my sins remembered—

Suddenly, the conductor shouted "All aboard!" with such vehemence that Artemus jumped. "We have to move this train," said Mister Nussbaum. "We need to get up the road."

Miles Duvall waved from the baggage car. The engineer was watching from the cab, and Mister Danly was strolling back down the platform. "You're late, Ira," said Mister Danly.

"I've heard enough of that," snapped the conductor. He turned to Artemus. "Now get this train moving," he said. "Hurry up." Then he was gone into the coach.

Artemus watched his conductor go, and after a moment waved his hand and got the whistle signal in response. The train began to glide into motion, and Artemus stepped aboard the moving coach.

Once again, Mister Danly hurried alongside. "What's the matter with your captain? He seems awful prickly."

"He's late," said Artemus.

"Well, ain't we all," said Danly.

Artemus watched from the open vestibule window as the agent dropped farther and farther behind. When the train outran him at last, Mister Danly stopped, winded, bending over with his hands on his knees. Yet the pale oval of his face was still lifted toward them, watching as they fled away into time. Artemus had seen this same thing before, a hundred times, but now the growing distance seemed unimaginable, like that which lay between the stars.

* * *

Though the sun was hidden, the Silver Star made a faint shadow in its passage over the land. Artemus Kane stood in the vestibule and watched the shadow of his coach racing along beside. It leapt over fencerows and grade crossings, flickered over the trunks of trees. The shadow kept the shape of the car, but it was distorted, too, as the features of the land pulled at it.

Artemus found himself suspended in the deafening noise of the space between cars. Such a racket—the drumming of the wheels, the rattle of the steel buffer plates—was hypnotic if you gave in to it. Beyond the window, the shadow fled along. White clouds of egrets lifted from the fields, and flocks of blackbirds. Rabbits ran from the shadow, or seemed to, though Artemus knew it was the train itself that frightened them. Cattle only lifted their heads, unafraid, curious. In one broad pasture, a horse, tail and mane streaming, galloped alongside and was quickly left behind. For years, Artemus had known this horse to race the trains in all seasons. In fact, Artemus had never seen him do anything else, as though his sole purpose, the reason his people fed and doctored and curried him, were this futile pursuit.

He was about to proceed when he noticed a slip of paper tucked behind the sign on the bulkhead that said *Passengers May Not Stand in Vestibule*. The cleaning crews rarely missed such a detail. Artemus plucked it out, unfolded it. Scrawled in pencil were the words

T.J.—Dont forget see Agt Ch'ville about s.o. 905.

K.S.

That was yesterday, probably, long hours before Artemus climbed aboard the southbound Silver Star at Meridian. Away up in Virginia, where it was no doubt bitter cold, where dirty snow caked on the wheel trucks, one trainman had reminded another about setting out coach 905 at Charlottesville. Artemus had no idea who these men were, of course, but the note made them real and alive, as if they had spoken to him. One of them had stood in this vestibule, right where Artemus Kane was standing, hearing the same sounds and perhaps watching his train's shadow pass along beside. If Artemus cared to make the calculation, he could guess if they were off duty right now, or riding the southbound version of the Silver Star as it rambled through the Blue Ridge.

Sometimes it was easy to forget that other men worked these same cars in climes and landscapes far removed from Pelican Road. A long-haul passenger train was passed along from division to division, and only at the crew-change points did the men know one another. Within the theoretically inflexible limits of the timetable, the Silver Star was mutable as its own shadow. Cars were added or dropped off, engines were swapped out, the road grime dulled the flanks and streaked the windows of the hurrying coaches. Along the way, the train was given to the care of strangers with their own personalities and squabbles and folklore, their own Mister Nussbaums and Sonny Leekes. Their own Anna Roses and Arabellas too, and their own rivers they liked to cross. Artemus found comfort in the thought that if he ever met T.J. or K.S., they would not be strangers. He would be bound to them by mutual experience and a common language, and if they asked Artemus Kane to set out coach 905 at Charlottesville, he would know how to do it.

Men got fired, or they got laid off in hard times. Maybe a girlfriend was in the family way, a wife was clamoring for divorce, or the law was closing in. For numberless reasons, or for none at all, a man sometimes grew restless, needed a little travel, some room to think, a landscape where fresh possibilities might present themselves and old sins be forgotten. Then the railroad, like the vanished frontier, offered opportunities for escape. With no more than a union card and the practical knowledge of his craft, a man could seek out other roads that needed extra crews in boom times: a grain harvest on the Milwaukee, a big run of West Virginia coal on the Norfolk & Western, a lumber boom on the Great Northern. Such men were known as Boomers, and rare was the trainmaster or superintendent who was not glad to see them when the yards were crowded and the trains couldn't move.

A man who went out on the boomer trail might find himself on some remote railroad he had never even heard of, with only a few varying details—home-grown signals, for example, or the different names of stations and grades—and these quickly gotten used to. Usually it took an experienced man no more than two trips to settle in, to learn that such-and-such a place was always switched with air, that here you worked from one end of the siding, there another, that a caboose was called a way-car here and a van there, and you might find Chinamen or Mexicans or Indians where, at home, you would expect to see only Negroes.

Artemus had never gone booming himself, but he heard traveling men talk about working narrow-gauge lines in Colorado and how odd the three-foot gauge looked, the delicate rail and miniature switches. In Alaska, they said, there was a rifle in every caboose in case a bear decided to climb aboard. They spoke of crossing the barren deserts of Texas and Arizona and even Mexico, told what it was like to pound through the snow sheds on the Union Pacific, or ride the Great Northern in the shadow of the Rockies, or pass under the Royal Gorge on the swaying, ice-caked roof of a boxcar. Old Hoot Gibson never forgot the approach out of the mountains above Denver on the D&RGW, circling down to the clean, glittering nighttime city with fire rimming the wheels. Others spoke of gloomier cities far to the north— Utica and Albany and Buffalo—and of short lines in Maine and New Hampshire where grass grew between the rails. They waxed astonished on the bewildering array of tracks in New York or Gary or East St. Louis and told how these places made Meridian look like a Lionel train set. Up there, everything was blackened by coal soot, they said, and sometimes people shot at you for amusement. Up there, they said, every transfer caboose had bars on the windows, and an armed special agent was part of every crew.

In Chicago, the Polacks who crewed the electric South Shore trains rarely made jokes and never made friends with strangers. The Irishmen on the B&O carried guns as a matter of course, not in their bags, but in holsters on their belts. East St. Louis was the worst place of all. There, the Terminal Railroad Company supplied every interlocking tower with a .45 automatic and a hundred rounds of ammunition. Jean Chauvin once fired a switch engine in East St. Louis, in the Q yards under the Eades Bridge. He told how, for lunchtime fun, the Polack switchmen liked to build a scrap-lumber fire under an empty oil drum and toss in a stray cat.

In the Southwest, on the other hand, everybody was friendly. A train crew might stop in the middle of a run to negotiate with a Mexican farmer for a brace of hens, or entice a comely senorita to sweep out the cab. Across the Mississippi River, boomers on the L&A encountered descendents of Haitian and Santa Domingo slaves who spoke island French and perfect English, and whose dignity was intractable. In California, American Indian track gangs could not be induced to smile or wave by any means, while the Chinese bowed solemnly to the passing trains.

Among all these landscapes and races and cultures, the railroad man spoke his own language and knew the truths peculiar to his trade. He leaned out his cab window, watched from his cupola or vestibule, listened to the click of wheels on the rail joints and the echo of his engine's whistle in the dark. His peril was universal and familiar. Night was still night and cold still cold—hot still hot, too, though the bugs might be different—and a man coupled an air hose in Utah or Iowa or Vermont the same way he did in Louisiana. Cabooses came in all colors, but they all smelled the same. Order forms might be green or yellow, timetables red or white, but they all told the same story and carried the same message: be safe, look out, pay attention. Meanwhile, the trains, long or short, never ceased. They crawled over the vast continent night and day, and on their steel axles they carried the American dream of plentitude and freedom.

One of these was the Silver Star, running sixty miles an hour now through the Louisiana winter morning. Pretty soon, Rufus Payne the engineer and Jean Chauvin the fireman, making up time, would have them at seventy, at eighty on the straightways, at a hundred if they thought the train could stand it. And the Silver Star would stand it in this flat country, the heavy cars gliding over the heavy rail, all eager for speed, ready to race time as surely as the galloping horse raced their passing. Artemus knew that somewhere along the train, Mister Nussbaum was taking tickets, Stanfield beside him, each swaying to the train's movement. Whatever Mister Nussbaum was feeling right now, he would see to his duty because that was the kind of man he was. Meanwhile, villages and depots, boatyards and sawmills, telegraph poles, houses, fences all fled past in a blur of color and form and registered in the trainmen's minds, each detail important, each one fixing their moment in time.

They were to pass the northbound freight drag at Gant's siding. Artemus held on to his cap and leaned far out the vestibule window, and in a moment, sure enough, he saw the marker lights of the caboose tucked safely away in the passing track. As the trains grew closer together, Artemus saw the rear-end crew of the freight gathered on the roadbed—Bruce Butler, Will Prescott, Kenny Speed, all men he knew and had worked with. The freight men lifted their hands and hollered a greeting to Artemus, their words snatched away by the wind and noise. The Silver Star sped along down the length of the long drag, the clatter of its wheels echoing off the cars. Across an empty flat car, Artemus caught a glimpse of Gant's store, but no girl on the porch. Surely, though, old Demeter Gant was in there, gripping his knees with his little withered claws. The thought filled Artemus with disgust, but he offered a quick prayer for the old man's peace just in case somebody might be watching over them.

On the north end, the passing ritual was repeated with the men on the engine—Richard Whiddon, Johnny Hadden, Marion Wigley. Then the freight train was behind them, and the men with it, down the long corridor of time. *Farewell, boys*, Artemus thought, and in a little while, the Silver Star was rattling over the Pearl River bridge.

* * *

In spite of the clearance, the Silver Star couldn't seem to make up time. They found the snow at Picayune: wet, sloppy flakes that didn't stick but made the streets wet and the town lights shine brighter. Motorcars crawled along the main street, feeling their way, and the citizens stepped gingerly on the sidewalks.

The agent had two typed copies of a message for them:

> Extra 4512 South delayed Pachuta acct. derailment. Main
> line not effected. Extra 4512 will wait at Purvis for No. 6.

Artemus, standing under the train shed, puzzled over the message. First, he wondered why people simply could not understand the distinction between "effected" and "affected." Second, it seemed unnecessary to hold Frank Smith's train at Purvis when they could clearly make Talowah, even Lumberton farther south. Mister Nussbaum and the other trainmen were of the same opinion.

Mister Nussbaum had left the cars without his overcoat, but the cold didn't seem to bother him. "We will be their first opposing train out of Hattiesburg," the conductor pointed out. "Why not let them run?"

"What if he meant Lumberton instead of Purvis?" said Bomar.

"It's happened before," Stanfield said.

The agent, a new man who had come here from another division, had been annoying everyone with his talk about the weather. He went on and on as if it were something entirely new and unexpected, as if it had never been cold in December in all the history of man. Now the agent said, "I called him up, asked him the same thing. He said the 4512 has an order to be in the hole at Purvis." The agent hunched in his overcoat. "He was short with me," he added.

"I would like a copy of that order," said Mister Nussbaum. The agent went into the depot and returned a few minutes later with a new order and clearance card specifically for Number 6:

NO. 6 HAS RIGHTS OVER ALL TRAINS PICAYUNE
TO MERIDIAN.

Mister Nussbaum shook the new order at the agent. "I asked for the local's wait order," he said. "What is this nonsense?"

The agent shrugged. "Man said to ask you how many more orders you needed today. Said to get your train moving."

"Well, no shit," said Stanfield.

"Sure is cold, ain't it?" said the agent.

The color rose in Mister Nussbaum's face. "All right," he said. Then, to the flagman: "Oliver, take the engineer his copies. But tell him I said to run Lumberton to Purvis as if he had a yellow board, and tell him to watch out for the 4512. Do you understand me?"

"Yes, sir," said Oliver Bomar, and stood uncomfortably for a moment, holding the message and the order between his fingers like a soiled napkin. "Mister Nussbaum—" he began, but the conductor cut him off.

"Do as I say, Oliver. Be quick."

The flagman looked at Artemus, then at Mister Nussbaum again. Finally, he moved off toward the engine, walking fast. The conductor watched him go, then walked off himself without another word. He paced up and down the platform through the steam that rose in warm billows from the coaches, and every few minutes, he would look at his watch.

Stanfield said, "Something is eating the captain."

"He don't like to be late," said Artemus.

"He don't like engineers, either," said Stanfield, though the comment was pointless since everybody knew it. Many of the old trainmen and enginemen—the really old ones like Mister Nussbaum and Rufus Payne, the engineer of the Silver Star—had spent their working lives in contempt for each others' craft, a dark element of their pride and experience that worked against them sometimes. A.P. Dunn was an exception, as he was in most things, and Artemus wished Mister Nussbaum could be an exception, too, but, beyond the demands of the job, Artemus had never known Mister Nussbaum to speak with anybody in engine service, neither engineer nor fireman nor hostler, not even the mechanics and lowly engine wipers at the roundhouse.

Even so, Artemus thought the conductor should have delivered the verbal order to Mister Payne himself. It was part of the job, nothing more. Now Payne would be insulted, and Oliver Bomar was put in an awkward position.

"We been late before," said Stanfield. "It's something else today."

"It's Christmas Eve," said Artemus.

"No disrespect," said Stanfield, "but that don't mean anything to his people."

"It does to him, Vernon," said Artemus, and tapped his sleeve.

Stanfield looked puzzled by the gesture until its meaning dawned on him. "The mourning band," he said. "Christ, I never even…I mean, I never even *noticed* it."

"It's all right, Vernon," said Artemus. "We can't notice everything."

"It's not all right," said Stanfield. "We got to look out for him."

"I will speak to him," said Artemus.

He left Stanfield then, and moved along the train. He felt it pull at him with its restlessness. It wanted to be gone. They all wanted to be gone, as if the simple act of passing were the most important thing in the world. The next minute, the next hour, was not soon enough. Artemus knew that was a foolish notion; passing on was their business, and time was the medium, always time. Then he arrived at the place where Mister Nussbaum was standing. The conductor was no longer pacing, but staring straight ahead at the brick wall of the depot. His watch lay forgotten in his palm. Artemus said, "Captain, let me fix this."

The conductor stiffened as Artemus unpinned the band around his uniform sleeve, but he said no word. Artemus straightened the band, smoothed it, fastened it so that the safety pin was hidden.

"Now, then," said Artemus. "It's hard to do it right by yourself."

For a moment, the conductor gave no sign that he had heard. After a moment, he shook himself, glanced at his watch, and returned it. Then he smiled, a little. "You are worse than my mother," he said.

"Aw!" said Artemus. "You mean you had a mother?"

"Get back to your station, my boy," said Mister Nussbaum. "We are forty-five minutes late, and we need to get underway."

* * *

On the head end of the Silver Star, Mister Rufus Payne fidgeted with anger. He wore his customary soft felt hat, a white shirt buttoned at the neck, starched white overalls, and leather gauntlets with a white mule on the cuff. He was a round, sharp-eyed, florid, immaculate man whose blood rose to his face when he was mad. When that happened, as it was happening now, his hair seemed even whiter, and his eyebrows arched like white tomato worms.

Payne, like many old-time enginemen, felt a whiff of contempt toward the trainmen whose lives, by comparison, were comfortable and easy. The engine crews, after all, were on the sharp end, always vigilant, peering ahead into storm and darkness, expecting every moment a catastrophe, not only possible but inevitable, that they would be the first to see and therefore have long seconds to fear. Plenty of time to contemplate their deaths while the conductors and brakemen and flagmen, unawares, played cards and drank coffee and read lurid magazines in the caboose. Even the head-end brakemen on freight trains were not exempt from Mister Payne's scorn: Sonny Leeke, for example, who sat behind the fireman and gabbed about baseball and worked crossword puzzles.

Payne had been out on all manner of jobs with Ira Nussbaum, and in all those years they had never had a conversation. What little discussion they did have—beyond the mandatory comparing of watches and orders—always tilted toward the conductor's will and expectations. Now, Mister Nussbaum had not even bothered to consult with Rufus Payne, but sent his decree by the hand of a functionary. Payne had no chance to argue his firm belief that the southbound 4512 would be in the hole at Purvis. As evidence, he had the dispatcher's typed message and the order giving the Silver Star rights over everything all the way to Meridian. He saw no need to delay his train any further.

Across the broad, spotless cabin, Jean Chauvin studied his chief and recognized the signs of trouble. Chauvin had worked stoker engines for years; it had been ages since he had bent to an actual coal scoop. Nevertheless, his gaunt face, pale as rice paper, was always smeared with grease and soot, and it glistened with sweat in all weathers. No force of nature—not the heat of the boiler backhead, not the hot sun of July streaming through his window—relieved his ghostly pallor. Every trip, he wore black overalls, a black welder's cap backward on his head, and a black neckerchief over a black clip-on bow tie. He was one of the few operating men who wore glasses, and these spectacles slipped down the slope of his long nose every few minutes. Now Chauvin pushed his glasses up with a gloved finger. He said, "C'mon, Rufus. Tell me the last time Mister Ira was wrong."

The engineer knew that Ira Nussbaum, the cranky old Jew, had made an informed decision. The 4512 was piloted by A.P. Dunn, a man near the end of his tether, who had worked too long and needed to be watched closely. Rufus Payne accepted that. But he was tired and bilious, and he no longer wished to argue, not with his spectral fireman, not with his conductor, not even with death itself. He wanted only to be home in Meridian on Christmas Eve with the assembled generations of his enormous, annoying, long-lived family, most of whom, especially the children, he despised. He had promised his tired, bilious wife, whom he despised most of all, that he would retire in two years when he was seventy. Then he would die, he told her. Do you promise that, too? she asked. He promised her that, too, and she had gone straight downtown and taken out a big insurance policy with Jacob Luttrell the bank president.

"He is wrong this time," said Payne.

* * *

Artemus went back to his place near the end of the train. In Picayune, as in Slidell, the colored waiting room was overflowed with families dressed for travel, each group gathered around its scarved and hatted matriarch. Their luggage was pasteboard, mostly, and their lunches in baskets and in cardboard boxes tied with string. No diner, coaches only, on the "Ol' Zip Coon." Artemus knew from the steamed-up windows that the stove was roaring in there. He could see the women's fans batting like moths through the glaze. He knew the heavy perfume and damp wool suits and boxes of fried chicken made for a rich atmosphere, and he wondered how the people bore it.

Not all of them did, apparently. A half-dozen black children, in frilly dresses and miniature suits, were lined up on an empty baggage wagon, watching the snow. Artemus waved at them, and they grinned and hugged themselves and waved back with their stubby fingers. A tall, thin, light-skinned man in a homburg hat, supporting himself on a brass-knobbed cane, was with them. At Artemus's gesture, the man spoke sharply to the children, and they fell silent and still. Then the man moved away from them and limped across the platform. The man stopped a few paces distant and removed his hat. He said, "Sir, are you from Meridian?" His voice was smooth and musical, but not a Southern Negro's voice. Maybe once, but not now.

"That's right, uncle," said Artemus.

The man smiled at the term, a little ironically, thought Artemus, who was not used to overt irony in Negroes, though they were good at the subtle kind, which Artemus admired. The man wore a good dark suit with a watch chain looped across the waistcoat. From the chain dangled the key of a scholastic fraternity. Here, apparently, was a black man well educated at the North. Artemus was familiar with the type and found them disagreeable, for they seemed dissatisfied with most people and superior to all. In this, Artemus thought, they differed little from their white counterparts.

The man said, "I have learned, over the years, that it is useless to ask a Negro directions to anywhere. Has that been your experience, sir?"

"Yes, it has," said Artemus. "I always figured it's because I'm white. Or maybe they're just stupid."

"Well, your being white probably has more to do with it," said the man. He paused a moment, waiting for a response perhaps. Finally, he replaced his hat and leaned forward on his cane. "But, you know, it's true even among our own kind. We believe that if you name a thing, you take its power away."

Aw, bullshit, thought Artemus, annoyed by the man's tone.

"Can I ask you something, sir? Some reliable directions from a white gentleman?"

"Ask away," said Artemus.

The man settled back on his heels. He said, "We get off at Meridian. When we walk out the depot, how do we find the colored funeral home in…Jumpertown? Is that what you all call the Negro district?"

"That's what we call it," said Artemus. "You walk out the depot, turn right down Front Street, go three blocks, turn right again, and there you are. It's a house with columns on the porch, right by the railroad. Used to be a mill owner's place, a white man's. There's a colored taxi will take you, if you want—and your family."

"Thank you so much," said the man. Artemus expected him to tip his hat ironically and move on, but he didn't. Instead, he plucked from his waistcoat pocket a wrinkled telegram and smoothed it out. "Now, I know you are surely busy," said the man, "but just let me ask you one more thing."

"Yes, yes," said Artemus.

A little wind caught a plume of steam and sent it swirling around the figure of the Negro man, and the snow, grayish-white like his hair, drifted down beyond the shed. "A trifling inquiry," he said, "just to satisfy an old man's curiosity."

"Get on with it," said Artemus.

"Ah!" cried the man suddenly, and thrust his cane angrily at the Silver Star as he might at a poisonous snake, and his voice was all at once high and tremulous. "Tell me how it is possible—" he began, and paused, as if the words he needed were overwhelmed by sheer amazement. He set his cane against the bricks and bowed his head.

"You can ask it," said Artemus.

When the man tried to speak again, Artemus barely heard him. "What sin does a man have to commit—" the old man began, but his voice broke once more. "My God," he said in disgust. He shook himself and tapped his stick. He lifted the telegram and held it out to Artemus, his eyes clear, his voice steady now. "For a man to be caught in the couplers of a train car," he said. "What would he have to do to deserve that? Can you tell me, sir?"

* * *

Far behind the lines, Artemus and Gideon and a French corporal are strolling in an ancient wood under a high, leafless canopy. The sun is hidden, yet the trees make dim, lacy shadows over the earth. Their great muscular limbs creak, and the tops sough and rattle in the wind. The air is cool, drifted of smoke, smelling of mold and decay.

The corporal has but one eye. The other was lost at Verdun, yet still he serves, for Frenchmen are scarce after so many years of war. He is short and stout like a barrel, with a carefully trimmed beard. He wears the sky-blue overcoat of the French poilu, its skirts pinned back, and a red kepi that seems silly and useless to the Americans. He was born here, in a cottage at the edge of the wood, and he entertains his companions with tales of robber bands and knights and wraiths who had passed this way. He tells of a certain lost maiden—how her soldier lover died in the wars in Holland, and how, when she heard the news, she shed all her fine brocaded clothes and all her sparkling jewels and walked alone into the wood and was never seen again. When the tale is done, and the Americans are pondering whether they could ever inspire such a reaction in a girl, a pair of black ravens glides silkily overhead. Let us follow them, says the corporal. Then, after a little way, the three men hear the voices of other birds in a low muttering, punctuated by shrill cries as if in anger or argument.

Aha, says the Frenchman. Come closer, and I will show you something of interest.

They creep silently over the leaf mold until they find a deep rectangular depression surrounded by younger trees and hedges grown wild. The limbs of tree and hedge are black with birds. The Frenchman says in a whisper that this was the foundation of a great house sacked by the Hessians in a vanished war, and it is here, since then, that the ravens gather to hold their court.

Their court? says Artemus.

My uncle showed me once, says the Frenchman. He moves forward to a low stone wall. We stood in this very place, he says. I was a child then, but I remember it still.

Christ, says Gideon, pointing. There's a skeleton yonder.

Sure enough, the bones of a man, draped in rags leached of color, are propped against the far wall of the old cellar. The legs are covered in leaves, the cracked skull tilted, jaw agape.

Allemande, says the corporal. He spits, then crosses himself. They were through here in '15, he says. But, he says, l'ossature is not the birds' object now. Observe.

Down in the pit, within the dead man's reach, a bird huddles motionless, feathers in disarray, beak pressed to the ground. The ravens are bigger than crows, but this one seems to have been diminished as if he were slowly growing invisible. Presently, five birds glide down and make a circle around the one, solemn and still. All the birds are silent now. The air ceases to move, and the trees seem to lean inward, listening.

A single bird, bigger than the rest, clearly an elder of ravens, drifts down to a chimney stone. Even in the dim light, his feathers gleam with blue iridescence like no other among them. He adjusts himself on the perch, then tilts his eye toward the gathered host. A cawing, a terrible croaking, rises to the canopy and the gray sky beyond.

So he is condemned, whispers the Frenchman.

The birds are silent now. The elder raven cocks his head as though waiting, but no more sound comes from the laden branches. The old bird thrusts out his great black wings. The five executioners move in with a rustling, a jostling of feathered backs, all silent. They do not take long, but long enough, perhaps, for the one under the stabbing beaks. When they are finished, they move away, turning their backs on the dying one in the pit. Then, as if on signal, all the birds around begin to lift from the earth, rising up past the canopy to the open sky where they swirl like smoke. In a moment they are gone.

The men remain motionless behind the low stone wall. A light rain begins; they hear it first in the high branches, then feel it on their faces.

Artemus picks up a black feather left behind. You were a child, he says after a moment.

Yes, says the French corporal.

Gideon goes down into the pit and lifts the bird's black body in his palm. It quivers yet, just as dying men will do; then it is still, the yellow eyes gone dull.

What do you suppose it did? asks Gideon, and he and the bird seem small and far away in the antique wood, in the gray afternoon.

* * *

The Silver Star, now fifty minutes late, pulled away from Picayune without its usual smooth start: so fast, in fact, that the passengers were jostled in the coaches. Black smoke and soot from the engine's stack swirled under the platform shed in a poisonous cloud, and Artemus understood clearly that Mister Rufus Payne was angry and working the throttle hard. This was embarrassing. This was not the way a first-class train, late or not, made its farewell. However, the abrupt departure saved Artemus from the old Negro. Without a word, he ran for the steps and pulled them up. Watching behind, he saw the old man hobble forward past the yellow line on the platform, shouting now, though the words were lost. He shook his telegram at the Silver Star and struck the flanks of the coaches with his stick while they passed inches from his face. Artemus thought sure the old man would go under the wheels, and he considered pulling the air, but in a moment the train leaned around a curve and hid the man from view.

Artemus closed the window, vaguely troubled by the encounter, by the power turned loose on the train by so much anger. The Negro's anger seemed to pursue the Silver Star like a shade, like a curse, just as Rufus Payne's anger pulled the train along. Artemus did not believe in curses, but he believed in the dark power of madness, and a fraternity key dangling from a gold watch chain was no sign that old knowledge had been forgotten. He tried to put the man and his infernal question out of his mind. Nevertheless, as people will do, and now that it was too late, he tried to think of things he might have said. *It's not always a question of sin*, he thought. *Sometimes you don't have to do anything.*

"Fuck," he said aloud. He didn't owe the man anything. He hadn't invited the question, and he might have stood there a hundred years without giving an answer. After all, the French corporal in the wood had not answered Gideon's question either.

The coach door opened, and Oliver Bomar passed through. He stopped when he saw Artemus, and joined him at the window. "Well," said the flagman, "I gave old Rufus the message, and he treated me like a redheaded stepchild."

"Well, fuck him," said Artemus, pressing his fist hard against the window. "The old son of a bitch."

"Yeah," said Oliver. "Anyway, I'll be glad when this trip is over." He clapped Artemus once on the shoulder and passed on up the train.

The flagman's remark lingered in Artemus's mind. Oliver could not be blamed for thinking it, but it was bad luck to say it. "The old son of a bitch," Artemus said of Rufus Payne to the empty vestibule, and suddenly his own anger, nameless and irrepressible, seemed to fill the space with a red glow like the companionway lights on the troop ships. They were red, he remembered, so a man going topside could see better in the dark.

Artemus made himself think on Anna Rose. Usually, the thought of her made him see better in the dark. She had a way of cleansing things, of turning them back to what was real and true. He only had to know that she was out there in the spaces beyond what he could see.

Now, once again, he had no confidence in the empty places. He had left her behind this morning, as he had a hundred mornings, framed in the crooked door, her hair mussed from sleeping, her eyes half-closed and wanting to sleep again. *This is not the same as leaving*, she had said, but in fact, he thought, all leaving was the same, an emptiness without guarantee that it would be filled again. Artemus wished he could say that to Anna Rose. He wanted to touch her face as he could the cold glass of the window before him, only her face would be living and warm, and he could trace the shape of it, and she would speak to him. But he couldn't touch her, for he was way out on Pelican Road, and Anna Rose was sleeping, and he could tell her nothing about what leaving her meant.

THE DARK WOMEN

The 4512 rolled south from Belle Roman, and Mister Dunn felt better than he had in a long time. His leg still ached, but his head was clear and his heart strangely lightened. Whatever had happened back in Meridian, whatever he had done to upset his crew, was evidently forgotten, or forgiven, which amounted to the same thing. Even Frank Smith had been his old self at Pachuta, willing to take a chance, trusting in his crew to get the job done, trusting in Mister Dunn most of all.

That fact was not lost on the engineer. The truth was, he could not remember much about their trip before the derailment. He recalled a collection of vague images. He heard disconnected voices spread across an indeterminate time. Something had been amiss, but it meant nothing now. They were running fine, everything in order, and Mister Dunn owned the men's trust again. He would be careful to hold on to it, to cling to himself and not lose his way again. He would pay attention, not just to the job but to the world about, and to himself.

In a little while, Necaise began to ask about the mechanics of steam propulsion. Eddie Cox surprised Mister Dunn by speaking learnedly to the boy about firebox ratios and boiler capacity, drive-rod lengths and the diameter of cylinders. Eddie laid out the complex process whereby mild and inoffensive tap water was transformed into a thing of terrible power, and how the power was controlled, and how it was used to turn the wheels of the 4512. Their dialogue grew intense, and Mister Dunn had to admonish them to keep watch ahead.

The snow was a white tunnel down which they fled, distance a blurred, indefinite pool. The little country crossings slipped by, all empty of traffic, but still the whistle cried out for each and echoed in the woods and against the yellow-clay cuts. Mister Dunn felt the great engine moving under him, the sum of power and a myriad moving parts all balanced on the point of catastrophe, all under his hand.

* * *

One summer night, under a rising moon, Mister Dunn waits in the clear on Richburg Hill. Eddie Cox and Dutch Ladner sit with him in the dark cab, yawning, smoking, slapping at mosquitoes, talking quietly of nothing. Whippoorwills query in the deep, shadowed woods around them, and crickets sing in the grass. The opposing train, southbound, is a few minutes late but appears pretty soon, the engine working hard up the grade. They can see its shimmering headlight and a shower of sparks from the stack. They hear the hammering of the locomotive as the engineer opens his throttle. Eddie and Dutch lean out the window, and Mister Dunn has left his seat to join them, when all at once the hammering ceases, the headlight vanishes, and the whole countryside lights up in a white flash as if the moon itself exploded. A pillar of pure fire lances skyward then turns on itself in a dirty roiling fist of black smoke, fire and smoke rising as the sound reaches them, a terrific detonation that sucks the air out of the cab.

Mister Dunn and Eddie Cox and Dutch Ladner drop to the ground and run toward the wreck. It is hard to run along the rails, and dangerous—pieces of the engine fall around them, crashing in the trees, thudding and clanging on the roadbed—and futile, for the men to whom they run are dead. Of this they are certain, but they run still, out of unspoken protocol and simple courtesy.

In a moment, they come upon the remains of the southbound locomotive. Though they have brought no lanterns, they can see clearly the thing looming before them in a mist of steam and moonlight. The engine has rolled a quarter mile beyond the place where it died. The driving wheels are still on the rail, and the blackened, twisted frame, but above that, only stars and the lingering shroud of steam. A curl of smoke, too thin even for a ghost, rises from some crevice where hot ash has collected. Nothing remains of the cab, the boiler, the men who a few moments before were riding along, making up time. It is as if those men had breached an invisible rampart and passed into the country of time itself, swallowed up by tomorrow, or yesterday, or trapped forever in a present of unimaginable violence.

After a moment, the whippoorwills take up their calls again, and the crickets, one by one, begin to talk in the weedy ditches. Mister Dunn and his comrades do not speak. They do not pray aloud, though Eddie Cox kneels in the gravel, and Mister Dunn remembers, *Eternal rest grant them, O Lord, and let perpetual light shine upon them.* The men gather close and listen to their own breathing. They hear the groan of air in the tangled cars, the tick of hot metal, the whine of mosquitoes. To the south, the bobbing lanterns of their own rear-end crew appear, small as fireflies, but no lanterns come from the north: nothing there but moonlight and silence.

And no houses in that desolate place, nor telephones, and no time to dally, and men injured, no doubt. So they must leave their train in the siding and back the light engine two miles to a call box against a following train that might appear at any second. The conductor and flagman stand on the tender, popping one fusee after another, the red glare spreading over the rails and the trunks of trees. Mister Dunn keeps the whistle blowing, and Eddie the bell tolling, making as much noise as they can. They reach the call box with no time to spare, with the following train's headlight glittering to the south.

Hours later, when he finds sleep at last, Mister Dunn dreams of a monstrous shape, black under the pale moon, shrieking through the maw of hell's own furnace, while a great bell tolls and tolls for the lost lives of men.

* * *

Mister Dunn said, "Bobby, come over here." The boy crossed the cab, and Mister Dunn moved out of his seat. "Sit here," he said, and the boy looked at him. "Go on," said Mister Dunn.

Necaise took the engineer's seat. He looked small sitting there. Mister Dunn guided the boy's left hand to the brake valve, his right to the throttle bar. "Now take hold of it," said Mister Dunn. Necaise tightened his grip and sat up straight in the seat so that he seemed to grow a little. Mister Dunn leaned down and spoke in the boy's ear: "Feel it under your hands, how it wants to get away. But you won't let it. You have to sit here and feel it and listen to it, and you have to know you are part of it."

"Like a horse," said Necaise, who had never ridden one, but had read in boy's books of "the iron horse" and "the iron steed" and so on.

"Not at all," said Mister Dunn, who had never ridden one either. "A horse has just enough mind to be stupid and unpredictable and willful. This thing runs off the law, and that's all. If you're man enough or mean enough, you can force your will on a horse, but not on a steam engine. You cannot knock a locomotive in the head with a two-by-four and get its attention. All you can do is know the law and be careful, and all the attention has to be your own."

For you cannot alter the Law, Mister Dunn thought.

For God has made the Law that governs the world and all that dwells and moves therein, but He will not save you from it. You can bury a murdered cat under the walls, and they will come down just the same.

The fireman perhaps—no one would ever know for sure—turned away to watch the moon or think of his wife, and the water fell in the glass, and the men died.

The inspector in his rounds laughed at a joke or thought of his mistress as she looked when last night she opened her door to him, and for the sake of these things missed the crack, no more than a hair-breadth, in the riveted fabric of the boiler. Perhaps. And three men died on their way up Richburg Hill, trying to fool time.

For the Law will suffer no dreaming.

"Bobby," said Mister Dunn, "it is not God sitting here, it is you, and you only get the one chance."

"Yes, sir," said Necaise, and turned his eyes ahead.

They passed a whistle post, and Eddie Cox began to ring the bell. Without being told, Necaise lifted his hand and closed it on the whistle cord and pulled. A feather of steam slipped out of the bronze whistle's mouth and was flicked away by the wind. Then the sound followed, echoing in the woods, as the deserted highway crossing passed beneath them.

* * *

George Watson was tired of the sound of the whistle. He had lived the soft life too long and lost the patience that hardship demanded. He was tired of the train whistle and tired of riding and sick of being cold and hungry. He was so cold that he couldn't feel his toes anymore, and he wanted to sleep, wanted to crawl under the cardboard and curl himself into a ball and dream some more, no matter what the dreams brought him. The trouble was, if he went to sleep now, the cold might take him.

He blamed Lucy Falls for his presence on this raggedy-ass local. All he wanted to do was take her out, have a little fun, maybe lay up with her over Christmas. Then she sprung the bad news, and here he was.

Nailing a drag was always chancy; you could never tell what might happen out on the road. An experienced rider tried to find a long train, one that was going on through to someplace, one that wouldn't have to do a lot of switching and maybe set your car out on some godforsaken spur track. George Watson knew all that. He had been a traveling man all his life, and he knew about trains. Still, Lucy Falls and her ice pick had clouded his judgment. If not for her, George would not have climbed in the first empty boxcar he found. In fact, he wouldn't have had to leave at all. He might have seen his brother laid out, even. Now that chance was gone, like his money.

The sporting clothes George Watson wore, that he put on last night just for Lucy Falls, were wrinkled and stained and stank of coal smoke. All the shine was gone from his two-tone shoes, and the slag had gouged the leather. The damp air had undone the pomade in his hair. He had run off scared and left two hundred god damned dollars, and sometimes when he thought about it, he felt like bailing off the train right then and going back and killing some people if he had to—niggers, police, it didn't matter—so long as he got his stash and his raccoon coat.

But not Lucy Falls. Somehow, he could not imagine killing her. Maybe Sweet Willie could, but George could not. She was the one needed it most, of course, but when he tried to imagine the act, he failed. He might as well try to imagine marrying her, a prospect unlikely as his own salvation.

He cursed himself as a fool for ever thinking he would be in New Orleans by suppertime. Even without the derailment, they were bound to go dead in the wasteland along Ponchartrain.

Back in the little town, George suffered with impatience as the train was backed into the yards. He saw the depot sign: Pachuta, a place he never heard of and didn't want to see again. He was surprised when the train got underway again so soon, the engine snorting and blowing black smoke past the door, the slack slamming in and out. In the mad race that ensued—Who knew what the fuck was going on?—

George could hardly keep his feet in the swaying, bouncing car and got knocked around pretty bad. His idea was to close the door, but, as often happened, it was stuck, and the wind howled around in the empty box, stirring up dust and cornmeal and fluttering the cardboard. Once a big piece went sailing out the door like a monstrous brown bird. Finally, all George could do was hunker down in the corner and hope that he would survive the wreck when it came. The boxcar like to have beat him to death, and the sudden, unexpected clamor of the reefer train bursting past the door had scared him worse than any apparition.

At least the ride was smoother now that the race was over. George wondered what it would be like to ride inside a nice warm passenger train. He never took one in his life, not even a Jim Crow car. He tried to ride the blinds once, between the lead coach and the tender—an experience so terrifying and disorienting that he never tried it again.

George thought about all the things he was afraid of. People believed Sweet Willie Wine wasn't scared of anything, but that was only a lie George Watson used to protect himself. George Watson would not ride the blinds or the hog rods. He wouldn't go outside when it was thundering. He was scared of snakes and wasps, of being burned to death, of being stabbed with an ice pick. Once, when they were little black, bullet-headed spawn, he and June snuck into a circus on a dare and found no joy there, only the horror of wild beasts, of painted clowns and midgets. George was scared of empty churches. He was scared of funeral homes and wide, empty spaces, and close, tight spaces. If people knew these things about him, his reputation as a bad man would be ruined, and that reputation, in the end, was the only thing that protected him.

But what good was it doing him now? Here he was on the lam, nearly broke, going to a place where he had no reputation at all. Still, that's what he was after. If he wanted Sweet Willie Wine dead, then he would have to kill his reputation, too.

Of course, that meant George Watson would have to replace the old rep with a new one. That seemed like a lot of trouble so late in life, and maybe it wasn't worth it. He was too old to change, and too old and soft to be out on the cholly in the wintertime. He felt the weight of the pistol in his pocket. He began to think how easy it would be to just put the pistol to his head and go to Jesus, as the saying went. But George was scared of that, too. Jesus would not be waiting for him, no matter what the people said.

He had too much time to think, and while he was thinking, he understood what really scared him about Lucy Falls. George Watson would not have taken her to Memphis. George Watson would have tried to marry her and bring out the child into the world to suffer. That was more fearsome than anything he could conjure. George Watson was a god damned fool.

And now George Watson discovered that, along with everything else, he had to take a shit. Foul his own nest, and no escape.

He rose and staggered across the car to the far corner, took off his coat and dropped his suspenders and dropped his breeches and backed up against the bulkhead, his privates shriveling in the cold. Though the call was urgent, nothing came at once. He was forced to balance himself while he strained and strained, until at last he dropped a half-dozen little pellets so hard and cold that they bounced. They had almost no smell. George was thankful for that, anyhow; only dog shit smelt worse than a man's. He tore off some cardboard to clean himself, then, eyes averted, scraped a pile of cornmeal over his poor leavings.

The slack ran in and nearly knocked him down. Most likely a town was coming up, for the train began to slow, and George could see motorcars and junkyards, and houses with lamps in the windows burning bright and cheerful. No doubt they would do some switching here, more delay, more hours carved out of whatever life he had left.

The whistle blew steadily, grating on his nerves. George Watson leaned against the door and rolled a cigarette, no longer caring if anybody saw him or not. Out there, beyond the door, the world seemed distant and strangely pure under the snow, all its meanness hidden. The echoing void of the boxcar lay behind. George Watson let his ruined two-tone shoes teeter on the door sill while he smoked. It was one of the best smokes he'd ever had. All at once, he felt pretty good, and he thought maybe he would lie down again after his smoke, just for a little while.

* * *

Mister Dunn was back in his seat as the 4512 came into Laurel and pulled into the clear. At the depot, they were given a list of eleven empty boxcars to pull off the Gulf & Ship Island interchange. Frank Smith delivered this news to the head end and personally uncoupled the engine from the train and rode the tender stirrups to the switch and lined them in.

To get to the G&SI interchange, they had to back down through the edge of town, clumping past backyards under the bare arches of oak trees, sometimes so close to the houses that the engine seemed to be passing through the yards themselves. Dogs came running and barking. Children threw snowballs and ran away, and people waved from their back porches. The air was filled with the smell of coal and wood smoke and of dinners cooking, and through the windows, the men could see the lights of Christmas trees. Out on Pelican Road, a train went whistling by, and another whistled on the M&O line, and still another downtown in the yards.

Necaise and Smith walked together, the snow crunching under their shoes, the engine moving close behind them. They worked their fingers inside their leather gloves and touched the palings of fences. Necaise picked up a handful of rocks and threw them one by one at a Nu-Grape sign on a barn. They drew deeply of the air, the vapor of their breath mixing with the steam. The cold, brittle rails rang sharply and groaned and creaked as the wheels passed over them. Once Necaise had to run ahead and pull a child's Radio Flyer wagon from the engine's path.

The cut lay strung out in a curve and was broken over three crossings, which meant that four separate couplings had to be made. Necaise flagged the crossings and made the joints. Frank had to pass signals to the head end, meanwhile checking numbers against his switch list. When everything was together, they came out, with Necaise and Smith riding the top of the last car.

They had to sit down to get under the tree branches. No word had been spoken between them until now when Necaise began, "Frank, I'm sorry you had to come up here—"

"Don't misunderstand," said Smith. "It takes two to make this switch. I could've sent Sonny, but I just like the ride."

Necaise said, "You know, A.P. is doing all right. He let me run the engine a while. He and Eddie was learning me—" Then he stopped, knowing from the look on the conductor's face that he had told too much.

For a moment, Smith said nothing. He sat cross-legged on the wooden walkway that ran along the top of the car. In his cap was the pigeon feather he found at Pachuta. Finally, he said, "You need to learn how to run an engine, that's good. But not on this trip. You understand me?"

"But, Frank—"

"God dammit," said Smith, shaking his head, "I'll put you back on the shanty, I swear to God."

"Yes, sir," said the brakeman. He snatched at a branch and came away with a sprig of mistletoe. "But it's not A.P.'s fault. He was—"

"I don't want to hear about it," said Smith. He shook his head again. "Jesus Christ," he said.

* * *

The truth was, Mister Dunn was not all right, and he was not running the engine now. When the brakemen got off, he had given the engine to Eddie. He sat in the fireman's seat, leaning out the window, thinking.

He was tired now, all at once, and he found it hard to keep his mind on what was happening. Snatches of early morning had been returning to him: how he had fallen, how he had spoken strangely to Bobby Necaise, how Frank Smith had looked at him in the yard. He remembered Nettie's voice in the dark of the bedroom. One after another, these things broke across the moment he was in, drawing him away into another time where he still seemed to have business. He was so bothered with remembering that, when the engine whistled for the first crossing, he was shocked. Beyond the tender, he could see Frank and Necaise walking along. He could see a line of boxcars leaning in a curve, a rusty open knuckle at the head of the cut.

Suddenly, Mister Dunn was on the ground too, in two places at once, watching himself from the engine cab. He saw himself stop walking alone. The engine squealed to a halt beside him. Mister Dunn stood by the frost-rimed tender, listening to the clank and breathing of the locomotive, the slosh of water in the tank, the sudden throb of the air pump. The whistle had ceased, but the bell went on ringing.

Mister Dunn crossed the frozen dirt road and summoned the engine. It backed slowly. Mister Dunn beckoned, moved his arm in a circle slower and slower, dropped his hand to signal stop. The couplers clashed together, and the pins fell. He knelt between the cars and wrestled the air hose couplings together and turned the angle cocks to let the air flow. When he stood out again, the engine was vanished, and the cars, and all of his crew, but the bell was still tolling somewhere, and he was not alone.

From the backyards, through leaning gates and cattle gaps, came a crowd of women all in black, heads bowed, their hands clasped before them, all silent but for their slippered feet in the snow and the rustling of their dresses: white women, colored women, old and young. A great round silver moon cast the women's shadows before them, long shadows that fell across the snow in dark imitation as the women approached. Mister Dunn could not move. The women flowed around him, and as each one passed, she raised her head and spoke a man's name. Mister Dunn knew them for the names of the dead, though he did not know them all, there were so many.

Some shaped the name bitterly: the old fat wife of Rodney Felder whom he knew, and Marquette's lean, battered consort. There was a yellow woman with a hard face and long red nails like a harlot who was a stranger to him. Some names were offered with gladness, as if it were a relief to let them go; some were uttered with tenderness and regret. The young bride, Bruce Herrington's, could barely speak; she let the boy's name pass away in a whisper, like the vapor of breath.

They all looked at Mister Dunn, spoke the names, then turned away, drawing their black shawls over their heads and vanishing into the cold mist. The last one came slowly, as if she did not know her way. Mister Dunn felt he knew her, and he wanted to hear the name she bore to speak. She was almost by, almost gone, when she lifted her face.

Nettie? he said.

Eddie touched his shoulder, and he jerked awake. The familiar confines of the cab came in sharp focus all at once and he stood so quickly that he nearly fell over. "What?" he said. "What is it?"

"We all coupled up," said Eddie. "We ready to go."

"To follow?" said Mister Dunn.

"Come on, now, Mist' A.P.," said Eddie. He guided Mister Dunn gently. "The captain is comin'. We best swap places."

Mister Dunn was just in his seat again, his hand settling on the brake lever, when Necaise clambered up the gangway and the conductor close behind. Necaise sat down without speaking, still holding his sprig of mistletoe. Eddie Cox took up the coal rake and clanged opened the firebox door and peered inside, muttering to himself. Frank

Smith stood in the cab, in the glow of the fire, tapping the folded switch list against his leg. He looked at Mister Dunn. "A.P.," he said.

"Come in and warm yourself," said Mister Dunn.

"Sir, we have a long way yet," said Frank Smith.

"Not so long, sir," said Mister Dunn.

The gray sky seemed to lower, and a little wind came and stirred in the branches. The locomotive breathed softly beneath them like a woman in her sleep, while blackbirds left tracks across the snow, among the frozen laundry and barren hedges of the yards. The birds had a curious way of walking, too much like men for comfort. In the world out there, people moved about their houses, moved across the light, and motorcars puttered in the streets, and way off a mill whistle blew.

Frank Smith reached up and took the bell rope and sent a pealing through the morning. He listened to it dying away, as if it were a sound he had never heard before. "Fuck it," he said at last, and turned away. He was almost down the ladder before he said, "When you are ready, Mister Dunn."

* * *

Thanks to Mister Dunn's fast running, the 4512 was close to time into Hattiesburg. A northbound passenger train occupied the main line at the depot, so Necaise lined them into a clear yard track, and they crawled along through a canyon of snow-covered boxcars and gondolas and tanks. Near the south end, they were stopped by the conductor of a switch engine whose cut was blocking the lead. They sat there, the minutes ticking by, until the track was clear again. When they pulled up to the yard office at last, the order board was down.

Necaise took the order on the engine. When Frank Smith got the order on his end, he pulled the air and stopped the train and got off.

The yard office was hot, dim, smoky, littered of papers and ledgers and hulking black typewriters. On the walls were the usual collection of bulletins and calendars and job notices, the call board for switch engine crews, and the cartoonish safety posters everyone ignored. Festooned from the ceiling fans were some garish dime-store Christmas decorations that only made the office seem more dreary.

The telegraph was clattering away, but for someone else apparently, for the operator, Mangum Fentress, sat with his feet up on his desk, smoking a pipe. When Smith entered, the telegrapher swiveled around in his chair and smiled and got to his feet. Mangum Fentress was a tall man in vest and shirtsleeves and spectacles, his hair parted neatly in the middle.

"Hello, Mannie," said the conductor. He was suddenly embarrassed, unsure how to proceed. Fentress had just copied an order instructing Extra 4512 to meet No. 6, the Silver Star, at Lumberton. Smith had expected the meet to take place at Talowah, a matter of only a few miles, but a world of distance in the operation of trains. Something about it seemed wrong, and Smith was bothered because he could not say what it was, and he did not want to lay it off on Mangum Fentress.

The telegrapher laughed. "I know what you came in for," he said. "Number Six is late. You want some coffee?"

"No," said Smith. "I want to make a phone call."

Fentress pushed a squat black telephone across the counter. Smith dialed the dispatcher in Meridian. The voice on the other end was one he did not recognize.

"Yes, Number Six is late," said the voice testily. "That happens sometimes."

"Six is never late," said Smith

"Well, he is today," the voice said, tightening with irritation. "You can make Lumberton easy," it said, this time with the confidence of a man in a warm office, his train sheet neatly inscribed before him and the yellow lights lit on his board.

"Are you sure?"

"You think I made it up?" said the voice.

Frank Smith hung up on the man. "Fuck you," he said.

The clerks looked up. Fentress said, "Beg pardon?"

"Not you, Mannie," said the conductor. He pointed to the tele-phone. "Who is that dispatcher?"

"His name is James Harris," said the operator, and lifted his hands. "I don't know him. He's just trying to get you over the road, I guess."

"Ah," said Smith. "Well, we best get on then. Merry Christmas."

"Hold on," said the operator, pulling on his overcoat. "I'll walk out with you."

The two men stood a moment on the narrow wooden platform, watching the snow where it blew in clouds off the roofs of standing cars. It covered the stone-gray slag and the dark cinders, was drifted against the sides of oil drums and the pale yellow flank of a mainte-nance shed. A switching cut was passing deep in the yard. A man riding the tops, his hands shoved in his coat pockets, drifted by like a revenant. The air smelled of hogs and smoke and grease. Meanwhile, the X-630 waited on the main line, slightly canted, with a plume of smoke rising from the stovepipe. The whole train was in sight, down to the fore-shortened locomotive in its cloud of steam.

Fentress pulled up his coat collar. He said, "The road is emptying out. There's nothing ahead of you, and nothing against you but Number Six all the way to the Pearl River. If you're doubtful, wait in the hole at Talowah. Nobody will be there."

"We can make Lumberton all right," said Smith. "I didn't mean to insult you in there."

"You didn't," said the other. He lit his pipe and flicked the match away. "I get tired of this shit sometimes."

Smith nodded. "I know," he said. The smell of the pipe tobacco made him want a cigar. He waved a highball and was glad to hear the whistle make answer; if the day got any gloomier, they would have to break out the lanterns. "Goodbye, Mannie," he said.

"Be careful," said Fentress, and turned back into the office.

They set out the hogs on a house track at the packing plant. A row of lightbulbs burned under the shed roof, and the whole place reeked of blood. Sonny Leeke made the switch, and when he returned to the caboose, he arranged his gloves on the stove to dry. "Poor sons of bitches," he said. "Tomorrow is Christmas, and all they got to look forward to is getting knocked in the head."

Dutch Ladner looked up from his copy of the *Police Gazette*. "You was raised in the country," he said. "Since when was you sentimental about livestock?"

"I ain't," said Sonny. "I'm just saying."

"Well, don't," said Ladner. "Them hogs don't know it's Christmas, for Christ's sake."

"How you know they don't know?" said Sonny Leeke.

Frank Smith lit a cigar at his desk and went over his orders one more time in the glow of his Aladdin lamp. They were perfectly clear, indicted in graphite on the green 19 forms and signed by the operators in Meridian and Hattiesburg, and no matter how many times Smith looked at them, they read the same. The 4512 would not leave a register ticket at Talowah. The 4512 would wait for the Silver Star at Lumberton.

Smith thought about Artemus Kane and Mister Nussbaum, who were out there somewhere in the snow. They would chafe at being late, and they would try to make up the time. Well, so would the 4512. Their train was longer now, but it was all empties, unless you counted George Watson as a load.

The Bergeron's Auto Repair girl smiled down from the calendar, reminding everyone that it was Christmas Eve. Frank wished he did not know about George Watson in the boxcar. He wondered again if the man knew how his brother June was killed. The man would be cold and hungry, like the hogs.

Frank Smith was conductor. If he wanted, he could pull George out of his boxcar and let him ride in the warm caboose. Every instinct told him that was the right thing to do, but the right thing was not always the right thing. It might put a colored man in an uncomfortable situation, and the other boys might not appreciate the precedent. Moreover, Smith had Mister Dunn to worry about.

In the end, it was better to let things alone, Smith thought. George Watson was out there by his own choice, and it was unlikely he would die of the cold, and if he did, it was his own fault. Mister Dunn would keep his wits, and the crew of the Silver Star would follow their orders and be careful. The 4512 would get over the road this one last time, then Frank would sort it all out in New Orleans. The worst that could happen was that they would be caught by the law out in the marshes, and over this, Frank Smith had some control. Today, he decided, they were going to run. No more pickups, no more stopping to switch out a bunch of god damned empty cars that could wait for tomorrow. If he was called on the carpet, that would be all right, too, for Frank Smith had gone a long while, since summer, without any time off. Maybe he could lay up at Gideon's house in the Quarter and drink some real whiskey and smoke a little dope. In any case, Smith told himself, the train they had now was the one they would drag into New Orleans.

The conductor pushed back his chair. "Grab a handhold, boys," he said.

"Fuck 'em, let's run," said Sonny Leeke, rubbing his hands together. "It's Christmas Eve on Basin Street."

"Way down in New Or*leens*," said Ladner.

Smith climbed into the cupola and leaned out the window and gave an exaggerated highball signal. The whistle answered, the train jerked into motion, and Frank Smith settled back into the worn leather seat to watch the country go by. Out on the main again, the wheels hammered over the rail joints. Smith looked at his watch: it was straight up noon, and Lumberton was thirty minutes away. *Don't let me fuck up*, thought Frank, turning the watch in his fingers. *Just don't let me fuck up.*

* * *

At noon, the snow was falling heavy at Talowah. Donny Luttrell had seen all the morning trains by, and he had read the order releasing conductors from their obligation to drop a register ticket at his station. Donny thought this odd, but he had never worked a holiday before, and he supposed this was how it was done. In any event, he did not question the order; no doubt the dispatcher knew what he was doing. Donny also had the message reading

> Extra 4512 South delayed Pachuta acct. derailment. Main line not effected. Extra 4512 will wait at Purvis for No. 6.

Purvis was six miles to the north. Donny would not have to watch for the southbound 4512 until Number 6 had passed going north, which gave him opportunity to go to the graveyard as he had planned. He was not worried. He always heard a passenger train from miles away, and he would have plenty of time to get back to the depot for the Silver Star.

Donny took a ham sandwich and Thermos jug of coffee and made his way through the trees, through the ruin of the old town. Along the way, he cut sprigs of cedars, thinking to lay them on the lonely graves.

He enjoyed how the snow crunched under the soles of the logger's boots he had ordered from a catalog before Thanksgiving. He listened to the sparrows rustling among the pine needles, and the twitter of juncos and fussing of squirrels. He admired the scarlet flash of cardinals, and he watched for the hawk. Another thing to watch for was the pack of wild hogs that, in the last week or so, had taken residence in the woods. He hoped the hogs would show up, for just yesterday he had bought a chrome-plated .45 automatic from a brakeman who needed money. He imagined himself holding off an attack by the fierce razorbacks. In any event, the boots and the pistol made him feel as if he had finally become one with his surroundings. He thought himself ready for anything.

And foolish, a little, strolling along with a bouquet of evergreens and a .45 stuck in his waistband. Moreover, he was thinking of Rosamond Lake, of what it would be like to make this passage through the snow with her. He tried to imagine what he would say to the girl he had betrayed, and who had betrayed him in turn.

Once, Donny had taken Rosamond Lake to the Confederate cemetery that lay on the crown of a hill behind the university. The rotten wood markers had long since been removed from the graves and the sunken places filled so that the cemetery, surrounded by cedars, enclosed in a low stone wall twined with poison ivy, was smooth and featureless now, with no monument to speak its calling, and no one left to say which narrow parcels of ground held the bones of a man. It was a place much visited by students, but only because it was remote and peaceful, conducive to romance in a narrow, watchful world that offered scant privacy. Beyond that, the students, most of them, found little purpose there, and no meaning at all. Being young, they could discern no connection between their own lives and the rumor of nameless men long dead, who had come out of Shiloh and Stones River, suffered their wounds in the old chapel hospital, perished in unimaginable ways, and been buried at last on a muddy hilltop—laid to rest far from home in the company of strangers, attended by strangers, strangers themselves.

Donny Luttrell brought Rosamond to the cemetery at twilight in a bleak April. The trees were new-budded, the ground strewn with yellow daffodils, but too much rain had fallen, too much yet to come, and the woods around were gray and sodden and crowded of blackbirds. No matter. Donny spread a blanket by the wall, in a bank of nodding, glistening flowers, and there Rosamond gave of herself. When it was done—it was only a moment, less time than it took to be born—when the night was just beginning, and Rosamond was pressed against him in the damp, Donny could feel the quick beating of her heart. He could not know it was the last time he would feel it. In return, the ground beneath gave only of silence, save a fleeting whisper that might have been no more than the moving air: Don't be fooled, it said. You are strangers, too, sine nomine, even to yourselves.

They never spoke after that. When she refused to see him, sent word that she could not bear his company now, Donny Luttrell quit his classes and sold his books and, with his stipend, rented a room in town. All that long month, in every twilight, he returned alone to the soldiers' cemetery and sat with his jug against the stone wall. No sign remained of his and Rosamond's passing there: the grass had sprung upright, and the daffodils lifted their bells again, and the moss was green. All those evenings, Donny waited until the night was accomplished, listening for voices that never came. He listened while the daffodils faded and the trees came into full leaf, until the night in May when Rosamond summoned him at last and told him what had happened, and he began the journey that had brought him to these cold Piney Woods.

The cemetery at Talowah was no longer hidden by the vines and creepers and the tangled, gnarled privet. In the early fall evenings, Donny had worked with ax and swing-blade to clear the ground. Sometimes, when the day shift closed down, the loggers would come out to help, working silently for a while, then squatting on their heels with a jug and hand-rolled cigarettes. If they wondered the reason for all this trouble, they never asked; instead, while the night grew cool around them, they told stories of the old town and of Pelican Road. They taught Donny to wear stovepipes on his legs for the snakes, and they drove many a timber rattler and copperhead from his ancestral haunts. They showed the boy how to smoke out hornets with journal-box waste, and how to up-end a jar of gasoline over a yellow-jacket nest. One by one, they cleared the broken stones and brought them into the light, and sometimes they had stories of the people who lay beneath their feet.

Now, in bleak December, the loggers were gone, and Donny came into the burying ground alone. He walked among the scattered stones, telling their names to Rosamond and telling of them he knew: Captain Ronan Montieth of the 9th Mississippi; Celeste Condon, beloved consort of Randall Jung; the nameless twins of James and Nancy Falkner; the unknown traveler murdered on Pelican Road; Frank and Ann Smith, early settlers buried side by side, so close their graves made a single depression. So long silent, these vanished ones had a voice at last, and to each, and to the unmarked sunken places and the Negro graves marked only by fragments of stone, Donny Luttrell brought his tokens of life.

When he was finished, Donny found himself alone again. Somewhere Rosamond had left him, but that was all right, for she never went far in time.

He went down into the shelter of the sunken road and took dinner in his solitude, and for a long while he listened. He heard the winter birds, the hawks' keening far above, the furtive shuffling of sparrows in the leaves, the sift of snow. A westerly wind blew strongly in the pine tops, driving the weather from across the great river. Donny wrapped his coat around him and leaned against the bank of old Pelican Road, thinking of them who had traveled this way in winter hardship, some looking for promise in the new ground, some looking no further than the next meanness they could do. The cold wind blew for them all, and took them all away, as it must Donny Luttrell one day, a stranger like the rest. But not now. For now, he had a name and could still believe in tomorrow. He could sleep for a little while above the soft earth, knowing there would come time enough to sleep beneath it.

And so he slept and dreamed, though in all his long years he would never recall what he dreamed of. For honor's sake, he liked to think that Rosamond returned to him there in the sunken road, or his mother perhaps, two dark women with kindly voices that spoke in vain to save him, to save them all.

He slept and never heard the Silver Star climbing the grade below Talowah siding, nor the 4512 passing his station. Mister Dunn never called for signals, for the order board was green, and the empty cars made only the faintest rustle in their passing beyond the woods, in their hurrying down toward Lumberton on Pelican Road.

LES PECHES DU MONDE

Artemus went up through the coaches of the Silver Star. He was in a bad humor, though, as often happened, he could not say why. In the vestibules, the deck plates shifted under his feet, and beneath them, invisible, the ground rushed backward in a blur of cross-ties and slag and dead possums, the stubs of burnt-out fusees, spatters of grease and oil, shreds of toilet paper, all the detritus of Pelican Road stretching back to Basin Street, to Artemus Kane's locker, to the streetcars on Canal and the narrow stairs that led to Anna Rose's flat.

And more to come, miles and miles unreeling beneath the Silver Star. Down the long serpentine of the rails, over grades and over bridges, through mazes of yard tracks, the train would pass in time toward the familiar outlines of the town that borned Artemus Kane. There, he would stand in this vestibule or another and watch the vine-covered backs of buildings drift by, raise his hand to men he knew, throw the station switch behind for the main line. In time, he would gather up his bag and lantern and step down on the platform, talk a while in the crews' washroom, start his motorcycle—if it would start at all—and ride through the wet snow, under the colored lights, to the house where every room was filled with his mother's furniture but nothing else, no longer even ghosts.

In one of the vestibules, Artemus discovered a passenger violating the rules. This person had opened the window and was leaning out the half-door, letting the cold wind pour over him. Citizens, as the sign plainly declared, were forbidden to loiter in a vestibule while the train was in motion, and it was a trainman's duty to remove offenders. Usually, Artemus could care less; he only chased away those whom he instinctively disliked. Now, however, he was primed for any target.

He opened his mouth to speak, thinking to speak curtly, supported by the rules and regulations of the Operating Department of the Southern Railway that gave him authority over the conduct of passengers on the fast train designated Numbers 5 and 6 on the timecard but known far and wide as the Silver Star, extra-fare, all-Pullman, New Orleans to New York City, upon which Barbara Stanwyck herself had once complimented him on his uniform.

Except that the courteous Tulane student, the handsome lad who had inquired after the coach for Atlanta, turned away from the window, drawn perhaps by the presence of another person in the emptiness. At the sight of the boy's face, all the elements of Artemus's reprimand evaporated.

"Oh, hello," said the boy. He forced a smile and tapped the accusing brass sign with his finger. "I guess I'm not supposed to be here."

Artemus shook his head. "It's all right. Just be careful."

"Oh, sure," said the boy. "Thanks."

Artemus moved closer, and now he could see clearly what he thought he had seen, that the boy's face was shiny with tears. The smile was gone, replaced, in the sudden, guileless way young people have, by a quick turning toward the shadows. The boy dragged the sleeve of his sweater across his eyes, embarrassed and wanting to deny it.

They stood awkwardly for a moment. Artemus knew from experience that it was useless, for him at least, to try to follow a young person into his dark spaces. They were too closely guarded. Still, he could not turn away. "Are you in trouble?" he asked bluntly.

"Oh, no," said the boy. "It's just the wind."

Bullshit, thought Artemus. He said, "Well, it's poor practice to lean out the window. The train throws up rocks sometimes."

The boy nodded. He looked away and rested his fingers on the door ledge. "Did you ever know anybody to jump out?"

At first, the boy's question, spoken in a whisper, fled away amid the noise. Then the words seemed to come together all at once, and Artemus understood. In fact, he had seen such a thing a few years before. He remembered, in a sudden burst of color and sound, the screaming passengers, the squealing and shuddering of the train, the jumper, now a pile of sorry rags, who lay just off the roadbed a half mile behind. They could see the man clearly even at that distance, and they walked toward him through the smell of overheated brakes: conductor Troy Guider, flagman Stanfield, and Artemus, each man walking slowly, wrapped in his own silence, carrying his own particular dread and sorrow as he would no doubt bear them to his own death one day.

Artemus shivered at the memory, and his face, apparently, betrayed him, for the boy held up a hand. "Wait," he said. "I didn't mean…I was only asking—"

"Well, don't," said Artemus sharply. "That is not a thing to have in your head." He reached across the boy and unlatched the window and slammed it shut. In the comparative quiet, the boy shrank back as if Artemus had made to strike him.

"Easy," said Artemus. "It's all right." They stood together for a moment, watching the white-dusted pines flicker by, and the fields, glazed with snow, that opened out now and then. The world was going about its business, unmindful of the train and the people who fled past behind the lighted windows.

"What do you study down yonder?" Artemus asked.

"Architecture," said the boy, once more in a whisper. "I was going to be—" Then he stopped, his voice dying away. He pressed his fingers to the cold glass. "I was expelled," he said.

Artemus, surprised, spoke before he thought. "You?" he said. "Why?"

The boy smiled again. "Why not?" he said.

* * *

In memory, Artemus views the scene as he might an etching in a museum: a November sky ballooned with rain; gray fields glazed with water; gray, stricken trees. Along the horizon stretches a leafless wood like a bank of fog, interrupted for a space by the clustered roofs of a village where a black curtain of smoke darkens the sky, fading at its upper reaches so that it is indistinguishable from the clouds.

In the middle distance is a spectral windmill. Closer looms a church of Norman architecture, centuries old. It is a ruin now. The apse and roof are gone, but three walls remain, pierced by narrow windows empty of glass. Outside, along the walls, the glass lies scattered in shards amid the lead strips that bound it: shattered images of saints, the only bright color in the landscape. Through the windows, barely visible, are the collapsed rafters and arches of the roof and the indistinct shapes of men.

The churchyard is crowded with a company of Marines, some seventy-five men this late in the war. The church is surrounded by a stone wall just higher than a man. In a niche, under a Gothic arch set in the stones, a statue of Our Lady stands with her arms outstretched, her face tilted downward toward the serpent coiled at her feet. Beyond the wall is the parish cemetery, headstones and crosses and humble statuary all toppled and jumbled. The occupants, many of them, have been evicted by the pounding of artillery. Their clothes and cerements decorate the limbs of nearby trees, their bones and caskets litter the churned ground. Someone has harvested a score of antique Gallic skulls and set them in a row on the wall, where they stare blankly and breathe silent lessons of mortality. A few have the lower jaw still attached; between the brown teeth of one, Squarehead has inserted the stump of a cigar.

Lombardy poplars rise from the churchyard, their tops shattered. In the garden, the phallic snouts of a mysterious yellowish vegetable probe upward, each parting the ground in perfect wedges as if it were emerging from a pie. The city men call them dickheads. The country men have squatted on their heels, squeezed the sprouts, and declared them cabbages perhaps, but maybe not. Some argue for asparagus. No one knows what grows in the French winter, and no one cares. They are too tired. There is too much rain, and the Germans are in the village.

Artemus Kane's memory, for an instant, holds all this in silence, all in stillness. Then, gradually, sounds resume, and movement. The Marines, jerkily at first, like the beginning of a film, begin to stir. Soon, their actions take on the peculiar fluid grace of young men. They pace, they pose, they scratch themselves and adjust their equipment. Now and then, one looks off toward the village, then looks away. Despite the rain, they smoke pipes and cigarettes. They speak in low voices, and laugh, and cough. The windmill creaks to life. Swallows come and go from its eaves as the tattered arms are driven by the wind, and the birds driven by the wind, darting and swirling. Ravens croak in the broken poplars, and from the tree line comes the monotonous, intermittent tat-tat-tat of a Maxim gun firing toward the church, though it is just barely out of range. The men within the church begin to move about. They are Marines trying to start a fire for coffee. The crowns of their helmets are faintly medieval, as if the shades of Longshank's men had returned to pillage.

Artemus and Gideon Kane are standing by the stone wall, which offers shelter from the wind and thus from the blowing rain. Nevertheless, their overcoats are soaked, and they are splattered and caked with mud. Artemus has planted his rifle between his feet, an empty ration tin over the muzzle. Gideon's shotgun is slung muzzle-down; to the stock is affixed a canvas bandolier with five brass shells, the primers already little circles of green from the damp.

Gideon had finally gone to a field hospital to see about his bronchitis, and the brothers have not seen each other in two weeks. They spend a few minutes trading news. Gideon studies Artemus's wound from the Belleau Wood and is glad to see it healing well. For himself, Gideon is better now, his lungs cleared up, he says. Neither has received a letter from home. Then they are silent. They do not reminisce on old times, and they do not speak of the future which, after all, is nothing more than the burning village they will have to attack pretty soon, in open order across the fields.

They are, in fact, strangers in a way that each man understands, though neither can voice it. They know that war is all the same save in its narrow spaces, in the minutes, hours, weeks through which a man passes alone, the little increments he perceives and suffers in a way no other before him has in all of time. It is a truth that touches every man in sight, and every man beyond sight across the broad stroke of war, and it makes them all brothers, all strangers forever.

Artemus Kane is overcome with loneliness by the wall of the ruined church, and at the same time seized by a profound sense that he is among strangers and thus the only people he will ever truly love. He wonders how he will explain this if anyone he meets—not in the future, but in some unformed universe beyond death—should ever need to ask. Meanwhile, over the village, a futile illumination flare arcs into the sky, sputters and goes out, leaving a trail of white smoke like a question mark.

Frank Smith, now the company first sergeant, crosses the garden, trampling the sprouts, his face still and solemn. When he draws near, he sees the skulls lined up on the wall. Who did that? he asks, and Artemus and Gideon shake their heads. Smith stands for a moment, his rifle between his feet, the muscles in his jaws working. Like god damn children, he says at last, and lifts his Springfield by the barrel and scrapes the skulls off the wall. They plop and roll in the mud. Smith looks at Artemus Kane. The captain wants somebody in that windmill, he says. Guess who it is?

Ah, the windmill, says Artemus. He looks in that direction, though he cannot see the windmill through the wall.

Gideon coughs wetly and spits an ample gob of white sputum into the mud. I'll go with them, First Sergeant, he says.

Smith looks at Artemus, then at Gideon. As you will, he says.

Artemus Kane's regular squad is down to seven men: Squarehead, Round Man, Tall Man, the Preacher, the Artist, and two Mormon brothers. Gideon makes eight, Artemus nine. They gather around the first sergeant and receive their instructions: occupy the windmill, watch for movement, don't die.

Stay leeward, says Smith finally. That gun down there has the range of the mill.

Aye, aye, Top, says Artemus. Then he asks: What if the Krauts are there already.

Well, Kane, says Smith, if they are in there, then run them the fuck out. Get a prisoner if you can.

Maybe we can paint it, too, says Squarehead, while we're at it.

Get moving, says Smith.

The men adjust their equipment and fix bayonets, and in a moment they are moving across the stubble field in the rain, leaving the company and the church behind. It is lonesome out there. They walk at port arms, keeping their distance from one another, pulling hard against the mud, splashing through the water in the rows. Artemus wishes his brother hadn't come, but there is no sense arguing, for Gideon has his own way. In any case, Artemus does not watch his brother; rather, he watches carefully the windmill, tall and silent and grotesque, and the thing seems to watch in return through its narrow blank windows. The Marines move closer. The blades turn lazily, patiently. Artemus can hear the machinery creak in the mill, and it may as well be his own legs moving, his own lungs drawing in the cold air.

The rain comes harder now and pours off the rim of Artemus

Kane's helmet in a silver curtain. All the day past is a flat pane, like something painted on glass, each moment frozen in tableau, each one clearly visible but unreachable now, as distant as an old tale told by old men. Only the present is real, the step in the icy water, the slight adjustment of the hand along the rifle stock, the unconscious gauging of distance from the next man. Yet the present is enough. It will suffice. In the present is contained all the beauty of the world, all the blood quick with life, all the possibility yet unborn nor even conceived. Artemus is once more seized with loneliness, but he knows he must ignore it, he must pay attention. One day, if he lives, he can think about it, but not now. He is trying mightily to focus his attention when the sniper fires from the windmill.

The shooter must have been a distance back from the window, for the shot is a metallic *pank* barely heard. Squarehead falls like a stone, face-down in the mud, his arms beneath him. He does not twitch nor quiver nor make a sound, he is quickly dead and now almost indistinguishable from the earth and water that received him. His comrades, too, have made themselves part of the ground, burrowing like turtles into the mud, all but Gideon, who is still walking.

The windows! Artemus cries. Put your fire on the windows! It is an unnecessary command; the men are already firing, working their bolts, firing again. Gideon, still wearing his barracks cap, walks on. He carries his shotgun in one hand by the balance, the sling drooping down. In his overcoat and equipment, outlined against the sky, he seems hulking, gigantic, an unmissable target, like an elephant. Artemus shouts, Gideon! Gideon, what the fuck you doin'!

In the midst of their own fire, they do not hear the next shot from the windmill. A hole appears in the crown of the Artist's helmet, and he, too, is still.

Now the Maxim gun in the village has found them, and angry splatters and spurts erupt in the mud around them, and the rounds snap overhead. Artemus thinks, *We can't stay here*. Let's go! he says.

Move. Get moving.

The men set out at the double-quick, hunched over, their shoes sucking in the mud. The windmill seems to grow no closer, but floats above the mud, beckoning with its arms, and the men, laden with impossible burdens, run as though in a dream. At last, they catch up with Gideon, who is still strolling along. A bullet has struck his canteen; the water arcs out in a silver stream, then dies away. Artemus snatches the boy's overcoat sleeve, pulls him forward. Why are you doing this? he says.

Gideon smiles at his brother. Why not? he says.

* * *

"That's stupid," said Artemus. "That's not an answer." He had the Tulane student tightly by the arm, and the boy was looking at him in astonishment and fright. Artemus, suddenly aware, let go of the boy. "Sorry," he said. "It's none of my business."

The boy relaxed then. "You're being kind," he said, and held out his hand. "I'm Jeff Brown."

Artemus told his name and shook the boy's hand. He was conscious that the boy was studying his marred face, circumspectly, perhaps thinking the question that everybody wanted to ask but never did, save children sometimes, and Anna Rose in Gideon's courtyard once. The train rattled noisily over a switch point, and the couplers banged. The machinery in the windmill was quieter, Artemus remembered. It was muted, a distant grinding. When they got there, the Marines swept the place, but the sniper was long gone, of course, only his ejected brass left behind. Afterward, they sat against the walls of the little rooms or peered carefully out the windows, watching for movement. Gideon sat in a cramped tower room by himself, cleaning his shotgun. When Artemus found him, Gideon said, I should have picked up a rifle. Artemus said, Why did you do that, fool? Gideon smiled again. Don't fuck with me, he said. You have always known.

So what? Artemus said. So fucking what?

"I can't give you an answer," the boy from Tulane said.

Artemus shook his head. "I haven't earned one," he said. "Just be careful, and promise to leave this window closed."

"Honor bright, Mister Kane," said the boy, and pressed his hand over the embroidered football letter that, Artemus perceived, he'd been proud of once. Why not, after all?

* * *

The Silver Star, still fifty minutes late, slid to a squealing halt at Poplarville, Mississippi, its last stop before Hattiesburg. The train lingered only a moment to snatch up a family and two bags of mail, then it was off again, racing its pale shadow across the land.

Mister Rufus Payne, the engineer, had fifteen minutes good running to Lumberton, Mississippi. That was as far as he could push it, however. Beyond Lumberton, he was to proceed slowly and watch for the 4512 on orders of Conductor Nussbaum. That would delay them another thirty minutes, and they still had to stop at Hattiesburg and Laurel.

When Mister Payne got the highball, he jerked back on the throttle and let the engine run. It was a good machine, the finest, newest engine on the Crescent Division, and it was running hot, the drive rods and tall driving wheels a white blur of motion, heat shimmering off the boiler in little waves. Maybe he would let it run all the way, he thought. He was still the engineer. The message, putting the local in the hole at Purvis, and the green 19 order, giving them rights over all trains, had come down from the dispatcher. Nussbaum's verbal slow order was given secondhand. In his pride, the conductor had not bothered to deliver it himself. How much weight could it carry, then?

Mister Payne lowered his goggles and peered out the open cab window, feeling the bite of the wind. The long boiler of the engine rocked back and forth, snow dancing in the spear of the headlight. The rails were wet, but Mister Payne had plenty of sand. He spoke silently to the engine, after his custom. Come on, come on, darlin', he said. Then he thought of A.P. Dunn, wherever he was way off in the morning. You better find a hole, old man, he said, and in that moment Rufus Payne decided that, no matter what, he would bring the Silver Star into Meridian on the money, on time. That's what he was paid for, anyhow.

* * *

Back in the flying train, Artemus and his cousin were walking the coaches for the second time since Slidell. They began at the head end and started aft, touching the seat backs as they swayed from side to side. They studied the passengers' faces, fixing them in memory so they could be matched to the green slips of paper in the brass clips over the seats. These were done in Mister Nussbaum's hand, and bore the number of the station where each occupant would depart into the wide world. Passengers, however, were always changing seats and wandering around the train, and one of a brakeman's duties was to see that an errant citizen did not miss his stop. When that occurred, it was a nuisance for everybody, and the wrath of Mister Nussbaum came down on them all.

Artemus could not stop thinking about the Tulane student. He had left the boy with nothing, and this time, he could not even think of what he *might* have said. He scanned the coaches, but the boy was nowhere to be found. In the car for Atlanta, his seat, marked by the green slip, was empty, though a magazine, *Architectural Digest*, lay open in his place.

"You lookin' for somebody?" asked Stanfield.

"Nope," said Artemus.

At one point, the two brakemen paused instinctively and listened to the wheels under their feet. The usual interval between rail joints was reduced to a steady hammering.

"Old Rufus is hauling ass," said Stanfield. He spoke in a whisper, conscious of the passengers.

"He can run to Lumberton however fast he pleases," said Artemus.

"Yes," said Stanfield, "but this is between him and the captain. I will bet five dollars he don't slow down until he gets to Hattiesburg, just for stubbornness."

"He is stubborn," said Artemus, "but he will do what Ira told him."

"Ira himself never told him a damn thing," replied Stanfield, "and Rufus will do as the train orders say. I guarantee you he is counting on the 4512 being at Purvis. Five dollars."

"All right," said Artemus, "but if you win, you may not live to spend it." He spoke lightly, but the fact was, he knew he had already lost the bet. Rufus Payne was going to ignore Mister Nussbaum. He was going to run for home, sure as the world, the stubborn old son of a bitch.

The last coach, just ahead of the club car, was filled with college students and heavy with cigarette smoke and perfume. The girls were fresh and lively, excited to be going home. They chattered to one another and flirted with the boys, and now and then adjourned by squads to the ladies' washroom.

"What do you suppose they do in there?" asked Stanfield.

"They talk about me, mostly," said Artemus glumly, for the girls depressed him.

They were almost to the door when it slid open and a girl unlike the others stumbled through, pulling the cold and the racket behind her. She caught herself and stopped, as if she had entered the wrong hotel room: a fat, shapeless child, dark of hair, with a wisp of mustache over her lip and beads of sweat on her forehead. Her cheeks were wet with tears, her eyes uncertain as they touched on the laughing girls and handsome boys whose world was not her own. Watching her, Artemus knew she was in the kind of trouble that nothing could prepare her for, the kind a person was never ready to meet.

"Is everything—" Artemus began, but no sooner did he speak than the girl flung herself at him and wrapped her nail-bitten fingers in his coat lapel. "I'm looking for Artemus Kane," she said

Artemus grasped her hand. "You found him. What is it?"

"It's Jeff," she said. "You talked to him. You have to come." She pushed Artemus away and turned, and ran headlong into the closed door. She slumped against it, her fingers pawing at the latch. "Please," she said. "He has a gun."

THE LAST MEET

Artemus and Stanfield followed the girl into the vestibule where Artemus caught her arm. "Tell me what's the matter." The girl said, "Jeff told you he got kicked out of Tulane. What he couldn't tell you was that it was for…" The girl's face flushed red, and she caught herself as if the words she might have spoken had choked her. She herself could not say it. She began again, "His daddy—"

"Never mind," said Artemus. He understood then, all at once, what the boy's trouble was. He realized he had known all along, just as he had known with Gideon. There was nothing in the manner of either boy that betrayed him; rather, it was the air around them, as if God, knowing they would have trouble all their lives, had surrounded them with a particular grace. That is how Artemus chose to think of it, when he could stand to think of it at all. And this girl, ugly and alone, she would think of it that way, too. She would understand it better than Artemus ever could, maybe better than Gideon or Jeff Brown ever could, even if she couldn't say it. Artemus took the girl by the shoulders. "What's he doing?"

"He's out on the porch thing at the end of the train."

"And he has a gun?" said Stanfield.

"Yes," she said, breaking down again. "What am I supposed to think?"

Artemus cursed himself for a fool. Passengers were not allowed to ride on the rear platform when the train was running at such a speed. The door was supposed to be locked, and it was Artemus's job to see that it was, and Artemus, caught up in his bad thoughts, had forgotten. On the other hand, the boy and his gun, if he really had a gun, were isolated from the passengers back there. "Listen, darlin'," he said to the girl. "You go in the ladies' room, clean your face, get back to your seat. I'll take care of the boy."

"But—"

"I promise," said Artemus. "Just try to settle down, and don't scare the citizens." He took her face in his hands. "Can you do that?"

The girl nodded. "Good," said Artemus, and touched her brittle hair and turned her. Stanfield opened the coach door, and in a moment, she was gone.

In the club car, the citizens were drinking and talking as if nothing at all had happened.

The black bartender was polishing a glass. "What about it, Pete?" said Artemus.

"People havin' a good time," said the bartender. He waved his towel at the crowd. "They don't care how late we are."

"Did a boy come through here?" asked Artemus. "College boy in a Tulane sweater?"

The bartender tilted his head toward the back of the car. "He's out on the platform," he said. "I thought the door was locked, but it ain't. I figured—"

"Give me a shot," said Artemus. "Some of that Jack Daniel's."

Stanfield leaned his arm on the bar beside Artemus. "Me, too," he said.

"Now, gentlemen," said the bartender, "you know I can't—"

"Just this once," said Artemus. "Be quick."

The bartender poured the drinks and set them on the bar, and the trainmen downed them in a single draught. "What'll we do now?" asked Stanfield.

Artemus turned to the door. Through the porthole, he could see the rails pointing back toward Basin Street. "Best we not gang up on him," he said. "I'll go out and talk to him. You fetch the captain."

"I need to go with you," said Stanfield.

"It's nothing," said Artemus. "Just a kid. Now, go on."

Artemus did not wait for a reply, but walked aft and pushed the door open and stepped out onto the platform.

It was scary out there at such a speed. The snow swirled up behind in a wild demon mist, and the noise, the passage of the wind and the hammering of the wheels, was deafening. The platform itself shivered and bounced as if it were attached with baling wire. Artemus slammed the door behind him and went out to the rail with only a glance at Brown, who was pressed against the bulkhead. He took in the boy's frightened face and the pistol held down along his leg. Artemus gripped the back rail, though it was freezing, and he wore no gloves. The wind snatched his cap away at once and sent it spinning and tumbling along the track behind, lost forever. The snow stung him, half-blinded him as he bent over the rail, over the blur of the cross-ties. He could feel the boy watching him.

In a moment, the boy spoke. "You won't stop me!" he yelled over the racket. It was like something from the movies, and Artemus, expecting better, was disappointed. He turned, leaning against the cold blade of the rail. "Brown, what the fuck you doin'!" he shouted.

The boy, from his face, was shocked, thrown off balance by the remark; perhaps he was expecting something different as well. Artemus could easily believe that the boy had never been cussed in his life, so language might be a virtue here in an unexpected way. "The fuck you doin', you little prick!" he said with all the meanness he could muster. He pushed off from the rail and took a step.

The boy raised the pistol. "Don't come any closer! I mean it!"

Jesus Christ, thought Artemus. He saw now that the gun was an old Colt Peacemaker, all the bluing worn away, and he wondered what in God's name a kid like this one was doing with such a piece. Artemus said, "It's a single-action, dipshit. You have to cock it first."

Artemus was sorry at once for his cleverness. He was certain he would not be shot on purpose, but the boy was using both thumbs to cock the pistol. The barrel was wavering, and the bore seemed big enough for a man to crawl into. Artemus prayed, *Don't let him slip, don't let him slip*. Then the boy had the hammer back, locked in place, and Artemus relaxed a little, for the safest place would be wherever the kid was aiming. He took another step. The boy waved the gun. "I mean it," he said, but quieter now.

Artemus saw that the football letter was half-torn from the boy's sweater. Artemus pointed. "What's that about?"

The boy looked down as if seeing his work for the first time. "I don't deserve it."

"Why not?" said Artemus. "Didn't you earn it? Is that somebody else's sweater?"

"No, god dammit," said the boy. "Why don't you just leave me alone?"

Around them, the landscape shifted momentarily, opened out into yards and houses, the main street of a town, storefronts, a water tower. Artemus heard the urgent clang-clang of a crossing signal. Some part of his mind ticked off *Lumberton*.

"So why?" said Artemus.

Now the boy's face twisted in anger. "Why, why, why?"

Artemus backed off, hands held open before him. They were in the woods again, still rolling fast like Stanfield predicted, like Artemus himself had known they would. He thought, *I have got to finish this*. "Just tell me," he said. "Then we can go inside. I'm freezing my ass off out here."

"You know what I am," said the boy. "I can see it in your face."

"I know you're a god damned lunatic," said Artemus. "What else? You think I can't stand it? You think I never saw a swish before?"

"Swish, queen, queer, twist!" shouted the boy.

"Don't point the gun at me," said Artemus. "Put it in your ear. That's the best way. It's a .44-40. It will blow the side of your head off."

Obediently, the boy stuck the muzzle in his ear.

Shit, thought Artemus. He said, "Only one thing left now. Pull the fuckin' trigger. Go ahead. It's easy."

"You want me to, I will!"

"Oh, don't lay it off on me," said Artemus. He was moving closer now, though they were on an ascending grade, and he had to pull against a little gravity, balancing himself. He saw Mister Nussbaum's face in the door's porthole and motioned him away. "It's what you want, ain't it?" he shouted at the boy. "Pull the trigger—that'll fix every-thing! Then your daddy will be proud of you!"

The boy leaned away from the bulkhead and shut his eyes. *Good*, thought Artemus, and took two quick steps and put out his hand. The boy's eyes were shut tight. "Go ahead, Jeff," said Artemus, and slipped the web of his thumb delicately between the hammer and the frame. The boy pulled the trigger.

When nothing happened, Jeff Brown opened his eyes again. "Damn you," he said.

"Well, I misjudged you," said Artemus, breathing hard, for it hurt like hell when the hammer came down. He closed his hand around the pistol and took it away, thinking to fling it over the platform railing, but it was a good old piece, and he hadn't the heart. Instead, he thrust the pistol in the waistband of his trousers. He said, "I really didn't think you were that fucking stupid."

* * *

The Silver Star passed Lumberton in a blur of stores and houses and motorcars. Rufus Payne opened out the throttle for the grade beyond, making for the crest a half mile distant. Just beyond the crest was the Talowah siding, and then Purvis in six minutes, maybe five, where he would give old A.P. Dunn a good dusting. He leaned out the window, feeling the speed, feeling the engine under his hand. The rails were in a long perspective that ended at the top of the grade. The roadbed made a tunnel through the pines, through the white swirl of snow: the edge of the world up there, then a downward grade running fast, keeping the power on and the slack run out. Mister Payne turned to his fireman, thinking to say how all was well, but Jean Chauvin was standing, pointing out the narrow window of the cab. Mister Payne looked and saw the headlight glimmering at the crest of the grade.

"Aw, god," said Mister Payne, barely an exhalation. He slammed off the throttle and set the brakes and pulled back on the Johnson bar and grabbed the whistle cord, all he could do. "Chauvin!" he cried while the whistle screamed in a single note across the afternoon. "Jump, man!" But Jean Chauvin would not jump. He crossed himself and began, "Hail Mary, full of grace—"

* * *

The 4512 hammered over the switch at the north end of Talowah siding, and Mister Dunn opened out the throttle for the little grade ahead. He would have to be careful on the other side lest the slack bunch up. He planned to come off the hill under power so as not to shake up the boys in the back too bad; they had had a rough ride already.

Since Hattiesburg, Mister Dunn had allowed himself to do some thinking. Time, it seemed, had run off and left him, just as it had Eddie Cox. Blood kept running down his nose, and he had to keep taking off his glove to wipe it away. Necaise had offered to bandage the wound, but Mister Dunn wouldn't let him. He wanted to see the blood. It was red as ever, but Mister Dunn knew it was old now, too old to trust anymore, maybe too old to climb to his head where he needed it. He had decided that tomorrow would be his last trip, like it would for Eddie. They would go together, stepping out of life into the dusk that time left behind in its passage. He thought about his warm kitchen and how, maybe not tomorrow, but soon enough, he would think about what his life had meant. That it meant something, he had no doubt; it was only a matter of touching it, looking at it with clarity in a way he had not had time for. He turned to look across the cab, thinking to tell Eddie, but caught himself and turned to the window again. There was plenty of time to talk, away from the racket, away from the things they had to pay attention to right now.

They topped the grade, running hot and fast, and there was a headlight shimmering with speed and staring them in the face.

Mister Dunn thought *This is not right* even as his hands were moving. He closed the throttle and touched the brake. If he blew out the air at this speed, the cars would pile all over them, and they would die, and the men in the back would die—but he had to try, had to slow them down. He opened the throttle again, then slammed the brake lever and heard the train dynamite behind him, a terrific explosion of air followed by the screech of brake shoes against the wheels. He reached up and pulled the whistle cord.

"Jump, boys!" he shouted over the screaming whistle. "I can't stop 'em!"

Eddie Cox was staring ahead. The headlight of the Silver Star was already lighting up his face, but there was no fear in it, only a deep sorrow. He only moved to take up his Bible and press it to his chest.

"Jump, Bobby!" cried Mister Dunn.

Bobby Necaise looked out the window at the ground speeding past. It was too far. *If it was water*, he thought, *I could do it*. He thought, *They will teach me that in boot camp*. He looked ahead at the light that was no longer just a light, but the shape of a locomotive, and no longer shining at them, but illuminating the trees by the roadside. The passenger engine's pilot trucks had left the rails, and now it was beginning to tilt and crab sideways, pushing up a little mountain of slag before it. Bobby could see the top of the boiler now, and the cab lurching upward from the pressure of the heavy cars behind. He felt his own cab shift under his feet, saw Mister Dunn cover his face with his hands. *That is God sitting there*, thought Necaise. Then he closed his eyes and waited.

* * *

On the back platform of the Silver Star, the boy collapsed, sliding down the bulkhead. Artemus caught and held him by the front of his sweater. "I ought to slap the shit out of you," he said.

"I don't want to go home!" cried the boy. He began to weep then, so Artemus backhanded him twice, not hard, just as he had struck Gideon in the windmill that day. "So don't go home," said Artemus.

"Where else?" said the boy, wiping at his face.

"Stop your sniveling and listen to me," said Artemus. "My brother—"

The door opened, and Mister Nussbaum emerged. "Kane?" he said.

"We're all right," said Artemus.

"Your brother?" said Jeff Brown.

"He finally learned how little difference it made," said Artemus. He slapped the boy again. "So what?" he shouted. "So fucking what?"

"Mister Kane," said the conductor calmly, "why don't we all go in and sit down?"

"In a minute, sir, for Christ's sake!" said Artemus. He took the boy's cheeks in his hand, squeezing hard. "You got too much to do," he said. "You can't let—"

Suddenly the brakes blew out beneath them. Artemus and Mister Nussbaum looked at one another, each one knowing. The train lurched and shuddered, squealing like a beast in pain. Foul smoke swirled across the platform, the stench of friction. Mister Nussbaum took hold of Artemus then. The old man's grip was stronger than Artemus could ever have imagined. "It's the 4512," he said.

A great noise ascended, from the ground it seemed, though not of the ground, but of steel and iron grinding. The car twisted sideways, wheels bumping along the ties. Artemus felt Mister Nussbaum fall away, but still he held tightly to the boy and went on talking, trying to tell him everything was all right. Only now his voice was gone. It seemed to be nowhere but in his own head. He lost his hold on the boy's face, lost sight of it, and felt himself being lifted away in a sudden darkness filled with tumult. "You got too much to do!" he tried across the empty place, but he could not be sure the boy heard him before the darkness closed around them both.

APOLLO'S ILLUSION

Anna Rose Dangerfield woke with a start as if from a bad dream, but she had not been dreaming. She had been in that sweet blue region of half-sleep, listening to the voices on the street below, and sometime in her dozing, Artemus had come back to her. She had seen him clearly, standing at the foot of her bed in his uniform. The shoulders of his coat were damp, and he wore no cap. The light from the jalousies latticed his face with brightness and shadow, as if the sun were shining. Back so soon? she said, her heart suddenly joyful. He had smiled and spoken in return, though she could not remember what he said. Then all at once he was gone again.

She sat up, drawing the afghan close. On the dressing table, between the candles, the corpus of Our Lord sagged on the cross, remembering, in his last moments, his nativity perhaps. The clock there said half past noon, and Anna Rose remembered vaguely the tolling of the cathedral bell. The room was silent now, save for the hiss of the gas heater, and empty.

It was only a dream after all, she thought, and felt the disappointment that always accompanied the collapse of fond wishes and illusions.

The hour was late for rising, even for her. She got out of bed, stretched, pulled on her robe and crossed the cold floor. She cracked

the door and peered out into the hall. It was empty and still. It lay in
unfamiliar darkness, too, and Anna Rose saw, with a momentary sadness and surprise, that the antique Edison bulb had burned out at last.
The only lumination came from a narrow window at the end that
looked out on the courtyard. She made her way quickly down the hall
to the bathroom and was sick again, as she had been these several
mornings past. She washed her face and considered herself in the
cloudy mirror over the sink. Her hand touched her belly and felt, she
believed, a little swelling there already. *You have to tell him sooner or
later*, she thought, and she wondered if he would be glad. *It will make
him happy*, she told herself. Maybe he knew already, and that is why he
smiled at her in the vision. In any event, tomorrow night, Christmas
night, she would meet the Silver Star at Basin Street, and she and
Artemus would have supper, and they would go to Mass. She would tell
him afterward, in the twilit nave of Immaculate Conception, among the
smell of snuffed candles. Then she would not be so afraid.

* * *

At first, there was no pain, nor anything to harm, and no longer any
fear that something bad must happen. There was only the darkness,
vast and still, all empty of sound and movement like the dark before
time must have been. *So this is death*, he thought, and it was all right.
He was glad to know what death was, after so long wondering.

He would have liked to remain, but after a season, the darkness
began to shift, as if it had weight and substance. He felt it glide across
him, passing away, and for a moment he was filled with regret. Then a
globe of light appeared, and he was drawn into it, and soon he found
himself in a landscape of shadows. *This is better*, he thought, for the
light was soft, like the full moon walking over the woods, and he was no
longer alone; others were there with him, moving among the shadows.
He could not see their faces, but he knew them just the same, and knew

their voices. *All is well*, he thought, and believed it for a time.

Then a coldness touched him, and with it came a deep sorrow, for he understood it was not death after all, but life that held him. The light grew, and by it he saw the others moving away, following the shadows. He called to them, but they would not stay, and he could not follow. Soon they were gone, and he knew they would not return. He watched them pass away until only the light remained, then he turned back reluctantly into the world.

"Get up, Frank," said Sonny Leeke.

He tried to obey, but a bright lance of pain struck him in the spine, and he fell back again. His knees were bent, and he saw that he was jammed against the forward door of the caboose. "I can't," he said.

Pale sunlight slanted through the windows of the X-630. The air was bitter with the smell of dust and burning brakes, and dense with coal smoke. "Get your ass up," said Leeke.

"Goddamn it," said Smith.

Leeke took him by the arms and lifted him to his feet. He stood unsteadily, the spasmed muscles around his spine pulling him sideways. He put his arm around the brakeman's neck, and together they moved toward the open back door. It seemed a long journey. Leeke kicked the overturned desk chair from their path. They crunched over broken glass, among a shambles of strewn cushions and Christmas presents, scattered books and papers, coal spilled from the bunker, dislodged raingear and fusees and torpedoes. The stove was hot when they passed it, boiling smoke where the stovepipe had broken loose.

"Wait a minute," said Leeke. "I got to fix that." He hunted around and found his gloves, and with his gloved hands forced the stovepipe back in place. "We might want a stove directly," he said, and shucked the gloves, and took Smith's arm again. Finally they passed through the door and into the cold, into a terrible silence where the snow fell swiftly, urgently, as if it wanted to hurry and cover up what had been done. Smith had no idea what that might be, for he could remember nothing beyond the dark.

"Something bad has happened," he said.

"Yes," said Leeke. "I think we hit the Silver Star."

* * *

It was the worst dream George Watson ever had, of a big bird like an owl that swept down out of the snow and covered him with its wings. They had a terrible struggle, and George Watson was flung against the walls of the boxcar, and dragged across the splintered floor, and smashed against the bulkhead, and all the while the bird screamed with a sound like nothing of the earth or of hell even. Then everything was quiet, the bird gone limp and soft, weightless as if only its feathers remained. Watson pushed the thing off him, the light returned, and he saw that it was not a bird at all, but only the sheet of cardboard.

Still, there had been a fight of some kind, for he was hurting all over, and there was blood on the front of his silk shirt. Watson lay still for a moment, trying to gather himself. He found that the blood was leaking from his nose, and he had to blow hard to clear his nostrils so he could breathe. Then he noticed other things that were wrong. The train was not moving. He was lying, not on the floor, but on the side of the car, and the door yawned above him. Snow was falling straight down through it, and he could see the sky.

He sat up and looked around. The air was thick with dust. He had lost one of his shoes, and his pistol was gone. Then he began to shiver, and he had to crawl back under the cardboard and hug himself until the shivering stopped. While he was under there, the car gave a groan and shifted, and Watson was on the floor again. When he emerged at last, he found that, if he wanted to, he could step right out the boxcar door and onto the ground. He wondered how that could be, so he decided to get up and see for himself. Getting up was hard, for he was stiff and aching with cold, but he managed it in time. He crossed the floor and stepped out, and fell flat on his face in a tangle of vines. He lay still a moment, then rose stiffly to his feet again. He was way up in a stand of pine trees. It came to him that someone, Mister Leeke probably, had played a joke on him, took the wheels from under the car and slid the whole god damn thing into the woods.

"That just ain't right," said George, and all at once he was madder than he had ever been. He went back into the car and found his pistol and the lost shoe, then folded some of the cardboard around him so that he resembled a great brown moth. He went out again and started around the boxcar, thinking to find Mister Frank Smith and raise hell. Even if George Watson was only a nigger, and a bad one at that, and riding for free, he ought not to be treated in such a way when he had done no harm to anybody, at least not lately.

He came out in the middle of a sandy road, and stopped. His breathing stopped, and even his heart perhaps, long enough to make him dizzy. He tried to make himself believe what he was seeing, but his mind was shook up and confused.

He was surrounded by a mountain of boxcars, all piled on top of one another, spread from woods to woods on either side of the main line. Or where the main line used to be, for now, where it showed at all, there was only torn-up ties, and mounds of slag, and rails twisted and bent. One of the cars sat on the very top of the pile, slanted toward the sky, and as George watched, it creaked and groaned and settled itself. The whole pile creaked and groaned, in fact, and air hissed from the cylinders, and there was a ticking from the overheated brakes. A journal box had caught fire and was leaking oily smoke.

George Watson looked, and believed, and as soon as he believed, all feeling left him. He did not own a feeling that could touch what he saw, only a numbness that left him curiously at peace. Time had ceased, and everything he had worried about no longer mattered. It was freedom, in a way—the most freedom he had ever known, and the most peace.

He had to go through the woods to get around the wreckage. It was quiet in there, except for the sifting of the snow, and he liked the smell of the pines and the softness of the needles under his feet. Presently, he glimpsed the freight engine through the trees. The locomotive lay on its side, leaking steam at every joint and groaning like a dying beast. He could see the top of the boiler and the crushed roof of the cab. The tender had turned over, too, and was lying at an angle, all the coal spilled out. He knew there were men in there, and he knew he should go over, but he was afraid of what he would see. Not the dead—he had seen plenty of dead men—but those who might be alive, all torn up and begging him for help when he had none to give.

In fact, he didn't know *what* to do. He had no idea where he was, though it was clear that he was still in the Piney Woods. He could hear automobiles passing to the east, tires thump-thumping over pavement joints: the New Orleans highway, most likely. He could go over there, stand by the road, and hope some colored people came along to give him a ride. But what if the highway police came by, or a truckload of white boys looking for sport? Maybe he should just keep walking until he got to a house. But there would be dogs at a house. He knew that out in the country even the colored people had dogs, and nigger dogs were the worst of all. Or maybe he should go back and find the caboose, only there might be injured men there, too. Watson touched the tobacco can in his pocket. *Aw man*, he thought. He was trying to make up his mind what to do when he got tangled up in a thicket of briars and had to push out onto the sandy road. There, he was made to stop again and reach for an understanding of what he saw.

A second locomotive, northbound, lay on its side, coal spilled out, steam rising in a cloud, the boiler buried for half its length under a great mound of slag. Behind it sprawled the ruins of a long passenger train. Some of the cars remained upright, jackknifed across the main. Most were turned over, and these seemed longer, bigger, than they ought to be. They were streaked and dented as though they had been flailed with chains. A coach had telescoped the baggage car so that the two occupied a single space where nothing could live. Dismounted wheels and trucks lay everywhere. Rails were twisted; ties were pushed up; broken window glass sparkled in the gray light.

George Watson walked south along the wreck, clutching the cardboard tight around him. His shoes and socks were soaked through, and his feet were freezing, but it was not the cold that troubled him. He was afraid that he had fallen into another dream where all the world he had known was come to an end in a haze of snow. He had been alone most of his life, but he had never felt more alone than he did now. A profound silence settled around him, as if the violence of the world's end had made an empty place in the air and sucked away all the possibility of sound.

But this was no dream, and he was not alone. Those were not empty boxcars out there, but fine green Pullman coaches where hundreds of people were trapped. Some of them, maybe most, were dead, their souls rising even now into the gray afternoon. But others were stirring into movement again, groping for the light, trying to understand what had happened to them. He could sense them struggling behind the darkened windows, and pretty soon they would begin to emerge. What would George Watson do then?

He realized that it wasn't quiet, either. Some part of him, for a little while, and without his will, had simply refused to listen. He listened now, and heard the same groaning of air and ticking of brakes—and then something else, more terrible than the shrieking of the dream bird had been.

It started softly, a whimpering no louder than the snow sifting in the pines. George Watson knew it was coming from the passenger coaches, but the sound was elusive, rising from everywhere, but nowhere in particular. It was like when the people began to sing in church, soft at first, and only a few, so you couldn't tell who was singing and who wasn't. But then it began to swell, like the voices of the people as the song took hold, and in a moment it was a mourning and a crying, a wailing, a jumble of words pleading, a tangle of questions that no one could answer, least of all George Watson.

Now the fear enclosed him, and he dropped his cardboard wings and knelt in the road. Maybe Sweet Willie Wine would have liked to go over there and see what he could find—jewelry, money, fat watches— but all George Watson wanted to do was clap his hands over his ears. He felt like he had come upon a door to hell left open, and he knew there would be no closing of it again; he knew he would hear these sounds for all his life remaining.

His numbness deserted him, and his peace, and in their place came a great sorrow for the strangers who needed so much help. They seemed to be crying to him; nobody else was around for them to cry to, after all. The thought came to him that he should pray, but he had no words for praying, nor any notion of what praying was. All he could do was kneel in the road and be afraid. He shut his eyes tight, trying to clear his mind, but that only made him dizzy again. When he opened his eyes, he saw the girl.

He didn't know how she got out, or when, but there she was coming toward him through the veil of snow. Her hair was dark, but her face was ghostly white, the blood on her clothes bright red. She was shoe- less, walking up the track in her stocking feet, seeming unmindful of the rough slag, the shards of glass.

George Watson stood up. He wanted to flee, to be gone before she noticed him, but he couldn't make up his mind to do it. Meanwhile the girl had come closer until he could hear the ragged sound of her breathing. Something was wrong with the shape of her, and at first he couldn't grasp what it was. Then she stopped, walked in a little circle as if trying to determine her way, and he saw that her right arm was gone at the shoulder. He cried out then—he couldn't help it—and the girl turned toward the sound of his voice. "Oh," she said, and sat down in the snow.

A moment passed, and George Watson spent it trying to make up his mind. He wondered if he would ever know what he should do, and if he had ever known. He looked at the girl again, who seemed to have forgotten him. She was sitting with her bare legs straight out, her face twisted in a puzzled frown. As he watched, she began to move in a curious way, jerking her right shoulder, panting with the effort. Somehow, he understood. The girl was trying to pull her dress over her knees with the hand that wasn't there.

So George Watson made up his mind, or had it made up for him, no matter. A shallow ditch ran alongside the road, and Watson crossed it and came to the place where the girl sat. He put out his hand. "Let me help you, missy," he said.

The girl was still frowning. "Get away," she said. "Don't you touch me." Then her face relaxed, and she brushed absently at her hair with her good hand. "Can I have some water?" she asked.

He went back to the ditch and scooped up a double handful of snow. It was like carrying live coals, but he made his way back to the girl, and knelt, and held the snow just under her chin. "See can you take some," he said, but it was no use. He watched the light go out of her eyes, and just that quick, in the time it would take to turn down a lamp, she was past all wanting.

He rose and brushed the snow from his hands. More people were around now, climbing from windows, dropping from the open diaphragms where once the cars had come together. In fact, the wreck was crawling with movement all down its length, and George Watson knew it was time to go. Still, there was one more thing he could do, and to this he gave no thought at all. He took off his checkered wool suit coat and laid it across the girl's bare legs. Then he backed away, across the ditch, across the road, to the wood line.

A man shouted at him. "You boy! What you think you're doin'!"

George Watson realized, too late, that he had left his pistol in his coat pocket. Well, no matter, he could worry about that another day. Right now, he had to get through the woods and out to the highway before he froze to death. He looked one last time at the girl where she sat alone, bent forward at the waist like a broken doll. "You be all right," he said. Then he was gone.

* * *

When they got outside, away from the dense smoke, Frank Smith found he could breathe easier. He sat down on the platform of the X-630 and pressed his back against the cold handrail. He was trying to put in order all the things he had to do, but they were swimming around in his head like fishes in a pool. Twenty-one years he had traveled up and down Pelican Road, and he had been in all manner of bad situations, but this was the first one where he couldn't remember what happened.

He told himself they could not possibly have hit the Silver Star. They had an order, crystal-clear, to meet the passenger train at Lumberton. The last station they had passed was Talowah, and he could see that they were not far past it now. Lumberton was five miles to the south. "Sonny, why would you say we hit Number Six?" he asked.

The brakeman was slumped against the door frame. "Can you think of any other reason A.P. would dynamite this train way out here?"

There were many reasons, Smith knew, but he could not seem to think of any. In fact, he could hardly think at all. He shook his head to clear it, and suddenly he remembered what they had to do—the first thing they always did when something bad happened. They had to flag behind, had to protect the rear. The marker lamps were still burning on the caboose, but that was not enough. "Where's Dutch?" said the conductor. "We got to put out a flag."

Leeke did not seem to be injured, but his face was gray, his hands shaking. He coughed violently and spat over the steps. Smith thought the man might be hurt inside where it didn't show. He was about to remark on the possibility when the brakeman said, "Dutch is still up in the cupola."

"Well, get his ass out here," said Smith.

The brakeman shook his head. "He's dead, Frank. He went through the window and broke his neck."

Smith looked away, feeling the anger rise in him. They had so much to do, and here was Sonny Leeke fucking around. "No—" he began, but Leeke was rummaging around inside the caboose. Presently, he emerged with a handful of torpedoes and a fusee. "I'll set out the flag," he said.

"No," said Smith. "Ladner is the flagman. You need to go up and see—"

"Listen to me," said Sonny Leeke. "Dutch has gone west, and there is not a god damn thing we can do about it. I'll put the flag out, then I'm comin' back here. Understand?"

Leeke pushed by and went down the steps. Smith watched him stumble away like a drunk man, saw him stoop to bend the torpedoes around the rail a quarter mile up the main. Then a fusee blossomed bright and red in the snowfall. It would only last five minutes, then Ladner would light another one, and another, and stand out in the cold as long as he had to—

But no, Ladner was dead, and that was Sonny Leeke out there. Smith knew he had to accept that, had to get his mind in order. He knew that pretty soon he would have to accept other things as well, but right now there was too much to do. He crawled a little way into the caboose, cursing the bones that God had made too fragile. "Dutch!" he shouted, but there was only the soft whisper of the stove and a hiss of air from the brake line.

Time passed. Smith's watch was shattered—the hands were stopped at twelve twenty-six—so when Sonny Leeke returned, Smith had to ask what time it was. One thirteen.

Smith refused to lie on a cushion as Sonny Leeke suggested. Instead, he sat stiffly in his conductor's chair and watched as Leeke pulled the flagman's body down from the cupola. Leeke dragged the man outside, where he laid him in the slag and covered him with a blanket. Frank Smith could not help at all. Then the brakeman went back and lit another fusee and returned once more, shivering with cold.

Leeke stood now with his back to the stove. He said. "We got one car still coupled ahead, the rest are spread out all over the main and up in the woods. I couldn't see past that."

Smith tried to remember. He had been at his desk. Sonny Leeke was sitting on a seat cushion, reading a comic book. Ladner had just climbed into the cupola. Ladner must have seen what was going to happen, but he couldn't tell about it now.

"It's bad," said Leeke. "Worst I ever seen."

Frank Smith wished he could go back to the place where he had been, to the quiet dark where everything was peaceful and he had nothing to do. He said, "You got to go up there. You got to see what happened."

"In a minute," said Leeke. "In a minute, I'll go."

Smith wanted him to go right now, but it was not in him to insist. The two trainmen waited a while in silence. The second fusee burned out, but Leeke made no move to go out and light another. It was just as well; the brakeman had other things to attend to. The torpedoes and the marker lamps would have to do for now. Presently, Leeke said, "I had a thought out there, about Sweet Willie Wine."

Smith made no answer. He had forgotten about the rider, but he remembered now, and remembered how he had considered bringing him back to ride on the caboose, then hadn't.

"Well, most likely he would of froze to death anyhow," said Leeke. He stood up then, and pulled on a rain slicker. "Guess I'll leave my umbrella this time," he said, and grinned in his old way. "If you want to take a stroll, you can use it for a cane."

"I might," said Smith. "Willie Wine was in one of those Maryland boxes."

"I'll look in on him," said Leeke.

"No," said the conductor. "No, you got to get to the head end." He thought for a moment about what that meant. He said, "It don't matter if you're afraid to go. I'd be afraid myself."

Sonny Leeke looked down at his hands. "I'm not afraid," he said.

"I meant there's no shame in it," said Smith.

Leeke nodded. "I know what you meant," he said. He put on his gloves, and took up a lantern that wasn't broken, and then he was gone. Smith heard him go down the steps, heard him pause at the place where Dutch was lying. Then Sonny Leeke's footsteps crunched on in the slag, and after a moment, they died away.

Frank Smith sat alone in the quiet caboose. His mother's picture still hung beside the lamp, and he reached up and straightened it. In a little while, he took his orders out of his overalls pocket. He thumbed through them and found the one they had received at Hattiesburg:

EXTRA 4512 SOUTH WAIT AT LUMBERTON FOR
NO. 6 UNTIL 2:01 PM.

He smoothed it out on the desk, knowing that sooner or later somebody would want to see it. Then he tried to think about what he needed to be doing right now. There was nothing. He had done all he could, and he could only wait while others acted out their parts. The fact was, Frank Smith was no longer in charge of anything.

He was glad Leeke had fixed the stovepipe. If he'd had to wait in the cold, his back would have set up like concrete. He slept a while, though he tried not to. When he awoke, Roy Jack Lucas was standing at the stove, warming himself. "Hey, Jackie," said Smith in surprise.

The detective jumped as if he had not known anyone was there. "Hello, Frank. How you feelin'?"

Smith's initial surprise turned uncomfortable all at once. He was usually glad to see Roy Jack, but he was not glad to see him now, for his presence boded ill. "You came all the way from Meridian," Smith said.

"Yes," said the detective, "in a car with no windows. The chief let

Hido drive, so we made good time."

Smith had no idea what that meant, but it didn't matter. He said, "What happened, Jackie?"

The detective's overcoat and pants and shoes were caked with yellow mud. His eyes were red, his face lined with fatigue, dark with two day's growth of beard. When he spoke, it was barely above a whisper. "Well, it's pretty bad," he said.

Goddammit, thought Smith. "Just tell me," he said. "Did we hit the Silver Star?"

"Yes, Frank, you did," said Lucas.

Smith felt the words like a physical blow, even though he had expected them. "But how?" Smith asked.

Lucas shrugged. "I can't say yet. Sonny told me you couldn't walk. Are you all right?"

"Never mind," said Smith. "Just tell me what's going on."

So Lucas told what he had seen, and all that had come to pass in the hours since the news went out over Donny Luttrell's telegraph. He described the wreck of the Silver Star and how, right now, the sandy road was crowded with curious spectators. The Army was coming over from Shelby, he said, bringing a hospital tent and doctors and military policemen. The big hook was on the way, and section gangs were already working on a temporary track so that trains could pass. Frank only half-listened, for he had seen all that before at other wrecks. He knew that the night, when it came, would be lit by searchlights, by the blue arc of cutting torches, by the headlamps of work trains. Men would build fires to warm themselves, and the smoke would drift through the lights. It was what Lucas wasn't saying that ate at him.

Then Lucas mentioned that a special train was to run out of Hattiesburg to carry off the dead and injured. "He ought to be showing up pretty soon," said the detective. "I need to go back and flag for you."

"No," said Smith. "I'll do it."

Once he had something to do, Smith was able to move around a little, though slowly, carefully, mindful of the live nerves that would bring him to his knees if he made the least misstep. He pointed to the corner of the caboose. "Fetch me that umbrella, if you please," he said.

With Sonny Leeke's umbrella for a cane, the conductor found he could stand upright as a proper man should. He said, "Jackie, I have not asked you yet, but I am asking you now."

"I know, Frank," said the detective. "I'm sorry. Can I sit in your chair?"

Smith had to smile at that. It was an old-time courtesy, a deference that new men hardly ever understood. "Of course, Jackie," he said.

Lucas sat, and rubbed his face with his hands. Then he took a notebook from his coat pocket and turned the pages until he found the one he wanted. He stared at the page for a moment. He said, "Somebody else has the passengers' names. All I got are the railroad—"

"Please, Jackie," said Smith. "Just read."

"All right," said Lucas, and began. He read reluctantly in a low, inflectionless voice, tolling the old, familiar names, pausing over some as if he wanted to remember them before he went on. He read a long time, so long that Smith thought he would never get to the end, so long that he would not have been surprised to find his own name among them.

When all the names of the dead were spoken, Lucas closed his notebook. The two men sat in silence a while. "Well, thank you, Jackie," said Smith at last. "I'm going out now. If you want to make some coffee, the pot's layin' around here someplace, and there's some French Market in the locker there."

Lucas put his notebook away and sat looking at his hands. "Sure," he said. "I can do that anyhow."

Smith took up a clutch of fusees and went out the back door and lowered himself carefully to the ground. He did not look at the place where Dutch Ladner lay, but northward where soon the relief train must appear. He was surprised to find that evening had come. The snow had stopped, and the sky was clearing from the west. A smear of lavender clouds hung over the tree line, and Smith caught a glimpse of the sun as it slid behind them. Apollo and his chariot were falling away into the sea somewhere, leaving behind the illusion that time meant something. They had made so much of time, with their watches and train orders and timetables, and now it had tricked them in the end and lured them down to the place where everything must go at last, where hours and years meant nothing.

Smith remembered how he had seen the sun that morning, and how he had taken it as a sign. Now another sign presented itself: the evening star, bright and solitary in the twilight. Whatever meaning it had, Smith would leave to the gods who placed it there. Instead, he spoke aloud the names Lucas had read, in case the gods were interested.

He had a good deal yet to do, he thought, as he followed the star up the main line. He had to stay quick so that, when he got back to Meridian, he could start Artemus Kane's motorcycle and ride it to the house on 7th Street and put it safely in the shed next to his own. He had to call Gideon before the papers came out in the morning, and he had to call Anna Rose. Surely Artemus had her number around somewhere, and Smith did not want her to hear the news from a stranger. Of course, he had to think of what he would say to them both; he would do that on the train going north. He would write it down, in fact, so that he could be sure it was the right thing. Then, when all that was in order, he would waken Maggie in the middle of the night and tell her what happened, and maybe she would let him stay the night, just this once. Maybe tomorrow, they could all have Christmas together after all.

He would ask Maggie to have his suit cleaned so he could go to the funerals. Later, he would go see Mister Dunn's old wife, and Bobby Necaise's mother, and try to explain how they came to be where they were when death took them. He would go down to Jumpertown and search until he found Eddie Cox's wife, and search until he found somebody kin to Sweet Willie Wine. In time, he would sit before boards of inquiry and show them the order from Hattiesburg and try to explain that they were supposed to meet the Silver Star at Lumberton. After that, he would lie on steel tables in Meridian and New Orleans while company doctors poked and prodded him, and he would have to figure out something to do when they told him that his back was too far gone, that he couldn't work as a trainman anymore. Maybe they would let him be a crossing guard. Maybe he could be a yard clerk. Maybe the Army would take him, who would take anybody, it was said.

So much to do, and so far to travel yet on the journey. He would have to learn not to look around him, not to expect the same company he had known so long. This would be hardest of all, for right now he could see them all plainly, just as they were before, all laughing, all in movement through time. But not with him. He had to learn that. He had to learn that he could no longer follow where they had gone.

So much to do, but that was all in the future, near and far. Right now, he had to protect the rear of his train. In the last of light, he spotted a prize between the rails: a crow's pinion, black and shiny. Slowly, painfully, he bent and picked it up. When he was straight again, and balanced on the umbrella, he turned it in his fingers. In time, if he listened closely, he would know why it came to be here. That was something else he could do tomorrow.

Smith popped a fusee and stood waiting in its red glare. In a little while, the headlight of the relief train appeared from the north, coming slowly, circumspectly, feeling its way down Pelican Road. Out of the darkness, a flagman appeared, a walking apparition in the cone of the headlight.

"Hello, Frank," said the flagman when he was close enough. "My God, how you feelin'?"

"I'm all right," said Smith. "I just fucked up, is all." Then he turned away and walked slowly, carefully, back to the X-630 where Roy Jack was making coffee.